Praise for
JUST AN ORDINARY DAY

"*Just an Ordinary Day* is a long-overdue collection of Jackson's short fiction. . . . Jackson at her best: plumbing the extraordinary from the depths of mid-20th-century common.
It is a gift to a new generation."
—*San Francisco Chronicle Book Review*

"[Jackson] will make you laugh, contemplate your own mortality, and scare you into a wakeful night. And she appears to have done it all equally deftly."
—*The Miami Herald*

"An unsettling tale-spinner in complete command of her craft."
—*San Diego Union-Tribune*

"For Jackson devotees, as well as first-time readers, this is a feast. . . . A virtuoso collection."
—*Publishers Weekly* (starred review)

"A welcome new collection."
—*Newsweek*

"Psychologically complex and deliciously horrifying."
—*Sun-Sentinel,* Fort Lauderdale

Other books by Shirley Jackson

THE ROAD THROUGH THE WALL
THE LOTTERY: AND OTHER STORIES
HANGSAMAN
LIFE AMONG THE SAVAGES
THE BIRD'S NEST
RAISING DEMONS
THE SUNDIAL
THE HAUNTING OF HILL HOUSE
WE HAVE ALWAYS LIVED IN THE CASTLE
THE MAGIC OF SHIRLEY JACKSON
COME ALONG WITH ME

JUST AN ORDINARY DAY

Shirley Jackson

Edited by
Laurence Jackson Hyman
and Sarah Hyman Stewart

BANTAM BOOKS

New York Toronto London Sydney Auckland

JUST AN ORDINARY DAY

A Bantam Book / January 1998

PUBLISHING HISTORY
Bantam hardcover edition / January 1997
Bantam trade paperback edition / January 1998

Cover art copyright © Tom Hallman.
Library of Congress Catalog Card Number 96-23871

ISBN 0-553-37833-3

Published simultaneously in the United States and Canada

Bantam Books are published by Bantam Books, a division of Bantam Doubleday Dell Publishing Group, Inc. Its trademark, consisting of the words "Bantam Books" and the portrayal of a
rooster, is Registered in U.S. Patent and Trademark Office and in other countries. Marca
Registrada. Bantam Books, 1540 Broadway, New York, New York 10036.

Contents

✍

PART TWO: UNCOLLECTED STORIES

Contents

𝒟

PART TWO: UNCOLLECTED STORIES

Introduction

S EVERAL YEARS AGO, A carton of cobwebbed files discovered in a Vermont barn more than a quarter century after our
mother's death arrived without notice in the mail. Within it were the
original manuscript of *The Haunting of Hill House,* together with
Shirley Jackson's handwritten notes on character and scene development for the novel, as well as half a dozen unpublished short stories—the yellow bond carbons she kept for her files. The stories were
mostly unknown to us, and we began to consider publishing a new
collection of our mother's work.

Soon we located other stories, some never published anywhere,
and some published only once, decades ago, in periodicals, many long
defunct. Shirley's brother and sister-in-law, Barry and Marylou Jackson, supplied more stories in well-preserved copies of magazines;
other pieces our sister, Jai Holly, and brother, Barry Hyman, had
filed away over the years. Many more were found in the archives at
the San Francisco Public Library. A windfall came when we learned
that the Library of Congress held twenty-six cartons of our mother's
papers—journals, poetry, plays, parts of unfinished novels, and stories, lots of stories. After a week spent there photocopying, we began
to feel we had the makings of a book, the first new work by Shirley
Jackson since *The Magic of Shirley Jackson* and *Come Along with Me,*
both published shortly after her death in 1965 at the age of forty-
eight. We hoped Shirley Jackson's work could now be discovered by
a whole new generation of readers.

We uncovered a wealth of early writing from the late thirties and early forties, but very little from her precollege years. She claimed to have burned all her writings just before she left home to go to the University of Rochester, in 1934, and she may have done so, although some of her high school journals are among her preserved papers at the Library of Congress. While we could place them in a general time frame, none of the new stories we discovered had dates on them or any indication of when they were first written. Rather than be inaccurate we have left the stories in Part One undated.

Later visits to the Library of Congress enabled us to find missing parts of incomplete stories or versions that we liked better. Soon we had assembled more than 130 stories, and of these we agreed on the fifty-four presented here, those that we feel are finished and up to Shirley Jackson's finely tuned standards. When we approached Bantam we were met with considerable enthusiasm for the project, and the book began to take shape as a significant collection of Jackson's short fiction. Of the stories included in this collection, thirty-one have never been published before. The remaining stories had been previously published in magazines, but never before included in a collection of Jackson's short fiction; and of these, only two or three have appeared in book form at all, mostly anthologies. One of those anthologized (and very hard to find) is "One Ordinary Day, with Peanuts."

Many of the stories we found untitled or with working titles, since she often waited until publication to name them. In these instances we have created titles in the best muted Jackson style we could manage. In other instances we decided to change repetitive character names, often arbitrarily assigned by Jackson and intended to be changed before publication. We decided not to alter the archaic money references in these stories, however dated they may be, feeling that the integrity and understanding of the stories ought not be compromised.

We include a full range of Jackson's many types of short fiction, from lighthearted romantic pieces to the macabre to the truly frightening. We also include a few of the humorous pieces she wrote about our family, since those, too, were what Shirley Jackson pioneered with as a writer, as well as her shocking and twisted explorations of the supernatural and the psyche. We want this collection to represent the great diversity of her work, and to show the writer's craft evolving through a variety of forms and styles.

Our mother lived and wrote in a time—the thirties through the sixties—when smoking and drinking were both widespread and fashionable. Her characters grimly and gleefully chain-smoke and throw down drink after drink, in between boiling their coffee and spanking their children. But underneath these literary folkways of her time the universal themes glitter.

The stories we include here are not all charismatic heart-stoppers on the level of "The Lottery." Most of her short fiction was written for publication in the popular magazines of her day (*Charm, Look, Harper's, Ladies' Home Companion, Mademoiselle, Cosmopolitan, The Magazine of Fantasy and Science Fiction, Reader's Digest, The New Yorker, Playboy, Good Housekeeping, Woman's Home Companion*, etc.). She actually wrote very few horror stories, and not many stories of fantasy or the supernatural, probably preferring to develop those themes more thoroughly in her novels. She had the courage to deal with unfashionable topics and to twist popular icons. Some of the stories gathered here are so unusual in style or point of view that they resemble almost none of the rest of her work.

We discovered that some stories tried to get themselves written over and over throughout Jackson's life. "The Honeymoon of Mrs. Smith" is shockingly different in attitude, theme, and climax from the version it precedes here, "The Mystery of the Murdered Bride." They are the same story, told years apart and from almost opposing viewpoints. This is the only instance—but a fascinating one for students of short fiction—in which we have chosen to include two versions of the same story. We have also included a few "feel-good" stories beloved by readers of the (mostly women's) magazines of the fifties and sixties. They are tucked between tales of murder and trickery, among ghostly rambles and poetic fables, between hugely funny family chronicles and dark tales of perfect, unexpected justice.

Our mother tried to write every day, and treated writing in every way as her professional livelihood. She would typically work all morning, after all the children went off to school, and usually again well into the evening and night. There was always the sound of typing. And our house was more often than not filled with luminaries in literature and the arts. There were legendary parties and poker games with visiting painters, sculptors, musicians, composers, poets, teachers, and writers of every leaning. But always there was the sound of her typewriter, pounding away into the night.

This collection of short fiction, taken as a whole, adds significantly to the body of Shirley Jackson's published work. These stories range from those she wrote in college and as a budding writer living in

Greenwich Village in the early forties, to those she churned out steadily during the 1950s, to those nearly perfect, terrifying pieces crafted toward the end of her life in the mid-sixties. This collection demonstrates her lifelong commitment to writing, her development as an artist, and her courage to explore universal themes of evil, madness, cruelty, and the humorous ironies of child-raising. She took the craft of writing every bit as seriously as the subject matter she chose (the *Minneapolis Tribune* once said: "Miss Jackson seemingly cannot write a poor sentence") and in the work presented here the reader will find the wit and delight in storytelling that were her trademarks.

LAURENCE JACKSON HYMAN
SARAH HYMAN STEWART
San Francisco
August 1995

Preface

🖉

All I Can Remember

ALL I CAN REMEMBER clearly about being sixteen is that
it was a particularly agonizing age; our family was in the
process of moving East from California, and I settled down into a
new high school and new manners and ways, all things that I believe
produce a great uneasiness in a sixteen-year-old. I know that a chemistry class in the new high school was suspended so that I could see
my first snowfall; the entire class stepped outside and amused itself
watching my reactions to something I had never dreamed was real.

I also remember such a tremendous and frustrated irritation with
whatever I was reading at the time—heaven knows what it could
have been, considering some of the things I put away about that
time—that I decided one evening that since there were no books in
the world fit to read, I would write one.

After dismissing the poetic drama as outmoded and poetry as far
too difficult, I finally settled on a mystery story as easiest to write and
probably easiest to read. It occurred to me that if I wrote all of the
story except for the end, I might put the names of all the characters
into a hat and draw out one to be the murderer, thus managing to
surprise even myself with the ending. I remember that I sat all day
upstairs in my room, writing wildly in order to set up a situation in
which one of my characters (all most unsavory, and given to adolescent wisecracks) could be chosen as the murderer. After the first two
or three murders, the story got rather sketchy, because I had not
enough patience to waste all that time with investigation, so I put the

names of my characters together and took my manuscript downstairs to read to my family.

My mother was knitting, my father was reading a newspaper, and my brother was doing something—probably carving his initials in the coffee table—and I persuaded them all to listen to me; I read them the entire manuscript, and when I had finished, the conversation went approximately like this:

BROTHER: Whaddyou call *that*?

MOTHER: It's very nice, dear.

FATHER: Very nice, very nice. *(to my mother)* You call the man about the furnace?

BROTHER: Only thing is, you ought to get *all* those people killed. *(raucous laughter)*

MOTHER: Shirley, in all that time upstairs I hope you remembered to make your bed.

I do not remember what character eventually came out of the hat with blood on his hands, but I do remember that I decided never to read another mystery story and never to write another mystery story; never, as a matter of fact, to write anything ever again. I had already decided finally that I was never going to be married and *certainly* would never have any children. It may have been about that time that I came to believe that being a private detective was the work I was meant to do.

—SHIRLEY JACKSON

PART ONE

THE SMOKING ROOM

H E WAS TALLER THAN I had imagined him. And noisier. Here I was, all by myself, downstairs in the dormitory smoking room with my typewriter, and all of a sudden there was this terrific crash and sort of sizzle, and I turned around and there he was.

"Can't you be a little quieter?" I said. "I'm trying to work."

He just stood there, with smoke rolling off his head. "This is as quietly as I can do it," he said apologetically. "It takes a lot of explosive power, you know."

"Well, explode somewhere else," I said. "Men aren't allowed in here."

"I know," he said.

I turned around to get a good look at him. He was still smoking a little, but otherwise he seemed quite a charming young man. The horns were barely noticeable, and he was wearing pointed patent leather shoes that covered his cloven hoofs. He seemed to be waiting for me to make conversation.

"You must be the devil," I said politely, and added: "I presume."

"Yes," he said, pleased. "I *am* the devil."

"Where's your tail?" I demanded. He blushed and made a vague gesture with his hand.

"Circumstances . . ." he murmured. He came over to the table where I was working. "What're you doing?" he asked.

"I'm writing a paper," I said.

"Let's see." He reached over to the typewriter and I shoved his hand away, getting quite a nasty burn from it, too.

"Mind your own business," I told him.

He sat down meekly. "Look," he said, "do you have an extra cigarette?"

I threw the pack over to him and watched him light one with the tip of his finger. My hand was all inflamed where I had touched him, and it hurt.

I held out my hand to him. "You oughtn't to treat people like that," I said. "It makes enemies."

He looked at my hand sympathetically, then murmured over it, and the burn vanished. "That's better," I said.

We sat back and smoked for a minute, looking at each other. He was a good-looking guy.

"By the way," I said finally, "do you mind telling me what you're here for?"

"This is a college, isn't it?"

I looked at him for a minute, but he didn't seem to mean anything nasty, so I said: "You are at present in the smoking room of the largest girls' dormitory on the campus of State University, and the housemother will raise hell if she finds you here."

He began to laugh, and I realized that my choice of words had been a little silly, to say the least.

"I'd like to meet this housemother," he said.

I tried to imagine what *that* would be like, and gave up. "She's the closest thing to you you'll find on earth," I said earnestly.

He raised his eyebrows, and then suddenly seemed to think of something, because he reached into a pocket and pulled out a piece of paper.

"I wonder if you'd mind signing this?" he asked casually.

I picked up the paper. "May I read it first?"

He shrugged. "It isn't important, but go ahead."

I read: " 'This gives the devil my soul,' " and a space was left blank for my name. "This isn't awfully legal," I said.

He looked anxiously over my shoulder. "Isn't it?" he said. "What's wrong with it?"

"Well, obviously!" I threw the paper down on the table and pointed at it scornfully. "Who's ever going to think that holds in a court of law? No witnesses, a thousand loopholes for a smart lawyer . . ."

He had picked up the paper and was frowning over it miserably. "It's always been perfectly all right before," he said.

"Well, I'm just surprised at your methods of doing business, that's all. No court would even look at it."

"Look," he said. "We'll make out another contract . . . one *you* think is all right. I don't want to do this thing wrong, after all."

I thought. "All right," I said. "I'll make one up. Mind you, I'm not awfully sure of the legal terminology, but I think I can manage."

"Go ahead," he said. "If it suits you, it suits me."

I pulled the paper out of the typewriter and found a carbon and two new sheets.

He looked at the carbon suspiciously.

"What's that?"

"I'm making two copies," I told him. "I've got to keep one myself. That makes it binding."

He continued to regard me suspiciously while I worked over the contract.

"How long is this contract good for?" I asked at once.

"Oh, eternity," he said easily.

I finally finished and took the sheets out of the typewriter. Due to the fact that my knowledge of legal documents is restricted to the notices the dean sends out about poor grades, the contract was just a little confused. It read:

> I (here a space was left blank for a name), hereinafter
> to be known as the party of the first part, do hereby sell
> and consign my soul, hereinafter to be known as the
> party of the second part, to the custody and careful
> watchfulness of (here another space was left blank),
> hereinafter to be known as the party of the third part,
> who does hereby swear and promise the sum of one
> dollar in return, also other unnamed considerations,
> admitting and conceding that it is a fair and just
> bargain, and no complaints afterward; this agreement to
> be binding, by mutual consent of the parties concerned,
> in any court of law, wherever conducted. (signed)
> (witnessed)

The devil read it twice. "I don't understand it," he said.

"It says the same thing as yours did," I told him, "except that it's more binding." I pointed over his shoulder. "You see all those things about the parties of the first and second parts? And about the court of law? That all makes it legal."

"Well, sign it, then," he said.

I thought. "We need a witness," I said. "I'll go upstairs and get my roommate."

I left before he could say anything. My roommate was asleep.

"Look, Bobbie," I said. I shook her. She turned over and said, "Go away."

"Bobbie," I said, "you've got to come and witness a contract."

"What the hell," Bobbie said.

"I've got the devil waiting downstairs."

"Let him wait," Bobbie said. She had both eyes open but she wouldn't move. I rolled her out of bed and stood her up. "Come on," I said. "He'll get impatient."

"Signing contracts with the devil," Bobbie said in disgust. "At three in the morning. How's a person ever going to get any sleep."

"Come *on*!" I said.

Bobbie sat down on the edge of her bed. "If he's been waiting all these thousands of years," she said, "he can wait until I get some lipstick on."

By the time I got her downstairs, the devil had smoked four more of my cigarettes. He got up when we entered and bowed very low to Bobbie.

"Charmed," he said.

Bobbie smiled at him invitingly. "Hello," she said.

"Come on, you two," I told them, "I've got to get this over with and get back to work."

"What do I have to do?" Bobbie said, looking at the devil out of the corner of her eye.

"Just sign," the devil said, taking her arm to lead her over to the table.

Bobbie let out a yell that ought to have waked the housemother and the whole dormitory. The devil backed away and began to apologize, but Bobbie stood there rubbing her arm and glaring.

"Look," she said belligerently, "I'm not fooling around with any guy sets fire to you when he touches you." The devil looked at Bobbie's arm and made the burn go away, but after that Bobbie kept the table between them. I took up the contract.

"I'll sign first," I said. I wrote my name quickly in the *second* blank and handed the paper to the devil.

"You have to sign, too," I said.

"Where?" He looked blankly at the paper. I showed him the first place and handed him my pen. He blushed, and looked from me to Bobbie. "I'm afraid . . ." he began, "do you mind if . . ." he shrugged and made an X in the space. "I never learned . . ." he said apologetically. Bobbie's jaw dropped and she just stood there until I kicked her in the ankle.

"Sign here," I said, and she signed in the witness space.

Then the devil and I signed again at the bottom, and signed the duplicate the same way, and I handed him one sheet and kept the other.

"Now," I said as casually as I could, "I guess I owe you a dollar."

"What for?" he said.

"Bobbie," I said rapidly, "run upstairs and borrow a buck from someone."

"What the hell," Bobbie said. But she turned around and started up the stairs.

"Well," said the devil, rubbing his hands, "what can I do for you now?"

I began to polish my nails on my hand. "Let's see," I said. "I'll start out with an A in Chemistry 186, the power to be invisible when I come in after hours, a date with the captain of the football team for the senior ball—"

"Throw in something for me," said Bobbie, coming through the door.

"Let's see," I said, "give her—"

"A date with that blond guy," said Bobbie, "*you* know." She handed me a dollar.

"I guess that's about all," I said to the devil.

"Except, of course," Bobbie put in, "except for a couple of hundred thousand dollars."

"You shall have all those things," the devil promised eagerly.

"Oh, yes," I said. "And you get this out of it." I handed him the dollar.

"What's this for?" he asked.

I looked at the contract. "That's for your soul," I said.

The devil looked at his contract. "*Your* soul," he said.

"No." I showed him the contract. "Where you signed, it says you give me your soul for the sum of one dollar, also other unnamed considerations. Those would be the cigarettes of mine you smoked."

"And getting me out of bed," Bobbie added.

The devil read the contract again. Then he began to stamp his feet, and flames came out of his mouth. Bobbie and I looked at each other.

"Golly," she said. "What a date *this* guy would be!"

Just then the devil seemed to get a little pale, and he backed up against the wall, staring in back of us. Bobbie and I turned around, and there was the housemother. She stood in the doorway, in a bathrobe, with curlpapers on her hair, and she was an awe-inspiring sight.

She looked at the devil. "Young man," she said, "what are you doing here?"

"Ma'am . . ." the devil began.

"You're a fire hazard," she snapped.

"Yes'm," the devil said.

"Leave at once," she said ominously, "before I report you to the dean of women."

The devil cast one dreadful look at Bobbie and me, and then tried to vanish in a puff of smoke. All he succeeded in, however, was a weak sizzle, and then he was gone.

"All *right*," said the housemother. Then she turned to Bobbie and me.

"Well?" she said.

"Look," Bobbie began.

"You see, it was like this—" I said.

"Hmph," said the housemother. "Devils, indeed!" And she went back to bed.

I Don't Kiss

Strangers

⚜

EVERY TIME HE CAME over to where she was sitting he
would start to say something and then decide not to; there were
too many people around for him to say anything sentimental, and her
attitude discouraged whatever humorous comments the situation
suggested. Once he sat down next to her and took hold of her hand,
but she only smiled at him vaguely and went on staring straight in
front of her.

The room was so full of people and there was so much noise and
he wanted to get her outside somewhere into the night, but there was
nothing to say to her to get her there. He told someone about it,
somewhere along in the evening. "You can't just go up to a girl in the
middle of a party and say 'come on outside into the air, we gotta say
goodbye somehow.'"

But the guy he told about it said only, "For Christ sake take her in
the bedroom, it's empty now," and wandered away.

Finally, when the party was good and drunk, and the singing was
loud enough to cover most conversations, he went over and sat down
next to her again.

"Look," he said, "I'd sort of like to talk to you."

"Sure," she said. "I'm listening."

There wasn't anything to say from there; he thought of reminding
her that this was their last evening together, but discarded that as
tactless; he also wanted to ask her why their last time together should

be spent with the two of them out of joint, but knew he could never get an answer. He said: "I keep looking at you all the time."

"I don't want to look at you now," she said very quickly, "I've got enough to remember you now."

"You'll come see me, won't you?" He grabbed her hand and tugged at it, trying to make her look at him. "You'll come be a camp follower, won't you?"

"Nope," she said. "I'm going home. To mother."

"And you'll spend all day sitting in a nice cool bridge luncheon while I slave away over a hot Garand rifle."

"Shut up," she said.

Now was the time, and he said it. "Come away. Let's get out of here."

"I don't want to get too far from the liquor," she said.

"Just outside for a few minutes."

"No." Then she said, "Wait a minute. Come on." She picked up her drink and a box of cigarettes and waved at him to follow her. She took him into the bathroom and locked the door.

"Here," she said. "Now we aren't too far away and there aren't any people."

"Suppose someone wants to come in," he said, sitting on the edge of the bathtub.

"Let them wait. We won't be long."

"Such a cheerful place," he said, looking around. "Dedicated, like our publishing houses, to the least pleasant waste of humanity."

"Goody," she said. "We're going to have a drawing room parting. You must be Noel Coward and go on saying things like that."

"What's the matter with you, for God's sake—you just drunk?"

"No," she said.

It seemed that now he could say anything that had seemed too tactless or too useless before, so he began: "Darling, it's our last evening together, and I don't want it spoiled . . ."

"Why should our last evening be any different from any other? I spoiled enough of them before, didn't I?"

"But I don't want to keep thinking of you like—"

"Listen," she said. "This isn't one of our good times together—didn't you know that? Can't you see that there's a difference between us being in love and having fun, and you being drafted and us being in love?"

"It's different?" he asked.

"Sure, it's different. Up to last night everything was the same, but the minute it started being your last day with me it got to be different. And it's going to be different for a hell of a long time."

"A year."

"Stop the crap about a year," she said. "Even if you do come back you'll be an ex-soldier. You'll have all sorts of dreadful things to remember and you'll be different."

"Anyone would think you were the one got the draft number," he said.

"You think I didn't? I can sit here and say yes, it'll be a long time before I see you again, and not even intimate what a long time means. How I'll sit around and read letters. Or find me another guy. I haven't even got an idea what this new guy looks like. I don't even know how his voice will sound. That's what a long time means. And all the things I'll have to do without you. I can't even comprehend right now the number of times I'll get into bed by myself. Or with somebody else—this guy I don't know. Or how many times I'll run out of cigarettes without having you to run out and get them."

"Yeah," he said, "but which one of us has to lie on his belly in the mud?"

"Which one of us has to readdress your mail?" she said. "Who's going to have to wind the clock now, or remember to take out the garbage every night?"

"You'll get used to it."

"Then I'll be different too. I'll be someone who's living without you, like you're someone who goes to army camp tomorrow."

"But why can't we be happy tonight, at least?" he demanded. "Why the hell do we have to bawl about it? We're fighting because I'm going away—that's silly."

"Nobody's fighting," she said, "and nobody's bawling. You'd like nothing better than a chance to pat me on the back and say 'there there, it's only a year,' but I won't let you. I won't even feel bad—just different."

"But why?"

"Because this saying goodbye is the only thing I've got now," she said. "Because I've got to go on doing the same old things forever afterward, that's why, and nothing stays the same when you're different."

"That doesn't make sense," he said. "You mean I'm different because I'm going away."

"Can't you see?" she said. Then: "Look, I'll try again. You're not just the guy I love anymore. You're the guy I love who's been drafted. And all I get out of it is this few minutes saying goodbye to you. When you go away I won't have anything at all except what you leave me. And I don't want to spend these last few minutes with the guy I love who's been drafted."

"I'm sorry," he said. "I don't get it."

"No," she said. "Well, I'll write you a letter."

Someone began to pound on the door, then, and he said, "The party sounds like it's breaking up."

"Yeah," she said. She stood up. "Well . . ."

He stopped at the door and turned around. "You're not going to cry, are you?"

"No," she said.

She walked around him and unlocked the door, and he put out his arms to her, but she turned away.

"No," she said. "I don't kiss strangers. You ought to know that by now."

Summer

Afternoon

$\mathcal{D}$

R OSABELLE JEMIMA HENDERSON, WHO could open and close her eyes and had real hair that could be curled and braided, lay back comfortably against the pink pillow in her doll stroller. Beside her, Amelia Marian Dawson, who could take real walking steps when her hands were held, and could say Mama and Dada upon request, slept, her long lashes shadowing her delicately colored cheeks under the roof of her doll carriage. On the front steps of the Dawson house, their maternal duties suspended for a minute, Jeannie Dawson and Carrie Henderson bent solemnly over their second-favorite game, which between themselves they called Flower People. Jeannie had fair hair pulled back into a pony tail tied with a pink ribbon, and Carrie had square-cut dark hair and wore a red shirt. Carrie thought that Jeannie's mother was the second-nicest mother in the world, and Carrie's father could make Jeannie laugh until she squeaked, when he made funny faces.

When they played Flower People they made tiny houses of leaves and grass, and the little bells from the bush next to Jeannie's front porch were dainty pink and white ladies. From the low tree around the side of Jeannie's house they gathered green pods which made cradles for the little flower children. Jeannie had a nutshell for a table in her house, and Carrie had a scrap of silver paper for a rug in her house. "My lady is coming to visit your lady," Jeannie said, and minced a pink blossom over to Carrie's house. "How do you do, Mrs. Brown?" the pink lady asked. "I have come to see you for lunch."

"How do you do, Mrs. Smith," Carrie's white lady said, flouncing to her own front door. "Will you come in and sit down in my living room with the silver carpet and I will make some lunch for us."

The pink lady and the white lady sat in leaf chairs and between them Carrie set a rose petal with two bird berries on it. "Will you have some ice cream?" the white lady asked. "And some cake and cookies? I made them myself."

"Thank you very very much," the pink lady said. "They are certainly very very delicious."

"Listen," Carrie said, white lady poised. "Listen, my mother *did* make some cookies today."

"Then let's go over to your house," Jeannie said.

"We'll ask her will she give us cookies and milk," Carrie said.

Leaving the pink and white ladies at lunch, and Rosabelle and Amelia sound asleep by the steps, they moved down the front walk, stopping once to examine a small creature, which Carrie thought was most probably a daddy longlegs and Jeannie thought was almost certainly a baby caterpillar, and then paused again on the sidewalk to wonder if the moving van might possibly be going to stop on their block; when it continued on past them, they went lingeringly up the front walk to Carrie's house. There was a path through the hedge that stood between the two houses; this was used by Jeannie's mother and Carrie's mother and by their fathers, going back and forth, but Carrie and Jeannie used the front walks, because they always had plenty of time.

Carrie's mother had indeed made cookies, but it was too close to dinnertime for more than one cookie each and so, nibbling carefully around the edges to make the cookies last longer, they came out of Carrie's house and wandered down the sidewalk again.

"I don't want to play Flower People anymore," Jeannie said.

"I don't want to either," Carrie said. "We could play hopscotch."

"Hopscotch is really only about my fifteenth-favorite thing to do," Jeannie said. "We could play jumprope."

"Jumproping is only about my hundredth-favorite thing to do. We could play dancing."

"We could color with crayons."

"We could climb the walnut tree."

"We could play dancing."

Carrie thought. "We could go see Tippie," she said.

"Yes." Jeannie nodded so that her long hair flopped over her face. "We can go see Tippie."

Just of a size, they moved with slow grace along the sidewalk, nibbling at their cookies. "We haven't been to see Tippie for a very very long time," Jeannie said.

"Maybe Tippie's been wishing we could come to see her."

"Maybe Tippie's been sad because we never came."

"It's been days and days since we went to see Tippie."

Without planning, they both began to skip on the same step. They did not need to ask each other if skipping might be a good idea just along here, because at this point they always began to skip, and skipped until they came just past the Browns' driveway, where the sidewalk was broken. Then they walked again, going solemnly single file along the broken place in the sidewalk and then walking again side by side to the corner and around it, past the vacant lot where, one evening, the big boys in the neighborhood had made a Boy Scout campfire and roasted potatoes, and Carrie and Jeannie, watching curiously from the sidewalk, had each been given a toasted marshmallow, which was sticky but nice. The vacant lot belonged to the Browns, but all the big kids in the neighborhood played there, and once the boys had built a kind of hut, and no girls were allowed. Jeannie and Carrie were not allowed to play in the vacant lot because they were small, but they were allowed to walk around the block so long as they did not put one foot, not even one toe, into the street. Even when it rained and the water ran raging down the gutters and the big kids built dams and sailed leaf boats, Jeannie and Carrie were not allowed to put one toe off the sidewalk into the street. This was perfectly fair. When Jeannie and Carrie were big kids they would play in the gutter when it rained and would go to school all day and make snow forts in the vacant lot. While Jeannie and Carrie were small—it was perfectly fair—they could go all around the block, even pushing their doll carriages if they liked, but not put one toe into the street.

Once, along this block past the vacant lot, the Harris boy had given first Carrie and then Jeannie a ride in his skate wagon, and sometimes in the early evening, just after dinner, when the sky was still green and voices sounded strangely far away, Carrie and Jeannie were allowed to walk together around the corner and watch the big kids play kick-the-can in the street, or hide-and-seek around the streetlight, or prisoner's base. One of the big girls who played prisoner's base came sometimes to baby-sit for Jeannie or Carrie when their mothers and fathers went out in the evening, and then she would read stories, and cut out paper dolls.

Around the next corner was the part that Carrie and Jeannie did not like so well, but it was where Tippie lived. Through the trees behind these houses they could see the backs of their own houses, where they lived, and it was funny to see your own house from the back, when it couldn't see you. One of the things that made this street less happy was Mrs. Branson's garden, which was long and dark and shadowy with big drooping trees, and not at all a good place to play, even when Mrs. Branson did not come out and say she would call the police if children kept running over her lawn.

"I wonder if Tippie's looking for us," Jeannie said, skipping again; they always skipped going past Mrs. Branson's house, because they liked to get past it quickly. "I bet she's been waiting and waiting and waiting for us to come again."

"I bet she's been asking her mother could she call us on the telephone," Carrie said.

Tippie's house was on the corner. It would have been shorter to go around the other way, up the other side of the block, but Carrie and Jeannie always went to Tippie's house along the street with the vacant lot; they always had plenty of time. The other way was the way to go home; after passing Tippie's house the only place to go was the way home. Besides, from this side they could see Tippie's window as they went along the street.

"I wonder if she's there today," Carrie said, stopping on the sidewalk to look up at the second-floor window. "I can see her dollhouse inside there."

They looked up anxiously. Sometimes the window caught the sun and then they could not see anything inside, but sometimes, like today, the window shone clean and sparkling in the afternoon light.

"I can see her teddy bear and her giraffe," Jeannie said.

"I bet she's got her toy shelf right along under the windowsill," Carrie said as she had said many times before. "That way, everyone can see her toys and when she comes home she can look right up and see them waiting there for her, her teddy bear and her dollhouse."

"The Noah's Ark is gone," Jeannie said. "I bet she's playing with her Noah's Ark today."

"And the pretty doll in the blue dress is gone. I bet she has her doll and is playing dolls with it, and then she's going to play with her Noah's Ark."

"I wish she'd even wave, or something," Jeannie said.

"I wish she'd even come to the window and look at us and wave," Carrie said.

"I wish she'd come outdoors and play sometimes," Jeannie said.

"Maybe she was disobedient and her mother said she had to stay in her room all day," Carrie said as she had said many times before.

"Maybe she was sick and her mother said she had to stay in bed till her temperature went down," Jeannie said as she had said many times before.

"Maybe she has a friend who comes to play with her every afternoon."

"Maybe she has a baby kitten and can't leave it all alone."

"I wish she'd even wave, sometimes," Carrie said.

"I bet she's glad when we come to see her, though."

Sighing, Carrie turned away. "I guess she doesn't want to play with us today, either."

They stood for a minute, looking up at the window. "Bye, Tippie," Jeannie said softly. "Bye, Tippie," Carrie said.

Then they began to skip, going on along the sidewalk, and skipped around the corner and most of the way down the next street; this was the longest skipping they did, because this street was not interesting at all, just houses with no children unless you counted the Andovers' little tiny baby which might just be outside in its baby carriage and Jeannie and Carrie could tiptoe up very very softly and peek in, smiling with incredulous delight at the tiny hands and the little pink sleeping face. Today not even the Andovers' baby was outside, and so they skipped all the way down to the corner and around that corner to Jeannie's front steps, where the flower ladies still lingered over their dainty lunch, and Rosabelle and Amelia slept on.

"I'm going to ask my mother why Tippie can't come out and play," Jeannie said suddenly.

"Then your mother could call her mother on the telephone and say could Tippie come over," Carrie pointed out. "I'm going to ask *my* mother can Tippie please come to my birthday party."

"I'm going to ask my mother can Tippie come over tomorrow."

"I'm going to ask my mother can Tippie come and live with us." Giggling wildly, they reeled down the sidewalk just as the back door of Carrie's house opened and Carrie's mother called, "Carrie? Carrie? Time to come in now."

Sitting in the kitchen on the high stool beside the counter, Jeannie watched her mother peeling potatoes, and sang quietly to herself. Outside it was getting darker; the leaves were changing color, and soon it would be the end of summer and the big kids would go back to school. In another year Jeannie and Carrie would go to school, would walk off each morning with the big kids, would even, perhaps, carry a book or a pencil box or lunch in a paper bag; "Mommy," Jeannie said absently, "will Tippie go to school someday?"

"I suppose so. Who is Tippie?"

"The little girl."

"If she's a little girl she will certainly go to school. Where does she live?"

"Around the corner. We go to see her all the time, me and Carrie."

Jeannie's mother hesitated, frowning. "Another little girl around here?" she asked, and then, worried, "Baby," she said, "have you and Carrie been crossing the street?"

"No, no, not a toe," Jeannie said, and giggled. "Tippie lives on *our* block. Around the corner. Past Mrs. Branson's dark old garden."

"Which house, baby?"

"On the corner, after Mrs. Branson's garden. We start from our own front walk and we go to the corner and we go around and we go past the vacant lot and then we go around *that* corner and we go past Mrs. Branson's and then on the *next* corner is Tippie's house."

Mrs. Dawson put down the potato she was peeling and came to lean on the counter across from Jeannie; she put out one finger and touched Jeannie's nose and both of them laughed. "Silly small thing," Mrs. Dawson said. "That's the Archers' house."

"And Tippie lives there. We go and look up at the window and we see her playing but she doesn't come outside. We go and watch her."

Mrs. Dawson stopped laughing and came around the end of the counter and gathered Jeannie up off the stool and then sat down with Jeannie in her lap. Jeannie curled herself up and sighed luxuriously. "Baby," Mrs. Dawson said, "did someone talk to you about Mrs. Archer and her little girl? Maybe Helen, when she came to babysit?"

"No," Jeannie said, wondering. "But can you call Mrs. Archer and ask her can Tippie come over and play sometime?"

"Baby," Mrs. Dawson said, and stopped. Then she took a breath and asked slowly, "Baby, did you ever hear of people dying?"

"Sure," Jeannie said, surprised. "Great-grandmother died, and Carrie's goldfish."

"Mrs. Archer had a little girl, and she died," Mrs. Dawson said, still speaking very carefully. "You must have heard someone talking about it; it didn't happen very long ago."

"Tippie stays in her room all the time. We watch her put her toys on the windowsill and take them down again. She has a Noah's Ark and a doll in a blue dress and a yellow giraffe."

"Jeannie." Mrs. Dawson gave her a little shake. "There *is* no little girl at the Archers' house. There are no children there at all now," and she held Jeannie tighter. "There are certainly no toys. I know." She hesitated again. "I packed them away myself," she said. "They gave everything away."

"Why did you have to pack the things if they belonged to Mrs. Archer's little girl? Why didn't Mrs. Archer pack them herself?"

"Mrs. Archer wasn't feeling very well. Carrie's mother and Mrs. Brown and I went over to help her."

"That was nice of you." Jeannie wriggled comfortably. "Helping her pack when she didn't feel well."

"But you must promise me something, baby. You must promise me that you will never *never* say anything to Mrs. Archer about pretending to see a little girl—"

Jeannie sat up indignantly. "It's not pretending," she said. "We go all the time and watch Tippie. It's our third-favorite game."

Mrs. Dawson started to speak, and then stopped. Instead, she put her cheek down on Jeannie's bright head. "Why do you call her Tippie?" she asked after a minute.

Jeannie giggled. "We thought sometimes we could see just the tip of her head or the tip of her hand waving, so we called her Tippie. It's a name we made up, Carrie and me."

"I see," Mrs. Dawson said. Then she went on brightly, "You know, young lady, if I don't get my potatoes peeled pretty soon, your daddy will come home and he'll say 'WHERE'S MY DINNER,' and when there isn't any dinner what do you think he'll do?"

"He'll spank us," Jeannie said delightedly. "He'll spank us both."

She slid off her mother's lap and landed on the floor, laughing and sitting. "Mommy," she asked, "would you feel bad if I died like Tippie?"

Mrs. Dawson reached out and touched Jeannie's nose quickly and lightly. "Yes," she said. "I would feel very bad indeed."

"Listen," Jeannie said, scrambling to her feet, "there's Carrie calling me. Why do you suppose she came over again just before dinner?"

Scurrying, she raced through the dining room and through the hall and tugged open the front door. "Hi, Carrie," she said.

"I forgot Rosabelle Jemima," Carrie said. "I had to come and get her so she wouldn't catch cold being outside so late."

"Did you ask your mother could Tippie come over?"

"Yes, but she said no," Carrie said. "Did you?"

"Yes, but she said no. Ask your mother can I come to your house for lunch tomorrow."

"I'll ask her. And you ask your mother can *I* come to *your* house for lunch tomorrow. Then we can call each other on the telephone and say."

"All right. You can bring Rosabelle Jemima if she doesn't catch cold."

"All right. Goodbye, Jeannie."

"Goodbye, Carrie."

Carrie turned the doll stroller and started off down the walk. "Listen," Jeannie called, "you ask your mother."

"I will. And you ask yours."

"Don't forget."

"You don't forget either."

"Goodbye, Carrie."

"Goodbye, Jeannie."

"See you tomorrow."

"See you tomorrow."

"Goodbye, Rosabelle Jemima."

"Goodbye, Amelia Marian."

"Goodbye."

"Goodbye."

Indians Live
in Tents

36 Elm St.
Tuesday

Dear Miss Griswold,
This is just a note of thanks, to say that I want you to know how much I certainly appreciate your kindness in letting me have this apartment. Every time I come home at night and look around my own little room-and-a-half I think of you, and I think of how if I didn't speak to Timmy Richards and Timmy Richards hadn't known Eve Martin and Eve Martin hadn't gotten in touch with Bill Ireland and Bill Ireland hadn't known you, then I would still be living out in Staten Island with my sister and her kids, and I remember how grateful I am to you for giving me your apartment. I wish you could see it now. Of course your stuff was good-looking, and I guess I could never make this place look as pretty as you had it, but of course the first thing I had to do was put away all that stuff with the ruffles and the curtains and things, and now I've got my ship models and my college pictures up and it sure looks swell. Whenever you want your stuff, of course, it's right here. I wouldn't touch it for anything.
Well, thanks again, and I sure hope you're happy in your new place. You sure were lucky to get it and whenever you want to send for your furniture I'll send it along to you and then get my furniture from Bill Ireland and he can get his stuff from Timmy Richards and Timmy can get his back from his mother. So thanks again, and yours very sincerely,
Allan Burlingame

101 Eastern Square
Thursday

Dear Mr. Burlingame,

I'm so glad you like my apartment, and of course I'm truly delighted that I was able to pass it along to you. Naturally I'm not even beginning to be settled here yet, so of course can't send for my furniture right away. However, as soon as I get my sublease straightened out, we can fix everything. As you know, I'm having a little trouble with the landlord, because we didn't want to tell him right away about how I was subleasing the place—he wanted it for his aunt or something—so of course it's not really legal yet, my being here. As a result I'd be very grateful if you didn't address your letters such as the last one to me direct. Address them to me care of Tuttle, which is the name of the people I'm subleasing from. Or better still, if you have any problems, telephone. The number is listed under the name of J. T. Maloney, which is the name of the people the Tuttles subleased from, and of course no one liked to have the phone changed because the landlord never really liked *having the Tuttles sublease from the Maloneys.*

As a matter of fact, it's just me and the telephone here now. I managed to wear two blankets in under my coat when I came in so I can roll up in them at night, and I had my toothbrush in my pocketbook and I've sneaked in a towel and a cake of soap, but otherwise it's sort of empty. The Tuttles took their furniture out piece by piece and put it into the back of their car covered with a rug, and yesterday the bed went and I must say it looked like the janitor was going to catch us taking the springs down the back stairs.

If you know of any way you can sneak some kind of a folding chair up to me, I'd appreciate it.

Yours very truly,
Marian Griswold

36 Elm St.
Monday

Dear Miss Griswold,

Sorry to hear of your roughing it. There is nothing I would like better than turning over all your furniture to you right away, since my friends think it is sort of funny my sleeping in a bed with a pink canopy and keeping my watch and loose change on a dresser with a gauze skirt thing on it. I finally found the telephone under that little doll effect you had, and would call you instead of writing except that the telephone book is holding up one foot of the bathtub and I can't get it out. I also wish you could get some of your clothes out of the closet partly because I could use the hangers and partly because my aunt brought me over a chocolate cake yesterday and when she went to the closet to hang up her coat I had a terrible time explaining to her. Can you think of anything?

Sincerely,
Allan Burlingame

101 Eastern Square
Wednesday

Dear Mr. Burlingame,

I am having enough trouble getting in and out of my apartment myself without trying to carry a dresser with a gauze skirt. If you don't like it, move. I have to go up the stairs one flight at a time, hiding in the shadows on every landing for fear someone should see me and tell the landlord there is someone strange living in the Tuttles' apartment. I gave the janitor five dollars and I told him I was visiting the Tuttles and they never came out of the apartment because they all had influenza, but I'm pretty sure he knows they moved out and I am living there because I think he saw the living room chairs in the elevator, and I know *he saw me moving in the cot, but I told him it was because the Tuttles didn't have enough beds, and then I gave him the five dollars.*

At any rate I have a place to sleep now and I hope to get in a coffeepot tomorrow or the next day. As soon as I tell the landlord that the Tuttles have moved and I am leasing the apartment I will be able to send for my furniture.

Yours very truly,
Marian Griswold

Shax, Asmodeus, Baal, and Co. Realtors

Dear Mrs. Tuttle,
In reference to the apartment 3C at 101 Eastern Square, subleased in your name from Mr. J. T. Maloney, we are sorry to be in a position to inform you that your sublease having expired, we have no choice but to inform you that your sublease on apartment 3C at 101 Eastern Square is no longer valid, and we shall expect to recover said premises on October 1st of this year, that being the date upon when your sublease expires. We are sorry to inform you that if you do not vacate said premises before said

date we shall have to service upon you first warning of a notice of eviction.

Yours extremely cordially,
B. H. Shax, Executive Vice President

101 Eastern Square
Monday

Dear Helen,
This just came. What shall I do?
Desperately,
Marian

95 Martin Lane
Wednesday

Dear Marian,
Hang on, if you can. Because we have trouble enough of our own—it turns out the owner of this apartment can't stand children and just because some old grouch complained about Butchie's tricycle in the halls, and anyway it's their own fault if the old halls are so dark, anyway, the landlord is being real nasty about it. So whatever you do do, don't let go of that apartment—we may be coming back.
Best,
Helen

36 Elm St.
Thursday

Dear Miss Griswold,
I am very sorry to keep bothering you like this, but the lady in the apartment down the hall here says that you owe her a dollar and sixty-five cents for a C.O.D. package which you never paid her, and I tried to give her your new address but she said she wanted the money so I had to give her the dollar sixty-five, which I am afraid left me rather pressed, since the rent here is higher than I was paying my sister when I lived with her. So I would be grateful if you could send it along. Also the bottom of your bookcase fell out and I tried to put it back but didn't do much of a job on it. And I'm sorry but I burned a hole in the top of your coffee table.

How are you getting along in your new place? I think I know where I can borrow a car and anytime you want your furniture I'd be glad to bring it over. Just let me know.
Sincerely,
Allan Burlingame

Thurs.

Dear Miss, Landlord came over today and made me let him into 3C to see if it was evicted and so here is your five back because I couldn't keep him out.
Charles E. Murphy (janitor)

Shax, Asmodeus, Baal, and Co. Realtors

Dear Mrs. Tuttle,
Thank you for leaving so promptly after my letter. We must now only trouble you for the amount ($65.75) of last month's rent.
Most extremely cordially,
B. H. Shax

101 Eastern Square
Friday

Dear Mr. Shax,
You were misinformed. The Tuttles have moved, but I have taken over this apartment with their permission. Enclosed is my check for the month's rent. Every human being has the right to shelter. Indians live in tents, Eskimos live in igloos, dogs live in kennels, and I am living here.
Sincerely,
Marian Griswold

Shax, Asmodeus, Baal, and Co. Realtors

Dear Miss Griswold,
Enclosed is your check for last month's rent of apartment 3C at 101 Eastern Square because we are returning it. If you are interested in the possibilities of renting a kennel or an igloo, I suggest you consult with some real estate firm that handles that type of business. Our firm handles

only apartments, and since you are not the legal resident of the apartment at 101 Eastern Square you cannot pay the rent. Since you believe that you are *the legal resident of the apartment you may consider this as first warning of notice to evict.*

Most extremely cordially,
B. H. Shax

101 Eastern Square
Wednesday

Dear Mr. Burlingame,
Bring over all my furniture as fast as you can. I intend to stay in this apartment until a gentleman named B. H. Shax comes personally and carries me out into the street, and that is going to be harder than he thinks, because I am not an easy person to carry down three flights of stairs.

Sincerely,
Marian Griswold

36 Elm St.
Thursday

Dear Bill,
Will you get together my stuff and bring it over as soon as you can? I'm finally getting this dame's stuff out of the place. Thank heaven,
Al

10 Oliver
Friday

Dear Timmy,
Sorry, but I'm afraid I'll be needing my furniture and things. Al wants his back because he is getting rid of the stuff that girl left in his place.
Bill

1249 Jones St.
Saturday

Dear Mom, would you mind sending along as soon as possible the bed and chairs and stuff you said once I could have? On account of the guy who owns the furniture in this apartment wants it. Can I have the little radio too? Will write soon.

Love,
Timmy

101 Eastern Square
Monday

Dear Mr. Shax,
I am enclosing again my check for last month's rent on this apartment. I have spoken to Mrs. Tuttle and she believes that her sublease gives her the right to sub-sublease, although it does not allow her to open a vegetable stand on the sidewalk, keep mockingbirds, or advertise clairvoyant readings in the front windows. So you can consider me as having sub-sublet the apartment and I suggest you keep the check.
Sincerely,
Marian Griswold

Shax, Asmodeus, Baal, and Co. Realtors

Dear Miss Griswold,
Enclosed please find your check for $65.75 to cover the rent for one month on apartment 3C at 101 Eastern Square. Since you are not the legal resident of this apartment it would not be legal for us to accept this check. Mrs. Tuttle is mistaken. Her lease gives her every right to keep mockingbirds, but none whatsoever to sub-sublet.
Most extremely cordially,
B. H. Shax
P.S. Please consider this as second warning of notice to evict.

101 Eastern Square
Friday

Dear Mr. Shax,
If I am not the legal resident of the apartment you cannot evict me. You cannot evict Mrs. Tuttle, who is the legal resident of the apartment, because she is not living here. Unless you accept my check you are not going to receive any rent for the apartment at all because you cannot rent it to anyone else while I am living here because you cannot evict me so

they could move in. Mrs. Tuttle will not pay the rent because she is not living here.

Sincerely,
Marian Griswold

95 Martin Lane
Friday

Marian dear,

I'm really awfully sorry, but I'm afraid we're coming back. To the apartment, I mean. They definitely won't let us stay here with Butchie, and they don't much like the dog, either. We figure there's no use fighting just to keep an old apartment we're not crazy about, so back we come. I'm really terribly sorry about your moving and all, but you do understand, don't you?

Love,
Helen

Shax, Asmodeus, Baal, and Co. Realtors

Dear Miss Griswold,

I am not a hard-hearted man, and even though the real estate business is one of dog-eat-dog you must try to understand that it is only because the real estate business is like that, that we frequently seem to be unpleasant and hard-hearted. I could not sleep nights if I put a young girl out onto the street to starve. I am not really a hard-hearted man, so you may keep the apartment. Will you please forward by return mail your check for last month's rent on apartment 3C at 101 Eastern Square plus your check for next month's rent and a signed statement to the effect that you will not sub-sub-sublet. I assume that you have no intention of opening a sidewalk vegetable stand, keeping dogs or children, hanging pictures on the walls, making unnecessary noise, leaving garbage in the hall, blocking the stairway or the elevator, putting scratches on the floors, renting rooms for money, or opening any business for profit on the premises. As I say, I am not a hard-hearted man, and I could not sleep nights if I had to forcibly evict you.

Most extremely cordially,
B. H. Shax

101 Eastern Square
Tuesday

Dear Mr. Burlingame,

This is a terrible thing to do, but I guess I will have to have my old apartment back, and just as everything was all right here, too. The people

I got this one from want it back because they can't stay in their new place with a baby. So don't bring over my furniture. I'll probably be wanting to come back next week sometime.
  Sincerely,
  Marian Griswold

36 Elm St.
Wednesday

Dear Bill,
Never mind about the stuff. The dame wants the place back.
Al

10 Oliver
Thursday

Dear Timmy,
I won't be needing my furniture for a while yet. Al got kicked out of his apartment by the dame who's coming back.
  Bill

1249 Jones St.
Friday

Dear Mom,
It's O.K. about the furniture. Hope you haven't already sent it, because I won't be needing it now. Will write soon.
  Love,
  Timmy

36 Elm St.
Friday

Dear Felicia,
I am sure you will forgive my taking this method of asking you this question, when you realize how much it means to me, and how whenever I am with you I find it impossible to gather my courage to speak. I know that you have for a long time been aware of my feelings for you, and if by some lucky chance you feel the same way about me, it would certainly be wonderful.
  Could you possibly consider becoming my wife? We would have to live with your family for a while until we found an apartment, but as you know, I have a good job with good prospects and it would be the ambition

of my life to support you in a comfortable fashion, and of course for a while we would save money on rent.

Please let me know at once. You will make me the happiest of men.
Your own,
Allan

95 Martin Lane
Monday

Marian dear,
The most wonderful *thing has happened, and just* wait *till you hear. You know we are being thrown out of this apartment and honestly I was just* desperate, *but then last Sunday we went out to Connecticut to visit Eve Crawley and her new husband—you remember Eve, don't you? With that amazing hair?—and* what *do* you *think? We just by pure blind luck found the most* adorable *little cottage for sale, and well, to make a long story short, we grabbed all our money on the spot and made a down payment on it, and we're moving in next week. What do you think of that? It's got four rooms and of course there's some work to be done around the place—putting in a bathroom and whatnot, and fixing one corner of the roof, but Bill can do that nights when he comes home, because of course he'll have to commute, and there's nearly an acre of ground, and the* loveliest *old trees, and I'm going to drive him to the station every morning and meet him every night, and then during the day I can do the painting and papering around the house. And it cost only sixteen thousand, with the most* miserable *down payment, and we can take the rest of our lives to pay off the mortgage, if we want to—the bank was* terribly *nice about it. Aren't you jealous of us, living in the* country? *And of course you'll come and visit us just every chance you get, and we can all have* loads of fun getting together and fixing the place up. Must go now—we're signing the last papers this afternoon.*
Love,
Helen

101 Eastern Square
Tuesday

Dear Mr. Burlingame,
If you still want my apartment you can have it. Heaven has just passed a miracle in my favor.
Sincerely,
Marian Griswold

36 Elm St.
Wednesday

Dear Bill . . .

10 Oliver
Thursday

Dear Timmy . . .

1249 Jones
Friday

Dear Mom . . .

16 Arden's Court
Saturday

Dear Allan,
I can't tell you how pleased and flattered and happy I was at your
letter, and I guess you knew all the time what I would say when you
finally got around to asking me. Of course I will marry you, and I think
it's wonderful.
Mother and Dad are also very happy at the idea and Dad says that now
that their last child is getting married it's time for them to move back to
California, where they always wanted to be, anyway. So they are going to
let us have this apartment and most of the furniture as a wedding present,
and even though twelve rooms might be a little large for us at first, we can
always manage to use the space for giving parties and such. Mother says
come for dinner tomorrow night and we can talk it over.
Love, from your
Felicia

THE VERY HOT
SUN IN BERMUDA

※

IT WAS THE FIRST false summer of the college year, the time when the lawns first come out green and the sky is first really blue; the apple trees had chosen to occupy themselves with faint pink blossoms; the campus buildings were beginning to look old and dusty and red between the fresh trees and the really blue sky. In another week it might be snowing again, with the sudden treacherous weather that goes with spring dances and precommencement engagement parties, and ends, finally, in a blaze of heat and lethargy, with final exams and the last tortured words of the term paper.

It was Saturday; Katie Collins had spent all morning in the sun, starting the tan on her long legs and smooth back; by fall she would be startlingly brown, and could wear white evening dresses to set it off. Walking across campus, she watched her legs, still a little tan from last year, perhaps faintly reddened by this morning's sun. Ought to have a black bathing suit this year, she was thinking, strapless, two-piece, make the men whistle when I go along the beach. Thinking of the men whistling made her smile while she walked. Hot sun, hot sand; in another month she would be swimming, playing tennis, dancing, sailing; thinking about it made the sun seem hotter already; or green, she reflected, I could get a wicked green bathing suit, green is always good on me.

She was wearing yellow shorts, in honor of the sun, and she felt appropriate to the grass and the trees; walking across campus, it suddenly occurred to her that the next spring, unlike this spring and last spring and the one before that, she would spend somewhere else; married, probably, she thought, I ought to get married right after I graduate; girls like me aren't safe single. She smiled again at the quiet campus. Everyone was studying, or sunbathing, or lying around drinking Cokes; no one was walking outdoors except Katie.

Maybe not go home at all, she decided, just go off somewhere like Bermuda for a honeymoon. It made her laugh to think of herself lying in the very hot sun in Bermuda while some of her friends were still in college.

Tall and long-legged and alone, she walked quickly across the campus to where the grass ended and the ground sloped down to a brook; turning, she followed the brook a little way until she came in sight of a small one-story building set back from the trees along the brook. Then she began to walk more slowly, stopping to look down at the brook, putting her hands in her pockets to saunter along until something far off caught her attention; when she was very close to the building she said, "Hi!" She waited for a minute, and then went over and tapped imperatively on the window next to the door. "Hi," she said again.

She waited for another minute, and then the key turned and the door opened. "Keep you waiting?" Katie said cheerfully. She walked up to the door and stood against the doorway, smiling. "You been waiting long?" she demanded.

"*Please* come in," the man said.

"No one's around," Katie said, but she went inside and closed the door behind her. The windows made the studio very light, and on this sunny day there was a rich pale glow in the room that touched the colors on the pictures around the wall, and brightened completely the canvas on the easel, a still life of an apple, a book, and a copper candlestick. Katie walked over to a bench along one wall and sat down, stretching her legs out in front of her. "I'm worn out," she said. "I ran most of the way."

"You didn't look it, coming along the path."

Katie laughed, regarding her long legs approvingly. "I was teasing you," she said.

"You didn't even look at the picture," he said.

Katie stood up leisurely and came over to look at the still life on the easel. "Gets prettier every day," she said, "and so do you." She turned around and looked at him critically. "But you look so sad." She went over and pulled childishly at the sleeve of his old corduroy jacket, and he looked at her quickly and then back at the picture.

"Why wouldn't I be sad?" he said. He gestured at the picture. "I've been working at it all day."

"It looks swell," Katie said. "Honestly, I think it looks fine."

He rubbed his hand wearily across his long, thin forehead. When he smiled at her, finally, his face seemed more helpless, with a sort of sullen intention at helplessness. He took her hand, and said, "I needed you to come."

"Well, I'm here," Katie said. "And the picture's okay." She pulled away from him and started to walk around the room, her hands in her pockets. "You've changed things around again," she said. When there was no answer she said sharply, "Peter, wake up! I said you've been changing things around again."

He said, "I thought 'Mood' would look better in the center. Stand out more." He was still standing helplessly in front of the easel, watching her when she walked across to stand in front of the picture he called "Mood." It was a painting of a girl sitting by a window; she was a very pretty girl with long dark hair down her back; she was wearing a white dress and she was staring at the moon. "It looks swell here," Katie said. "Just fine." She began to laugh, not turning around. "Were you late for dinner yesterday?" she asked.

"Not very."

"Was she sore?"

"Katie," he said desperately, "for God's sake, stop walking around and come talk to me." His voice trailed off weakly. "I don't know what to do," he said.

"Poor old Peter," Katie said. She came over and took his arm, leading him to the bench. "Poor old Peter," she said again. "She gives you a hell of a time."

He put his head in his hands, saying shakily, "Sometimes I think I can't stand it much longer. What am I going to do?"

"Don't get all upset," Katie said. Impatient again, she got up and reached into the pocket of her shorts for a cigarette. Lighting it, she walked over to the easel and said to the picture, "Don't pay any attention to her."

"I think if she doesn't leave me alone—" he said.

Katie moved closer to the picture, frowning. "Why is this part blue?" she asked. "You told us in class . . ."

He lifted his head. "I wanted to see how it would look there. It's a sort of departure to give a greater effect." He sighed. "I suppose it looks awful."

"It'll do," Katie said. She moved restlessly away from the picture and along the nearest wall, seeing without interest the familiar pictures one after another, still lifes of vases and books and violins and china cats, portraits of his children, an occasional abstract in vicious reds and yellows, a landscape with a rusty barn, a picture of a beautiful girl with dark hair knee-deep in a moonlit pool, another of a beautiful girl with dark hair gathering roses by moonlight. "I passed her on campus this morning and she wouldn't speak to me," Katie said.

He was frowning, staring at an imaginary picture. "It needs *something* there," he said. "Blue seemed like the thing."

"I wanted to walk right up to her and slap her face," Katie said. "What a worn-out old hag."

"Don't talk like that," he said.

"Excuse me," Katie said formally. "I forgot she was your wife. What a well-preserved old hag." She laughed, and he smiled reluctantly. "Cheer up," she went on, "don't let her make you miserable." Her tour of the room brought her back to the easel, and she said, "It's a *swell* picture, honestly."

"I made it as good as I could for you," he said. "I only wish I weren't a third-rate artist." He waited for a minute. "If I could make it better, I would," he said.

Katie dropped her cigarette on the floor and put her shoe on it. "I don't want to make her mad, though," she said. "She could get me thrown out of college if she got mad enough."

"She's waiting for you to graduate." He stood up wearily and went over to the easel, looking at the picture while he felt out for the brushes and palette beside it. "She says that after a few weeks I'll never see you again."

"She better not make any kind of a fuss," Katie said.

He began to paint cautiously. "I've let her go on thinking that I won't see you again."

"I certainly wish you could come out to the beach," Katie said.

"I don't know." He pursed up his lips doubtfully. "She may go away somewhere with the children."

Katie said quickly, "But of course there's my family and all my friends. Maybe I could meet you in New York or someplace."

"New York would be easy," he said, turning around to her. "I told you I could manage New York."

"I'll see how things come out," Katie said. Going to the window near the door, she said, "This weather is driving me crazy. Let's go outside for a while, go wading in the brook."

"Too many people around on a day like this," he said. "I don't want her to get any more suspicious than she already is."

"Oh, Lord," Katie said. "Were you ever in Bermuda?" She tapped her fingers irritably on the window glass. "I'd like to go to Bermuda."

"Come away from the window," he said. "You're not supposed to be here."

Katie stamped her feet walking to the bench; she sat down, pulling up her legs and wrapping her arms around them. "How nearly finished are you?"

"Another couple of days."

"Plenty of time," Katie said. "I don't have to have it till May fifteenth."

"I'll spend some time working it over," he said. "I'm not satisfied at all."

"I am," Katie said. "As long as I graduate. They don't expect me to be a genius." She yawned, and stood up. "I'm going."

He turned away from the easel, surprised. "I thought you'd stay awhile."

"I stayed awhile," Katie said. "I'm no help to you while you're painting, anyway." She stopped with one hand on the door and kissed one finger to him. "You work nice and hard," she said, "and I'll see you in class Monday."

He said desperately, "Katie, listen," and she hesitated, the door just open. "Can't you tell me something to say to her?" He stood without moving, looking at her eagerly, his shoulders weak. "Think of *some*thing," he said.

"Let me see." Katie stood in the doorway, chewing her lip. "Tell her," she said finally, "you tell her that I wouldn't hurt her for the world." She smiled and waved her hand. "Bye," she said, and slipped out the door, closing it gently behind her. Before she was more than a few steps away, she heard the key turn in the lock.

As though anyone cared, she thought, going along beside the brook; next spring I could be in Paris. As she started across the campus she thought suddenly, why not a poppy-red bathing suit? and laughed out loud. Boy, she said to herself, they could see me coming a mile away.

NIGHTMARE

IT WAS ONE OF those spring mornings in March; the sky between the buildings was bright and blue and the city air, warmed by motors and a million breaths, had a freshness and a sense of excitement that can come only from a breeze starting somewhere in the country, far away, and moving into the city while everyone is asleep, to freshen the air for morning. Miss Toni Morgan, going from the subway to her office, settled a soft, sweet smile on her face and let it stay there while her sharp tapping feet went swiftly along the pavement. She was wearing a royal blue hat with a waggish red feather in it, and her suit was blue and her topcoat a red and gray tweed, and her shoes were thin and pointed and ungraceful when she walked; they were dark blue, with the faintest line of red edging the sole. She carried a blue pocketbook with her initials in gold, and she wore dark blue gloves with red buttons. Her topcoat swirled around her as she turned in through the door of the tall office building, and when she entered her office sixty floors above, she took her topcoat off lovingly and hung it precisely in the closet, with her hat and gloves on the shelf above; she was precise about everything, so that it was exactly nine o'clock when she sat down at her desk, consulted her memorandum pad, tore the top leaf from the calendar, straightened her shoulders, and adjusted her smile. When her employer arrived at nine-thirty, he found her typing busily, so that she was able to look up and smile and say, "Good morning, Mr. Lang," and smile again.

At nine-forty Miss Fishman, the young lady who worked at the desk corresponding to Miss Morgan's, on the other side of the room, phoned in to say that she was ill and would not be in to work that day. At twelve-thirty Miss Morgan went out to lunch alone, because Miss Fishman was not there. She had a bacon, tomato, and lettuce sandwich and a cup of tea in the drugstore downstairs, and came back early because there was a letter she wanted to finish. During her lunch hour she noticed nothing unusual, nothing that had not happened every day of the six years she had been working for Mr. Lang.

At two-twenty by the office clock Mr. Lang came back from lunch; he said, "Any calls, Miss Morgan?" as he came through the door, and Miss Morgan smiled at him and said, "No calls, Mr. Lang." Mr. Lang went into his private office, and there were no calls until three-oh-five, when Mr. Lang came out of his office carrying a large package wrapped in brown paper and tied with an ordinary strong cord.

"Miss Fishman here?" he asked.

"She's ill," Miss Morgan said, smiling. "She won't be in today."

"Damn," Mr. Lang said. He looked around hopefully. Miss Fishman's desk was neatly empty; everything was in perfect order and Miss Morgan sat smiling at him. "I've got to get this package delivered," he said. "Very important." He looked at Miss Morgan as though he had never seen her before. "Would it be asking too much?" he asked.

Miss Morgan looked at him courteously for a minute before she understood. Then she said, "Not at all," with an extremely clear inflection, and stirred to rise from her desk.

"Good," Mr. Lang said heartily. "The address is on the label. Way over on the other side of town. Downtown. You won't have any trouble. Take you about"—he consulted his watch—"about an hour, I'd say, all told, there and back. Give the package directly to Mr. Shax. No secretaries. If he's out, wait. If he's not there, go to his home. Call me if you're going to be more than an hour. Damn Miss Fishman," he added, and went back into his office.

All up and down the hall, in offices directed and controlled by Mr. Lang, there were people alert and eager to run errands for him. Miss Morgan and Miss Fishman were only the receptionists, the outer bulwark of Mr. Lang's defense. Miss Morgan looked apprehensively at the closed door of Mr. Lang's office as she went to the closet to get her coat. Mr. Lang was being left defenseless, but it was spring outside, she had her red topcoat, and Miss Fishman had probably run off under cover of illness to the wide green fields and buttercups of the country. Miss Morgan settled her blue hat by the mirror on the inside of the closet door, slid luxuriously into her red topcoat, and picked up her pocketbook and gloves, and put her hand through the string of the package. It was unexpectedly light. Going toward the elevator, she found that she could carry it easily with the same hand that held her pocketbook, although its bulk would be awkward on the bus. She glanced at the address: "Mr. Ray Shax," and a street she had never heard of.

Once in the street in the spring afternoon, she decided to ask at the newspaper stand for the street; the little men in newspaper stands seem to know everything. This one was particularly nice to her, probably because it was spring. He took out a little red book that was a guide to New York, and searched through its columns until he found the street.

"You ought to take the bus on the corner," he said. "Going across town. Then get a bus going downtown until you get to the street. Then you'll have to walk, most likely. Probably a warehouse."

"Probably," Miss Morgan agreed absently. She was staring behind him, at a poster on the inside of the newspaper stand. "Find Miss X," the poster said in screaming red letters, "Find Miss X. Find Miss X. Find Miss X." The words were repeated over and over, each line smaller and in a different color; the bottom line was barely visible. "What's that Miss X thing?" Miss Morgan asked the newspaper man. He turned and looked over his shoulder and shrugged. "One of them contest things," he said.

Miss Morgan started for the bus. Probably because the poster had caught her eye, she was quicker to hear the sound truck; a voice was blaring from it: "Find Miss X! Win a mink coat valued at twelve thousand dollars, a trip to Tahiti; find Miss X."

Tahiti, Miss Morgan thought, on a day like this. She went swiftly down the sidewalk, and the sound truck progressed along the street, shouting, "Miss X, find Miss X. She is walking in the city, she is walking alone; find Miss X. Step up to the girl who is Miss X, and say 'You are Miss X,' and win a complete repainting and decorating job on your house, win these fabulous prizes."

There was no bus in sight and Miss Morgan waited on the corner for a minute before thinking, I have time to walk a ways in this lovely weather. Her topcoat swinging around her, she began to walk across town to catch a bus at the next corner.

The sound truck turned the corner in back of her; it was going very slowly, and she outdistanced it in a minute or so. She could hear, far away, the announcer's voice saying, ". . . and all your cosmetics for a year."

Now that she was aware of it, she noticed that there were "Find Miss X" posters on every lamppost; they were all like the one in the newsstand, with the words running smaller and smaller and in different colors. She was walking along a busy street, and she lingered past the shopwindows, looking at jewelry and custom-made shoes. She saw a hat something like her own, in a window of a store so expensive that only the hat lay in the window, soft against a fold of orange silk. Mine is almost the same, she thought as she turned away, and it cost only four ninety-eight. Because she lingered, the sound truck caught up with her; she heard it from a distance, forcing its way through the taxis and trucks in the street, its loudspeaker blaring music, something military. Then the announcer's voice began again: "Find Miss X, find Miss X. Win fifty thousand dollars in cash; Miss X is walking the streets of the city today, alone. She is wearing a blue hat with a red feather, a reddish tweed topcoat, and blue shoes. She is carrying a blue pocketbook and a large package. Listen carefully. Miss X is carrying a large package. Find Miss X, find Miss X. Walk right up to her and say 'You are Miss X,' and win a new home in any city in the world, with a town car and chauffeur, win all these magnificent prizes."

Any city in the world, Miss Morgan thought, I'd pick New York. Buy me a home in New York, mister, I'd sell it for enough to buy all the rest of your prizes.

Carrying a package, she thought suddenly, *I'm* carrying a package. She tried to ease the package around so she could carry it in her arms, but it was too bulky. Then she took it by the string and swung it as close to her side as she could; must be a thousand people in New York right now carrying large packages, she thought; no one will bother me. She could see the corner ahead where her bus would stop, and she wondered if she wanted to walk another block.

"Say 'You are Miss X,'" the sound truck screamed, "and win one of these gorgeous prizes. Your private yacht, completely fitted. A pearl necklace fit for a queen. Miss X is walking the streets of the city, completely alone. She is wearing a blue hat with a red feather, blue gloves, and dark blue shoes."

Good heavens, Miss Morgan thought; she stopped and looked down at her shoes; she was certainly wearing her blue ones. She turned and glared angrily at the sound truck. It was painted white, and had "Find Miss X" written on the side in great red letters.

"Find Miss X," the sound truck said.

Miss Morgan began to hurry. She reached the corner and mixed with the crowd of people waiting to get on the bus, but there were too many and the bus doors were shut in her face. She looked anxiously down the long block, but there were no other buses coming, and she began to walk hastily, going toward the next corner. I could take a taxi, she thought. That clown in the sound truck, he'll lose his job. With her free hand she reached up and felt that her hat was perched at the correct angle and her hair neat. I hope he *does* lose his job, she thought. What a thing to do! She could not help glancing over her shoulder to see what had become of the sound truck, and was shocked to find it creeping silently almost next to her, going along beside her in the street. When she looked around, the sound truck shouted, "Find Miss X, find Miss X."

"Listen," Miss Morgan told herself. She stopped and looked around, but the people going by were moving busily without noticing her. Even a man who almost crashed into her when she stopped suddenly said only "Excuse me," and went on by without a backward look. The sound truck was stopped by traffic, up against the curb, and Miss Morgan went over to it and knocked on the window until the driver turned around.

"I want to speak to you," Miss Morgan said ominously. The driver reached over and opened the door.

"You want something?" he asked wearily.

"I want to know why this truck is following me down the street," Miss Morgan said; since she did not know the truck driver, and would certainly never see him again, she was possessed of great courage. She made her voice very sharp and said, "What are you trying to do?"

"Me?" the truck driver said. "Look, lady, I'm not following anybody. I got a route I gotta go. See?" He held up a dirty scrap of paper, and Miss Morgan could see that it was marked in pencil, a series of lines numbered like streets, although she was too far away to see what the numbers were. "I go where it tells me," the truck driver said insistently. "See?"

"Well," Miss Morgan said, her voice losing conviction, "what do you mean, talking about people dressed like me? Blue hats, and so on?"

"Don't ask me," the truck driver said. "People hire this truck, I drive where they say. I don't have nothing to do with what happens back there." He waved his hand toward the back of the truck, which was separated from him by a partition behind the driver's seat. The traffic ahead of him started and he said quickly, "You want to know, you ask back there. Me, I don't hear it with the windows all shut." He closed the door, and the truck moved slowly away. Miss Morgan stood on the curb, staring at it, and the loudspeaker began, "Miss X is walking alone in the city."

The nerve of him, Miss Morgan thought, reverting to a culture securely hidden beneath six years of working for Mr. Lang, the god-damn nerve of him. She began to walk defiantly along the street, now slightly behind the sound truck. Serve them right, she thought, if anyone says to me, "Are you Miss What's-her-name?" I'll say "Why, yes, I am, here's your million dollars and you can go—"

"Reddish tweed topcoat," the sound truck roared, "blue shoes, blue hat." The corner Miss Morgan was approaching was a hub corner, where traffic moved heavily and quickly, where crowds of people stood waiting to cross the street, where the traffic lights changed often. Suppose I wait on the corner, Miss Morgan thought, the truck will have to go on. She stopped on the corner near the sign "bus stop," and fixed her face in the blank expression of a bus rider, waiting for the sound truck to go on. As it turned the corner it shouted back at her, "Find Miss X, find Miss X, she may be standing next to you now."

Miss Morgan looked around nervously, and found she was stand-ing next to a poster that began "Find Miss X, find Miss X," but went on to say, "Miss X will be walking the streets of New York TODAY. She will be wearing blue—a blue hat, a blue suit, blue shoes, blue gloves. Her coat will be red and gray tweed. SHE WILL BE CAR-RYING A LARGE PACKAGE. Find Miss X, and claim the prizes."

Good Lord, Miss Morgan thought, good Lord. A horrible idea crossed her mind: Could they sue her, take her into court, put her in jail for dressing like Miss X? What would Mr. Lang say? She real-ized that she could never prove that she wore these clothes inno-cently, without criminal knowledge; as a matter of fact, she remembered that that morning, out in Woodside, while she was drinking her coffee, her mother had said, "You won't be warm enough; the paper says it's going to turn cold later. Wear your heavy coat at least." How would Miss Morgan ever be able to explain to the police that the spring weather had caught her, made her take her new coat instead of her old one? How could she prove anything? Cold fear caught Miss Morgan, and she began to walk quickly, away from the poster. Now she realized that there were posters everywhere: on the lampposts, on the sides of the buildings, blown up huge against the wall of a high building. I've got to do something right away, she thought, no time to get back home and change.

Trying to do so unobtrusively, she slid off her blue gloves and rolled them up and put them into her pocketbook. The pocketbook itself she put down behind the package. She buttoned her coat to hide the blue suit, and thought, I'll go into a ladies' room somewhere and take the feather out of my hat; if they know I tried to look different, they can't blame me. Ahead of her on the sidewalk she saw a young man with a microphone; he was wearing a blue suit and she thought humorously, put a blue hat on him and he'd do, when she realized that he was trying to stop people and talk about Miss X.

"Are you Miss X?" he was saying. "Sorry, lady, red topcoat, you know, and carrying a package. Are you Miss X?" People were walking wider to avoid him, and he called to ladies passing, and sometimes they looked at him curiously. Now and then, apparently, he would catch hold of someone and try to ask them questions, but usually the women passed him without looking, and the men glanced at him once, and then away. He's going to catch me, Miss Morgan thought in panic, he's going to speak to *me*. She could see him looking through the crowds while he said into the microphone, loudly enough so that anyone passing could hear, "Miss X is due to come down this street, folks, and it's about time for Miss X to be passing by here. She'll be along any minute, folks, and maybe you'll be the one who walks up to her and says 'Are you Miss X?' and then you'll get those beautiful awards, folks, the golden tea service, and the library of ten thousand of the world's greatest books, folks, ten thousand books, and fifty thousand dollars. All you have to do is find Miss X, folks, just find the one girl who is walking around this city alone, and all you have to do is say 'You are Miss X,' folks, and the prizes are yours. And I'll tell you, folks, Miss X is now wearing her coat buttoned up so you can't see her blue suit, and she's taken off her gloves. It's getting colder, folks, let's find Miss X before her hands get cold without her gloves."

He's going to speak to me, Miss Morgan thought, and she slipped over to the curb and signaled wildly for a taxi. "Taxi," she called, raising her voice shrilly, "taxi!" Over her own voice she could hear the man with the microphone saying, "Find Miss X, folks, find Miss X." When no taxi would stop, Miss Morgan hurried to the other side of the sidewalk, next to the buildings, and tried to slip past the man at the microphone. He saw her, and his eyes jeered at her as she went by. "Find Miss X, folks," he said, "find the poor girl before her hands get cold."

I must be crazy, Miss Morgan thought. I'm just getting self-conscious because I'm tired of walking. I'll definitely get a taxi on the next corner.

"Find Miss X," the sound truck shouted from the curb next to her.

"She's gone past here now," the man with the microphone said behind her, "she's passed us now, folks, but she's gone on down the street, find Miss X, folks."

"Blue hat," the sound truck said, "blue shoes, carrying a large package." Miss Morgan went frantically out into the street, not looking where she was going, crossed directly in front of the sound truck, and reached the other side, to meet a man wearing a huge cardboard poster saying "Miss X, Miss X, find Miss X. CARRYING A LARGE PACKAGE. Blue shoes, blue hat, red and gray tweed coat, CARRYING A LARGE PACKAGE." The man was distributing leaflets right and left, and people let them fall to the ground without taking them. Miss Morgan stepped on one of the leaflets and "Find Miss X" glared up at her from the ground under her foot.

She was going past a millinery shop, when she had a sudden idea; moving quickly, she went inside, into the quiet. There were no posters in there, and Miss Morgan smiled gratefully at the quiet-looking woman who came forward to her. They don't do much business in *here,* Miss Morgan thought, they're so eager for customers, they come out right away. Her well-bred voice came back to her; "I beg your pardon," she said daintily, "but would it be possible, do you think, for you to let me have either a hat bag or a hatbox?"

"A hatbox?" the woman said vaguely. "You mean, empty?"

"I'd be willing to purchase it, of *course,*" Miss Morgan said, and laughed lightly. "It just so happens," she said, "that I have decided to carry my hat in this beautiful weather, and one feels so foolish going down the street *carry*ing a hat. So I thought a bag . . . or a hatbox . . ."

The woman's eyes lowered to the package Miss Morgan was carrying. "Another package?" she asked.

Miss Morgan made a nervous gesture of putting the package behind her, and said, her voice a little sharper, "Really, it doesn't seem like such a *strange* thing to *ask*. A hatbox or a bag."

"Well . . ." the woman said. She turned to the back of the shop and went to a counter behind which were stacked piles of hatboxes. "You see," she said, "I'm alone in the shop right now, and around here very often people come in just to make nuisances of themselves. There've been at least two burglaries in the neighborhood since we've been here, you know," she added, looking uneasily at Miss Morgan.

"Really?" Miss Morgan said, her voice casual. "And how long, may I ask, have you been here?"

"Well . . ." the woman said. "Seventeen years." She took down a hatbox, and then, suddenly struck with an idea, said, "Would you like to look at some hats while you're here?"

Miss Morgan started to say no, and then her eye was caught by a red and gray caplike hat, and she said with mild interest, "I might just try *that* one on, if I might."

"Indeed, yes," the woman said. She reached up and took the hat off the figure that held it. "This is one of our best numbers," she said, and Miss Morgan sat down in front of a mirror while the woman tried the hat on her.

"It's lovely on you," the woman said, and Miss Morgan nodded. "It's just the red in my coat," she said, pleased.

"You really ought to wear a red hat with that coat," the woman said.

Miss Morgan thought suddenly, what would Mr. Lang say if he knew I was in here trying on hats when I'm supposed to be going on his errands. "How much is it?" she asked hastily.

"Well . . ." the woman said. "Eight ninety-five."

"It's *far* too much for this hat," Miss Morgan said. "I'll just take the box."

"That's eight ninety-five *with* the box," the woman said unpleasantly.

Helplessly, Miss Morgan stared from the woman to the mirror to the package she had put down on the counter. There was a ten-dollar bill in her pocketbook. "All right," she said finally. "Put my old hat in a box and I'll wear this one."

"You'll never be sorry you bought that hat," the woman said. She picked up Miss Morgan's blue hat and set it inside a box. While she was tying the box she said cheerfully, "For a minute I was afraid you were one of the sort comes into a shop like this for no good. *You* know what I mean. Do you know, we've had two burglaries in the neighborhood since we've been here?"

Miss Morgan took the hatbox out of her hand and handed her the ten-dollar bill. "I'm in rather a hurry," Miss Morgan said. The woman disappeared behind a curtain at the back of the shop and came back after a minute with the change. Miss Morgan put the change in her pocketbook; I won't have enough for a taxi there and back, she thought.

Wearing the new hat, and carrying the hatbox and her pocketbook and the package, she left the shop, while the woman stared curiously after her. Miss Morgan found that she was a block and a half away from her bus stop, so she started again for it, and she was nearly on the corner before the sound truck came out of a side street, blaring, "Find Miss X, find Miss X, win a Thoroughbred horse and a castle on the Rhine."

Miss Morgan settled herself comfortably inside her coat. She had only to cross the street to get to her bus stop, and the bus was coming; she could see it a block away. She stopped to get the fare out of her pocketbook, shifting the package and the hatbox to do so, when the sound truck went slowly past her, shouting, "Miss X has changed her clothes now, but she is still walking alone through the streets of the city, find Miss X! Miss X is now wearing a gray and red hat, and is carrying *two* packages; don't forget, *two* packages."

Miss Morgan dropped her pocketbook and the hatbox, and stopped to pick up the small articles that had rolled out of her pocketbook, hiding her face. Her lipstick was in the gutter, her compact lay shattered, her cigarettes had fallen out of the case and rolled wide. She gathered them together as well as she could and turned and began to walk back the way she had come. When she came to a drugstore she went inside and to the phones. By the clock in the drugstore she had been gone just an hour and was only three or four blocks away from her office. Hastily, her hatbox and the package on the floor of the phone booth, she dialed her office number. A familiar voice answered—Miss Martin in the back room, Miss Walpole?— and Miss Morgan said, "Mr. Lang, please?"

"Who is calling, please?"

"This is Toni Morgan. I've got to speak to Mr. Lang right away, please."

"He's busy on another call. Will you wait, please?"

Miss Morgan waited; through the dirty glass of the phone booth she could see, dimly, the line of the soda fountain, the busy clerk, the office girls sitting on the high stools.

"Hello?" Miss Morgan said impatiently. "Hello, hello?"

"Who did you wish to speak to, please?" the voice said—it might have been Miss Kittredge, in accounting.

"Mr. Lang, please," Miss Morgan said urgently. "It's important."

"Just a moment, please." There was silence, and Miss Morgan waited. After a few minutes impatience seized her again and she hung up and found another nickel and dialed the number again. A different voice, a man's voice this time, one Miss Morgan did not know, answered.

"Mr. Lang, please," Miss Morgan said.

"Who's calling, please?"

"This is Miss Morgan, I must speak to Mr. Lang at once."

"Just a moment, please," the man said.

Miss Morgan waited, and then said, "Hello? Hello? What *is* the matter here?"

"Hello?" the man said.

"Is Mr. Lang there?" Miss Morgan said. "Let me speak to him at once."

"He's busy on another call. Will you wait?"

He's answering my other call, Miss Morgan thought wildly, and hung up. Carrying the package and the hatbox, she went out again into the street. The sound truck was gone and everything was quiet except for the "Find Miss X" posters on all the lampposts. They all described Miss X as wearing a red and gray cap and carrying two packages. One of the prizes, she noticed, was a bulletproof car, another was a life membership in the stock exchange.

She decided that whatever else, she must get as far from the neighborhood as she could, and when a taxi stopped providentially to let off passengers at the curb next to her, she stepped in, and gave the driver the address on the package. Then she leaned back, her hatbox and the package on the seat next to her, and lit one of the cigarettes she had rescued when her pocketbook fell. I've been dreaming, she told herself, this has all been so silly. The thing she most regretted was losing her presence enough, first, to speak so to the driver of the sound truck, and then to drop her pocketbook and make herself conspicuous stooping to pick everything up on the street corner. As the taxi drove downtown she noticed the posters on every lamppost, and smiled. Poor Miss X, she thought, I wonder if they *will* find her?

"I'll have to stop here, lady," the taxi driver said, turning around.

"Where are we?" Miss Morgan said.

"Times Square," the driver said. "No cars getting through downtown on account of the parade."

He opened the door and held out his hand for her money. Unable to think of anything else to do, Miss Morgan paid him and gathered her hatbox and package together and stepped out of the taxi. The street ahead was roped off and policemen were guarding the ropes. Miss Morgan tried to get through the crowd of people, but there were too many of them and she was forced to stand still. While she was wondering what to do, she heard the sound of a band and realized that the parade was approaching. Just then the policeman guarding the curb opened the ropes to let traffic cross the street for the last time before the parade, and all the people who had been standing with Miss Morgan crossed to the other side and all the people who had been on the other side crossed to stand on Miss Morgan's side, turning in order to cross again on the side street at right angles to the way they had crossed before, but the policemen and the crowds held them back and they waited, impatient for the next crossing. Miss Morgan had been forced to the curb and now she could see the parade coming downtown. The band was leading the parade; twelve drum majorettes in scarlet jackets and skirts and wearing silver boots and carrying silver batons marched six abreast down the street, stepping high and flinging their batons into the air in unison; following them was the band, all dressed in scarlet, and on each of the big drums was written a huge X in scarlet. Following the band were twelve heralds dressed in black velvet, blowing on silver trumpets, and they were followed by a man dressed in black velvet on a white horse with red plumes on its head; the man was shouting, "Find Miss X, find Miss X, find Miss X."

Then followed a float preceded by two girls in scarlet who carried a banner inscribed in red, "Win magnificent prizes," and the float represented, in miniature, a full symphony orchestra; all the performers were children in tiny dress suits, and the leader, who was very tiny, stood on a small platform on the float and led the orchestra in a small rendition of "Afternoon of a Faun"; following this float was one bearing a new refrigerator, fifty times larger than life, with the door swinging open to show its shelves stocked with food. Then a float bearing a model of an airplane, with twelve lovely girls dressed as clouds. Then a float holding a golden barrel full of enormous dollar bills, with a grinning mannequin who dipped into the barrel, brought up a handful of the great dollar bills, and ate them, then dipped into the barrel again.

Following this float were all the Manhattan troops of Boy Scouts; they marched in perfect line, their leaders going along beside and calling occasionally, "Keep it up, men, keep that step even."

At this point the side street was allowed open for cross traffic, and all the people standing near Miss Morgan crossed immediately, while all the people on the other side crossed also. Miss Morgan went along with the people she had been standing with, and once on the other side, all these people continued walking downtown until they reached the next corner and were stopped. The parade had halted here, and Miss Morgan found that she had caught up with the float representing the giant refrigerator. Farther back, the Boy Scouts had fallen out of their even lines, and were pushing and laughing. One of the children on the orchestra float was crying. While the parade halted, Miss Morgan and all the people she stood with were allowed to cross through the parade to the other side of the avenue. Once there, they waited to cross the next side street.

The parade started again. The Boy Scouts came even with Miss Morgan, their lines straightening, and then the cause of the delay became known; twelve elephants, draped in blue, moved ponderously down the street; on the head of each was a girl wearing blue, with a great plume of blue feathers on her head; the girls swayed and rocked with the motion of the elephants. Another band followed, this one dressed in blue and gold, but the big drums still said X in blue. A new banner followed, reading "Find Miss X," with twelve more heralds dressed in white, blowing on gold trumpets, and a man on a black horse who shouted through a megaphone, "Miss X is walking the streets of the city, she is watching the parade. Look around you, folks."

Then came a line of twelve girls, arm in arm, each one dressed as Miss X, with a red and gray hat, a red and gray tweed topcoat, and blue shoes. They were followed by twelve men each carrying two packages, the large brown package Miss Morgan was carrying, and the hatbox. They were all singing, a song of which Miss Morgan caught only the words "Find Miss X, get all those checks."

Leaning far out over the curb, Miss Morgan could see that the parade continued for blocks; she could see green and orange and purple, and far far away, yellow. Miss Morgan pulled uneasily at the sleeve of the woman next to her. "What's the parade for?" she asked, and the woman looked at her.

"Can't hear you," the woman said. She was a little woman, and had a pleasant face, and Miss Morgan smiled, and raised her voice to say, "I said, how long is this parade going to last?"

"What parade?" she asked. "*That* one?" She nodded at the street. "I haven't any idea, miss. I'm trying to get to Macy's."

"Do you know anything about this Miss X?" Miss Morgan said daringly.

The woman laughed. "It was over the radio," she said. "Someone's going to get a lot of prizes. You have to do some kind of a puzzle or something."

"What's it for?" Miss Morgan asked.

"Advertising," the woman said, surprised.

"Are *you* looking for Miss X?" Miss Morgan asked daringly.

The woman laughed again. "I'm no good at that sort of thing," she said. "Someone in the company of the people putting it on always wins those things, anyway."

Just then they were allowed to cross again, and Miss Morgan and the woman hurried across, and on down the next block. Walking beside the woman, Miss Morgan said finally, "I think I'm the Miss X they're talking about, but I don't know why."

The woman looked at her and said, "Don't ask *me,*" and then disappeared into the crowd of people ahead.

Out in the street a prominent cowboy movie star was going by on horseback, waving his hat.

Miss Morgan retreated along a quiet side street until she was far away from the crowds and the parade; she was lost, too far away from her office to get back without finding another taxi, and miles away from the address on the package. She saw a shoe repair shop, and struck by a sudden idea, went inside and sat down in one of the booths. The repair man came up to her and she handed him her shoes.

"Shine?" he said, looking at the shoes.

"Yes," Miss Morgan said. "Shine." She leaned back in the booth, her eyes shut. She was vaguely aware that the repair man had gone into the back of the shop, that she was alone, when she heard a footstep and looked up to see a man in a blue suit coming toward her.

"Are you Miss X?" the man in the blue suit asked her.

Miss Morgan opened her mouth, and then said, "Yes," tiredly.

"I've been looking all over for you," the man said. "How'd you get away from the sound truck?"

"I don't know," Miss Morgan said. "I ran."

"Listen," the man said, "this town's no good. No one spotted you." He opened the door of the booth and waited for Miss Morgan to come.

"My shoes," Miss Morgan said, and the man waved his hand impatiently. "You don't need shoes," he said. "The car's right outside."

He looked at Miss Morgan with yellow cat eyes and said, "Come on, hurry up."

She stood up and he took her arm and said, "We'll have to do it again tomorrow in Chicago, this town stinks."

That night, falling asleep in the big hotel, Miss Morgan thought briefly of Mr. Lang and the undelivered package she had left, along with her hatbox, in the shoe repair shop. Smiling, she pulled the satin quilt up to her chin and fell asleep.

Dinner for a
Gentleman

I<small>T IS NOT POSSIBLE</small>, I frequently think, to walk down the
street as fast as you can and kick yourself at the same time. You
can stop, of course, and try if you really *want* to, but, I mean, you're
apt to look a little foolish, and foolish, if you're me, is what you
generally look too much of already.

I mean, every time I try to show off I get caught; that's what it boils
down to. Every time I get into one of those conversations where I
don't really know what I'm talking about, but I pretend I do, first
thing I know there I am saying something I've got to back up with
proof, and then, I mean, where am I? Well, *this* day, at any rate, I was
walking down the street wishing I could kick myself, with both arms
full of bags of groceries and a great dismal cloud of foreboding located
somewhere around the back of my neck. So all right, Hugh Talley
was a cook. So I mean, I could have left it at that, couldn't I? I hadn't
needed to say anything, not a word; I hadn't even needed to listen. But
no. So here I was, going down the street, going home to cook dinner
for Hugh Talley, just because I wanted to show off, and if I thought I
looked foolish now, what was going to happen in about an hour when
Hugh Talley sat himself down at the little table in my apartment all
grinning and ready for dinner? I mean, I could have *kicked* myself.

I'm not stupid; I know it sounds like I am, and I suppose not
many people would get caught all the time the way I do. But I've
noticed that Hugh Talley has that effect on a lot of people—he's so
very handsome, in that man-to-man sort of way that's horribly effec-

tive in the movies, and just pretty awful when you meet it day after day in the office. He makes the other men in the office look pale and sort of shabby. He has a good sunlamp tan and he plays golf and he eats robustly and, more than anything else, Talley loves to put on a silly apron and get out in the kitchen and show the womenfolk how to cook. There is no woman in the world, Talley is fond of saying, who knows how to cook a steak the way a *man* likes it. Or spaghetti. Or fried chicken. Women—and you should see the look of pained disgust on Talley's face when he says it—take good meat and cover it with gooey sauces. *That,* not to put too fine a point on it, is Hugh Talley.

And me? Well, I don't play golf, and even though I've got a good healthy appetite, my tan tends to build up sort of spottily during the summer and disappear with the first frost. I'm like a thousand other girls in the city—I've got a job I like, and I used to share my apartment with another girl, but she got married and so now I live alone, and someday I'll probably get married to some nice fellow and have two children (a boy first, I think, and then a girl) and I'm strong and healthy and I have nice legs and my hair is naturally curly. And, like a thousand other girls, I *do* hate to have a man—any man—tell me anything in that faintly patronizing voice men use sometimes that begins: "The trouble with women . . ."

Except that of all the girls who had ever tried to make Hugh Talley eat his words with their cooking, I guess I'm the first one who ever tried it without first learning how to cook.

You see what I mean?

I'd skipped out of the office early that day to do my shopping for dinner and then get home and hunt up a cookbook. I knew there was one in my apartment somewhere; my roommate and I got it long ago to find out how to make fudge. When I got home and let myself into the apartment I went right over to the bookcase without putting my packages down and looked, and there it was, looking just as new as when we bought it. Right then a voice spoke up from in back of me:

"Dimity Baxter!" it said.

Well, I jumped, and I dropped my packages, and I turned around, and there was this little old lady standing there smiling at me, and while I stood there, still half bent down in front of the bookcase with my mouth open, she put her knitting down and came over and started to pick up the groceries, which had fallen to the floor.

"Let me just get these put away," she said. "What were you planning for dessert? Lemon pie?"

"What?" I said, and at that it was more than I thought I could say.

"Just ran over to see if I couldn't give you a hand," she said. She started for the kitchen, her arms full of packages.

"But listen—" I said.

"Your hired man let me in," she said, and sniffed. "Said he figured he could trust me."

Automatically, I had gathered together some of the stuff on the floor and followed her out into the kitchen with it. "My hired man?" I said stupidly. "You mean the super?"

"Super," she said. "He figured he could *trust* me. Call me Mallie," she added.

"Mallie," I said.

"From upstate," she said. "Guess you could call me an old friend of your mother's," and she laughed.

Well, it *was* rather too much. Not that my mother isn't the nicest person in the world, and this little lady was a lot like her, but somehow my mother and her friends just simply don't *look* right in a business girl's apartment, if you know what I mean. Mallie just sort of glanced around the little kitchenette there, and I could see her face when she saw the cup and saucer I'd left in the sink that morning (I *can* make coffee, after all, with hot water and one of those concentrates) and when she looked around still more and saw that I had only a couple of saucepans, and the rolling pin and mixing bowls were all that sort of small-sized, cute kind of stuff they turn out for people who don't cook much, and when she opened the cupboard door and I could see her looking at the two cans of soup and the can of sardines that were all that was in there, and *those* were left over from when I had a roommate—well, it was all pretty embarrassing, and I felt more like a fool than ever.

So, naturally, I had to go and be rude to her, because I felt like such a fool myself. "Will you excuse me," I said to her with that sort of deadly politeness you use when you really wish you weren't saying what you *are* saying—"Will you please excuse me if I go right ahead with my work? I'm having a guest for dinner and I really must hurry."

Well, that was not exactly the way I'd figured it might be. That is, to go right ahead with this dinner I was going to cook, while Mallie sat in the kitchen and watched me. She sort of belonged in a kitchen, if you know what I mean. She looked as though she could find the right shelf by instinct, and knew exactly how to pick things up to use them best, and she sort of melted comfortably into a corner between the sink and the stove. I mean, definitely not the sort of person to bring out a cookbook in front of.

All I could do, though, was say "Well . . ." sort of helplessly, and go on back into the living room and get the cookbook. "Got to make sure I do everything right," I said lamely to Mallie when I came back, and she nodded cheerfully over her knitting.

My first problem, and the one that weighed most heavily on my mind, was that lemon pie. I remembered too distinctly telling Hugh Talley in an absolutely insufferable tone that unless he could make a lemon pie he really wasn't much of a cook. I thought when I was telling him that, probably a lemon pie was easier than apple, or cherry, or something like that. Only one crust, you know.

I was fairly sure that Mallie was watching me out of the corner of her eye when I turned to the index of the cookbook and ran my finger casually down the list until I came to Lemon Meringue Pie. I turned to the page, trying hard to look as though I made a lemon pie every day of my life and just intended to refresh my memory a little. I read the recipe twice. I had been right; it *was* easy. All I had to do . . .

"Wash your hands first," Mallie said sharply.

I jumped, and then I went over to the sink and washed my hands. I was beginning to realize that when this Mallie said something as though she meant it, first you jumped, and then you did what she told you to do. After I had washed my hands and tied a bathtowel around my waist for an apron, I went to the bags of groceries I had brought home and took out the flour, the shortening, the lemons, the eggs, the condensed milk, the gelatin, the vanilla, the cream—all the things I had bought because it seemed to me that they might go into a lemon pie. "Now," I said gaily.

The first thing that happened was that I spilled the flour. I didn't have a measuring cup, of course, so while I tried to guess how much flour I needed I dropped the bag and it broke on the floor, but there was enough on the table for me to use. The recipe said I could use more flour if necessary, anyway. But the pie crust I was making never did come out exactly as I thought I remembered it ought to. Somehow, one minute it was all crumbs when I tried to roll it out, and the next minute, when I finally picked it up and kneaded it between my hands until it got solid, it was hard as a rock and wouldn't roll at all. Finally, after about four tries, I got the crust rolled into the right shape for the pie plate, although it got rolled too thin some places and I had to sort of piece it together and pinch it to make the edges stick, and even then it was pretty thick some places. "It won't matter when the filling's in," I told myself. Finally I put it into the oven and turned around and looked at Mallie.

"Well," I said with some satisfaction, "*that's* done."

Mallie hadn't said anything while I was making the pie crust. Once I had turned around to look at her because I wondered for a minute if maybe she hadn't been laughing at me—it was when the ball of dough I was working with had bounced out of my hands and across the table—but she had her head down over her knitting. The back of her neck and her ears were bright red, and she sounded like she was coughing, but I decided not to say anything if *she* didn't. She'd been nice enough to pick up the pieces of the mixing bowl when it fell on the floor.

When I put the pie in the oven and turned around to look at her she smiled at me innocently. "Better get those potatoes on," she said.

"I *know*," I said. "Don't worry about *me*."

I went back to the index of the cookbook. I really ought to start right in on the pie filling, but maybe if Mallie thought that the potatoes were next . . . Potatoes, Baked. I turned to the page and saw with dismay that the time given for potatoes, baked, was fifty minutes. And Hugh Talley would be here in forty-five minutes, allowing that he was five minutes late. "He'll have to wait," I told the clock grimly, and dived for the potatoes.

"Wouldn't of thought *any*one could mess up a baked potato," Mallie observed to her knitting.

I glared at her, but I was moving too fast to answer. By then I was squeezing the lemons for the pie filling; when I was on about my eighth lemon the squeezer skidded across the table and took a nose-dive onto the floor, and I had to finish the lemons by hand, and add a little canned lemon juice to get what I figured was a cupful. Then when I tried to beat the eggs I all of a sudden remembered the pie crust, and when I rushed to get it out of the oven, the eggbeater tipped over the bowl with the eggs in and *they* went down. But it didn't really matter because the pie crust was burned black anyway. I just stood in front of the stove with the pie dish in my hand.

"You put it in, in back of the potatoes," Mallie said softly. "Then with the potatoes in front, you forgot it."

"Never *mind*," I snarled at her. "I'll buy a lemon pie."

"*Buy* a lemon *pie*?" Mallie said as though I had suggested stealing one off a windowsill.

"Never *mind*," I said again.

I had planned to make biscuits, too, but the oven was getting so full and the time was getting so short that I gave up the idea. It was fifteen minutes before Hugh Talley was due to arrive—allowing that he was ten minutes late—and then I remembered vaguely that I had planned to have lamb chops, too.

"Lamb chops," I said. "Lamb chops."

"Lamb chops," Mallie said soothingly.

Could she be laughing at me? I looked at her again, and she looked back at me with those wide, friendly eyes.

"Lamb chops," I said doggedly. I searched among the litter of papers on the table and found the package of lamb chops. I knew they were to be fried, but the only frying pan I could find was too small for more than two, and knowing Hugh Talley's famous appetite, I had bought six. I would just have to fry them two at a time. I glanced suspiciously at Mallie; she had her eyes shut, briefly, and her lips moved. I thought she was saying "lamb chops" to herself.

There was absolutely no place in the kitchen to put down the package of lamb chops, so I held it in my hand while I turned the pages of the cookbook. It was also very hard to read the cookbook because by now the lemon pie filling had soaked through the pages and there was so much flour on my hands that it made a sort of paste. The page that told about lamb chops was also the page that told about lemon meringue pie, and was thoroughly stuck to the next one. I had to put the lamb chops down to separate the pages, and the only place I could find was the windowsill, and I had opened the window to let the odor of burning pie crust out, and, anyway, I suddenly smelled something else burning, and when I leaped to see what it was I joggled the package of lamb chops on the windowsill, and there I was. Mallie came over to the window beside me and looked out.

"Well," she said, "your lamb chops, down there on the sidewalk. From here," she added severely, "they don't look like first cut lamb chops, either."

I opened the oven door to see what was burning and found that the potatoes were still baking nicely, and so was my potholder, which I had left inside.

"That does it," I said with admirable restraint. I stood up and pushed my hair back with my floury paw. "That does it," I said again, without quite so much restraint. "I'll make him pay for this," I said. "I'll teach him to go tormenting nice girls with his old cooking. I'll fry the leaves of the cookbook one by one—" I was going on, but Mallie stopped me.

"You just calm down," she said. And, once again, I did what she told me to. I stopped yelling and looked around the kitchen. The sink was piled high with dirty dishes. I had set the broken lemon squeezer on top of the pile of dishes in the sink because I couldn't find anywhere else to put it, and half a lemon sat precariously on top of *that*. The mixing bowls were in the sink, too, except the one I broke. For some reason I had used four mixing bowls and a saucepan for that pie filling. On the table was a mess of eggshells and the wrappings from the food and the cookbook, sitting smack in the middle of the pool of pie filling. I had forgotten to turn on the heat under the coffeepot, which sat, cold and reproachful, next to the broken bag of flour, which, for some reason, I had set on the stove. There wasn't enough flour left in the bag, though, to worry about; it was mostly on the floor. The potholder was cooked to a turn. The doorbell rang.

I stared at the footprints in the flour on the floor. "Did I really walk that much?" I asked Mallie a little bit hysterically.

Mallie set down her knitting at last, and rose. "You go along now," she said. "You change into your blue dress; I pressed it this afternoon while I was waiting for you. You take a quick shower and get dressed, and *I'll* take care of your young man."

"But," I began helplessly. I waved one arm at the kitchen, and the doorbell rang again. "What shall I do?" I said.

"I just *told* you what to do," Mallie said sharply. "You run along and get dressed."

Well, I already knew what to do when Mallie spoke like that. There was no further question of hesitation or disobedience. I found myself heading for the shower and the blue dress. Just as I closed the bedroom door, I heard Mallie's voice saying, ". . . old friend of Dimity's mother. Just stopped in to say hello."

I confess frankly that I took an unreasonably long time over that shower. With anyone else, I suppose I could just have admitted honestly that I'd made a mess of things and talked big and then couldn't perform, but with Hugh Talley, that sort of admission was harder. He'd never forget it, for one thing. And he'd never let *me* forget it, for another. I thought of Hugh Talley's red face and complacent smile once when I was just ready to step out of the shower, and then I stepped back into the shower again and stayed there awhile longer. Go ahead, Dimity, I kept telling myself, go ahead, face up to it.

I felt somewhat better when I was dressed and had the smoke out of my hair and the flour out from under my fingernails. I felt a little bit cheerful—almost, as a matter of fact, as though someday, perhaps in ten years or so, living in some town maybe five hundred miles from Hugh Talley, this day might begin to seem less important to me, even, perhaps, funny.

I gathered all my pride together just inside the bedroom door, and I put my head as high as it would get with the stiff neck I had gotten from bending over that stove, and I straightened my shoulders, and finally I opened the door and I marched bravely out into the living room and up to Hugh Talley, where he was sitting in the only comfortable chair with his feet up on the hassock.

"Sorry to keep you waiting, Hugh," I said with my brave smile, "but as a matter of fact, I might just as well admit—"

"Dimity," Mallie said sharply, "best run into the kitchen and look to that pie."

"I might as well admit," I went on, "that after all I said—"

"I looked in on it a minute ago," Mallie said, "and it wants to come out of the oven right now. *Right* now," she insisted, and then added sweetly, "Of course, that's only what *I* think, of course. Dimity knows best."

It began to sink into my mind, what she had said. I was so wound up for my courageous speech to Hugh Talley that it took a minute or so before I even realized that Mallie was speaking to me. Anyway, I turned around and looked at her and she gave me a prodigious wink, and waved toward the kitchen with her hand. Then, when I turned back to stare at Hugh Talley, I saw something I also had not noticed before. The little table in the living room was set for dinner for two. The tablecloth was shining, the glasses were glittering, the silverware was reflecting the light of the two tall candles set in the center of the table. It looked pretty.

Mallie said, "I've got to run along in a minute, but first I'd like to see how your pie came out, Dimity."

It occurred to me, now, that she wanted me to go into the kitchen. So I went and she followed me. Hugh Talley said as we left, "Hope Dimity didn't put on too much style for *me*. I wasn't expecting much, you know." And he laughed in an unpleasant sort of way.

I stood in the kitchen doorway. I could have sworn that when I left it a short time before there had been dirty dishes in the sink, flour on the floor, and no dinner worth speaking of in the stove. Now, however, the kitchen was spotless—a good deal cleaner, I blush to say, than it had ever been before. Everything had been put away. It seemed likely that the floor had been scrubbed.

"What?" I said—my usual intelligent remark when astonished.

"If you don't shut your mouth soon," Mallie said tartly, "I won't be answerable for what falls into it."

"But—" I said—another intelligent comment of mine.

"No time for silly questions," Mallie said. "You listen to me, Dimity Baxter. For a while there I figured I'd let you work along on things yourself, and then come through and say right out you were wrong. But I'll tell you something. I don't like that young man in there one bit. First thing he says to me when he sits down, 'Did Dimity really make this dinner herself?' Now, I don't call that fair at all, so I said to him, 'She spent all afternoon in the kitchen,' and of course *that* was true." She looked me up and down reflectively. "Blue's a good color for you," she said, and then went on. "That's the sort of young man you have to edge around the truth with. So don't you tell him anything, you hear? And for heaven's sake, get that pie out of the oven."

I opened the oven and took out the pie, noticing dully as I did so that the meringue was perfect, and little flakes of the crust fell off the edges. "Pie," I said.

"What else would it be if I called it a pie?" Mallie demanded. "Don't you ever have that young man here for dinner again, you hear?"

"I won't," I told her fervently.

"I borrowed your piggy bank, by the way," Mallie said.

"The piggy bank?" I said. "But there was only six—"

"Never you mind," Mallie said. "Those lamb chops were a bad cut, anyway. Now, here's a cookbook for you instead of that old one I threw out, and maybe someday I'll run in and say hello again."

Briefly, quickly, she kissed me on the cheek, a swift brush of soft old lips, and then the front door closed softly and I was standing in the middle of my clean kitchen with dinner smelling good and a cookbook in my hand.

"Hey!" It was Hugh Talley calling me from the living room. "When do we eat?"

I moved numbly toward the stove. I lifted the napkin off one of the dishes keeping warm; it was hot biscuits, light and brown and not like anything I had seen for quite a while. Another dish held the baked potatoes; a third dish held the chops. There was the pie. And there was, I discovered, a salad in the refrigerator.

There was nothing for me to do but start carrying it in to Hugh Talley, which I did.

Sitting at the table, Hugh Talley looked down comfortably at his plate. "Doesn't look bad," he said. He had taken three biscuits, remarking that they were probably like lead. He had taken a baked potato, with the comment that it looked a little bit hard. He had served himself two chops, noting as he did so that for a wonder they weren't covered with some kind of fancy sauce. When he helped himself to salad, he observed that the salad dressing probably contained whipped cream. But he had supplied himself nicely just the same. I just sat and stared at my own plate; it certainly *looked* like food.

"You know," Talley said with his mouth full, "these biscuits are really pretty good." He swallowed, and gestured with the piece of biscuit still in his hand. He had plenty of butter on it, I noticed. "You know," he said again, "I'll bet there's a trick or two about biscuits you haven't caught on to yet. I bet you just use any old flour to make them—isn't that so?" I nodded—what else could I do? "Well," he said, consuming the piece of biscuit in his hand, "that's allllll wrong. That's the way all women cook. Just take any old flour and use it for everything. But now, you take a *real* cook—" He gestured largely, and ended his gesture over the plate of biscuits. He hesitated, and then took another. "You take a real cook, *he* knows about flour. Why, when I want to make biscuits I go to a special little flour place I know of, way downtown, and I say to them, 'Listen,' I say, 'I don't want any of your ordinary flour, I want that *special* flour you keep for Hugh Talley.' And by golly, that's what I get."

"*What's* what you get?" I asked him, but he didn't hear me.

"Same thing with applesauce," Hugh Talley said. "You take applesauce—I bet you put cinnamon in it?" I nodded again; I supposed I did put cinnamon in it. "Well," Talley said, "I guess about *every*one puts cinnamon, or some such thing, in applesauce—but not Hugh Talley." He shook his head violently and had another biscuit. "What you want to do—that is, what a *real* cook would do is get some of this special seasoning they have at a little place I know of; it's not like cinnamon, exactly, has more of a flavor, you might say. I go down there whenever I want to make *real* applesauce, and I say to them—"

I tasted a biscuit. It tasted real and more than real; it tasted like biscuits I remembered from the time I was about twelve and eating was practically all I lived for. It tasted, as a matter of fact, perfectly fine.

"And you take chops," Hugh Talley was going on; how he could eat so much and talk so much and do both together without stopping made me wonder for a minute, and the sweet thought that he might choke himself to death occurred to me. "Pork chops, you know," he said, "you have to treat a good pork chop right or it just simply tastes like any other pork chop. Now, *I* always take *my* pork chops, and I marinate them. Now, most people will tell you that marinating pork chops is all wrong, but not Hugh Talley." He shook his head positively. "The trouble is, most people think that by marinating pork chops I just mean simply marinating them, but no *real* cook would do *that*. Not," he said, "to a pork chop. You want to take a special combination of french dressing—not the french dressing you *buy,* of course." He stopped and looked at me aggressively, and I nodded again, because I was, by now, just nodding every time he stopped. "Naturally not," he said. "So you take french dressing, and you add this special—"

Pork chops? I thought suddenly. Pork chops? I looked down at my plate, took a taste. I was certain that I had bought lamb chops. Then I remembered the lamb chops down on the sidewalk and Mallie saying "I borrowed your piggy bank, by the way."

"Excuse me," I said hastily. I ran into the kitchen; the piggy bank was gone and the six cents it had contained lay on the shelf.

"Where's that lemon pie I heard so much about?" I heard Talley shouting from the dining room.

It didn't seem possible, after the dinner he had put away, but I picked up the pie and started in with it. As I entered the room, he began again. "Now, you take lobster," he said. "Most people, they don't cook lobster right." He watched approvingly while I brought over the pie. As I was about to set it down, he took a deep breath and began, "The trouble with women—"

I couldn't help it. Nobody could have helped it. Even *Mallie* couldn't have helped it, and I almost think she would have approved.

I thought it was terribly funny, and I'm afraid I began to laugh. Hugh Talley wiped the lemon pie off his face and glared at me. Then he stood up, brushing meringue from his sleeves and shaking crust off his hair, and he tried to catch his breath, and then, with his face red and his eyes glaring, he tried to think of something to say, something cutting enough, I suppose, to sound furious through a faceful of lemon pie.

"You—you—woman cook!" he shouted finally.

I heard the door slam behind him and I thought: small credit to me; I only threw the pie—Mallie baked it. And it seemed to me that perhaps Mallie had baked that pie for only one purpose, and that purpose had just been served.

I figured right then that there was one thing I really owed to Mallie and I'd better get started on it right away, and deal with the mess on the floor later. Anybody could clean up a mess, but Dimity Baxter was going to set herself out to learn to cook, and with no more nonsense about it, either.

I went into the kitchen and got the cookbook Mallie had left for me and came back and sat down in the comfortable chair Hugh Talley had so recently vacated. The cookbook was patterned in blue and white checks, and had "Dimity Baxter" written across the front in gold letters. Inside, on the flyleaf, it said "To Dimity from Mallie." And it had positively the strangest table of contents I had ever seen. It started with "Dinner for Mr. Arthur Clyde Brookson," a name I had never heard before, although, reading it, I said it over once or twice and liked the sound of it, oddly. Instructions for the dinner, which began on page one, started off: "Now, don't you get all flustered, Dimity. No need to worry about *this* dinner—he's going to like it, whatever you cook. Probably won't eat anything, anyway, either of you."

I turned back to the table of contents. Another item caught my eye. It read: "Luncheon for mother-in-law and two friends." I blinked, and giggled.

Another listing was "Dinner to be served to daughter's young man," and still another was "Family dinner, to serve fifteen." Also, "Dinner for husband's employer, and wife." That one made me laugh out loud.

Then one listing caught my eye, and, unable to resist, I turned to it. It was called: "First dinner of married life," and the instructions began: "Dimity, you take off that yellow organdy apron and put on the good practical one your mother sent you. Save the yellow one to serve dinner in. And don't let him get the idea he doesn't have to help do dishes."

There was only one thing I could think of to do, and, after a minute, I knew how to do it. I went out into the kitchen and said softly, "Thanks, Mallie."

PARTY OF BOYS

M Y OLDER SON, LAURIE, has a birthday early in October, so on good years he goes with his father to New York for the World Series; years when Brooklyn loses the pennant Laurie just has a birthday party at home. Toward the end of last summer, when it began to seem depressingly clear that Laurie would celebrate his twelfth birthday far away from Ebbets Field, he began a loving and detailed plan for the properest and gayest manner of celebrating a boy's only twelfth birthday. He began by proposing, as the only reasonable foundation upon which a happy birthday might be built, that both his younger sisters spend that weekend with their grandmother in California. I said that the distance between Vermont, where we live, and California, made this idea untenable, but that I would guarantee that both girls would spend the entire day visiting friends locally. Laurie then suggested that he invite eighteen friends and they play baseball on the side lawn. I said the side lawn was not an athletic field, and anyway I would not feed eighteen of his friends unless they ate in the barn. Laurie sighed, and offered to compromise on twelve, and volleyball. I said that the side lawn was not an athletic field, and besides I was fairly sure it was going to rain. Laurie thought for a minute and then asked with enormous courtesy whether it would be all right if he just asked Robert over for the afternoon, and they could play chess?

I told him that our dining room could hold eight twelve-year-old boys comfortably, provided they didn't run footraces or fence with the table knives—or perhaps, I suggested, he might like to have an evening party, with a little supper? In that case, I pointed out, I could make lots of sandwiches and a nice fruit punch, and he could invite as many as half a dozen boys and half a dozen gir— At that point Laurie left the room, remarking poignantly that sometimes he got to thinking that everyone in the world but him was crazy.

He finally decided that a Saturday afternoon movie was the thing, with supper afterward, and he invited his seven closest friends, all of whom could be depended upon to bring sensible presents, such as the latest popular records, and chemical retorts, and Tarzan books, which are very much in demand in Laurie's set. It was particularly specified in the invitations that formal dress was not expected. The guests arrived by bicycle, neatly wrapped packages dangling from the handlebars. The packages were put on the dining room table, to be opened at supper, the bicycles were lined up by our back porch, and Laurie and his seven friends wrestled one another happily into my car, to be driven into town to see "The Mad Fiend from the Lost Planet," and "Pride of the Rancho Grande," and "Tattooed by the Ape Men," and two serials and a cartoon, not to mention the newsreel and the coming attractions. I had cashed a check in the morning, and given Laurie enough money to pay eight admissions into the movie, with popcorn and a candy bar apiece, and I was to pick them up again after the movie.

My younger son, Barry, who is not quite three and regards his brother's friends with vast admiration as a superior order of being, infinitely tall and wise and able to fix any number of small toys, accompanied us to town, peering worshipfully over the car seat at the birthday party, which had crushed itself mercilessly into the back half of my station wagon. Barry and I had plenty of room in the front seat, since no party member was prepared to admit himself effeminate enough to sit with us. The eight of them seemed considerably jammed together in back—every now and then a wildly waving foot, or an arm upraised in protest, showed in the rearview mirror—and I kept wondering all the way into town if they were not all secretly hoping that I would run into something.

"Chees," came a voice from the back, which I was able to identify as Stuart's, "chees, I sure would hate to miss this week's serial. Remember—they were caught by the A-rabs?"

"Yeah, well, listen?" Oliver insisted. "You know they're going to get away?"

"Well, if it was you was that guy, well, now, what would *you* do?"

"But hey, he *lied,* din't he?"

"Yeah, but only because they said they were gonna shoot. I mean, what would *you* do? *Not* give up or something?"

"But sure, hey, because gosh—"

"But he *did.* You were there—he *did.*"

"Well, if it was me, I mean that guy there, *I* wouldn't of."

"Hey, you guys." It was Laurie, reminiscent. "Hey, remember *last* week? We sure heard from *that* usher, boy."

"Boys," I said. "Remember, no fighting. Behave like—"

"Jeeps," Laurie said. "I forgot you were here."

"I'm not," I said testily. "Barry is driving."

"I am driving," Barry confirmed. "I am right now turning on the wipeshield winders."

"Yeah, but." The conversation continued after a cautious pause. "Suppose it *was* you. Would you?"

"Well." This was Tommy, considering. "It's like if you took something din't belong to you. You wouldn't just *give* it back, would you, if you *meant* to take it? Just because they said?"

"No," said several voices at once. "But," Willie said, "suppose you *had* to? I mean, with the cops and all?"

"Well, *then,*" someone said. "If it was the cops."

"But he *didn't."* Two or three of them spoke at once. "And that *girl,*" said someone.

There was a brief, disapproving silence. Then Joey's voice rose. "If it was *me,*" Joey said, "if it was *me,* I'da done what was right."

"Yeah, you would." "Well, you sweet thing." "I believe *that.*"

I stopped the car in front of the theater. "Now, look, Laurie," I said. "Be careful with that money, and don't go running around town, and I'll be back at four-thirty and don't fill up on junk because dinner will be—"

"Sure, Ma, sure," Laurie said. "My old lady," he remarked generally. "She's tipped."

I bit my lip. "Have a nice time," I said.

"Yeah." They climbed out one after another, great feet stumbling, shoving and pushing; they had to go out the door next to Barry, and each one, struggling through, patted Barry on the head as he passed. Barry chuckled, I beamed nervously, trying to memorize hats and jackets to ensure returning our guests in the approximate order they came, and Laurie ordered everyone around. "Hey, wait," he kept saying.

"Be careful," I said involuntarily.

Laurie looked at me. "You're *tipped*," he said.

They crossed the street like the legions of Mars coming out of their flying saucer; halfway across, Laurie hesitated, thought, and turned back.

"Hey," he said, coming to the car window, "I almost forgot. Get some old piece of junk for Joey, will you? Model car or something?"

"For Joey?"

"It's his birthday, too. Hey, wait up." And he turned and raced back across the street while I was still saying, "But why didn't you tell me? I would have—"

I craned my neck out the car window, still asking, and watched them go into the movie, snatching at one another and clearly heading for the popcorn counter. Then, telling myself firmly that they would all probably grow up to be nice boys someday, I dug into my change purse for a penny for the parking meter, gathered Barry out of the car, and headed, still telling myself about how they would surely, surely be nice boys someday, for the toy shop and a piece of junk for Joey.

With the delayed reaction that I believe to be common to all mothers, I still feel toward Joey a mingled irritation and tolerance; he is six inches taller than the other boys and used to beat Laurie up every morning on the way to school. Although he is now a completely accepted member of Laurie's group of friends, I cannot lose the uneasy feeling that, crossed, Joey is always apt to heave a rock at something, even though he always calls me "Ma'am," and is one of the few boys who remembers to take off his hat when he comes into the house. I am not altogether successful at concealing my nervousness, so I make a great point of smiling largely at Joey when he comes into the house (he is, after all, two inches taller than I) and at P.T.A. meetings Oliver's mother and Tommy's mother and Willie's mother and I tell one another that a boy like Joey is, after all, someone who needs *sympathy*, not punishment; that kind of mischief making, we tell one another, is only because Joey feels insecure. Joey lives with his grandmother because his parents are dead, and the day Joey's older brother went off to reform school Willie's mother called me and we told each other that if Joey would be made to feel that he was, after all, an accepted member of the group, he might yet grow up to be a credit to his old grandmother. We have all made a point of being very earnest about this, and of course no one can actually prove that it was Joey who dumped the cement into the school furnace, but all the same I could not help feeling slightly wild-eyed at the idea that Joey had birthdays like other children.

However, if Joey was not to receive an irrevocable setback in the process of reformation, I knew I had better get into action right away, so I settled Barry down next to a toy tractor and went into the toy shop phone booth and called Willie's mother. She thought immediately that something had gone wrong with the birthday party and all the boys were coming over to her house, and I had to reassure her and then tell her that I had just heard that poor Joey had a birthday today, too, and none of us had known about it. She said good Lord, what a time to find out, and what was I planning to do, the poor child? I said I guessed I had no choice, the poor child, but to pick up a gift and an extra cake, since the one I had at home plainly said Happy Birthday to Laurie, and it would be next to impossible to add a postscript in pink icing which would include Joey. She said wait a minute, she was going to ice a cake for the church bake sale, and why didn't she decorate it for Joey instead? She could give the bake sale the apple pie and pick up something for dessert when she dropped the cake off at my house. I said gratefully that that would just about save my life, because I had enough extra candles, and Joey would never know that his birthday celebration was a last-minute affair. She said the poor kid, she hated to see a kid go without a party on his birthday, and she was sure Helen and Sylvia and Jean would be just sick when they knew, so why not call them, and she'd leave the cake on the kitchen table.

Encouraged, I called Oliver's mother and said did she know it was Joey's birthday today, too, and she said that did it, that was all she needed on a day like this was turning out to be, and what on earth could we do? I said that I had just dropped the boys off at the movie, and was still in town, and if she wanted some small remembrance for Joey I would be glad to pick up something.

"Oh, fine, then," she said. "Get him a book, maybe."

"A book?" I said. "For Joey?"

"Oh, Lord," she said. "A knife, then, and say it's from Oliver and I'll settle with you when I see you."

I said I'd also get a nice card and sign it "Oliver" and she asked if the boys were all safely in the movie and I said well anyway they were *in*, and she said she was glad it was me feeding them tonight and not her.

Then I called Tommy's mother, and *she* said that if I got a chance to get into the Boy's Shop I might pick up a light sweater or half a dozen pairs of socks, because it was her opinion that the poor child had absolutely *no* clothes. That seemed like such a good idea that I suggested it to Stuart's mother, who said what a time to find out, and all the boys always needed blue jeans anyway, and I could charge it to her account in the Boy's Shop if I was beginning to run short of ready cash.

By the time I headed home, then, I had made six phone calls and had seven birthday presents for Joey and a cowboy suit for Barry, which I had somehow gotten myself talked into buying. The cake was sitting on the kitchen table when I got home, and it was a handsome thing, half again as large as Laurie's, and reading "A very happy birthday to Joey."

Fortunately the boys were having spaghetti for dinner and I had made it in the morning, so all I really had to do was butter lots of bread and make a plain salad. ("None of that junk you put on salads," Laurie had said explicitly. "Just lettuce and sliced tomatoes and radishes, and no marshmallows or pineapple or junk." "I never put marshmallows in a salad in my life," I said indignantly. "Well, can't ever tell when you're going to start," Laurie said pessimistically.) I set the table with care ("Now, look, don't try to hand out little baskets of *candy* or something"), using plain paper napkins, ordinary glassware, my good silver, and my plain dark blue plates, hoping that Laurie would not regard the blue as an attempt at decorating the birthday table. With a certain cynical satisfaction I set a silver dish of salted nuts at each end of the table, a gesture I ordinarily make only at Thanksgiving, when the whole family is assembled. Laurie had conceded that it might not embarrass his friends overmuch if each one found a small favor at his place; he suggested beanshooters or water pistols, but I substituted yo-yos.

Barry had been cordially invited to take a seat next to the birthday boy, and to participate fully in the dinner festivities. My husband had assured us fervently that he had no intention of coming out of the study, and I had been told sternly that all I had to do was put dinner on the table and not make a pest of myself. ("At Jimmie's party, his old lady was always hanging around," Laurie said. "Chees!" "Please do not refer to people's mothers as old ladies," I said. "Jimmie's mother is not much older than—" "Tipped," Laurie said, sighing.) Entertainment at dinner was to be provided by one of those little cardboard games where everyone punches out a slip of paper describing a trick or stunt to do, and—although I was not, naturally, informed of this, if indeed it was planned ahead of time—by throwing tomatoes. Altogether, as planned, a wholly satisfying and nicely calculated birthday supper, provided I didn't lose one of the boys in the movies or drop the cake.

At four-thirty I was parked in front of the movie in a space marked "No Parking," and at four thirty-five the boys began to emerge, one by one, blinking and discarding candy papers. Each one patted Barry on the head as he climbed into the car, and I made nervous estimates about hats, jackets, and the policeman on the corner. When Laurie got in I turned, counted, and said, "Is everyone here? Stuart?"

"Here," said a voice from the mass in the back of the station wagon.

"Joey?" I said, peering.

"Yeah?"

"Oliver's not here," someone said, and several voices added, "No, Oliver, Oliver's not here, where's Ollie?"

"He went back for his shoe," Willie said.

"What happened to his shoe?" I asked, turning. "His *shoe*?"

"Oh, *Ma*," Laurie said, and there was a deep silence in the back of the car.

"Look," I said at last, "someone better go and get him. Because that policeman—"

"Here he comes," Laurie said. "Hurry *up*, Ollie, you think the old lady *wants* to get arrested? Besides, we got to get back and *eat*, for heaven's sake."

"Ice cream," Barry confided, smiling broadly over the back of the seat. "Ice cream, Laurie."

Once Oliver was in the car I counted twice more, announced that anyone not now in the car would probably have to walk, and headed home. Barry sang, "Ice cream, ice cream," softly to himself, and after a minute someone in the back said, "Hey, you *remember* that guy?"

"Gosh," someone said, and someone else said, "Boy," with a sigh.

"And those guys with the space guns—"

"And the octopus—"

"And in the serial—"

"Ice cream, ice cream," Barry sang.

"And when the cops were searching the house—"

"And the master brain—"

"And boy, was that usher *sore*."

I relaxed. Get dinner on the table, light the candles, make a fair attempt at getting sixteen hands washed. I felt a strong glow of satisfaction, too, remembering the presents and cake for Joey. "Ice cream and cake and ice cream," Barry sang.

Laurie sat at one end of the table and Joey at the other. The boys crowded around while the presents were opened; one or two of them looked mildly surprised to find that they had given presents to Joey, but no one said anything. I stood discreetly in the kitchen doorway, appreciating the rare pleasure of a task well done; Joey was deeply gratified, and went so far as to try on the sweater he had received from Tommy. Later, when the spaghetti was going around and Robert was doing a stunt that required that he imitate a fat lady getting into a telephone booth with an armful of packages, Joey left the table and came into the kitchen, where I was buttering more bread. "Thanks very much," he said awkwardly.

"Many happy returns," I said, wondering that I had ever been wary of this pleasant boy.

"Thanks, ma'am," he said again; he went back to the table and I went on buttering bread; Willie was trying to pat his head and rub his stomach, and Barry's voice rose anxiously, inquiring where was the ice cream.

I persuaded my husband out of the study to carry Laurie's cake, and I carried Joey's.

"Happy birthday," everyone sang, "happy birthday to Laurie and Joey."

"Happy birthday," Barry sang individually, "happy and ice cream."

I went back into the study with my husband, unaware that it was almost time for the tomato throwing to begin. "Who's that other boy?" my husband asked.

"It's little Joey. He's really getting on so well, now that he's got friends and he plays baseball now and—"

"That the kid shot out the post office window?"

"—And Mrs. Moore says it's wonderful the way he's settled down to his schoolwork with a little encouragement—"

"Turned the Henleys' cat into the chicken house?"

"You would have been touched to see him opening those presents."

"I understand," my husband said, "that if he tries to walk down Pleasant Street, old man Martin's going to be waiting for him with a shotgun."

"Of course," I said, "if you don't believe that a little kindness and patience—"

"Just make sure you count the silverware," my husband said.

Barry opened the study door. "When is supper?" he asked. "Come and see all the tomatoes on Laurie."

Later, disregarding the tomatoes and shreds of lettuce and bread and thin lines of spaghetti and torn paper and nuts and scraps of ribbon and the overturned chairs, I stood at the back door with Laurie, waving goodbye to his guests. "Thank you for a very nice time and for all the presents and cake," Joey said.

"You're very welcome," I said.

"See ya, Joe," Laurie said. "Gosh," he added to me as the last bike pulled away, "gosh, that Joey sure gets all the luck."

"I'm glad you told me," I said. "I would have felt awful if we hadn't known it was his birthday, too."

"Yeah, but you know what he's *getting?* His uncle's taking him out to the racetrack tonight, and Joey gets to bet on every single race. Gosh." I began to laugh, and Laurie turned and looked at me curiously. "Something funny?" he inquired.

"Nothing," I said. "I'm just tipped, I guess."

"What?"

"Tipped," I said. "Don't tell your father."

Laurie looked at me for a minute and then he shook his head hopelessly, and reached out and patted me approvingly on the shoulder. "Pretty dingy party, anyway," he said. "Come on, old lady, let's start cleaning up this mess."

JACK THE RIPPER

✥

THE MAN HESITATED ON the corner under the traffic light, then started off down the side street, walking slowly and watching the few people who passed him. It was long past midnight, and the streets were as nearly deserted as they ever get; as the man went down the dark street he stopped for a minute, thinking he saw a dead girl on the sidewalk. She was nearly against the wall of a building; a few feet beyond her was the small sign of a bar, and seeing that, the man started to walk on, and then turned back to the girl.

She was so drunk that when he shook her and tried to sit her up she sagged backward, her eyes half closed and her hands rolling on the sidewalk. The man stood and looked at her for a minute, and then turned again and went down to the bar. When he opened the door and went in he saw that the place was nearly empty, with only a group of three or four sailors at the farther end of the bar, and the bartender with them, talking and laughing. There was one man standing at the bar near the doorway, and after looking around for a minute, the man who had come in walked over and stood at the end of the bar.

"Listen," he said, "there's a girl lying out on the street outside."

The man farther down the bar looked at him quietly.

"I just happened to be passing down this way," the man who had just come in went on more urgently, "and I saw her, and I think something had better be done. She can't stay out there." The man farther down the bar went on looking. "She isn't but about seventeen."

"There's a phone out back," the man standing down the bar said. "Call the mayor."

The bartender came easily down to the end of the bar, the smile leaving his face as he came. When he got to the end of the bar, beside the man who had just come in, he stood unsmiling, waiting.

"Listen," the man said again, "there's a girl sixteen, seventeen lying outside in the street. We better get her inside."

"Call the mayor," the man down the bar said, "his number's in the book."

"I was just walking by," the man said, "and she was lying there."

"I know," the bartender said.

"Mention my name," the man down the bar said. "Tell him I told you to call."

"I saw that she was nice and comfortable," the bartender said, "and I put her pocketbook beside her, all nice and convenient." He smiled tenderly. "I hope you didn't disturb her," he said.

The man raised his voice slightly. "She can't keep on lying there," he said. "You're not going to say you intend to leave her there?"

"He'll remember me all right," the man down the bar said, nodding. "He won't forget me in a hurry."

"She likes it there," the bartender said. "Sleeps there nearly every night."

"But a girl fifteen, sixteen!" the man cried.

The bartender's voice became harder; he put both hands on the edge of the bar and leaned over toward the man. "Anytime she likes," he said, "she can get up and go home. She doesn't have to stay there. Let her get up and walk home."

"Not in any sort of a hurry he won't," the man down the bar said.

"Comes in here every night and gets drunk," the bartender went on. "I let her have a beer now and then without money, do you want I should rent her a room, too?" He leaned back again and his voice softened. "Sleeps like a baby, don't she?" He turned around abruptly and walked back down the bar to the sailors. "Another drunk," he said to them.

The man turned to the door and opened it, still hesitating. Then he went out. "Don't forget to tell him what I told you," the man down the bar called after him.

When he got back to the girl he saw that she still lay in the same position, face against the sidewalk, with her knees against the wall.

Her pocketbook lay on the sidewalk beside her, and the man picked it up and opened it. There was no money; there was a lipstick from the five and ten, and a key, a comb, and a little notebook. The man put everything back except the notebook; he opened it and found, on the first page, the girl's name and address. When he turned the first page he found a list of about twenty bars, with addresses and, in some cases, names of the bartenders. A few pages later he found another list, this time of sailors, each name followed by the name of a ship, and a date, apparently the date of the last time the ship was in New York. The entries were written in a big, childish writing, with uncrossed T's and an occasional misspelling. Toward the end of the notebook, a picture had been put between the pages. It showed the girl with two sailors, one on each side, their heads together, and all three smiling. The girl in the picture looked pleased and unattractive; lying on the ground, she seemed thin and almost lovely. The man put the picture back into the notebook and the notebook back into the pocketbook, and then, carrying the pocketbook, walked down to the corner and waved down a taxi. With the taxi waiting, he went back to the girl, lifted her, and put her in, and then got in after her. The girl was sprawled out on the seat, and the man had to sit on a corner to give her room. He gave the driver the address he had seen in the notebook, and the driver, after raising his eyes once to the mirror to look at the man, shrugged and drove off.

The house was in a bad neighborhood, old and dirty, and the driver, stopping the taxi, said: "This is it, mister." He turned and looked at the girl, and added doubtfully, "Do I help you?"

The man pulled the girl out of the taxi by taking hold of her legs and dragging her until he could put her feet on the ground, and then taking her by the waist and swinging her over his shoulder. He held her over his shoulder while he took change from his pocket to pay the driver, and then, still holding her by the legs, he went into the house.

The hall was lighted by gaslights, and the stairway was incredibly narrow and steep. The man knocked on the first door, first with his knuckles, and then, grimly, with the girl's shoes, swinging her legs back and forth.

From somewhere on the other side of the door, a woman's voice asked, "What is it?" and finally the door opened a crack and the woman put her face out. It was too dark for the man to see what she looked like, but she said: "Who is it? Rose? She lives on the sixth floor. Last door on the right." The door closed again. The man surveyed the stairway and thought. There was no room in the hall-way to put the girl down, so he tightened his grip on her legs and started up the stairs. He stopped for breath on every landing, but by the time he reached the sixth floor he was breathing heavily and moving slowly, putting both feet on each step. He leaned against the wall at the top for a minute, trying to shift the girl's weight, and then went down to the last door on the right. Putting the girl down on the floor, he opened her pocketbook and took out the key and opened the door. It was too dark in the hall to see what was in the room, so he lighted a match and went in, trying to find some light. After lighting three matches he found a candle, which he lit and set on the dresser in its own wax. The room was large enough for a cot and the dresser; on the back of the door were three hooks, on which were hanging a torn silk kimono and a pair of dirty stockings. The bed had a blanket on it, over the mattress, and a dirty, uncovered pillow. On the dresser were a few bobby pins and a package of matches. The man opened the four dresser drawers; all of them were empty except for the top one, which contained a bottle opener and a couple of beer bottle caps. When he had examined the room, the man went outside, where he had left the girl, and picked her up under the arms and dragged her into the room. He dumped her onto the bed and threw the blanket over her. He opened her pocketbook and took out the notebook, glancing through it until he found the picture, which he put in his pocket. He put the key on the dresser and the pocketbook beside it, and then, just before blowing out the candle, took out his knife. It had a polished bone handle, and a long and incredibly sharp blade.

He took a taxi on the corner near the tenement, giving the driver an address in the east seventies, and was home in a few minutes. When he got out of the elevator in his apartment house he stopped for a minute, looked at his hands and down at his shoes, and care-fully took a piece of lint off his sleeve. He let himself into his apart-ment with his key, and walked softly into the bedroom. When he turned on the light his wife stirred in her bed, and then opened her eyes. "What time is it?" she murmured.

"Late," he said. He went over and kissed her.

"What kept you so long?" she asked.

"I stopped and had a few drinks after the meeting," he said. He went over to the dresser to put down his keys, and looked at his wife's picture in the tall plastic frame. Reaching in his pocket, he found the picture of the girl with the two sailors and thought for a minute; then he went to his wife's dressing table, and with her plastic-handled nail scissors cut the two sailors out of the picture, leaving the girl alone. This fragment of picture he put into the lower corner of the frame holding his wife's picture. He lighted a cigarette and stood looking at it.

"Aren't you coming to bed?" his wife asked sleepily.

"No," he said. "Believe I'll take a bath."

THE HONEYMOON

OF MRS. SMITH

(Version I)

WHEN SHE CAME INTO the grocery she was sure that she had interrupted a conversation about herself and her husband. The grocer, leaning across the counter to speak confidentially to a customer, straightened up abruptly and signaled with his eyes, and suddenly everyone in the store, clerks and customers, found reason to interest themselves stubbornly in food displays or grocery lists, or shopping bags. Wherever she looked it seemed that she had all but caught a swift, eager glance that dropped as she turned, and then the grocer said loudly and clearly, "Afternoon, Mrs. Smith," and a slow sigh, almost imperceptible, swept through the store.

"Good afternoon," Mrs. Smith said.

"What'll it be for you today?" he asked, moving his hands nervously on the counter. "Big weekend order?" They were phrases he used with nearly all his customers, even shoppers so new as little Mrs. Smith, but when he spoke to Mrs. Smith his voice came out with an unusual heartiness, and he coughed, embarrassed.

"I don't need very much," Mrs. Smith said. "My husband thought we might be going away for the weekend." Again that long sigh went through the store; she had a clear sense of people moving closer, listening to every word she spoke. "A loaf of bread," she said. "A half pint of cream. A little can of peas." She looked down steadily at the list she had made a few minutes ago in her apartment; at first, a few days ago, she had wandered around the store as the other women did, but now that she knew their moving away from her and their side glances were deliberate and directed at her, she stood directly before the counter and read her order to the grocer. How silly they all are, she thought, and said, "And a quarter pound of butter, and three lamb chops." One, she wanted to say to their faces, one lamb chop for me, and two for my husband. For my husband, she wanted to tell them, turning to look at them one by one, because even an old maid of thirty-eight can *some*times find herself a man to protect her and be fond of her; it's just as well, she remembered ruefully, that they don't know how we met.

"Coffee?" said the grocer. "Tea?"

"A pound of coffee," she said, smiling at him. "I love coffee. I could drink coffee all day long, if I let myself."

"A *whole* pound?" the grocer said, startled.

"Yes." She took tight hold of the edge of the counter so that she would not stumble over the words. "My husband," she said, "is not fond of coffee. But I love it."

Again, although she was ready for it, she heard that distant sigh, and again the waiting silence. What do they want me to *do*, she wondered—pretend I'm a widow? The butcher, who had heard her order, came silently across the store and put down the wrapped package of lamb chops, gave her one quick look over his shoulder, and hurried back to the meat counter on the other side of the store. "Thank you," Mrs. Smith said, and the grocer began a fierce rattling of paper bags to open one for her order. One good thing about being so conspicuous, Mrs. Smith was thinking, I never have to *wait* anywhere; all these women were here ahead of me, and yet I have my groceries and—

The grocer leaned toward her suddenly. "Mrs. Smith," he said, "I guess it's not my place to speak, but around here people try to be neighborly and sooner or later someone's got to let you know—" He stopped, helpless, and the silence was immense. "Won't *any*body tell her?" the grocer demanded, and no one moved or spoke.

Mrs. Smith laughed shyly. "You don't need to tell me anything," she said. "I know I'm kind of new at things like keeping house and I suppose I'll make all kinds of foolish mistakes"—she hesitated, hearing again that expectant sigh—"but you've all been so kind," she said, "and I'm grateful to you for wanting to help me."

"Oh, my goodness," said the grocer. He gestured widely around the store; "Won't *any*one?" he said, and still there was no sound.

"Well," Mrs. Smith said uncertainly. "Thank you very much." She gave a little smile toward the other women, and took up her bag of groceries. "I expect we'll be back on Monday," she told the grocer. "Have a nice weekend."

The grocer stared at her with his mouth open, and Mrs. Smith turned to the door. As she closed it behind her she heard the grocer saying wildly, "You all just *stand* there—" Funny people, Mrs. Smith thought; city neighborhoods are really just like small towns, always edgy about new people. And I'm a new person, she thought happily; after thirty-eight years I've turned into a new person. Mrs. Charles Smith, she thought; I suppose I embarrass them because I'm a little foolish about it.

It was not really new to her, this attitude of odd surprise she encountered everywhere; as a matter of fact, the first person to show it had been herself, Helen Bertram, when Charles Smith, looking nervously down at the rice cookie by his teacup, had said, almost stammering, "I don't suppose you've ever thought about . . . getting married, have you?" Surprise, Mrs. Smith reflected now, had very likely been the outstanding emotion showing on her face, surprise and then, quickly, incredulous happiness; it's lucky he never looked at me that minute, Mrs. Smith thought now, and almost laughed. Mrs. Charles Smith. She realized then that she had stopped in front of a dress shop and to anyone passing might seem to be regarding wistfully a display of black lace nightgowns; good heavens, she thought, backing away and blushing; I hope no one saw me *then;* imagine such things at *my* age.

"I hope you won't think me forward," he had said to her on that golden morning now two weeks and three days past, "I hope you won't think me forward if I open a conversation with you?"

She had thought him unbelievably forward, had been astonished, had for a moment almost drawn her black shawl around her and moved coldly away, and then at last, changing her life, she had smiled back and said, "No, of course not."

"It is such a lovely day," he said.

"Lovely," she said.

"And the sea air is refreshing."

"Most refreshing."

And that night at dinner, in a restaurant on the pier, he had told her, soberly, about his wife who had died, about the little house now closed up and abandoned after fifteen years of married life, about the kindly employers who had sent him on a month's leave of absence to indulge his grief. "But a man gets very lonely, I find," he told her, and she nodded, sorrowful, and yet envious of the wife who had had at least those fifteen years. She told him, then, about her father and her long, lonely years keeping house, never getting any younger, and the insurance money that would be just enough, if she took care, to provide for her modestly; "At least," she said bravely, "I won't have to go out and try to find a . . . *job,* or anything like that."

"You must be very lonely, too," he said, and gave her hand a quick, shy pat.

Even the napkins in the restaurant on the pier smelled of fish, and the table had a faint salty grain. "That's really why I spoke to you, I guess," he said. "I knew I was being forward, but I guess I just thought that maybe you were all alone, too."

"I'm very glad," she said timidly. "That you spoke to me, that is."

"My wife," he said, "my *former* wife—Janet, that is—*she* would have been very angry. I guess I was afraid you would be angry, too. *She* would have gotten up and walked away."

Remembering how nearly she had come to getting up and walking away, Helen Bertram, so soon to be Mrs. Charles Smith, gave a little laugh and said, "I would call that silly. People who are all alone have every right to be friends with one another."

And then, three days later, they had taken tea together at a Chinese tea shop, and, looking uncomfortably down at his rice cookie, he had asked her if she ever thought about getting married. Now, turning in through the doorway of the apartment house where they were to live until the house was ready, little Mrs. Smith wondered, as she had so many times in the past few days, how it could happen that the lives of two people might be wholly changed by a chance, by the combination of a lovely day and the sea air, by a sudden sympathetic word, and the awareness of an unexpected comfort to be found in a shared melancholy—although, Mrs. Smith told herself conscientiously, she had not really been so *terribly* sad these past few days. She remembered with some tenderness the first wife, the lost Janet, and again, as she had before during these past few days, she made a small promise to Janet that Mr. Smith should not be less happy in his second wife than he had been in his first.

Mr. Smith had their little apartment on the third floor, and it was a long climb for Mrs. Smith, who was not getting any younger, and particularly with a bag of groceries. She stopped to rest on the second floor landing, and then remembered too late that Mrs. Armstrong lived on the second floor and that Mrs. Armstrong had already shown almost excessive interest in being neighborly; coming down, on her way to the store, Mrs. Smith had hurried past Mrs. Armstrong's door and heard it open behind her, and now it opened again and she was fairly caught.

"Mrs. Smith, is that you?"

"Good afternoon," Mrs. Smith called over her shoulder, moving with some haste toward the stairs.

"Wait a minute, I'm coming." The lock on Mrs. Armstrong's door snapped, and the door closed behind her. Mrs. Armstrong came hastily, a little out of breath, along the hallway and to the stairs where Mrs. Smith waited. "Thought I'd miss you," Mrs. Armstrong said. "I was waiting for you to come back. Where you been—shopping?"

Since Mrs. Smith was carrying her bag of groceries she had only to nod, and attempt to back on up the stairs, but Mrs. Armstrong followed her resolutely. "Well, I thought you'd never get back," Mrs. Armstrong said, panting. "I said to Ed that I wasn't going to let another day go by, not *one more day,* without having it out with you. *You* know, *you'd* do as much for *me.* Being your nearest neighbor and all."

She followed Mrs. Smith onto the third floor landing and waited, holding her side and breathing heavily while Mrs. Smith unlocked the door of the little apartment where she and Mr. Smith were living until Mr. Smith's little house was ready for them; Mrs. Armstrong was the first outsider to penetrate the little apartment, and Mrs. Smith realized nervously that she was not, after all, very well equipped to receive guests; they had unpacked so little, and lived so sketchily from day to day, waiting for the house, that the apartment seemed bare, and without warmth. "We're not really moved in yet," Mrs. Smith said apologetically, gesturing at the inadequate furnishings. "Actually, we're staying here only until—"

"Of course, you poor poor dear. I guess he told you to stay away from your neighbors?"

"No," said Mrs. Smith, surprised. "I've always been very slow about making friends, and so I suppose I—"

"You poor *poor* dear. But it's going to be all right now. I'm almighty glad I made up my mind to talk to you."

Mrs. Smith put her bag of groceries down on the kitchen table and came back into the living room to hang her coat in the hall closet, next to the unfamiliar raincoat that belonged to Mr. Smith, and it amused her, in spite of Mrs. Armstrong, to think of sharing her closet with someone else; later, when her clothes were fully unpacked in Mr. Smith's house, she would have a closet of her own, the cedar-lined closet, Mr. Smith had explained, that had once held the clothes of the first Mrs. Smith.

Mrs. Armstrong had moved busily into the kitchen, and was unpacking the groceries. "Didn't get much, did you?" she asked. "Shall I put on some coffee for us? Or do you expect *him* back?"

"He won't be back until dinnertime," Mrs. Smith said, trying to be friendly. "Thank you, I would like some coffee. And I bought very little at the grocery because we expect to be away tomorrow; we are going to do some work in our house, which has been empty for quite a while." There, she thought, now I have told her everything and perhaps we can sit down and drink coffee and talk about the weather until it is time for her to go.

"Going away *tomorrow*?" said Mrs. Armstrong, and her face was, alarmingly, white. *"Tomorrow?"* She sat down heavily on a kitchen chair, staring.

"Mr. Smith has a house about fifteen miles out of the city. It has been empty for several months." Mrs. Smith came into the kitchen and sat down, wondering how much detail Mrs. Armstrong might feel her due from a new bride. "We have taken this apartment for a few weeks so that we will have a chance to fix up the house before we move in. The cellar—"

"The cellar," Mrs. Armstrong repeated in a whisper.

"The cellar needs a new floor. While Mr. Smith puts down a new floor in the cellar I am going to wash windows, and scrub—"

"You poor poor dear," Mrs. Armstrong said.

"I hardly think I need sympathy, Mrs. Armstrong." Mrs. Smith made her voice a little sharper; all of this sounded like implied criticism of her husband, and Mrs. Smith had a stern view of the obligations of a wife, particularly one who had been rescued from loneliness and unhappiness at what was surely the very last moment. "Mr. Smith has been married before, certainly, but I hardly think that his former wife—"

"His former wife," Mrs. Armstrong said. "Sure. All six of them."

"I beg your pardon?"

"Why do you think everyone around here has been wondering and talking and some of us thought we ought to go to the police but of course they always take such a dim view if you're wrong? You think people around here are *blind*?"

"I think the people around here have been very thoughtful, and I certainly appreciate—"

"It's been in the papers," Mrs. Armstrong said desperately, "didn't you know it's been in the papers?"

"I do not read newspapers, Mrs. Armstrong. Mr. Smith and I agree on that, I am thankful to say. Newspapers, radio, all forms of mass—"

"Maybe," Mrs. Armstrong said heavily, "maybe it wouldn't hurt you this once—wouldn't *hurt* you, listen to me!—just to glance a little at a clipping I got here. Just look at the picture, maybe."

Mrs. Smith, a little amused, looked down briefly at the clipping Mrs. Armstrong took from her apron pocket. Sensationalism, Mrs. Smith was thinking; how these people do thrive on it. "Very interesting," Mrs. Smith said politely.

"How about the picture?" said Mrs. Armstrong. "That look like anyone you know?"

"Hardly, Mrs. Armstrong. I do not have acquaintances who put their pictures into the newspapers."

"Well." Mrs. Armstrong sat back and sighed deeply. "You know what this fellow did, this fellow in the paper?"

"I confess I did not read it."

Mrs. Armstrong picked up the clipping and looked at it again. "Six wives," she said. "Drowned them in the bathtub and they found them buried in the cellar. Six."

Mrs. Smith laughed aloud. "I know this fascinates *you,*" she began, but Mrs. Armstrong interrupted her.

"They got this picture because a neighbor just happened to take a snapshot of him going into the cottage. *The* cottage. Afterward, after they found . . . dug up the cellar . . . they got this snapshot and enlarged it. It's supposed to be a *very* good likeness."

"Mrs. Armstrong, *really,* I—"

"Now, this fellow is still loose somewhere, and they don't know where. A wife slayer. He drowns them in the bathtub and then buries—"

The coffee boiled, and Mrs. Smith moved thankfully over to the stove, set the coffee aside, and turned to take out cups and saucers. I won't offer her a second cup of coffee, Mrs. Smith was thinking, as soon as she finishes her first I'll start to pick up, and if she keeps on telling me these vulgar horrors I shall positively turn her out of the house; in any case, Mrs. Smith was thinking, I shall be very cold to her when we meet next; she is not at all the kind of acquaintance Mr. Smith would like me to have—suppose she considered herself a close enough friend to come calling when we are in our new house? What,

Mrs. Smith wondered, and smiled to herself, what would dear Janet think, at such a person in her house? "Sugar?" said Mrs. Smith politely.

Mrs. Armstrong had been drumming her fingers impatiently upon the table. "Look, dearie," she said as soon as Mrs. Smith turned around. "I'm not trying to be nosy, but *please* try to look at it our way. We—and that's all of us, all of us around this neighborhood, because we all saw the picture and we're all just about agreed and there's even some, as I say, wants to go to the police—we have kind of gotten to like you. You're hard to make friends with, I must say, but even so there's not a harsh word going around about you. And if we're wrong, we'll be the first to say so."

"It's very kind of all of you to think so well of me. I *am* a very shy person, although I try not to be."

"Did he make you take out insurance?" Mrs. Armstrong asked bluntly.

Mrs. Smith was puzzled. "He? You mean Mr. Smith?"

"I mean Mr. Smith."

"Why . . . yes. I mean, don't most married people? It's the least we could do for one another," Mrs. Smith said, repeating what Mr. Smith had told her, "to make sure that if anything happened to one of us, the other would be provided for. Money, of course, could never make up for the loss of a treasured companion, but we are neither of us as young as we used—"

"I don't want to frighten you," Mrs. Armstrong said. "If all of us around here should turn out to be wrong, as I say, we'd be the first to come forward handsomely and say so. How did you come to meet him?"

"Really," said Mrs. Smith, blushing deeply. "I hardly think—"

"Has he said anything funny? Anything that might make you suspicious?"

"Mr. Smith was married before," Mrs. Smith explained patiently. "He was married to a splendid, upright woman, and he told me so himself. We have discussed the situation thoroughly, and I assure you that I have no intention of trying to take her place. Mr. Smith and I were both very lonely people, and we can hardly expect our marriage to resemble that of a pair of twenty-year-olds. I have no reason to suspect that Mr. Smith has acted suspiciously or dishonorably toward me in any fashion."

"Have you searched his things?"

"Mrs. Armstrong!"

"The least you could do is find out whether he has a knife or a gun . . . but no. He doesn't do it that way, does he?" She shivered. "I don't know but what I'd prefer a knife," she said. "There's bathtubs *every*where."

Mrs. Smith spoke as politely as she could manage. "Mrs. Armstrong," she said, "I assure you, emphatically, that I have absolutely no interest in sordid crime. I am not, of course, attempting to criticize your pleasure in murder and sudden death, but it is simply not a subject that appeals to me. Suppose we talk about something else while we finish our coffee?"

"I don't think I want any coffee," Mrs. Armstrong said almost sullenly. She got up from her chair. "Well," she said darkly, "just don't ever say I didn't warn you."

Mrs. Smith laughed, privately pleased that her visitor was leaving so delightfully soon. "Living in a city sometimes makes you dwell on horrible things," she said. "I'm glad that we'll be out in the country soon."

Mrs. Armstrong stopped in the doorway and held out her hands eloquently. "*Look,*" she said, "all I can say is if you need any help—*any* help, *any*time—just open your mouth and scream, see? Because my Ed will be up as fast as he can come. All you have to do is scream, or stamp on the floor, or if you can get away, make it downstairs to our place. One of us is sure to be there. Just remember—all you have to do is scream."

"Thank you," Mrs. Smith said. "I'll be sure to call on you if I need anything."

Mrs. Armstrong started to close the door behind her, and then opened it again and said in a voice which she tried to make humorous, "Just don't take any baths," and closed the door. Her voice trailed up from the stairs. "Thanks for the coffee," she said.

Mrs. Smith sighed with relief, and went into the kitchen to clean up the coffee cups. After she had washed and dried the two cups and saucers she took a clean cup for herself and filled it with coffee and went to sit by the living room window. Looking out and down onto the dark and dirty street below, she fell once more into her state of quiet happiness; three weeks ago, she told herself, I was miserable and without a friend in the world. Father was gone, and there I sat, all alone and—she skipped hastily over the thought—even wondering what it would be like to walk out into the sea and just keep walking on and on, and then he sat down beside me; "I hope you won't think me forward," he said. Mrs. Smith gave a little secret laugh, and sipped her coffee.

She was broiling the lamb chops when the sound of her husband's key in the door brought her out of the kitchen and into the living room. They were still a little awkward with each other, so that Mrs. Smith did not quite dare to run to the door to greet him, and was touched when he came inside and nearly across the room to kiss her gently on the forehead. "How's my wife?" he asked.

"I missed you all day," she said. "Did your business go well?"

"Yes," he said. "I think I've settled everything."

"I just realized," she said, hurrying into the kitchen, "that I don't even know whether you *like* lamb chops; I hope you do."

"A particular favorite of mine," he said. He came into the kitchen and sat down in the chair Mrs. Armstrong had used earlier. "Anything particular happen today?"

"No." Mrs. Smith, concentrating deeply, regarded the little dinner table set, now, with odds and ends; when she had her house she would have matched dishes and silverware. "The woman downstairs came up for a while," she said.

There was a minute's silence. Then, "What did she want?" Mr. Smith asked indifferently.

Mrs. Smith carefully served the lamb chops and the peas, and put a baked potato on Mr. Smith's plate. "Just to gossip," she said; "we had coffee, and she chattered on and on till I thought she'd never leave."

"About what? I mean, what could someone like that have to say to *you*?"

"I didn't listen, really; I was just wishing she would leave. She's one of those people who loves gory details of murders, and I almost thought I would never be able to drink my coffee, the way she was talking."

"Anything in particular?"

"The plot of some movie she'd seen, I think," Mrs. Smith said vaguely. "Is the lamb chop all right?"

"Fine." Mr. Smith attacked his second lamb chop. "You're a fine cook," he said, as though surprised. "Imagine your being a fine cook in addition to everything else."

Mrs. Smith giggled. "*What* else, silly?" she said. "I thought you married me only to keep house for you."

"Speaking of keeping house," Mr. Smith said. He swallowed his mouthful of lamb chop and set down his fork. "I was thinking," he said, "we'd be better off and save a lot of time if we went down tonight, right after dinner, instead of waiting till tomorrow."

"I'd like to," Mrs. Smith said shyly. "I can't wait to see it."

"Just get right in the car and take off—there's no one cares what we do or when. We can stay there tonight—the electricity's on, and the water—and we'll be comfortable enough."

"Fine," Mrs. Smith said. "*I* don't mind a little discomfort; after all, there will be plenty of time to fix things the way we like them."

"And that way," Mr. Smith said, as though talking to himself, "I can get started on the cellar first thing tomorrow morning."

The Honeymoon of
Mrs. Smith

❦

(Version II)
The Mystery
of the Murdered Bride

WHEN SHE CAME INTO the grocery she obviously interrupted a conversation about herself and her husband. The
grocer leaning across the counter to speak confidentially to a customer straightened up abruptly and signaled at her with his eyes, so
that the customer, in a fairly obvious attempt at dissimulation, looked
stubbornly in the opposite direction for almost a minute before turning quickly to take one swift, eager look.

"Good morning," she said.

"What'll it be for you this morning?" he asked, his eyes moving to
the right and left to insure that all present observed him speaking
boldly to Mrs. Smith.

"I don't need very much," she said. "I may be going away over the
weekend."

A long sigh swept through the store; she had a clear sense of
people moving closer, as though the dozen other customers, the grocer, the butcher, the clerks, were pressing against her, listening av-
idly.

"A small loaf of bread," she said clearly. "A pint of milk. The
smallest possible can of peas."

"Not laying in much for the weekend," the grocer said with satisfaction.

"I may be going away," she said, and again there was that long
breath of satisfaction. She thought: how silly of all of us—I'm not
sure any more than *they* are, we all of us only suspect, and of course

there won't be any way of knowing for sure . . . but still it would be a shame to have all that food in the kitchen, and let it go to waste, just rotting there while . . .

"Coffee?" the grocer said. "Tea?"

"I'm going to get a pound of coffee," she said, smiling at him. "After all, I like coffee. I can probably drink up a pound before . . ."

The anticipatory pause made her say quickly, "And I'll want a quarter pound of butter, and I guess two lamb chops."

The butcher, although he had been trying to pretend indifference, turned immediately to get the lamb chops, and he came the width of the store and set the small package on the counter before the grocer had finished adding up her order.

One good thing, she was thinking about all this—I never have to *wait* anywhere. It's as though everyone knew I was in a hurry to get small things done. And I suppose no one really wants me around for very long, not after they've had their good look at me and gotten something to talk about.

When her groceries were all in a bag and the grocer was ready to hand it to her across the counter, he hesitated, as he had done several times before, as though he tried to gather courage to say something to her; she was aware of this, and knew fairly well what he wanted to say—listen, Mrs. Smith, it would start, we don't want to make any trouble or anything, and of course it isn't as though anyone around here was *sure,* but I guess you must know by now that it all looks mighty suspicious, and we just figured—with an inclusive glance around, for support from the butcher and the clerks—we all got talking, and we figured—well, we figured someone ought to say something to you about it. I guess people must have made this mistake before about you? Or your husband? Because of course no one likes to come right out and *say* a thing like that, when they could so easily be wrong. And of course the more everyone talks about this kind of thing, the harder it is to know whether you're right or not . . .

The man in the liquor store had said substantially that to her, fumbling and letting his voice die away under her cool, inquiring stare. The man in the drugstore had begun to say it, and then, blushing, had concluded, "Well, it's not *my* business, anyway." The woman in the lending library, the landlady, had given her the nervous, appraising look, wondering if she knew, if anyone had told her, wondering if they dared, and had ended by treating her with extreme gentleness and a sweet forbearance, as they would have treated some uncomplaining, incurable invalid. She was different in their eyes, she was marked; if the dreadful fact were not true (and they all hoped it was), she was in a position of such incredible, extreme embarrassment that their solicitude was even more deserved. If the dreadful fact *were* true (and they all hoped it was), they had none of them, the landlady, the grocer, the clerks, the druggist, lived in vain, gone through their days without the supreme excitement of being close to and yet secure from an unbearable situation. If the dreadful fact *were* true (and they all hoped it was), Mrs. Smith was, for them, a salvation and a heroine, a fragile, lovely creature whose preservation was in hands other than theirs.

Some of this Mrs. Smith realized dimly as she walked back to her apartment with the bag of groceries. She, at least, was almost not in doubt; she had known almost certainly that the dreadful fact was true for three weeks and six days, since she had met it face-to-face on a bench facing the ocean.

"I hope you won't think I'm rude," Mr. Smith had said at that moment, "if I open a conversation by saying that it's a lovely day."

She thought he was incredibly daring, she thought he was unbelievably vulgar, but she did not think he was rude; it was a word ridiculous when applied to him.

"No," she had said, recognizing him, "I don't think you're rude."

If she had ever tried to phrase it to herself—it would hardly be possible to describe it to anyone else—she might have said, in the faintly clerical idiom she had learned so thoroughly, that she had been chosen for this, or that it was like being carried unresisting on the surface of a river which took her on inevitably into the sea. Or she might have said that, just as in her whole life before she had not questioned the decisions of her father but had done quietly as she was told, so it was a relief to know that there was now someone again to decide for her, and that her life, inevitable as it had been before, was now clear as well. Or she might have said—with a blush for a possible double meaning, that they, like all other married couples, were two halves of what was essentially one natural act.

"A man gets very lonesome, I think," he had told her at dinner that night, in a restaurant near the sea, where even the napkins smelled of fish and the bare wood of the table had an indefinable salty grain, "a man alone needs to find himself some kind of company." And then, as though the words had perhaps not been complimentary enough, he added hastily, "Except not everyone is lucky enough to meet a charming young lady like yourself." She had smiled and simpered, by then fully aware of these preliminaries to her destiny.

Three weeks and six days later, turning to go in through the door of the shabby apartment house, she wondered briefly about the week-end ahead; she had been naturally reluctant to buy too much food, but then, if it turned out that she *should* be there, there would be no way to buy more food on Sunday; a restaurant, she thought, we will have to go to a restaurant—although they had not been together to a restaurant since that first dinner together since, even though they did not actually have to economize, they both felt soberly that the fairly large mutual bank account they now had ought not to be squandered unnecessarily, but should be kept as nearly intact as possible; they had not discussed this, but Mrs. Smith's instinctive tactful respect for her husband's methods led her to fall in with him silently in his routine of economy.

The three flights of stairs were narrow and high, and Mrs. Smith, with the immediate recognition of symbols she had inherited, had always had, potentially, and was now using almost exclusively, saw the eternal steps going up and up as an irrevocable design for her life; she had really no choice but to go up, wearily if she chose; if she turned and went down again, retracing laboriously the small progress she had made, she would merely have to go up another way, begin-ning, as she now almost realized, beginning again a search which could only, for her, have but one ending. "It happens to everybody," she told herself consolingly as she climbed.

Pride would not allow her to make any concessions to her position, so she did not try particularly to walk silently on the second floor landing; for a minute, going on up the next flight, she thought she had got safely past, but then, almost as she reached her own door, the door on the second landing opened and Mrs. Jones called, piercingly and as though she had run from some back recess of her apartment to the door when she heard footsteps.

"Mrs. Smith, is that you?"

"Hello," Mrs. Smith called back down the stairs.

"Wait a minute, I'm coming up." The lock on Mrs. Jones's door snapped, and the door closed. Mrs. Jones came hurriedly, still a little out of breath, down the landing and up the stairs to the third floor. "Thought I'd missed you," she said on the stairs, and, "Good heav-ens, you look tired."

It was part of the attitude that treated Mrs. Smith as a precious vessel. Her slightest deviation from the normal, in the course of more than a week, was noted and passed from gossip to gossip, a faint paling of her cheeks became the subject of nervous speculation, any change in her voice, a dullness of her eye, a disarrangement in her dress—these were what her neighbors lived on. Mrs. Smith had thought early in the week that a loud crash from her apartment would be the sweetest thing she could do for Mrs. Jones, but by now it no longer seemed important: Mrs. Jones could live as well on the most minute crumbs.

"Thought you'd never get home," Mrs. Jones said. She followed Mrs. Smith into the bare little room which, with a small bedroom, a dirty kitchen, and a bath, was the honeymoon home of Mr. and Mrs. Smith. Mrs. Jones took the package of groceries into the kitchen while Mrs. Smith hung up her coat in the closet; she had not bothered to unpack many things and the closet looked empty; there were two or three dresses and a light overcoat and extra suit of Mr. Smith's; this was so obviously only a temporary home for them both, a stopping-place. Mrs. Smith did not regard her three dresses with regret, nor did she particularly admire the suits of Mr. Smith, although they were still a little unfamiliar to her, hung up next to her own clothes (as his underwear in the dresser, lying quietly beside her own); neither Mr. nor Mrs. Smith were of the abandoned sort who indulge recklessly in trousseaus or other loving detail for a preliminary purification.

"Well," said Mrs. Jones, coming out of the kitchen, "*you* certainly aren't planning to do much cooking this weekend."

Privacy was not one of the blessings of Mrs. Smith's position. "I thought I might be going away," she said.

Again there was that soft, anticipatory moment; Mrs. Jones looked quickly, and then away, and then, sitting herself down firmly upon the meager couch, obviously decided to come to the point.

"Now, look, Mrs. Smith," she began, and then interrupted herself. "Look, why this 'Mrs.' all the time? You call me Polly, and from now on I'll call you Helen. All right?" She smiled, and Mrs. Smith, smiling back, thought, how do they find out your first name? "Well, now, look here, Helen," Mrs. Jones went on, determined to establish her new familiarity immediately, "I think it's time someone sat down and talked sensibly to you. I mean, you must know by now pretty well what people are saying."

Here we are, Helen Smith was thinking, two women of the singular type woman, one standing uneasily and embarrassed in front of a window, wearing a brown dress and brown hair and brown shoes and differing in no essential respect from the other, sitting solidly and earnestly, wearing a green and pink flowered housedress and bedroom slippers—differing, actually in no essential, although we would both deny indignantly that we were the same person, seeking the same destiny. And we are about to enter into a conversation upon a fantastic subject.

"I've noticed," Mrs. Smith said carefully, "that there's a lot of unusual interest in us. I've never been on a honeymoon before, of course, so I can't really tell whether it's only that." She laughed weakly, but Mrs. Jones was not to be put off by sentiment.

"I think you must know better than that," she said. "You're not *that* wrapped up in your husband."

"Well . . . no," Mrs. Smith had to say.

"And furthermore," Mrs. Jones went on, looking cynically at Mrs. Smith, "you're not any blushing eighteen-year-old girl, you know, and Mr. Smith isn't any young man. You're both people of a reasonably mature age." Mrs. Jones seemed to feel that she had made a point here, and she said it again. "You are both people who have outlived their youth," she said, "and naturally no one expects that you're going to go around billing and cooing. And *furthermore* you yourself are old enough to show some intelligence about this terrible business."

"I don't know what kind of intelligence I ought to show," Mrs. Smith said meekly.

"Well, good heavens!" Mrs. Jones spread her hands helplessly. "Don't you realize your position? *Everyone* knows it. Look." She settled back, prepared to demonstrate reasonably. "You came here a week ago, newly married, and moved into this apartment with your husband. The very first day you were here, people thought there was something funny. In the first place, you two didn't act like you were the types for each other at all. You know what I mean—you so sort of refined and ladylike, and him . . ."

Rude, Mrs. Smith thought, wanting to laugh; he said he was rude.

Mrs. Jones shrugged. "In the second place," she said, "you didn't look like you belonged in this house, or in this neighborhood, because you always had plenty of money, which, believe me, the rest of us don't, and you always acted sort of as though you ought to be in a better kind of situation. And in the *third* place," Mrs. Jones said, hurrying on to her climax, "it wasn't two days before people began to think they recognized your husband from the pictures in the paper."

"I see what you mean," Mrs. Smith said. "But a picture in the paper—"

"That's just what started us really thinking," Mrs. Jones said. She enumerated on her fingers. "New bride. Cheap apartment. You made a will in his favor? Insurance?"

"Yes, but that is only natural—" said Mrs. Smith.

"Natural? And him looking just like the man in the paper who mur—" She stopped abruptly. "I don't want to frighten you," she said. "But you should know all about him."

"I appreciate your concern," Mrs. Smith said in her turn, coming away from the window, to stand in front of Mrs. Jones so that Mrs. Jones had to look up from her seat on the couch. "I know all these things. But how many newly married couples are there who make wills in each other's favor? Or take out insurance? And how many women over thirty get married to men over forty? And maybe sometimes the men look like pictures in the paper? And with all this talk and gossip about us all around the neighborhood, you notice no one's been even sure enough to say anything?"

"I wanted to call the police two, three days ago," Mrs. Jones said sullenly. "Ed wouldn't let me."

"He probably said," Mrs. Smith said, "that it was none of your business."

"But everybody's *wondering*," Mrs. Jones said. "And of course no one can know for sure."

"You won't know for sure until . . ." Mrs. Smith tried not to smile.

Mrs. Jones sighed. "I wish you wouldn't talk like that," she said.

"Well," said Mrs. Smith reasonably, "what exactly is it you want me to do?"

"You could get some kind of information," Mrs. Jones said. "Something that would let you know for sure."

"I keep telling you," Mrs. Smith said, "there's only one way I can ever know for sure."

"Don't *talk* like that," Mrs. Jones said.

"I could run away from my husband," Mrs. Smith said.

Mrs. Jones was surprised. "You can't run away from your *husband*," she said. "Not if it isn't true, you couldn't do that."

"I have really no grounds for divorce," Mrs. Smith said. "It is a very difficult subject to mention to him."

"Naturally, you wouldn't have discussed it," Mrs. Jones said.

"Naturally," Mrs. Smith said. "I could hardly search his clothes—

there is nothing, I happen to know, in the pockets of the suit hanging in the closet and searching his overcoat pockets and his dresser drawers would hardly turn up anything convincing."

"Why not?"

"Well, I mean," said Mrs. Smith in explanation, "even if I discovered, say, a knife—what difference would it make?"

"But he doesn't do it with—" Mrs. Jones began, and stopped abruptly again.

"I know," Mrs. Smith said. "As I recall the details—and I haven't read much about them, after all—he generally does it—"

"In the bathtub," Mrs. Jones said, and shivered. "I don't know but what a knife would be better," she said.

"It's not our choice," Mrs. Smith said wryly. "You see how silly we sound? Here we are, talking as though we were children telling ghost stories. We'll end up convincing each other of some horrible notion."

Mrs. Jones hesitated for a minute over her own reactions, and finally decided to be mildly offended. "I really only came up," she explained with dignity, "to let you know what people were saying. If you stop to *think* about it for a minute, you ought to be able to understand why someone might want to help you. After all, it's not me."

"That's why I think you ought not to worry," Mrs. Smith said gently.

Mrs. Jones rose, but as she reached the door she was unable to keep herself from turning and saying urgently, "Look, I just want you to know that if you ever *ever* need any help—of *any* kind—just open your mouth and scream, see? Because my Ed will be up as fast as he can come. All you have to do is scream, or stamp on the floor, or, if you can, race downstairs to our place. We'll be waiting for you." She opened the door, said with a voice that she tried to make humorous, "Don't take any baths," and went out. Her voice trailed up from the stairs, "And remember—all you have to do is scream. We'll be waiting."

Mrs. Smith closed the door rather quickly and, before she started to think, went out to the kitchen to see to her groceries, but Mrs. Jones had put the things away. Mrs. Smith found the pound of coffee, and measured water into the coffeepot, thinking of her promise to the grocer that she would finish the pound of coffee herself. Mr. Smith drank coffee sparingly; it made him nervous.

Mrs. Smith, as she moved about the bleak little kitchen, thought, as she had often before, that she would not like to spend her whole life with things like this. It had not been so in her father's life, where a peaceful, well-ordered existence went placidly on among objects which, if not lovely, had at least the pleasures of familiarity, and the near-beauty of order, and Mrs. Smith, who had then been Helen Bertram, had been able to spend long days working in the garden, or mending her father's socks, or baking the nut cake she had learned from her mother, and pausing only occasionally to wonder what was going to happen to her in her life.

It had been clear to her after her father's death that this patterned existence was no longer meaningful, and had been a product of her father's life rather than hers. So that when Mr. Smith had said to her, "I don't suppose you'd ever consider marrying a fellow like me?" Helen Bertram had nodded, seeing then the repeated design which made the complete pattern.

She had worn her best dark blue dress to be married in, and Mr. Smith had worn a dark blue suit so that they looked unnervingly alike when they went down the street together. They had gone directly to the lawyer's, for the wills, and then to the insurance company. On the way, Mr. Smith had insisted on stopping and buying for the new Mrs. Smith a small felt dog which amused her; there had been a man selling these on the street corner, and all around his small stand were tiny wound-up dogs which ran in circles, squeaking in shrill imitation of a bark. Mrs. Smith brought the box with the dog in it into the insurance company and set it on the desk, and while they were waiting for the doctor she had opened the box and found that there was no key to wind the dog; Mr. Smith, saying irritably, "Those fellows always try to cheat you," had hurried back to the street corner and found the stand, the salesman, and the performing dogs gone.

"Nothing makes me more furious," he told Mrs. Smith, "than to be cheated by someone like that."

The small dog stood now on the shelf in the kitchen and Mrs. Smith, glancing at it, thought, I could not endure spending the rest of my life with that tawdry sort of thing. She sometimes thought poignantly of her father's house, realizing that such things were gone from her forever, but, as she told herself again now, "I had my eyes open." It will have to be soon, she thought immediately after, people are beginning to wonder too openly. Everyone is waiting; it will spoil everything if it is not soon. When her coffee was finished she took a cup into the living room and sat down on the couch where Mrs. Jones had been sitting, and thought, it will have to be soon; there's no food for the weekend, after all, and I would have to send my dress to the cleaners on Monday if I were here, and another week's rent due tomorrow. The pound of coffee would be the only detail unattended to.

She had finished her fourth cup of coffee—drinking by now hastily and even desperately—when she heard her husband's step on the stairs. They were still a little embarrassed with one another, so that she hesitated about going to meet him just long enough for him to open the door, and then she came over to him awkwardly and, not knowing still whether he wanted to kiss her when he came home, stood expectantly until he came politely over to her and kissed her cheek.

"Where have you been?" she asked, although it was not at all the sort of thing she wanted to say to him, and she knew as she spoke that he would not tell her.

"Shopping," he said. He had an armful of packages, one of which he selected and gave to her.

"Thank you," she said politely before she opened it; it was, she knew by the feel and the drugstore wrapping, a box of candy, and with a feeling which, when she felt it again later, she knew to be triumph, she thought, of course, it's supposed to be left over, it's to prove the new husband still brings presents to his bride. She opened the box, wanted to take a candy, thought: not before dinner, and then thought, it probably doesn't matter, tonight.

"Will you have one?" she said to him, and he took one.

His manner did not seem strange, or nervous, but when she said, "Mrs. Jones was up here this afternoon," he said quickly, "What did she want, the old busybody?"

"I think she was jealous," Mrs. Smith said. "It's been a long time since *her* husband has taken any interest in her."

"I can imagine," he said.

"Shall I start dinner?" Mrs. Smith asked. "Would you like to rest for a while first?"

"I'm not hungry," he said.

Now, for the first time, he seemed awkward, and Mrs. Smith thought quickly, I was right about the food for the weekend, I guessed right; he did not ask if she was hungry because—and each of them knew now that the other knew—it really did not matter.

Mrs. Smith told herself it would ruin everything to say anything now, and she sat down on the couch next to her husband and said, "I'm a little tired, I think."

"A week of marriage was too much for you," he said, and patted her hand. "We'll have to see that you get more rest."

Why does it take so long, why *does* it take so long? Mrs. Smith thought; she stood up again and walked across the room nervously to look out the window; Mr. Jones was just coming up the front steps and he looked up and saw her and waved. Why does it take so long? she thought again, and turned and said to her husband, "Well?"

"I suppose so," Mr. Smith said, and got up wearily from the couch.

THE SISTER

MARGARET LOOKED AT HER brother with the first conscious affection she had felt for him in her life. He looks big and awkward and childish, she thought, and whatever he's going to say is going to be right out of the movies. She watched him shut the door and stand just inside it for a minute, wondering how to start. Then he came slowly over and sat down uneasily in the pale blue slipper chair beside the bed.

"Golly," he said.

Margaret laughed. "Golly," she said.

"You really going?" her brother asked.

"Sure am," Margaret said.

Her brother ceremoniously took a package of cigarettes out of his pocket and offered her one. She shook her head, pointed at the lighted cigarette she had left on the edge of the dresser. Her brother lit his, and went across the room to the table and got an ashtray.

"You're going to burn the dresser scarf, leaving cigarettes around like that," he said.

"Been doing it ever since I started sneaking cigarettes in here," Margaret said.

"Mother put an ashtray in my room a couple of weeks ago," her brother said. "Guess she's started getting smarter. She never gave *you* an ashtray till you came home from college."

"I was smoking when I was fifteen," Margaret said.

Her brother rose and began to wander around the room. He came over to the bed and looked at the suitcase Margaret was packing. "I remember this dress," he said, lifting a corner of the hem, "you wore it the night I couldn't find a date for Dick and you came instead. We went to the country club dance."

"Those were the days when I still felt like an old maid," Margaret said.

Her brother hesitated. "Say," he said finally, "you really going to marry this guy?"

"I really am," Margaret said.

"You know what you're doing to your father and mother?" her brother said.

Margaret walked over to the dresser and picked up her cigarette. "You sound just like Dad," she said, "voice and everything. Now tell me I'm ungrateful and silly and don't know what I'm doing, and that I'll be home trying to beg pardon in a week."

"I don't think you will," her brother said. Margaret turned and looked at him. "You're too smart," he went on, "you went to college."

"I met him in college," Margaret said.

"I know," her brother said. "If I'd gone to college maybe I would have met a nice girl."

"Instead of the one you did meet."

"There's nothing wrong with Bobbie." Her brother frowned and stared firmly at Margaret's suitcase on the bed. "She's a nice kid. That's why we got married."

Margaret turned around to look at him. "What did you say?" she demanded. "Did you say you had married that little tramp?"

Her brother looked up and then down again, and Margaret suddenly began to laugh. "Do you know what *you're* doing to your father and mother?"

"I figured I'd tell them right afterward," her brother said, "but then you came home with this business about going out to Chicago to marry this guy, and that was bad enough."

"So I killed your story?" Margaret said. "What are you going to do?"

"Tell them later on, when they get used to you."

"They're going to get a shock."

"Margaret," her brother asked, "listen, what's wrong with them? No one else has children like us."

"What's wrong with us?" Margaret said. "We're good, honest, middle-class people belonging to a country club and owning one car.

I went to college because I wanted to, and you didn't go to college because Dad thought you ought to go to work. We play a family game of golf and a family game of bridge and not one of us ever said a nice word to any of the others. What do *you* think is wrong with us?"

"Bobbie says Dad was too strict with us," her brother said.

"Maybe so," Margaret said. "When were you married?"

"About a week ago."

"Where's Bobbie now?"

"With her family. They know about it. Her sister went with us."

"Should have taken me," Margaret said. "I would have liked to be there."

"I'd like to be at your wedding," her brother said. "We never talked like this before, did we?"

"Why should we?" Margaret said. "Nothing ever happened to us before."

She closed the suitcase and locked it, putting it on the floor. Her brother came over and helped her on with her coat, and she picked up the suitcase and looked around.

"Did I forget anything?" she asked.

"Look," her brother said, "do you want any money?"

Right out of the movies, Margaret thought. "Thanks," she said, "he sent me plenty."

"I have some cash with me," her brother insisted.

"Keep it for Bobbie," Margaret said, "she'll probably need it."

He followed her to the door of the bedroom. "Well," he said. He leaned over and kissed her on the cheek. "Good luck."

"Give Bobbie my love," Margaret said, and started down the stairs.

Her father came out of the living room with her mother in back of him. Margaret went straight on toward the front door, but her father held out his hand.

"Wait a minute," he said. "You won't change your mind?"

"You don't know what you're doing," her mother said.

"I'm really going," Margaret said to her father.

"A man none of us knows," her mother said, "out in Chicago."

"You can always come home, daughter," her father said, "we'll always make you welcome."

"Thanks," Margaret said.

"Margaret," her father said, "let me say this once more. Your mother and I are terribly hurt by all this, and yet we are trying to do only what is best for you. Maybe this news, so sudden and everything, has surprised us a little—"

"You and your brother," her mother said, "always such *obedient* children."

"Listen," Margaret said, turning around to her father and putting down the suitcase, "listen, you want to hear something that will *really* surprise you?"

ARCH-CRIMINAL

I SUPPOSE THE MOTHERS of most twelve-year-old boys live with the uneasy conviction that their sons are embarked upon a secret life of crime. In my case, this belief about my son Laurie is shared—not without reason—by Mrs. John R. Simpkins, of upper New York State, whose opinions on Laurie are even more forceful than those held by myself and, to a lesser extent, by my husband, who has recently been doing research into eighteenth-century crime, and points out that at that time *all* twelve-year-old boys were criminals—or, as he has it, cross coves—and many of them, as a matter of fact, were named Simpkins. "The gooseberry trick," he says reassuringly, "glomming the grapevine."

I refer, of course, to the Mrs. John R. Simpkins who lived next door to us the summer when Laurie was nine, and across the street from the Rowland boys, although of course when we rented the house for the summer we had no idea the Rowland boys were going to turn out to live nearby. Mrs. Simpkins still writes to me occasionally, when there is any news about people we used to know, and although she never comes right out and asks about Laurie's criminal record, and makes no mention of the less savory aspects of our six weeks next door, she writes in her most recent letter that she thought of us at once when she came across the newspaper story about the Rowland boy, clipping enclosed. In the next paragraph she says that her own dear little boy is receiving many compliments on his little poems in the school paper, and what is dear little Laurie doing these days? Still interested in all kinds of sports, Mrs. Simpkins supposes, and she wonders if he is as "lively" as ever?

"Look at this," I said, slamming the letter and the clipping down on the desk before my husband.

He regarded the clipping absently. "Got the tom on him, did they?"

"That woman ought to be locked up as a malicious gossip," I said. "I can imagine what that whole town thinks of us."

"The Rowlands—"

"Well," I said reasonably, "if she says it about the Rowlands it's probably true, because you know as well as I do that that older boy of theirs was never anything but a—"

"Choir bird," my husband said.

"But poor little Laurie—taken in by those juvenile delinquents— just following along and doing what they told him—"

"An outfielder," my husband suggested. "The outfielder on that last job."

I snatched my letter and the clipping and stormed out of the study. "Maybe," I said over my shoulder, "if Laurie had a father who spoke English—"

"That's what you said to Mrs. Rowland," my husband remarked amiably.

It was, too, almost. I went into the kitchen and decided to get even with Mrs. Simpkins and the Rowlands and my husband by serving vegetable soup for lunch again today, and put the cover on the saucepan wishing I had Spike Rowland's head inside. All I had said to Mrs. Rowland was that perhaps Spike's father should try to be a good example to his boys, and that was the only time I ever heard Mrs. Rowland laugh out loud. I never met Mr. Rowland myself, but Laurie did.

Spike was thirteen, Billy Rowland was ten, and Laurie was nine. The dear little Simpkins boy next door was about six months older than Laurie, and his young sister and our daughter Jannie were devoted friends all that summer. I thought it would be nice if Laurie and dear little Tommy Simpkins played together, and went so far as to invite the Simpkins children over for supper the first week we were there, but the party was a complete failure as far as Laurie was concerned, since after supper Tommy Simpkins settled down to play house with his sister and Jannie, and Laurie wandered outdoors in search of amusement, and met the Rowland boys shooting out streetlights.

We noticed, of course, that Laurie's general deportment had taken a turn for the worse as the summer wore on. He was impertinent, dirty, callous, and really treated little Tommy Simpkins most unkindly. He also became most evasive about his activities, and we only found out about the fire at all because he came home one evening with his jacket scorched and soot all over his face.

"What?" I demanded, dropping the jacket to seize Laurie and turn him around and around for signs of burns. "What?"

Laurie shook his head irritably. "I *told* him you'd be mad," he said.

"You were right. I am mad. Told who?"

"Spike. I told him he should use his own jacket."

"What for?"

"To put out the fire."

"What fire?"

"The one in our tree house."

"A fire? In your tree house? In our backya—is it out?"

"It's out all right," Laurie said as I turned and headed wildly for the back door. "Nothing to worry about *now*."

I sat down, counted to a hundred while Laurie absentmindedly rubbed soot on the curtains, and then, composed and lighting a cigarette with hands that shook only slightly, I said, "Now, Laurence, tell me all about this please. Your tree house caught fire?"

"Not at first."

"What do you mean?"

"It was all right before Billy poured on the kerosene."

"What?" I said faintly.

"He said it would burn better, but then the tree house burned too."

"What *started* the fire?"

"Spike did."

"Why?"

"To cook the potatoes."

"Potatoes?"

"The ones he hooked from old man Martin's store."

"He *stole* potatoes?"

"Well . . . he sort of had to."

"Why—why—why?"

"Because of Billy. So old man Martin would chase Spike instead."

"Young man," I said, "your father will be home at five o'clock, and you will spend the time until he comes in the bathtub. *He* will speak to you and decide what is to be done. I shall inform him that you have been associating with thieves and arsonists. Upstairs."

"No bath," said Laurie sullenly.

"Bath," I said. "Just one thing, though—what made Spike think that Mr. Martin wanted to chase Billy?"

"Because Billy put the cat in the meat counter. But *I* didn't do anything," Laurie said. "*I* just stood there."

Unfortunately Mrs. Simpkins had seen the fire in the tree house, and she made a number of fairly pointed remarks about little boys who played quietly with their little sisters as opposed to little boys who ran around with roughnecks. We absolutely forbade Laurie to see, contact, signal, or remember the Rowland boys, and it was the next morning that I dropped over and had my chat with Mrs. Rowland. She was a gray, tired woman, and she came to the door carrying the baby. Both of them looked weary and reluctant. I told her as politely as I could that I thought diplomatic relations between our houses must cease, and she nodded, sighing, as though we had been the last family who still spoke to them and now we were going, too. I asked if she would mention to her sons that their friendship with Laurie must be brought to an immediate halt.

"I'll tell them," she said, and the baby looked at me cynically.

I said that luckily the tree was not badly damaged, because of course we had only rented the house for the summer; "I *am* a little surprised," I added, "that a boy Spike's age would encourage such a thing."

"You are?" she said.

"Perhaps Mr. Rowland—"

She stepped back. "What about him?" she demanded, clutching the baby tighter.

"I meant only that perhaps Mr. Rowland could speak to the boys. Tell them that this kind of thing is dangerous."

"What kind of thing?" she said. "*He* never did anything, and you better not say he did."

"Well, if you call setting fire to a tree—"

"Oh, you mean Spikey," she said. "*He's* just a kid—I don't worry about *him*. But you better not say anything against his father—*he* didn't go setting fire to trees."

"I am only," I told her with vast patience, "suggesting that perhaps Mr. Rowland should set his sons a good example."

It was, as I say, the only time I ever heard Mrs. Rowland laugh.

We kept Laurie in solitary for a week. During that time his behavior was exemplary, and his morale astonishingly high. He read the greater part of "The Hardy Boys at Eagle Lodge," and spent a lot of time painting, although he declined a proposed correspondence with the Simpkins boy, who suggested that poor Laurie might enjoy playing chess by mail.

We believed optimistically that Laurie was a reformed character. I told my husband, on the last day of Laurie's confinement, that actually one good scare like that could probably mark a child for life, and my husband pointed out that kids frequently have an instinctive desire to follow the good example rather than the bad, once they find out which is which. We agreed that a good moral background and thorough grounding in the Hardy Boys would always tell in the long run.

The next day the policeman came. He knocked on the front door while my husband was reading the Sunday papers and I was basting the roast. He asked for Laurie.

"Laurie?" I said, and my husband said, "What?"

"You got a boy about ten years old?"

"Yes," my husband said, and I added defensively that Laurie was only nine.

"Well," the policeman said, and he seemed embarrassed. "I got kids of my own," he explained. "Girl ten, boy six."

We waited tensely, and after a minute he went on. "I better talk to the boy, I guess."

"Now, look here," I said, "Laurie didn't do anything," and my husband said, "What did he do?"

"Well, there's been a little trouble," the policeman said. "Your boy seems to have been mixed up in a little trouble."

A soft step on the stairs silenced him. Laurie, having ascertained the nature of our guest, was going back up to his room. His father went out and captured him, and when he was brought in, looking sullen and nervous, I had to resist a strong impulse to run over and gather him up bodily, crying out that he was my little baby and no one was going to touch him while I was around. Luckily the policeman spoke first.

"Now, then, son," he said. "Let's hear about this concrete mixer."

Laurie started to say, "*What* concrete mixer?" but caught his father's eye and said instead, "It was just an old concrete mixer, is all."

"Who turned it on?" the policeman asked.

"Spike," said Laurie almost inaudibly.

"Were you there?"

Laurie looked from me to his father to the policeman. "I guess so," he said.

"How did Spike start the concrete mixer?"

Laurie swallowed unhappily. "Wires," he said.

"Wires?"

"He twisted some wires together," Laurie said. " He said he was going to show me and Billy how you started a concrete mixer."

The policeman leaned forward. "Which wires?" he demanded. "You remember, son?"

Laurie shook his head, and the policeman sat back uneasily.

"*Spike* got inside," Laurie insisted. "We were just standing there."

The policeman regarded his fingernails casually. "Just where is this fellow Spike right now?" he asked. Laurie shook his head. "Well, anyplace you can think of where he *might* be?" Laurie shook his head. "You got any idea where he *usually* hides?"

"Whyn't you ask Billy?" Laurie said.

"He doesn't know either." The policeman sighed. "We'd sort of like to find that boy," he said.

"You going to arrest him?" Laurie asked.

The policeman hesitated. "As a matter of fact," he said at last, reluctantly, "I guess mostly we want him to go and turn the concrete mixer off again. The foreman's gone out of town," he explained to us, "and there's no one around can get the blasted thing turned off and it is just down there grinding and grinding away. Look, son," he said again pleadingly to Laurie, "you think of *any*where—anywhere at *all*—that kid might be?"

"Nope," Laurie said.

"Why don't you ask the boy's father?" I said.

Laurie snickered. The policeman glanced at me briefly and compassionately and then said to Laurie, "This all checks in pretty well with what the other boy—Billy—tells us. I don't think you'll be in any real trouble about it, but I think we better, you and me and Dad here, have a man-to-man talk about kids who get into mischief."

The application of this remark seemed pretty clear, so I excused myself and got back to my roast. After about half an hour I heard my husband and Laurie saying goodbye to the policeman at the front door. From the kitchen window I could see Mrs. Simpkins peering out of *her* kitchen window to see the policeman leave our house.

We got away fairly lightly; Laurie laboriously constructed a written apology for the company that owned the concrete mixer, which had finally burned itself out and gone off by itself. My husband offered to pay our share of the damage, but since Laurie had not been actually involved in the turning on of the concrete mixer the company declined, and the owner actually patted Laurie on the head when Laurie tearfully proffered his allowance for the week he had been confined. So far as I know, no attempt was ever made to collect from Mr. Rowland.

The clipping Mrs. Simpkins sent me, three years later, said only that Spike Rowland had been sentenced to two years in prison for stealing a large sum of money from the movie theater where he worked as an usher, and driving off with it in a stolen car. The father of the convicted youth was identified as John Rowland, owner of Honest John's Used Car Lot.

When Laurie came home from school and took his place at the lunch table, I set the clipping beside his plate without comment. "Vegetable soup?" he said.

"Again?" Jannie said, and my husband looked sadly down at his plate.

Our two younger children, Sally and Barry, had already begun their lunches; Barry had spilled his milk and Sally was thoughtfully smashing crackers with the back of her spoon.

"Look," Laurie said to me earnestly, "I work hard in school all day and I ought to have—" His eye fell on the clipping. "What?" he said. "I'm supposed to read this or something?" He read, scowled, read again, shrugged, dropped the clipping on the floor, and then said, "Hey!" in pleased surprise and picked it up again. "Hey," he said, "I didn't know old man Rowland sold cars. *That* guy?" He chuckled.

"You noticed that your friend has been sent to prison?" I asked.

"That? Oh, his old man'll take care of *that*. Spike used to say his father *owned* that town. Boy." Laurie sighed reminiscently. "We used to have times. You know that week I was supposed to be in my room?" he asked his father.

"Up the spout and charley wag," my husband said.

"Right," Laurie told him. "Boy," he said again. "They ever get that concrete mixer put back together again?" He addressed his sister Jannie. "You should of seen it," he said. "Cops all over the place and Billy and me—*we* didn't know a *thing*." He laughed.

"It was about four days before that boy turned up," I said.

"Well, *we* knew they couldn't find him," Laurie said. "He could of stayed there a year, I guess."

"Stayed where?" I asked, and my husband said, "You *did* know where he was, then?"

"Oh, sure," Laurie said. "He was in our cellar." He turned to Jannie again. "We had this Black Hand Society," he explained, "and Spike would cut off two of our fingers if we told, it was in the rules. And we took him lots to eat—Billy got him a box of graham crackers and a bag of apples he hooked, and I got that meat loaf was in our refrigerator." He turned to me. "You thought it was the dog, you remember?"

"Mrs. Simpkins," I said faintly.

"*You* were too little," Laurie told Jannie. "Boy, we used to hook potatoes and cook them on a fire, and Spike used to take us for rides in one of his father's cars—"

"What?" said my husband.

"—And a couple of times we sneaked out at night and went to the movies, and once Spike's old man gave him five bucks, and Spike bought a box of cigars, and—"

"Laurie," I said, wailing.

"Oh, *Mother,*" Laurie said. "You always think I'm a *baby.*" With a show of vast disgust he picked up his spoon. After a minute he chuckled again. "Boy!" he said.

MRS. ANDERSON

✵

Mr. ANDERSON, WATCHING HIS wife pour his second cup of breakfast coffee, took out a pack of cigarettes and put one in his mouth. Then he felt at his pockets, one by one, looked on the floor under his chair, moved his plate, and finally got up and went over to the stove, where he found a match and lighted his cigarette. "Left my damn lighter upstairs again," he said.

Mrs. Anderson put down the coffeepot, and sighed. "Thank *heaven* you said that," she said.

"What?" Mr. Anderson came back to his chair and sat down. "Said what?"

"About your lighter," Mrs. Anderson said. "You don't *know* how worried I've been."

"About my lighter?" Mr. Anderson frowned, and looked quickly at his coffee cup as though once his wife started worrying about his lighter, the next logical step was poisoning his coffee.

"About your saying it, and leaving your damn lighter upstairs again." Mrs. Anderson pushed the sugar bowl across the table and went on. "It was this dream I had—you see, you said—"

"I am not sure," Mr. Anderson said carefully, "that I am equal to hearing about your dreams at present. I—"

"But *this* one," Mrs. Anderson persisted, "this one has been *worrying* me. You see, *I* dreamed that you never said three or four—I guess it was really three—things you *always* said. Three times in my dream I sat there waiting and waiting for you to say these things you always say. Like leaving your lighter upstairs." She thought. "What I mean is, you say things over and over and this time you didn't."

"Please," Mr. Anderson said. "Please, Clara."

"Like leaving—"

"But I don't leave my lighter upstairs every morning," Mr. Anderson said.

"Yes, you do," Mrs. Anderson said. "Every single morning you take out a cigarette and you look for your lighter and then you go over to the stove and get a match and you say you left your damn lighter upstairs again. Every single morning."

Mr. Anderson started to answer, and then thought better of it. "Nearly eight-fifteen," he said instead.

"I'll get the car out," Mrs. Anderson said.

On the way to the station Mrs. Anderson resumed. "I just wish I could remember the other things you didn't say. Like at this corner you always say, 'Doesn't that light *ever* turn green?' "

Mr. Anderson, who had gotten as far as "Doesn't that light—" turned and looked at his wife. "I do not," he said.

"All right, dear," said Mrs. Anderson. "It's the ones I *don't* remember that worry me, the ones you left out."

"In your dream," Mr. Anderson asked elaborately, "what happened when I didn't say these things?"

Mrs. Anderson frowned, remembering. "Nothing, I *think*," she said. "I remember in my dream I worried and worried, and then the alarm went off and I thought I still had a knife in my hand when I woke up."

"Well, well," said Mr. Anderson. He leaned forward and looked through the windshield. "Plenty of time to get a paper," he said.

"*That's* not one of the ones I forgot," Mrs. Anderson said, pleased. "I remembered about the paper."

"Goodbye," Mr. Anderson said abruptly, and got out of the car. He went quickly up onto the station platform, turned to wave to Mrs. Anderson, and went into the newsstand. "Got a paper for me today?" he asked amiably, and then stopped, thinking.

"Same as usual, Mr. Anderson," said the girl at the newsstand. "Lovely day."

"Lovely," said Mr. Anderson absently. He put the paper under his arm and went out again onto the platform. "Morning," he said to someone he recognized but whose name he could not remember. "Morning."

"Morning, Andy, what's the word today?"

"Pretty good, thanks," Mr. Anderson said, "how's yourself?" and stopped, thinking. When the train came he stepped on so absent-mindedly that he stumbled and nearly fell, and inside he went without thinking to a seat on the left, the side away from the sun, and he had settled himself and his coat and opened his paper before he realized consciously that he was on the train at all. He held out his ticket and found himself saying, "Well, Jerry, feeling pretty fit?"

"Can't complain," said the conductor. "And you, Mr. Anderson?"

"Ten years younger than I ought to feel," said Mr. Anderson, and stopped, thinking.

By the time the train came into the city, Mr. Anderson had decided what he was going to say to his wife when he got home that night. "About this business of my saying the same things over and over," he was going to tell her, "about this dream of yours. I think you're overtired," he was going to say, "need to get away for a little while, maybe take a little vacation, go someplace for a week or so. Might even be able to go with you myself. Both of us getting into a rut," he was going to say, "too much the same old round. Better get away for a while," he was going to say.

Once he had concluded that Mrs. Anderson was overtired, he was able to get into his office without difficulty. "Top of the morning," he said to the receptionist; "Well, well, another day," he said to his secretary; "Daily grind starting again," he said to Joe Field.

"Same old treadmill," Joe Field said back.

Mr. Anderson stopped again, and thought. Heard Field say that pretty often, he thought, nearly every day, in fact. Matter of fact, Mr. Anderson thought, every morning for a matter of five years or so I have said "Daily grind starting again" to Joe Field and he has said "Same old treadmill" back to me. Mr. Anderson began to wonder seriously.

Toward noon Mr. Anderson said abruptly to his secretary, "Do you think I say the same things over and over?"

She looked up, surprised. "Well, you always end your letters 'Sincerely yours,' " she said.

"No," Mr. Anderson said, "when I talk, do I repeat myself?"

"You mean when I say 'I beg your pardon, I didn't hear you'?" she asked, blinking.

"Never mind," Mr. Anderson said. "I have a sort of headache, I guess."

At lunch he sat with Joe Field in the same restaurant where they had had lunch together for five years or so. "Well," Joe said as they sat down, sighing deeply, "good to get out for a while."

"Don't seem to have much appetite these days," Mr. Anderson said, studying the menu.

"Lentil soup again," Joe Field said.

"Look, Joe," Mr. Anderson said suddenly, "do you ever find that you're saying the same things over and over?"

"Sure," Joe said surprised. "I *do* the same things over and over."

"Ever find you're getting in a rut?"

"Sure," Joe said, "I'm *in* a rut. That's where I always *wanted* to be, in a rut."

"My wife told me this morning," Mr. Anderson said unhappily, "that every morning after breakfast I say 'Left my damn lighter upstairs.' "

"What?"

"Every morning after breakfast I say the same thing," Mr. Anderson said helplessly. "Every morning on the way to the station I say 'Won't that light *ever* turn green?' and 'Plenty of time to get a paper' and all sorts of things."

"Lentil soup," Joe was saying to the waitress, "and Spanish omelette. And coffee."

"I think I'll go home," Mr. Anderson said.

He telephoned his wife before he got on the train, and she met him at the station at home. When he got into the car he said, "The one thing I don't want to do is *talk*."

"Something wrong at the office?" she asked him.

"No," said Mr. Anderson.

"Are you well?" She turned and looked at him. "You look feverish," she said.

"I *am* feverish," Mr. Anderson said. "You turned too sharp at that corner."

Mrs. Anderson winced slightly, and Mr. Anderson shut his mouth tight and folded his arms and stared straight ahead of him. After a minute he said, "You're tired, Clara. Getting in a rut. Ought to get away for a while."

"I've been thinking," Mrs. Anderson said. "About the way people talk, I mean. And I sort of thought that maybe people *had* to talk that way, sort of saying the same things over and over because that way they can get along together without thinking." She stopped and thought. "Why I was so worried," she said, "was because if people didn't say those damn things over and over, then they wouldn't talk to each other at *all*."

"Some quiet place," Mr. Anderson said fervently. "Lie in the sun, loaf around, play a little tennis."

"We can't afford it," Mrs. Anderson said. She stopped the car in front of the house and Mr. Anderson climbed out wearily. He followed her up the front walk and through the door, put down his coat and hat and went into the living room and sat down with a sigh. His wife closed the door sharply. "I'd soon as not live with a man who doesn't talk at *all*," she said, her voice somehow different. "Even what you *do* say is better than nothing."

"I told you I didn't *feel* well," Mr. Anderson said.

"When I said we couldn't afford to go away, you didn't say 'Life's too short to worry,'" Mrs. Anderson said crossly.

Mr. Anderson sighed. "Life's too short to worry," he said.

"It doesn't do any good *now*," Mrs. Anderson said. "Besides, when you got off the train you didn't ask if it was time to change the oil in the car." Her voice had become almost tearful.

"I *told* you I had a headache," Mr. Anderson said. "I wish you wouldn't fidget with that knife."

"And when you left this morning," Mrs. Anderson said, her voice rising to a wail, "I sat there and sat there and sat there and you got on your old train without one *word* except goodbye."

"Clara, get control of yourself," Mr. Anderson said sharply. It was the last thing he ever did say.

Come to the Fair

After a great deal of most serious reflection, Miss Helen Spencer had decided that she was not going to the fair. "Granted," she told herself reasonably as she sat over her lonely cup of tea at dinnertime, "granted that they need the money. *No* one could say that I didn't want to spend the money for charity. *No* one," she told the cat, who stared long at her, and then she bent to give one quick touch to his front paw. "It's not that I grudge the money, not at all." Having lost the cat's attention, she addressed the teapot. "But what earthly sense is there in *my* going? I'd stand on the edge of the crowd, and say good evening to everyone, and laugh when everyone else was laughing, and buy myself an ice cream cone and maybe a balloon, and pretend I was having a wonderful time, and smile cheerfully at Mrs. Miller." She lowered her eyes before the teapot's steady regard. "And Dr. Atherton," she said, "of course." She broke off and sipped several times, very quickly, at her tea.

"*Any*way," she went on to the African violet on the windowsill, "who is going to notice whether I'm there or not? He'll be playing darts with Mrs. Miller and everyone will be having a good time and dancing on the green, so why should *I* go? *I* don't play darts." She thought for a minute and then, smiling ruefully at the sugar bowl, said, "Not that anyone ever *asks* me, of course."

She sighed, and perhaps the sugar bowl and the teapot and the violet sighed with her, since they should have known perfectly well that Helen Spencer was very lonely and, often, very unhappy, with the poignant misery that comes to lonely people who long to be social and cannot, somehow, step naturally and unselfconsciously into some friendly group; Helen Spencer was a lovely woman, to whose care was entrusted the fifth grade of the local school; she had been born and grown up in this town, and people who had known her all her life very often said to one another, "She's a *lovely* woman—I've often thought of asking her over for tea or something one of these days." As a result, Helen rarely went anywhere, and from the moment the first posters had begun to appear on the village trees ("Village Fair, July 25, 7 P.M. Come one, come all") she had known she would not go, as she followed her quiet daily round from home to school to post office to library to dinner alone with a faint miserable longing at the back of her mind, and perhaps even the faintest touch of self-pity.

Now, at six-thirty on the evening of the fair, with the first distant sounds of laughter and excitement coming from the wide lawn behind the courthouse, where the booths were almost set up, and the lights tested, and the bunting fluttering in the early evening breeze, Helen sat docilely at her coffee, pretending not to notice the untouched dinner before her. She thought sensibly, "I do believe I'll do my nails and wash my hair and go right to bed and read a magazine. I can always," she thought, "say I have a cold, if anyone should ask me. *If* anyone should ask me."

Then, because she knew self-pity when she saw it, she shook her head violently, said, "How silly I am," and got up, intending to set her uneaten dinner away in the refrigerator ("I'll certainly be hungry later," she thought) and told the cat, who stepped lithely between her ankles as she went toward the kitchen, "I'll do a penance for feeling sorry for myself. If the phone *should* just possibly ring—" and she hesitated, plate in hand, glancing hopefully over her shoulder at the phone, which was defiantly silent—"if the phone rings, I will let it ring seven times before I answer it." She reflected. "Six," she said. "Six times before I answer."

The phone rang then, briskly, and Helen tripped over the cat, caught the plate, set it down in a flying swoop on a chair, and answered before the phone had rung twice. "Yes?" she said. "Yes?"

"Helen, it's Dorothy Brandon. Look, dear, you've *got* to help us."

"I?"

"It's Wilma Arthur's mother. Oh, wouldn't you *know* she'd have to do it today?"

"Do what?"

"Fall down*stairs,* of course. It's such *horrible* luck."

"Poor woman."

"But couldn't she have done it *tomorrow?* I mean, of course, yes, the poor woman, she broke her leg and of course we're all *terribly* sorry, but of course look where that leaves us, and it's *already* after six."

"Six-thirty."

"Six-*thirty!*" Her voice rose to a wail. "And if *you* don't do it, I just think I'll go *crazy*—first it was that Williams boy forgetting to order the ice cream, and then the lights in the grab bag wouldn't work, and then that *horrible* trombone player—"

"A horr—?"

"He went and had a baby, I mean his wife did, this afternoon, and we had to ask the Hot Rock Trio to come over from South Arlen, and then Mr. French got mad and said he wouldn't play his musical saw if he had to compete with a jazz band, so by the time I got *him* smoothed down, then little Michael Willis was going to run the lemonade stand and his mother said because he threw a rock through the Perrins' window—"

"But," said Helen most practically, "I *can't* repair the Perrins' window, and when it comes to playing the trombone—"

"Helen, please *do* be sensible. All we want is—what?" she said to someone away from the phone. "What did you say? He did? Just now? What is the lemonade stand going to *do?* You tell them if I get my hands on that dog I'll—Helen," she said again into the phone, "I really don't have time to *talk.* Just hurry right on over and don't worry about a costume because we have loads of scarves and beads and stuff. But *hurry.*"

"But what—" Helen began, and then realized that she was talking into an empty phone. "What?" she said vaguely to the cat, hanging up slowly, and the cat yawned widely, eyes shut. "I guess I'd better hurry, then," Helen said, picking up her dinner plate and looking at it absently. "They *want* me," she explained, and set the plate down before the cat, who looked at it, startled, and then began hastily to bite at the slice of cold chicken, eyeing Helen with disbelief. Then the door slammed shut behind her and the cat settled down comfortably, finishing off the chicken first, going on to the cottage cheese in the salad, even tasting delicately at the lettuce. When nothing remained on the plate but lettuce and a slice of pineapple, the cat abandoned it and leaped softly onto the table, where he finished off the cream in the pitcher, took a lick at the butter, and then moved gracefully down and into the overstuffed chair, primped himself briefly, and fell beautifully asleep.

Helen Spencer, racing down the street with a completely meaningless sense of urgency, and no hat, ran onto the fair grounds, panting, between wooden booths advertising fish ponds and grab bags, lemonade and hot dogs, pony rides and homemade fudge; she made her way, pushing, through the little groups of women and men and children who fussed around the booths, the early comers, the ladies who had baked the home-baked cakes and contributed the embroidered aprons and donated painted ashtrays to go into the grab bag, the children ducking away from grown-up hands, standing big-eyed before the baseball-throwing concession and the little train made of borrowed wagons hitched to a jeep.

"Helen, *hurry*—there's a line waiting already."

"But what?" said Helen breathlessly as Mrs. Brandon took her arm and led her firmly across the lawn. "Where?"

"Come *along,* we've got to get something for your *head*."

Helplessly Helen, realizing that she had forgotten to comb her hair, pattered along behind Mrs. Brandon, asking at intervals, "What?" or "Where?" They came up behind a row of booths, going carefully between cartons and boxes where additional supplies were kept, and finally Mrs. Brandon raised a curtain on the back of a booth and said, "Here, now, as soon as we can get you dressed you can start, because if we keep these people waiting any longer, heaven only *knows* what they'll do, the Armstrong girl's been here fifteen minutes *already*."

The booth held two chairs, one on either side of a bridge table, a heap of bright-colored cloths, and nothing else. "We just need to tie these around you, any old way," Mrs. Brandon said, putting Helen forcibly down into one of the chairs and coming at her with a scarf of flaming scarlet, "and someone is going to bring some earrings and necklaces, but of course you can start without *those*. The Armstrong girl—" She stood off and looked at Helen, at the scarlet scarf wound around Helen's head. "You look real nice in that color," she said, "you ought to get a hat or something, let me see. Blue around your shoulders, and you'll be sitting down, so there really isn't any need for anything like a skirt or anything, we can throw this blue shawl over the table and that'll hide you, and now, where did they put the cards?"

"Cards?"

"Wilma said they'd be right . . . here. Now, why don't you just glance over them and I'll run outside and check your sign and then I can tell the Armstrong girl to come right in."

"Cards?" Helen said, appalled. Fingers shaking, she opened the deck of cards Mrs. Brandon handed her and stared at them in bewilderment. "But . . ." she said, but Mrs. Brandon had already gone and outside her voice said dimly, "And you can go on in, in just a minute, as soon as the Gypsy Queen is through—ah—communing with her spirits."

"But I don't know how—" Helen said, going to the front of the booth and parting the curtains, "Mrs. Brandon, I—" She broke off, looking back into the faces staring at her; in front of the booth was a waiting line that seemed to reach into the far distance, and, glancing down, Helen saw at her side an enormous sign, painted in bright reds and greens: "Madame Mystery. Knows All, Tells All, Reads the Future and Explains the Past. Fifty cents."

"Oh, golly," Helen said. Blindly, she made her way back to her chair and sat down, staring without comprehension at the deck of cards. As they spread out before her she saw one named "A sick person," with a picture of an invalid in bed attended by a doctor and a nurse, one named "The ring," picturing a bride and groom, one of a cupid, a broken mirror, a train, a house. Briefly, the thought of her quiet living room, her cat, her magazine, came across her mind, and if she had not been a person of good humor and good sense she might very well have tiptoed softly out through the back of the booth and fled home. In a small town, however, one does not unnecessarily leave the Mrs. Brandons marooned without a fortune-teller for their fairs, and Helen straightened her shoulders and tightened her lips, and called upon her memory and whatever good fairies were watching her, and said loudly, "Let the first seeker of truth come forward."

The curtains at the front of the booth parted and the Armstrong girl came in, moving cautiously in the dim light. Since she was a high-school junior in the school building where Helen taught fifth grade, she recognized Helen and smiled a little, saying, "I never knew *you* could tell fortunes," as she sat down. "I *love* having my fortune told," she added unnecessarily.

Helen pondered in what she trusted was the identifiable gypsy manner, her hands on the cards and her head bent. (Armstrong; Sally, was it? Susie? Not too bright, anyway—hadn't she failed geometry last year?—one of the cheerleaders, Helen rather thought; interested in that red-haired Watson boy.) "Choose a card," Helen said finally with vast authority.

The Armstrong girl giggled, debated with her hand hovering over the cards, and pounced at last. "*This* one," she said. Helen turned it over. "The clouds," she said, regarding the stormy landscape pictured on the card. "Well."

The feeling of being left out, of being always the one left alone at home, never regarded, never considered, never remembered, swept over her suddenly; here was a girl who would never, obviously, know that feeling, and, without thinking, Helen said, "You will never be lonely. *You'll* never be hurt. The trouble in your life will be small." (What troubles could she have, after all, a girl who couldn't pass geometry but had a redheaded young man?) "The invitation," Helen said, turning over the next card, "of course *you* know what *that* is?" The girl nodded, smiling. "You will have your wish about the invitation," Helen said, "and it will be one of the happiest occasions of your life." The girl leaned forward eagerly. "Will Mother let me *go?*" she asked, breathless. With great solemnity Helen turned over another card. "The stone wall," she said. "Well, you will be allowed to go, I think, but only because your mother knows that she can trust you to behave yourself and do as you are told. If you should disobey—come home late, or something—" She turned over another card. "The lightning. Well, you can count on getting into all kinds of trouble. *Serious* trouble," she said, raising her head to regard the girl ominously. "*Terrible* trouble."

The girl nodded, wide-eyed. "Am I going to get married?" she asked after a minute.

Helen turned up another card. "Broken mirror. Well. Not to the person you are thinking about now. You'll be older in another few years, and what looks so appealing to you now may then seem only a childish fancy. You will someday find"—she hesitated—"the man of your dreams," she finished grimly.

After all, she thought, there was nothing here that didn't make sense. And every girl thought she had a man of her dreams. Dr. Atherton wouldn't look much like a dream man to a sixteen-year-old, but who—Helen wondered while the Armstrong girl dwelt lovingly on her own future—was thinking about Dr. Atherton? I've known him since he had his first skate coaster, Helen thought; I'll be so happy when he finally settles down with Mrs. Miller.

"How old will I live to be?" asked the Armstrong girl.

"The flowers," Helen read. "Very old. You will be . . . hmm . . . wise, and respected, and have many grandchildren and you will have a fine life."

She paused, and the Armstrong girl gathered herself together reluctantly. "Well," she said. "Thanks so much, Miss Spencer." She started for the entrance to the booth and then stopped. "Look," she said, turning, "can you tell me just *any*thing more about that dance? That invitation, I mean?"

Agreeably Helen turned up another card. "The moon," she read, and lifted her head and grinned at the Armstrong girl, who grinned back. "Say, thanks," the girl said, and left.

At some time during the evening someone brought her a candle, which was set on the table and did little to dispel the gloom that surrounded Madame Mystery; by that time Helen had begun to feel that she had never known anything so well—not the plates she washed and dried at home, not the walls of her house, nor the clothes she wore every day—as she knew the pictures on these cards, the weddings and invitations and sicknesses and unexpected letters. She had told old Mrs. Langdon that her delphinium would surpass itself next year, young Bobbie Mills that his pitching arm would improve; she told all the pretty young girls that they would wait awhile, and look around, before they married, and she told all the plain young girls that they would find husbands sooner than they expected. She strongly advised fourteen-year-old Betsy Harvester not to run away to Hollywood, and refused laughingly to predict whether little Mrs. Martin's baby would be a boy or a girl. Still, the line in front of her booth continued, and it was not until Mrs. Brandon came in with a paper cup of lemonade that Helen realized that it was growing late, that the fair must be almost over.

"We're making a *fortune*," Mrs. Brandon said, patting Helen affectionately on the shoulder, "they say you're *wonderful*."

Helen straightened her back, and stretched. "Good to rest for a minute," she said. When she raised her eyes to Mrs. Brandon she blinked; she had been staring at the cards in candlelight for so long that the darkness of the rest of the booth dazed her. Mrs. Brandon went to the entrance and peeked out. "About six people waiting," she said. "Honestly, Helen, what you've *done* for us." She paused uncomfortably for a minute, and then said in a rush, "Never got to know you very well, *really*. Why don't you come for lunch tomorrow and help us figure out the profits? Like to have you."

"Why . . ." Helen said. "Thank you, I'd love to," she said. Then, hastily, "Better get back to work. Customers waiting."

"*Honestly,*" Mrs. Brandon said, patting Helen's shoulder again. "One o'clock, then, tomorrow." She departed through the back curtain of the booth and Helen heard her stumble against a carton. That will be nice tomorrow, Helen thought, maybe Bill Atherton . . . "Let the next approach," she said quickly, drowning out her own thought. After all, even if you'd known a person since he lost his first tooth, that still didn't give you any right to . . . "And what do you wish to learn from the cards?" Helen asked, and looked up and said, "Oh," weakly.

Mrs. Miller smiled. She was a woman who smiled charmingly, and walked charmingly, and spoke and laughed and dressed charmingly; if her charm was lost upon Helen Spencer, it was not because of malice in Mrs. Miller. "You've certainly been popular tonight," Mrs. Miller said. "I've been waiting in line for hours."

Deep embarrassment covered Helen, and she was hopeful that in the dim candlelight Mrs. Miller could not see that Helen, a grown woman and presumably a reasonable person, was blushing cruelly. "I'm only doing this—" she began weakly, and then thought, why am I apologizing? It's nothing to *her,* and said, "Are you interested in the future? Do you care to have the past explained?"

Now, most townspeople had had a fling at predicting Mrs. Miller's future, and although her past was perfectly clear, it had been obscured by the earnest efforts of well-meaning people to cast a blight upon it; Mrs. Miller had been married and divorced and, since she had not been born or raised locally, there was obviously something dangerous about Mrs. Miller; Helen Spencer, who was above petty gossip, detested Mrs. Miller cordially.

"I want to know," Mrs. Miller said, smiling demurely, "if I should accept an invitation I have received today. A most *important* invitation."

So she's caught him at last, Helen thought, and turned the cards one by one with tight hands, forcing herself to move slowly and gently. Pretend it's somebody else, she told herself, and said, "Here is the card for an invitation, and next to it the card for marriage." Mrs. Miller stirred, and smiled. "If it is an invitation to be married—of course, a proposal—it looks as though you must certainly accept. The next card is one for great good fortune. A long journey—perhaps a honeymoon?"

"Perhaps," said Mrs. Miller happily.

Probably Bermuda, thought Helen, who had always wanted passionately to go to Bermuda. "There will be few difficulties in the way of your happiness," she continued mournfully, "and you will be favored by great good fortune." With finality she gathered the cards together. "How happy you must be," she said, not without irony.

Mrs. Miller rose. "Thank you *very* much," she said. "I'm so excited." And she ran out.

I wish I hadn't come, Helen thought. I wish I'd washed my hair; now, I am not going to tell any more fortunes and I never want to see these cards again and why am I making a fool of myself here when other people . . . I wish I'd done my nails. I wish I had enough money to go to Bermuda by myself and settle down there; maybe I can apply to be transferred to some school in—say—Ruritania.

She turned over the cards miserably, one by one; the ring, she thought, the bridge, the sunlight. Someone came into the booth and she said without looking up, "No more tonight. I'm tired."

"Fine," said the voice of Bill Atherton. "I already know my future."

"Oh," said Helen, perceiving that it was beginning to seem that she could say nothing else. Of course, she thought, he *would* come in right after her; they came together, and she probably insisted gaily that they *must* have their fortunes told; I'm only surprised that they didn't come in together.

Helplessly she surveyed several possible remarks ("How nice to see you; I understand you're getting married"; "Mrs. Miller just told me; congratulations to you both"; "Will you both come someday for tea?") and intelligently remained silent. "I've come to the rescue," he said. "You've been long enough in the clutches of the gypsies."

Helen laughed, almost naturally. "It's been fun," she said.

"Then," he said, taking the cards from her, "I'll tell *your* fortune, just for a change." He spread the cards before him and looked at them, frowning. "I see," he said ominously, "a lady who is fond of gaiety, and people, and laughter."

"I know who *that* is," she said.

"Do you? I also see a lady who is lonely, and sad, and anxious to go far away."

"I know who *that* is."

"The first lady is awaiting a champion to defend her against black despair."

"I hope you'll be very happy," Helen said.

"The second lady has finally learned to accept the inevitable, and bows to it."

"Certainly," Helen said. "I—"

"The second lady," he continued smoothly, "is, as everybody knows by now, leaving this town as fast as she can, and for a good reason."

"I thought Ruritania," Helen said.

"But the *first* lady," he said, overriding her, "will probably live happily ever after. Eileen Miller," he said carelessly, as though it were of no importance whatsoever, "is leaving here tomorrow to go to Siam." He gathered the cards together. "She's had word from her future husband. He's a missionary." Then, for the first time, he looked directly at Helen. "Do you know," he said, "that tonight is the first time most of the people in this town have had any chance at all to talk to you easily?"

"But I—"

"Especially," he said, "me. Now, let's go play darts. You've done enough damage tonight." And he threw the cards into a corner.

At home Helen's cat, disturbed by some obscure cat-prescience, stirred on the chair and arose, yawning prodigiously. Perhaps he heard a mouse, or perhaps he recognized that his mistress had never been out so late in her life; at any rate, he slipped down from the chair and out into the kitchen, where one leap brought him onto the stove and the remains of the cold chicken. Thoughtfully, without fear of interruption, he selected a chicken leg and fell to work.

PORTRAIT

T HAT WAS THE WAY she talked, and I used to listen, and watch her sitting with her legs swung over the arm of her chair, talking and smiling but not laughing. I don't think I ever saw her laugh.

Go walking through the valley,
go walking through the valley,
go walking through the valley,
as we have done before.

. . . There was a child dancing in the garden and I went out and spoke to it.

"Child," I said, "you are stepping on my flowers."

"Yes," said the child, "I know."

"Child," I said, "you are walking on my garden."

"Yes," said the child, "I know."

"Why?" I said.

"I am dancing," said the child; "can't you see?"

Go in and out the windows,
go in and out the windows,
go in and out the windows,
as we have done before.

. . . The little boy looked at me and he was crying.

"Look," he said, "my hands are dirty."

"Why are they dirty?" I asked him.

"I was digging to get my father," he said.

"Is your father dead?" I asked him.

"They hanged him," he said.

"Why did they hang him?" I asked him.

"Because he was alive," he said.

"Then why were you trying to dig him up?" I asked him.

"Because now he is dead," he said, "and they can't hang him again."

Go forth and face your lover,
go forth and face your lover,
go forth and face your lover,
as we have done before.

. . . Far off among the trees there was a little girl sitting, and when I came to her she looked at me and frowned.

"Leaves will fall on you," I said.

"I don't mind; I'm hiding," she explained.

"Why are you hiding here?" I said.

"It's darker than most places," she explained.

"Who are you hiding from?" I said.

"Everybody," she explained.

"Why?" I asked.

"They want me to comb my hair," she explained.

And now you two are parted,
and now you two are parted,
and now you two are parted,
as we have done before.

That was the way she talked, but I don't think I ever saw her laugh.

GNARLY THE KING
OF THE JUNGLE

GNARLY THE KING OF the Jungle had been Ellen Jane's special property ever since her mother first told her about him; Gnarly was a lion who had been born years and years ago and had run away from the other lions to live with a little girl (like Ellen Jane) and had learned to talk to children, but not to grown-ups. "No matter how you try," Ellen Jane told her mother over and over again, "you can't hear Gnarly the King of the Jungle or even get him to talk to you." Gnarly's adventures were many: Sometimes he fought (and defeated) a band of monkeys who were teasing a small boy; once a cruel man made Gnarly substitute for a horse on a merry-go-round and his lot was made bearable only by the children who came to talk to him; once, even, Gnarly found a buried treasure and gave it to all the children in the world to spend on candy. (Ellen Jane got a piece of the candy; it was by her pillow one morning marked "From Gnarly the King of the Jungle.")

Ellen Jane's mother had invented Gnarly and all her friends told her she should put him in a book. "The way Ellen Jane loves it," her friends would say to her, "you could make a lot of money with a book."

Ellen Jane's mother was kept busy all day trying to invent new adventures for Gnarly to have each night before Ellen Jane went to bed. In all of his adventures Gnarly had to be friendly with children and talk to them. It was not until two weeks before Ellen Jane's sixth birthday that her mother completely solved the question of Gnarly's future adventures. "Ellen Jane," she had asked, "what would you like for your birthday?" And Ellen Jane had replied, as though it were the most natural thing in the world: "I only want Gnarly the King of the Jungle. I want him to come live with me."

And so Ellen Jane's mother, desperate, looked in the telephone book for places that might conceivably sell wooden lions, hunted through junk shops and secondhand stores, and finally found a huge wooden lion which had, incredibly, come off a merry-go-round, and which, with a new coat of paint and a pair of red jeweled eyes, might pass as Gnarly the King of the Jungle. Ellen Jane's mother took the lion to a carpenter and had it set on a pair of huge wooden rockers and had a cheerful grin carved on in place of the ferocious scowl that had graced the merry-go-round. Finally, she had her own dressmaker compose a green velvet saddle for Gnarly. He made an imposing picture at last, when he was smuggled into the house and placed beside the breakfast table, along with Ellen Jane's other birthday presents.

The morning of her sixth birthday, Ellen Jane came downstairs saying, "Has Gnarly come yet, Mother? Where is Gnarly?" and when her mother proudly escorted her to Gnarly, Ellen Jane only stood in the doorway with her hands clasped and said, "Hello, Gnarly."

While Ellen Jane's mother stood by the breakfast table, watching, Ellen Jane gravely climbed onto Gnarly's back, rocked tentatively three or four times, and then announced: "I want my breakfast here, and my lunch and my dinner and my breakfast tomorrow morning and my lunch tomorrow and my dinner tomorrow and my breakfast the next day and my lunch . . ." Ellen Jane became interested in Gnarly's ears. "Look, Mother," she said, "his ears are different, one is up and one is down."

"Shall I ask Veronica to serve your breakfast up there, then, dear?" asked Ellen Jane's mother.

"I'm going to live on Gnarly from now on," Ellen Jane said absently, twisting around to look into Gnarly's face.

Ellen Jane's mother opened the kitchen door. "Veronica," she said, "would you give Ellen Jane her breakfast on her rocking horse, please?"

"Rocking lion," said Ellen Jane. "Look, V'ronica. This is Gnarly."

Veronica had been doing general cooking and housework for Ellen Jane's mother long enough to have heard about Gnarly the King of the Jungle, and now she inspected the rocking lion cautiously from behind the tray with Ellen Jane's breakfast. "Ellen Jane," she said, "that's certainly a nice toy. You're certainly a lucky little girl."

"Not a toy," Ellen Jane said. "It's Gnarly."

"Gnarly," Veronica said.

"Look, V'ronica. He has eyes."

"Miz Curtain," Veronica said in sudden panic, "ain't Ellen Jane going to open her other presents? Her *other* presents?" she repeated significantly, gesturing toward the little heap of gifts on the table.

"Ellen Jane, dear," her mother said.

"*You* know," Veronica said, her voice rising, "that little box—" she pointed at herself, and then gestured violently at the gifts.

Ellen Jane's mother made her voice persuasive. "Dear," she said, "don't you want to see the pretty things everyone else has given you for your birthday?"

"Sure," Ellen Jane said. "Gnarly wants to see them, too. Bring them on over, V'ronica."

Veronica picked up one of the boxes. "Open this one first," she said eagerly. Ellen Jane ripped the tissue paper off the little box. "What is it?" she asked.

"It's a lovely gift, dear," her mother said.

Ellen Jane opened the box and took out a thick gold chain bracelet with a plaque set in. "It says 'Ellen Jane,'" she said, reading the engraving on the plaque. "Who's it from?" She hung the bracelet over the lion's ear. "There, Gnarly," she said. "You wear that while I open everything else."

"That's from me," Veronica said, pointing at the bracelet. "Ellen Jane, I gave you that bracelet."

"Did you?" Ellen Jane said, rocking on Gnarly so fast that the bracelet flew off. "It's pretty, V'ronica. Get it back for me, will you? It's under the table."

"Put the bracelet on, dear," her mother said as Ellen Jane took it from Veronica. "It's perfectly beautiful, Veronica, and *so* thoughtful of you."

"I got it from a fellow I know, Miz Curtain," Veronica said, pride in her voice. "He gets stuff like that wholesale and so I got this here bracelet for Ellen Jane when it was her birthday."

"Thank you, Veronica," Ellen Jane's mother said.

Satisfied, Veronica passed the other gifts up to Ellen Jane, one by one. A scarf was taken from its box and tied around Gnarly's neck, a pair of gloves sat comically on his ears, a painting set was placed on one rocker for his inspection, a lapel pin was fastened onto the saddle next to Ellen Jane.

"Well, dear, I think you've had a lovely birthday," Ellen Jane's mother said as Veronica carried out the tissue paper and ribbons. "I think we had better sit right down after breakfast and write little letters to everyone—your grandmothers and your aunt Alice and everyone to tell them how much you enjoyed the presents."

"We don't have to write V'ronica," Ellen Jane said, "she's right here."

"Dear," her mother said, "I thought that since it was your birthday we might go into town and have lunch and go to a movie—would you like that?"

"I can't go on Gnarly," Ellen Jane said.

"I see," said her mother. "Veronica, you can clear the breakfast dishes whenever you're ready."

She got up to leave the room but in the doorway she turned. "Lunch at Schrafft's?" she said pleadingly. But Ellen Jane was looking into Gnarly's face again and did not hear; her mother sighed and went out.

For a minute Ellen Jane hung with her arms around Gnarly's neck, carefully examining his face and front legs. Then she rose and turned around in the green velvet saddle and bent over again, looking at his hind feet and his tail. She was curled around the saddle, investigating his stomach, when Veronica came in to clear the breakfast dishes.

"Good God, child," Veronica gasped, "what are you doing?"

Ellen Jane lifted her head disdainfully. "I'm getting to know Gnarly," she said.

Veronica sat down in the chair recently occupied by Ellen Jane's mother. "You gave me a scare," she said. "I thought you was falling off that thing."

"Look at him, V'ronica. He has ears and red eyes and on his stomach he's all smooth and then up here it gets to be a mane and around his neck he's got a big collar of fur. *Look.*"

Veronica approached gingerly. "Is that supposed to be this here King of the Jungle your mother tells of?" she asked.

"This is Gnarly. Look at his ears, V'ronica. He can talk, too."

"Let's hear him," Veronica said immediately.

"He can't talk to *you;* he wouldn't talk to anyone but me. Not around here, anyway. He talks only to children. Look. Gnarly, this is

Ellen Jane talking. Tell me something." She bent around and put her ear to his mouth, and then rose, turning to Veronica. "He says this is the nicest place he was ever in and he likes me more than anything in the world."

Veronica was impressed. "Does he hear everything we say?"

"Sure. Ask him anything and I'll tell you what he says."

Veronica thought deeply. "Ask him how old I am," she said triumphantly.

Ellen Jane listened to Gnarly. "He says you're thirty-four."

Veronica, awed, approached to look more closely into Gnarly's face.

"I know that's right," Ellen Jane added, "because you told me only the other day how old you are, V'ronica. Just the other day you said to me that you were thirty-four years old."

Veronica giggled. "Ask him does he want to help me with these dishes?" She began to stack the dishes. Suddenly she started and turned around.

"Ellen Jane," she said, "did you say something?"

Ellen Jane stared, and Veronica shrugged. "I must be crazy," she said.

"What was it, V'ronica? What did you hear?"

"Oh, nothing," Veronica said teasingly. "I just thought I heard something, that's all."

"What, Veronica?"

"Well," Veronica began slowly. "I did think I heard someone say, 'Sure, I'll help you with those dishes.' As plain as day I heard it."

"It wasn't me," Ellen Jane said.

"I sure thought I heard it," Veronica said. She paused, a stack of dishes in each hand. "Couldn't have been that horse, now, could it?"

"Gnarly?" Ellen Jane began to laugh.

"Well . . ." Veronica shrugged again and went through the swinging doors to the kitchen.

Suddenly she put her head back through the doors. "You call me, Ellen Jane?"

"No," Ellen Jane said. "I didn't say anything."

Veronica looked at the lion and sighed. Then she frowned and walked over to Gnarly.

"Now, you stop teasing me, do you hear?" she said firmly to the lion. "I won't have my whole morning's work busted up by your making fun of me. If you want to come help with those dishes—"

"V'ronica!" Ellen Jane's voice was horrified. "Are you talking to Gnarly?"

Veronica looked at her. "I certainly am," she said. "And if this fresh horse thinks he can get away with any—"

Ellen Jane bounced up and down in the saddle angrily. "You're not," she screamed, "you're not talking to Gnarly at all. He's my lion and you can't have him talking to you. It's only your imagination, nasty V'ronica, and you're making believe he talks to you just to be mean!"

Veronica looked at her for a minute and then turned around and went back into the kitchen.

"Mother!" Ellen Jane shouted. "Mother, come here right away!"

"That's right, call your mother"—Veronica raised her voice from the kitchen—"and when she comes I'll tell her what a selfish little girl she has, and how you yelled at me just because Gnarly talks to me, too."

Ellen Jane's mother came running to the door. "Ellen Jane," she cried, "is something wrong, dear? Did you fall? What is it?"

Ellen Jane began to cry. "V'ronica did a terrible thing," she wailed.

"*Veronica* did?" Ellen Jane's mother was puzzled. She went to the kitchen door and swung it open. "Veronica?" she said. "What happened to Ellen Jane?"

Ellen Jane thought quickly. She and Gnarly had to do something bad to Veronica, something very bad. "She frightened me awfully, Mother," Ellen Jane said.

"But how, Ellen Jane?"

"By telling me about her brother, that's how," Ellen Jane said deliberately. "Her brother's a mean awful man and she told me he'd come and get me. He's in jail."

The kitchen door slammed back against the wall and Veronica cried, "Ellen Jane, you promised you'd never tell!"

Ellen Jane looked at her mother. "He's in jail for stealing and killing people and robbing a bank and all sorts of awful things."

"Miz Curtain," Veronica said, "please don't believe her."

"And for murdering and hitting policemen and taking a million dollars out of a man's pockets."

"Veronica," Ellen Jane's mother said, "how much truth is there in all this?"

"It's all true," Ellen Jane said, "she told me herself, a long time ago, and she made me promise not to tell anyone ever because she said if you knew you'd have her put in jail, too."

"Veronica," Ellen Jane's mother said, "I think we had better talk this over in the kitchen."

Veronica turned silently and held the kitchen door open for Ellen Jane's mother to pass through. Ellen Jane watched the door close behind Veronica, and then she threw her arms around the lion's neck and began to whisper in his ear, looking at the kitchen door and now and then giggling softly.

THE GOOD WIFE

𝕯

M<small>R. </small>J<small>AMES </small>B<small>ENJAMIN </small>P<small>OURED</small> a second cup of coffee for himself, sighed, and reached across the table for the cream. "Genevieve," he said without troubling to turn, "has Mrs. Benjamin had her breakfast tray yet?"

"She's still asleep, Mr. Benjamin. I went up ten minutes ago."

"Poor thing," said Mr. Benjamin, and helped himself to toast. He sighed again, discarded the newspaper as unworthy of notice, and was pleased to find that Genevieve was bringing in the mail.

"Any letters for me?" he asked, more to contribute to some human communication and desire, even so low a one as desiring the mail, than to secure information that he might very well have in a minute; "Anything for me?"

Genevieve was too well bred to turn over the letters, but she said "It's all here, Mr. Benjamin" as though he might have suspected her of abstracting vital letters, about business, perhaps, or from women.

There were of course—it was the third of the month—bills from various department stores, the latest of them dated on the tenth of the previous month, when Mrs. Benjamin had first taken to her room. They were trifling, and Mr. Benjamin set them aside, along with the circulars that advertised underwear, and dishes, and cosmetics, and furniture; it would amuse Mrs. Benjamin to look these over later. There was a bank statement, and Mr. Benjamin threw it irritably away toward the coffeepot, to be looked over later. There were three personal letters—one to himself, from a friend in Italy, praising the

weather there at the moment, and two for Mrs. Benjamin. The first
of these, which Mr. Benjamin opened without hesitation, was from
her mother, and read,

> Dear, just a hurried line to let you know that we're
> leaving on the tenth. I still hope you might come with
> us and of course up until the minute we leave for the
> boat we'll be waiting for word from you. You won't
> even need a trunk—we're planning to do all our
> shopping in Paris, of course, anyway, and of course you
> wouldn't need much for the boat. But do as you please.
> You know how we both counted on your coming and
> cannot understand your changing your mind at the last
> minute, but of course if James says so I suppose you
> have no choice. Anyway, if there's any chance of you
> and James both joining us later, do let me know. I'll
> send you our address. Meanwhile, take care of yourself,
> and remember we are always thinking of you, love,
> Mother.

Mr. Benjamin set this letter aside to be answered, and opened the
other letter addressed to his wife. It was, he assumed, from an old
school friend, because he did not know the name, and it read:

> Helen, darling, just saw your name in the paper, being
> married, and how *marvelous.* Do we know the lucky
> man? Anyway, we always said you'd be the first
> married and now here you are, the last—at least,
> Smithy hasn't married yet, but we never counted *her.*
> Anyway, Doug and I are just *dying* to see you, and now
> that we're in touch again I'll be waiting for word from
> you about when you and your new hubby can run up
> and pay us a visit. Any weekend at *all,* and let us know
> what train you'll make. Just *loads* of love and
> congratulations, Joanie.

This letter did not absolutely require an answer, but Mr. Benjamin
set it aside anyway, he poured himself a third cup of coffee, and
drank it peacefully, regarding the department store advertisements
superimposed upon the horrors of the morning paper. When he had
finished this cup of coffee, he rose, and collected the advertisements

and the paper and said, when he saw Genevieve standing in the kitchen doorway, "I'm finished, thanks, Genevieve. Is Mrs. Benjamin awake?"

"I just took up her tray, Mr. Benjamin," Genevieve said.

"Right," said Mr. Benjamin. "I'll be leaving for the office on the eleven-fifteen train, Genevieve. I'll drive myself to the station, and I'll be back about seven. You and Mrs. Carter will take care of Mrs. Benjamin while I'm gone?"

"Of course, Mr. Benjamin."

"Good." With his little collection of papers, Mr. Benjamin turned resolutely toward the stairs, leaving behind him the breakfast dishes and the coffeepot and Genevieve's incurious eyes.

His wife's room was at the head of the stairs, a heavy oaken door with brass-trimmed knobs and hinges. The key hung always on a hook just beside the doorway, and Mr. Benjamin sighed a third time as he lifted it down and weighed it for a minute in his hand. When he fitted the key to the lock in the door he heard the first split second of stunned silence within, and then the rattle of dishes as his wife set aside her breakfast tray and waited for the door to open. Sighing, Mr. Benjamin turned the key and opened the door.

"Good morning," he said, avoiding looking at her and going instead to the window, which showed him the same view of the garden that he had seen from the dining room, the same flowers a little farther away, the same street beyond, the same rows of houses. "How are you feeling this morning?"

"Very well, thank you."

The lawn, seen from this angle, showed more clearly that it needed trimming, and he said, "Have to get hold of that fellow to do the lawn."

"His name's in the little telephone book," she said. "The one where I keep numbers like the laundry's, and the grocer's." There was the sound of her coffee cup being moved. "Kept," she said.

"It's going to be another nice day," he said, still looking out.

"Splendid. Will you play golf?"

"You know I don't play golf on Mondays," he said, turning to her in surprise; once he had looked at her, even without intending to, he found it not difficult; she was always the same, these mornings now, and it came as more of a shock to him daily to realize that although, throughout the rest of the house, she existed as a presence made up half of recollection and half of intention, here in her room she was the same as always, and not influential at all. She sometimes wore a blue bed jacket and had an egg on her tray, and she sometimes put her hair onto the top of her head with combs instead of letting it fall about her shoulders, and she sometimes sat in the chair next to the window, and she was sometimes reading the books he brought her from the library, but essentially she was the same, and the same woman as the one he had married and probably the same woman that he might one day bury.

Her voice, when she spoke to him, was the one she had used for many years, although recently she had learned to keep it lower and without emotion; at first, that had been because she disliked the thought of Genevieve and Mrs. Carter hearing her, but now it was because it did so little good to shout at him, and frequently drove him away. "Any mail?" she asked.

"A letter from your mother, one from someone named Joanie."

"Joanie?" she said, frowning. "I don't know anyone named Joanie."

"Helen," he said irritably, "will you *please* stop talking like that?"

She hesitated, and then took up her coffee cup again with a gesture that made it clear that whatever she had intended to say, she was persuaded that there was no reason to say it again.

"I don't know her name," he said patiently, "but it was on her letter. She said Smitty wasn't married yet. She said how wonderful that you were married and would you and your hubby visit her soon."

"Joan Morris," she said. "Why didn't you say so instead of letting me—" She stopped.

"There were no other letters," he said deliberately.

"I wasn't expecting any but Mother's."

"Has Mr. Ferguson forgotten you, do you suppose? Or perhaps given up a difficult job?"

"I don't know Mr. Ferguson."

"So easily discouraged . . ." he said. "It could hardly have been a very . . . *passionate* affair."

"I don't know anyone named Ferguson." She kept her voice quiet, as she always did now, but she moved her coffee cup slightly in its saucer, and looked at it with interest, the thin cup moving in a tiny delicate circle on the saucer. "There wasn't any affair."

He went on, speaking as quietly as she did, and watching the coffee cup, but he sounded almost wistful. "You gave him up so easily," he said. "Hardly a word from me, and poor Mr. Ferguson was abandoned. And now he seems to be weakening in his efforts to release you." He thought. "I don't believe there's been a letter for nearly a week," he said.

"I don't know who writes the letters. I don't know anyone named Ferguson."

"Perhaps not. Perhaps he saw you in a bus, or across a restaurant, and had since that magic moment dedicated his life to you; perhaps, even, you succeeded in dropping a note out the window, or Genevieve took pity on you . . . perhaps Genevieve's fur coat was a bribe?"

"It hardly seemed likely that I should be needing a fur coat," she said.

"It was a present from me, originally, was it not? You will be pleased to know that Genevieve came directly to me and offered to return the coat."

"I suppose you *did* take it back?"

"I did," he said. "I prefer not to have Genevieve indebted to you."

He was already tired of her this morning; it was not possible to communicate with her because she would not abandon her coffee cup, and she knew already of course that he had taken the coat and the jewelry away from Genevieve. There was not even the hope between them that he believed she had actually dropped a note from the window, or somehow gotten word to the outside world; there was not even, they both knew, any way in which she might sit down and, hands trembling and with nervous glances at the door, set upon paper any statement of her position which might bring someone to unlock the door and let her out. Even if she had been allowed pencil and paper or had found it possible to scrawl with a lipstick upon a handkerchief, she was not capable anymore of expressions such as "I am kept prisoner by my husband, help me" or "Save an unfortunate woman unjustly confined" or "Get the police" or even "Help"; there had been a period when she had tried to force her way out of the room when the door was opened, but that had been only at first. She had then fallen into a sullen indifference and during that time he had watched her closely, since the (then almost daily) letters from Ferguson had suggested methods for release and he had suspected then that she was trying to communicate with her mother. Now, however, in this fairly new attitude of hers, which had begun when she gave away her clothes to Genevieve and began to stay in bed all day, and the letters from Ferguson were not as frequent, he had become easier in his mind about her, and even allowed her books and magazines, and had once brought her a dozen roses for her room. He did not for a minute believe that she was crafty enough to be planning an escape, or to use this apparent resigned state of mind to deceive him into thinking she had accepted his authority. "You still remember," he asked her, thinking of this, "that you may at any time resume your normal life, and wear your pretty clothes again, and return to normal?"

"I remember it," she said, and laughed.

He came toward her, toward the bed and the coffee cup and toward her blue bed jacket, until he could see clearly the combs on the top of her head and the small hairs that escaped. "Just tell me," he said beggingly. "All you have to do is to tell me—only a few words—tell me about Ferguson, and where you met him and what—" He stopped. "Confess," he said sternly, and she lifted her head to look at him. "I don't know anyone named Ferguson. I never loved anyone in my life. I never had any affairs. I have nothing to confess. I do not want to wear my pretty clothes again."

He sighed, and turned toward the door. "I wonder why not," he said.

"Don't forget to lock the door," she said, turning to take her book from the table.

Mr. Benjamin locked the door behind him and stood for a minute holding the key in his hand before he hung it again on its hook. Then he turned wearily and went down the stairs. Genevieve was dusting the living room and he stopped in the doorway and said, "Genevieve, Mrs. Benjamin would like something light for lunch; perhaps a salad."

"Certainly, Mr. Benjamin," Genevieve said.

"I won't have dinner home," Mr. Benjamin said. "I thought I might, but I believe I'll stay in town after all. I believe Mrs. Benjamin needs new library books; will you take care of that for her?"

"Certainly, Mr. Benjamin," Genevieve said again.

He felt oddly hesitant, almost as though he would rather stand there and talk to Genevieve than go on into his study; perhaps that was because Genevieve would certainly answer "Yes, Mr. Benjamin." He moved abruptly before he could say anything else, and went into his study and closed and locked the door, thinking as he did so, two rooms locked and shut away from the rest of the house, two rooms far apart, and all the house in between not being used, the living room and the dining room and the hall and the stairs and the bedrooms all just lying there, shutting two locked rooms away from each other. He shook his head violently; he was tired. He slept in the bedroom next to his wife's and sometimes at night the temptation to unlock her door and go inside and tell her she was forgiven was very strong for him; he was fortunately kept from this by the frightful recollection of the one time he had unlocked his wife's door during the night and she had driven him out with her fists and had locked the door from the inside, returning the key to him in the morning without a word; he suspected that soon it would not be possible for him to enter her room even by day.

He sat down at his desk and pressed his hand to his forehead irritably. It had to be done, however, and he took a sheet of her monogrammed notepaper and opened his fountain pen. "Dearest Mommy," he wrote, "my mean old finger is still too painful to write with—James says he thinks I may have sprained it, but I think he is just tired of taking dictation from me—as if he had ever done anything else; anyway, we're both just *sick* that we can't join you in Paris after all, but I really think we're wiser not to. After all, we only came back from our honeymoon in July, and James just *has* to spend *some* time at his old office. He says maybe this winter we can fly down to South America for a couple of weeks, and not let anyone know where we're going or when we're coming back or anything. Anyway, have a lovely time in Paris, and buy *lots* of lovely clothes, and *don't* forget to write me." Mr. Benjamin sat and regarded his letter and then, sighing, took up his pen and added, "Love, Helen and James." He sealed and addressed the letter and then, sitting quietly at his desk with his hands folded in front of him, he spent a moment thinking. He reached a sudden decision and opened the bottom drawer of the desk and took out a box of rather cheap notepaper, faintly colored, and a fountain pen filled with brown ink. With a sober air which made his gesture somehow ominous, he took the pen into his left hand and began to write in a bold hand, "My dearest, I have finally thought of a way to get around the jealous old fool. I've spoken to the girl a couple of times at the library and I think she'll help us if she's sure she won't get into trouble. Here's what I want to do . . ."

DEVIL OF A TALE

And the devil sat in the lonely silences of hell, lost in thought. There had been upon Earth a man, son of God, and he had put the devil to rout. And the world worshipped God's son, and through him God, and the devil sat alone.

"I will have a son," the devil said. "There will be a woman who will bear me a son."

And, taking himself to Earth, he sought out one Lady Katharine, wise and witty, mother of no children, but wife to a weak man. And the devil, speaking with Lady Katharine, put her his problem, and offered her the mothering of his son.

But Lady Katharine was wiser than that. "What assurance will I have," she said to the devil, "that you will reward me suitably?"

"You have my word, madam," said the devil courteously.

But Lady Katharine laughed, and said to the devil: "I will bear your son, and then you will forget your word and carry me off to hell. I will require adequate security."

"I will give you a throne in hell," the devil promised.

"I will take a throne on Earth," Lady Katharine replied.

"I will give you all you ask of me," said the devil, "and you will have my son as hostage."

"You will care for your son well enough without me," said Lady Katharine. "I will take your right eye as hostage."

So a bargain was struck, and the devil gave Lady Katharine his right eye as security for his bargain. And Lady Katharine bore a son to the devil, and kept the devil's eye in the form of a ruby in a box with a cross on the lid. And during her lifetime she possessed the wealth of the world, and all its joys, and she lived many long and pleasant years with the devil's right eye as hostage for her soul. And the devil's son grew and flourished under his father's watchful care, and he was the only son of Lady Katharine's life, and upon her death he would assume the wealth she had taken from the devil.

And Lady Katharine died, and the devil took her soul, and demanded his eye for her soul's freedom.

But the devil's son was possessed of all Lady Katharine's wealth, and the box with the cross as well, and having not his father's dread of the cross, he opened the box and found therein the ruby that was the devil's eye, and with it a note saying that it was Lady Katharine's wish that it be thrown into the sea to redeem her soul from hell.

But the devil's son, being his father's heir, laughed and closed the box upon the ruby. And the devil, wanting his eye, came to his son, and disclosed himself, and said: "I am your father, and I have protected and guided you all your life. You have my eye, and the redemption of your mother's soul; throw the box into the sea and free yourself from my anger."

But the devil's son, knowing his father well, said: "I am your only son, and you are not likely to have another; I will keep your eye as guarantee of your continued favors to me, and you dare not harm me; as for my mother's soul, let it lie in hell."

And he turned his back on the devil and went out into the world.

THE MOUSE

THE NEW APARTMENT INTO which Mrs. and Mr. Malkin moved on the first of October was large and comfortable. It had a woodburning fireplace, and a big kitchen, and was near Mr. Malkin's office; Mrs. Malkin had had the living room painted a soft rose, and the bedroom an equally soft blue, and the kitchen green, and then, in a sudden burst of what Mr. Malkin might have thought was wifely humor, she had taken the room Mr. Malkin had felt immediately was to be his study and had had it painted gray, a heavy slate gray. Mr. Malkin worked for an insurance company and had read somewhere that light, cheerful colors were best for work—Mr. Malkin's minor executive's office at the company had tan plaster walls and straight chairs—but Mrs. Malkin had been firm. "You're such a gloomy type anyway," she had said unkindly. She had relented to the extent of orange drapes and a bright rug, but Mr. Malkin never did like working in the room. Sundays, when Mrs. Malkin was moving cheerfully about in the kitchen, Mr. Malkin sat in his gray and orange room and pretended he was working, but at the end of the year, when he proposed repainting it, Mr. Malkin was to bring up as an unanswerable argument the fact that he felt he never had done any work in that room. And Mrs. Malkin was going to say that he never did any work anywhere anyway.

Mrs. Malkin had felt privately for a long time that it was her duty to see that her husband wasn't always as boyish as he intended to be; she had squashed with some enthusiasm his attempts to take up golf, had discouraged his friendship with an older member of the firm whom she thought patronizing, and had seen to it that at twenty-nine Mr. Malkin was always correctly dressed, good-mannered, childless, and taciturn.

Mr. Malkin liked his wife, or did until the terrible incident of the mouse.

The mice, both of them, had come with the apartment. The minute Mrs. Malkin had gone into the new kitchen and found the mousetrap the old tenant had left in the back of a cupboard, she had known she was going to have trouble. "They've been using this mousetrap right along," she told Mr. Malkin, "and you can see it hasn't done any good. Prints all over the kitchen."

"Trouble with this trap," said Mr. Malkin, getting down on his knees beside it, "they used the same trap over and over. Mice smell where traps have caught other mice, won't go near a trap that's been used."

Mrs. Malkin regarded her husband. "What makes you think you know anything about mice?" she asked.

"You get me a new trap," Mr. Malkin said, "and I'll have your mice caught for you."

Mrs. Malkin didn't remember to get a new trap until after the painters were finished and Mr. Malkin had put up the drapes and the pictures and she had had her new lampshades made and set them up. Then one night when she went out into her freshly painted kitchen to get a pack of cigarettes, Mrs. Malkin put her foot down on the mouse, which was racing for cover under the refrigerator. She screamed and ran into the living room, where Mr. Malkin was sitting and reading.

"I didn't know you were afraid of mice," Mr. Malkin said soothingly.

"I'm not," Mrs. Malkin said, "except I do hate to have one of them scare me like that."

"You get a trap in the morning," Mr. Malkin said, "and I'll have that mouse by night."

Mrs. Malkin got a trap the next morning, Mr. Malkin set it that night, and the mouse was caught, but just as Mr. Malkin was telling Mrs. Malkin, "You see, trouble with that old trap was that the mouse smelled where other mice had been caught," Mrs. Malkin heard a suspicious rustling in the newspapers behind the stove, and the next morning there were mouse tracks all over the sink.

"I'm going to have to get the exterminator," Mrs. Malkin said to

Mr. Malkin over the breakfast table, "this cannot go on. I'm not afraid of mice—you know that—but they're making me so nervous."

"No one needs an exterminator for a couple of mice," Mr. Malkin said. "You just get me a trap today . . ."

Mrs. Malkin nodded, helped her husband with his overcoat, and kissed him goodbye. "You get that trap," Mr. Malkin said as he went down the stairs, "and I'll see that your mouse is caught by night."

Later that morning Mrs. Malkin called her husband at the office. "You get me a trap?" Mr. Malkin asked right away.

"A trap?" Mrs. Malkin repeated vaguely.

Mr. Malkin thought he detected a strangeness in his wife's voice. "Is there something wrong?" he asked.

There was a brief silence. Then: "What I called you about," Mrs. Malkin said, "I was glancing through your desk."

Mr. Malkin thought swiftly. He had obviously done something wrong; however, at the moment, he could remember nothing in his desk that would offend his wife. "I keep a lot of junk—" he began.

"I know," Mrs. Malkin said, "there's a little bankbook."

"A bankbook?" Mr. Malkin said.

"It's made out to the name of—let me see." There was a pause while Mrs. Malkin looked at the bankbook. "Donald Emmett Malkin," she said.

"Donald Emmett Malkin," Mr. Malkin said.

"There's a balance of twenty-nine dollars," Mrs. Malkin said, "a dollar a week for about six months."

"Twenty-nine dollars," Mr. Malkin said. "Well."

"You'd better see if you can get that money back," Mrs. Malkin said. "After all, it's almost thirty dollars."

"Yes," said Mr. Malkin. "I had forgotten about it. I'll get the money back."

"Who's Donald Emmett Malkin?" Mrs. Malkin said.

"Just a name," Mr. Malkin said vaguely. "A joke I had at the time."

"Donald for your father, Emmett for my father," Mrs. Malkin said. "You say you'll get that money back? Shall I leave the book out for you?"

"Yes," Mr. Malkin said. "It was probably just a joke."

"Probably," Mrs. Malkin said. "I saw the mouse, by the way."

"Frighten you?" Mr. Malkin said.

"I hate mice," Mrs. Malkin said, "it was all fat and funny. Well, I'll throw this little book out then, if you're sure you won't want it."

"Sure," Mr. Malkin said. He hung up with some relief.

When he got home that night, Mrs. Malkin met him at the door. She was wearing her wine-colored housecoat and had her hair sleek and straight down her back.

"I got the mouse," Mrs. Malkin said.

"In the trap?"

"No," Mrs. Malkin said gently, "just the mouse. I was too quick for her."

"For her?" Mr. Malkin was saying as he followed his wife into his study. The mouse lay in the center of the floor, on a piece of white typing paper. The mouse was, too, just the color of the walls. "For her?" Mr. Malkin said with more strength.

"I hit her with the frying pan," Mrs. Malkin said. She looked at her husband. "I was very brave," she said.

"You certainly were," Mr. Malkin said heartily.

"Then I put her on the piece of paper with the broom," Mrs. Malkin said, "and brought her in here. And I know why she was so fat."

Mr. Malkin bent over the mouse and saw why she was so fat, and then he looked up at his wife. From the look on her face, Mr. Malkin realized that she was the most terrible woman he had ever seen.

My Grandmother
and the
World of Cats

S INCE MY GRANDMOTHER IS patient, and cats are long-
lived, I am not giving any sort of decent odds on the ultimate
outcome of their feud; although my money is privately on my grandmother, there is a lot of big dough coming from somewhere on the
cats, and I am not one to give anyone a tip on a losing proposition. I
can, however, give a brief résumé of the situation up to now, as a
constant observer, and I'd like to add that, taking the long view, I
have never thought that the cats had the staying power to match up
with the old lady. Nine lives, maybe, but not the staying power.

My grandmother is a charming, gentle woman, except for what
she does to cats. She is partial to them, too, and grieves constantly
over the cruel chance that has chosen her as their natural enemy. She
seems to appall them. Since she came to live with us, when my
grandfather died, about fifteen years ago, there have been no fewer
than forty or fifty cats that have bided their little hour with us,
developed their personality scars, and gone. Perhaps it is just that we
have gotten used to my grandmother, and it's too much to ask of a
cat.

I remember Flossie, who used to bite my grandmother. Nothing
more. Just walk up to my grandmother peacefully, get a firm grip on
her ankles, and hang on. For a while my grandmother thought it was
just affection, and was tremendously pleased at being singled out for
Flossie's friendship, but then, as Flossie grew older and bigger and
her teeth got longer, my grandmother developed a tendency to sit

with her feet tucked under her. Finally Flossie began to have kittens, thousands of them, and one day my grandmother was sitting resting her legs by putting them on the floor and Flossie, who my grandmother had thought was safely out of the room, came from under a table with one of her oldest kittens and began to teach him how to bite my grandmother's ankles. Since it is one of her cardinal principles never to have a cat killed, and never to dismiss one for any but a very adequate reason, my grandmother, who of course had no sort of proof against Flossie, went on sitting with her feet underneath her. However, Flossie finally made her mistake, and one day, in a fine jovial spirit, came running into a room and, mistaking my father for my grandmother, took a sizable piece out of his shin.

After Flossie was gone, my grandmother began to have trouble with the one kitten we had kept, a yellow half-Persian named Creampuff. Creampuff's approach tended more toward the psychological breakdown. He would leave the room pointedly whenever my grandmother entered, glancing over his shoulder with his lip curled as he left. If Creampuff was quietly eating in the kitchen and my grandmother came in, Creampuff would stop eating and walk out. When this had no effect except to make my grandmother lose a little weight, Creampuff began to kill flies and leave them around. Whenever my grandmother started to sit down anywhere, she would find seven or eight dead flies on the chair. One day I was sitting by the piano while my grandmother played and sang and Creampuff came into the room. He had not seen my grandmother, apparently, and she was delighted to think that he might be ready to make friends with her. "I'll just keep on singing," she said to me in a hurried whisper, "and you tell me what he does." So my grandmother went on singing "I passed by your window," and I watched Creampuff. He wandered around the room for a while, and then I noticed that all the time he was watching my grandmother out of the corner of his eye. Suddenly he jumped up on the piano bench, just as my grandmother reached "To bid you good morning, good morning, my dear," and was quavering on the high note. After one pained glance at my grandmother, Creampuff moved up onto the music stand and began killing flies. He waited until they landed on the music and then smashed them. My grandmother, torn between artistic integrity and absolute fury, finally left the room herself, upon which Creampuff grinned evilly at me, knocked the music off the stand, and went out of our lives. I don't know whatever happened to him; apparently he felt that his work in our house was finished.

After that my father put his foot down, and for a while there were no more cats in our house. Things went along quietly, no internal strife; my mother got herself a little dog, which became very fond of my grandmother, and used to come to her to have its stomach scratched.

Then one day I let a kitten follow me home, and it started again, worse than before. I named the kitten Nick, and since my grandmother was out of town the weekend I found him, he had time to make himself at home and adapt himself to the dog. He appeared to be a dear, lovable little kitten, until my grandmother walked in the front door. "Oh, a *kitten*!" my grandmother shrieked. "Wuz e a tweet 'ittle ting." Nick made a cat noise in his throat and charged. My grandmother, who had been bending over to look Nick in the eye, lost a good part of her coiffure.

From that time on, Nick turned into the prize of all our cats. He developed an attitude toward my grandmother that made Flossie and Creampuff seem like amateurs, and this time my grandmother lost her noncombatant bearing and tore into Nick, giving as good as she got. When Nick found a secret passageway through the furnace gratings that would lead him into my grandmother's room when she had all her doors and windows closed, and used this passageway to sneak in at night and jump up and down on her stomach, my grandmother filled the bathtub full of lukewarm water and dropped Nick in. Once my grandmother made a cake and left it, freshly iced, on the kitchen table to cool, and Nick walked around the top of it, making a pretty design. That time my grandmother caught Nick and put him under a dishpan turned upside down on the floor, and then she sat beside it and beat on the top with a spoon. It got so none of us were surprised when we would see Nick racing around the house and my grandmother after him with a broom.

"I think your grandmother's losing her mind, young woman," my mother said to me.

"Nick means no harm," I said.

"Your grandmother's plotting evil," my mother said.

When my brother ran the family car into a telephone pole, my grandmother was heard to say darkly that it was plainly more of that cat's doing, and then one morning the doorbell rang and my grandmother opened the door and a very small yellow bird was sitting on the porch. "What do *you* want?" my grandmother asked, but before the bird had a chance to answer, Nick, obviously concluding that this was a friend of my grandmother's, hurried out of the door and captured the bird, which he took away with him. My grandmother, looking very thoughtful, went out and bought a canary in a cage, which she presented to my mother. A few days later my grandmother rushed into the bedroom, where my mother was quietly teaching me how to make buttonholes, and screamed: "Hurry, that cat is after the canary, I always knew it!" My mother and I rushed downstairs, my mother armed with a darning egg, and found Nick on top of the canary's cage. The canary was swinging back and forth, caroling tenderly to Nick, who was eating the lettuce that my mother had put between the cage bars. My grandmother was staggered for a minute, but finally she recovered herself enough to point accusingly at Nick, who was watching her comfortably, with a little piece of lettuce hanging out of his mouth, and said dramatically: "Didn't I always say so? A born thief!"

Later on my grandmother went to bed with a cold cloth on her head, and my mother and I settled the question of Nick.

"Young woman, either that cat leaves this house, or I will not be responsible for your grandmother," my mother said.

"Possibly there is someone I could give him to, someone we don't know very well," I said. "Someone who doesn't come here very often."

"I'll speak to your father," my mother said. We both knew that my grandmother would never allow herself to be intimidated by a cat; either there had to be a good and sufficient reason for Nick to go, or my grandmother would fight it out on her home grounds until something gave. Apparently my mother spoke to my father; the next morning when she went up to see how my grandmother was feeling, she told my grandmother that Nick and my father had had a run-in, and Nick was leaving.

"Give him to me," my grandmother said. "I've been thinking of leaving myself."

"You want him?" my mother said, astounded.

"Think I'd let a fine cat like that go out of the family?" my grandmother said.

My grandmother and Nick went south for a while; we had weekly bulletins from my grandmother, saying that Nick had run away, Nick had bitten a train conductor, Nick had torn up all the hotel pillows, Nick had fallen into the ocean, Nick had hurt his paw in a fight with a crocodile (this was a subject to which we could never persuade my grandmother to return; she said she didn't like to think about it), Nick was tired of traveling and they were coming home.

They came home, my grandmother vigorous and brown, Nick thinner and looking rather tired.

"Traveling agrees with us," said my grandmother, "doesn't it, Nicky-boy?" She pulled Nick's ear affectionately. Nick purred.

Nick soon afterward died as a result of a run-in with a Chevrolet, and my grandmother got another cat, a sleek black creature with an angel face.

"Tough, isn't he?" said my grandmother when she brought him home. She had named him Mo after my grandfather. It soon developed that Mo was an eccentric; he lived entirely on salmon and cantaloupe; when cantaloupe was out of season he would eat strawberries. He used to sleep on the stairs, on the top stair but one. This led to a tiff with my brother, who used to come rushing in through the front door and up the stairs as fast as he could, and every time my brother started up the stairs fast, Mo would sit up and yawn just as my brother came to him, and my brother would trip.

One day my brother came in through the front door fast, and, suddenly remembering Mo, stopped and looked to see if Mo was there. Mo was. So my brother turned around to my grandmother, who was sitting in the living room knitting a hat for my father, and said that this time he was going to teach that cat a thing or two. Then my brother walked slowly up the stairs and picked Mo up and brought him downstairs and set him on the floor. With Mo sitting at the foot of the stairs watching, my brother walked up the stairs very carefully, and then turned around and walked down. "See, I didn't fall once," he said to Mo. He tried it once more, walking up very slowly and then down again. Then he said to Mo: "Okay, watch this." And he went outside the front door and then slammed it open, running in and up the stairs, and he got halfway up and he tripped and fell flat on his face. Mo sat down below with a serious expression, watching my brother lying there talking to himself. Then, still without speaking to Mo, my brother came down the stairs and turned around and raced up again as fast as he could go, and this time Mo ran, too, and he beat my brother to the top and my brother tripped over him and fell again.

My grandmother came out into the hall and asked pleasantly: "Fall down, dear?" Mo came walking down and followed my grandmother out into the kitchen, where she gave him a dish of strawberries, and my brother put his head through the banisters and lay there groaning until my mother came and picked him up.

My grandmother finally broke Mo's spirit. She first tied a ribbon around his neck; when this didn't seem to work, she put a bell on the ribbon. She explained to me that this also made him a good watch-cat; he could not endure having anyone come into the house without seeing if he could do something to them, and if he moved, my grand-mother, who was a light sleeper from the time when Nick used to jump up and down on her stomach—my grandmother would hear the bell and come down to get the burglars. This would probably have worked out very well, but unfortunately Mo had a fit because every time he tried to sleep the bell would ring.

My grandmother seemed very put out when Mo died.

"I always used to feel safe with him in the house," she said wistfully. "Much safer than I did with your grandfather."

MAYBE IT WAS
THE CAR

✑

Maybe it was the car. Or maybe it was the tree with elm blight, or the bathtub leaking again, or the laundry being late, or the thought of hamburger again tonight, or maybe after all it was the student of my husband's who asked me, wide-eyed and innocent, "How is your painting going?" When I told her the only painting I have done in twenty years was the lawn chairs, she stared, and frowned, and said, "But I thought you were supposed to be a painter." "I am supposed to be a writer," I told her with a certain tautness. "Funny," she said. "I always thought you were a painter. What kind of writing do you do?"

"Am I supposed to be a writer?" I asked my husband that evening.

"What?" he said. "I said, am I supposed to be a writer?" "I guess so," he said. "Why?" "I thought I was supposed to be a painter," I said.

"I don't understand anything you say anymore," he said. "How long till dinner?"

The car is new. It is a tiny English convertible, black and dancing and winsome. The children named it Toro at once because it has a picture of a bull on the steering wheel. I would rather be driving around in Toro than broiling hamburgers again tonight; I left my husband sitting in the living room reading the evening paper and went out into the kitchen and sat on my high stool in the corner and looked out at Toro parked in the driveway. My daughter had broken the zipper in her skirt. The rosebush I had planted by the porch was clearly not going to grow. I am a writer, I said to myself in the corner of the kitchen. I am a writer and here I sit broiling hamburgers. The dog had been down at the brook rolling in the mud again.

In a house with several thousand phonograph records, of all sizes and ages and speeds and degrees of loudness, I own two. One is a record of various music boxes playing. The other is a record of bullfight music. I went upstairs and borrowed one of the children's record players and brought it down to the kitchen and got my two records and put on the one where the steam calliope plays "The Sidewalks of New York." "Mother's gone batty again," my older son said to his father in the living room. "I wonder what she'll do this time."

"Everything," my husband said obscurely, "is either true or false or one of your mother's delusions."

"I wish she'd put on the bullfight music," my son said. "That calliope makes me nervous."

"The last time she played bullfight music we had vegetable soup four nights running," my husband said.

"You ought to take us out to dinner more," my son said.

"Usually after she's played the music boxes she goes up and cleans out the linen closet or sometimes she goes and reads the letters I used to write her when we were in college." My husband's voice shook.

"I just wish she'd put on the bullfight music," my son said.

I got off my stool and went into the living room. "Listen," I said, "am I a writer or am I a middle-aged housewife?"

"Oh, Lord," my son said, and my husband said, "A writer, dear. A writer."

"Yes indeed," my son said.

I went out the back door and down the steps and got into Toro. I could see my husband and my son looking out the living room window at me, and my daughter came to the window of her room upstairs and said, "Are you going out? Wait a minute till I put on another skirt and I'll come with you."

"You stay here and cook the hamburgers," I said. "There's ice cream in the freezer for dessert."

"Where are you going?" she asked me.

"I'm running away," I said. "I shall probably go out west and fight Indians."

"Again?" she said. "I thought you were playing the music boxes."

"Someday you will hear of me again," I said. "I will be running a bar in Singapore, or selling newspapers on a street corner in Algiers, or maybe a little old lady will come up to you many years from now and peer into your face and ask if you remember your mother and it will be me."

"Oh," she said. "Well, have a nice time."

I backed the car down the driveway and turned and headed out of town. It was five-thirty in the afternoon, very warm, and the country road was fresh and green. I am a writer, I told myself sternly, not someone who cooks and cleans and mends zippers. I am running away. I drove for about twenty miles and went through half a dozen small towns, but they were too close to home; I knew them all, knew the stores and houses and even some of the people. I have to go farther, I thought; I do not often go east, so I took the first road going east. It was a poor road, and got progressively less familiar, so I followed it until I came to an intersection and then turned south. By the time I had gone forty miles I could not recognize anything I passed, but it was getting dark. I came to a little town that had a sign saying "Settled 1684." There was a broad village green, and a handsome old colonial building called the Colonial Inn, and all around there were split-level ranch houses and glass-brick stores. I will stop here, I thought, and drove to the parking lot of the inn.

When I came into the lobby there was a dining room on my right named The Old Cow Shed and a bar on my left named The Trough. I went up to the desk and asked the lady there, who wore necklaces of copper beads, if I could get a room. She looked at me carefully and said, "Aren't you from around here somewhere?"

"No," I said. "I'm from Rio de Janeiro. I'm just passing through."

"I thought I seen you at the A and P supermarket," she said.

"No," I said, "I'm a tourist."

"Funny," she said. "Must of been someone else."

"Yep," I said.

"Going to stay long?"

"I don't know," I said. "I may get an emergency call from my boss. The old man. Secret service work, you know."

"Oh," she said again. "Maybe you'll recommend the inn when you go on?"

"Most certainly," I said. *"Muy bono."*

"All you Mexicans are rich, aren't you?"

"Oil," I said, and signed the little card she gave me. I signed it "Mrs. Pancho Villa" because I knew perfectly well she had seen me at the supermarket. She looked at it and said, "Glad to have you with us, Room Three," and gave me a key. I climbed the little narrow stairway and found Room 3, which had a fine old colonial spool bed and a modern maple desk. I combed my hair and washed my face and went down the stairs again and outside, and found a drugstore, where I bought a toothbrush, three mystery stories, and a box of caramels. Then I went back to the inn and went into The Old Cow Shed, and a hostess with her hair in pigtails found me a table in the corner. I ordered two daiquiris in memory of Rio, and a filet mignon. Three times the hostess came by and asked me if everything was all right, and each time I said yes, fine. I read a mystery story while I had my dinner, and with my coffee I had a drambuie. Then I went upstairs and got into the colonial spool bed and read my mystery story until I fell asleep, about nine-thirty.

When I woke up it was seven in the morning, and I went downstairs and into The Old Cow Shed and ate waffles and sausage. Then I paid my bill and went and got Toro out of the parking lot and drove down the main street of the town. Just at the edge of the town there was a cottage for sale and I stopped Toro and got out. The cottage had a big garden with a white picket fence around it, and a path of stepping-stones and a little gabled roof. While I stood at the gate looking, a man came around from the back and nodded at me. "Morning," he said. "Nice little house, ain't she?"

"Yes," I said. "Very nice."

"Good foundations. New roof. All new heating system. Storm windows."

"How many rooms?"

"Five. Three down, two up. Modern kitchen."

"No," I said, "it's too big."

"Too big for what?"

"Too big for me. I want only one room."

He shrugged. "Some people like a lot of space," he said.

"Not me. I'm a writer."

"A writer? Like on TV?"

"No," I said.

"Wouldn't of thought so," he said. "Would have figured you for someone with a family. Kids, you know. Baking pies and cakes and cookies. Would have said right off you were a good cook."

"I'm a writer."

"All right," he said. "So the house is too big for you."

"I was only looking anyway."

"No harm done," he said.

I got into Toro and drove off, back the twenty miles till I got to places I recognized, and then back twenty miles more home. When I came in they were sitting at the kitchen table having lunch. My daughter had made a shrimp salad and hot biscuits. "Hello," they said. "Have a nice time?"

"Sure," I said.

"Ninki had her kittens in the laundry basket," my daughter said.

"Something's gone wrong with the collar on my white shirt," my husband said.

"The garage called," my son said. "They said the vacuum cleaner wasn't worth fixing and you ought to get a new one."

"We put your records away," my daughter said. "Dad ate three hamburgers and the sole is coming off my sandal, the white one."

"Where did you go?" my husband asked me.

"I don't know," I said. "Around the world."

LOVERS MEETING

⌘

IT COULD NOT HAVE been accident, or a dream, or the quick small betrayal of the mind that caused her to hear the music; she knew that she had not turned on the radio, or put a record on the phonograph, and yet she heard it, clear and sweet and incredibly distinct, the words soft in her ear: "What's to come is still unsure, in delay there lies no plenty . . ."

So began the lonely, long terrible night that Phyllis spent in an adventure that ended . . . but first, to how it began. It began tidily, for Phyllis was a logical girl. She took fresh gloves, she tied her hair in a knot, she put a handkerchief in her purse. But she went out of the apartment without turning out any lights, and she did not look behind.

If she heard the footsteps when she left the apartment, she did not notice them particularly, or perhaps they merged perfectly with the sharp sound of her own high-heeled shoes going down the corridor; at any rate, it was not until she stepped out into the lonely street, walking easily and consciously and proudly, that she heard the sound of steps behind her, coming as surely along the street as she herself, and carrying with them the echo of the song . . . "What's to come is still unsure . . ."

Without surprise if not without fear she walked on. She walked quick and quicker, tense and alert. There were other sounds and she was aware of them, but also aware that she *knew* they were there though she heard nothing. Nothing except the following feet. And she walked without pause, yearning for the song to go on. The song said unsure, but it was sure, it was, it would be. *He* knows. So she walked through streets with crowds, faceless crowds, silent except for his feet.

If he is following me, she thought, trying to keep her mind level, reasonable, if he is, *could* he be, following me, is it because he is trying to tell me what to do? Am I doing wrong? Am I walking toward something I should be running away from? Or should I be running away from *him*? Wondering, she only just stopped in time at the street corner, and saw almost without surprise that the taxi driver sitting in his car at the corner was gesturing to her and calling, "Lady, lady."

"Yes," she whispered. "Yes. Certainly." Her lips formed the syllables carefully, consciously. She bent from the waist, stiffly. And looked at him. A familiar face, she thought. "Yes, fa—" Then she touched the cab's cold metal and the face changed. "This is no street for you to walk alone," the driver said. So she got into the cab, without looking back, and sat in the middle of the seat. "The bar," she directed. "Which bar, lady?" "Why, why, the Zanzibar! Of course."

The driver looked at her fleetingly in the mirror, and then back at the traffic again; the cab pulled out into the middle of the street and merged into the line of cars going uptown. "Lady," the driver said finally, "mind if I take you somewhere else? I mean, usually my fares tell me where they want to go and I take them there"—he laughed briefly, humorlessly—"but this time, lady, I really think you better let me take you somewhere else. At least, try to shake him off; he's still following."

The words clashed in her against those other words. The words did not fit. These sounds meant, why they meant there was someone who would say, "Hello, Phyllis, hello. Stop, it's Jack. I wanted to ask you to go to a concert." But that wasn't it, that couldn't be it. ". . . What's to come is still unsure." All right, my girl, she told herself. We'll see. We'll just see who will win. "Driver," she said. "Go ahead, lose him, lose him if you can."

"Right, lady," the driver said. The cab picked up speed, moving gradually over toward the curb and then suddenly, unexpectedly, turned against a red light and sped the wrong way down a one-way street. "If I get a ticket for this," the driver said, "you can have it, lady." He turned the wheel hard and they were going downtown again, and no car had turned out of the one-way street behind them.

Phyllis, shaken from the quick turning, almost laughed, in the back of the cab, to think that she and a friendly taxi driver were running from . . . running from . . . "How did you know anyone was following me?" she demanded suddenly, and the driver, looking at her quickly in the mirror again, said succinctly, "Saw him." "Saw who?" Phyllis asked. The taxi pulled to the curb and stopped. "You're okay now, lady," the driver said. "This is where we stop." He waved away the bill that Phyllis offered him. "Not from you, lady," he said. "I'd just as soon not take anything from you."

So he knew. She walked again. She skipped a little. She hummed. "La ci darem la mano . . ." And the melody fitted itself again to the voice inside. Goddamn. Goddamngoddamngoddamn. She let her pace break. Nothing could stop it now. Soon she would find it. It would open in front of her like a toy shop and she would go in and it would be like clouds of lilacs. And he would be in armor, damn it. And she laughed at her own audacity. Then she was at the door. A tall footman in wine-red velvet said, "How many, lady." And she answered, "One."

One. Why might she not buy two, seven, fifty-four, the whole great building with its lights and its flashing words and the tall red-velvet footman who bowed to her and smiled courteously as she passed; why might she not wander down the dark aisle alone, owning all she could not see? She knew abruptly that it was necessary for her to leave, go home perhaps, but not stay here, where the tall red-velvet footman bowed to her and smiled again as she passed him going out, as though he had not just seen her going in . . . and then he touched her gently on the shoulder and she half turned, conscious of quick movement behind her. "Pardon, madam," the footman said, his voice very soft as befitted the voice of a man who spent all day on the immense threshold of recorded sound, "Pardon, but you had better hurry. You are being followed. If you choose, you may leave by the side entrance." He bowed and smiled impersonally, and added, "But hurry. Please, please hurry."

She nodded and moved past him. She felt his eyes follow her until she turned and went up the stair to where his eyes could not follow and again she could hear the steps. They were soft on the carpet, but quite distinct. And the music, too. And now she sauntered. On the left was a tall mirror misted as an old woman's eye. And on the right wall a man regarding her with humor. "You certainly came just in time, so far," he said. "Go to the end of the corridor and wait there."

So she went on and through the curtain, where for the moment she could not see, she heard, "Hurry, hurry, there's just time."

"Hurry, hurry," the voice from the enormous screen picked up and mocked her, but the voice was wrong and the music was different. She went quickly, without consciousness of the darkness, down the aisle toward a door surmounted by a red sign saying "Exit," opened it somehow, and slipped through. She went clumsily but quickly down the open steel stairway without looking back, and, once in the street, almost ran, because the footsteps were still behind her. She reached the corner just as a bus pulled up, and the bus driver opened the door for her, leaned forward to give her a hand as she stepped in. "I'm going home," she said to him helplessly, and he nodded, without looking at her, and said, "I should think so. We'll get you there as fast as we can." She opened her pocketbook to find change, and the bus driver put his hand over the money box and said, "Never mind. I don't want it." He started the bus and she moved back to find a seat. The bus was nearly full and she went almost to the back and sat down next to an old lady whose lap was piled high with bundles. The old lady smiled at her over the bundles and said, "Poor dear. We all saw it." "I'm going home," Phyllis said, and the old lady said, "Of course you are, dear. I think it's a shame. He should be arrested, *I* think. People like that." She craned her neck to see out the window past the bundles, and clicked her tongue reprovingly. "And there he is still," she said. "Following right along."

Phyllis offered a strained grin that she meant for a smile and said nothing. "Let them try," she muttered. It will be mine now. They know and they think I am afraid. Let them try to get me away. When I get home and can sit still I'll have it all to myself. It will sing for me like a copper whistling kettle.

And she stepped out at the side door swiftly as the vehicle stopped, while the old woman leaned over whispering to the driver and the other passengers lifted themselves in their seats to look after her. And she went on, hardly feeling the pavement, toward home.

Did the footsteps still follow? She almost ran down the dark street toward home, but stopped suddenly; was that one last footstep, unable to stop as soon as she? "What's to come is still unsure," came sweetly and distinctly to her, and she began to run again. The door of her apartment house opened to her push, and she ran across the lobby, debated as she ran over to the elevator, and decided on the stairs. She ran up (was that a footstep on the marble of the stairs behind her?) past the landing on the first floor onto the stairs to the second floor, up to the third and down the corridor to her own apartment. Hastily, fumbling, she found her key and put it into the lock, opened the door and slammed it shut behind her, closed the bolt, and leaned breathless against the cool, safe wood. Ahead of her, at the far end of the room against the windows, a shape rose up in the darkness from the heavy chair. "You took long enough getting here," he said.

Nodding, she went to the mirror. She let down her hair and brushed it. She took up the vial. "Such a tiny glass," she said. "No, plenty," he answered. "There lies their lies." The music swelled. "Drink. In delay there lies no plenty . . . In delay there lies repentance . . . What's to come is sweet and sure . . ."

My Recollections

of S. B. Fairchild

✹

TWO AND A HALF years ago my husband and I decided
that for our fifteenth anniversary we would give ourselves a
tape recorder. We believed that with a tape recorder we could preserve, permanently, the small, shrill voices of our children and, with
the further record taken with the movie camera, preserve fond memories against the future. We thought sentimentally of sitting in an
evening, gray, worn, palsied, and blessedly alone, watching as the
projector reeled off endless series of pictures of our children dancing,
swimming, shooting off fireworks, playing baseball, and taking their
first faltering steps, and listening at the same time to their recorded
voices reciting "The Night Before Christmas" and singing "Three
Blind Mice."

The glories of a tape recorder were suggested to us, first, by an ad
in the Sunday paper, pointing out that a big store in New York
where we had a charge account, was selling "reconditioned" tape
recorders for ninety-nine dollars and ninety-nine cents, a saving, the
ad pointed out, of almost forty percent. Although we observed that
ninety-nine dollars and ninety-nine cents was as close to a hundred
dollars as made no difference, and was surely an extravagantly large
sum to be lavished on nothing but a fifteenth anniversary, we were
seduced into believing that a hundred dollars was little enough, after
all, to pay for the pleasure of hearing our children's voices in years to
come, when we sat in front of our home movie screen. I wrote to the
store in New York, which was called Fairchild's, and ordered the

tape recorder, asking that the ninety-nine dollars and ninety-nine cents be charged to our account.

Since we had already ordered, that month, some coin books for my husband and a box of chocolate apples, our monthly bill, which arrived some days before the tape recorder, was a hundred and eleven dollars and fifty-three cents. When the tape recorder arrived I had to pay three dollars and seventeen cents express charges. The tape recorder was in a kind of wooden crate, and when my husband came home he and our older son had to use hammers and a screwdriver to take apart the wooden crate and get the tape recorder out. Although there was a book of directions tucked inside the tape recorder, there was no tape, and while my husband and our son read the book of directions and examined the various pushbuttons and spools, I went into town to the music store and bought a package of tape recorder tape. It cost me five dollars and ninety-five cents, and the man in the music store, whom I have known for several years, was quite snippity about our buying a tape recorder from a store in New York instead of doing business through him.

All during dinner my husband and the children discussed the tape recorder, and after dinner the children retired to their bedrooms, where they practiced privately the several songs and recitations they planned to record on the tape recorder, so they could be safely stored away until the distant future day when their father and I could finally sit down for a few minutes and play over our memories. After the dinner dishes were done, we called all the children downstairs into the study and they waited, giggling and coughing nervously, while their father reread the book of directions and got the tape recorder ready to record. Everyone kept telling everyone else to be quiet. Our older son with his trumpet recorded one chorus of "Tin Roof Blues," and the baby half whispered a little tuneless thing he greatly fancied, called "Riding with an Engineer." Our younger daughter sang, loudly and with great attention to enunciation, a song about visiting a candy shop, and our older daughter chose to record a ballad she had learned from her grandfather, called "Your Baby Has Gone Down the Drainpipe (He Should Have Been Bathed in a Jug)." When we played back the tape, all the children were first astonished and then amused, and everyone wanted to record something else. My husband's voice was on the tape saying that unless everyone was quiet he would not record anything at all, and my voice was on the tape saying that did everyone hear what Daddy just said? because the next child to snicker would leave the room.

We played our tape over several times, and quite a few times after that for people who dropped in, and the children asked to have it played for their friends, and we played it to their grandparents over the phone. We were quite pleased with our recording, and thought we would record more when the children, particularly the baby, had learned new numbers. However, one evening when we were playing the tape for some friends of ours who had dropped in for a bridge game (and that, as it turned out, was the evening when the nine of spades disappeared so unaccountably in the middle of the second rubber and has not come back yet) the tape machine gave a kind of agonized groan, sang "—has gone down the drain—" and stopped. My husband and our guests fussed over it for a while, but nothing could persuade it to sing another note.

The next day my husband and older son carried the tape recorder out to the car and I drove it into town to the music store. The man in the music store and one of his clerks carried it into their repair shop and I told them how we had been playing our tape and the machine had stopped. They promised to check it over and see if it needed oiling or some such thing, and the man in the music store said that since I had not bought it there he would have to charge me for the overhaul; if I had bought the machine from him, he explained, he could have fixed it free of charge under his regular service guarantee, but since I had bought it somewhere else I would have to pay a regular repair bill. I said that was all right, it was no more than I deserved for buying it from the store in New York, and the music man said he certainly hoped I had learned a good lesson.

About three days later he telephoned me and said he could not repair the tape recorder. It had clearly, he said, been sent out by mistake, a mistake which of course could not happen with a machine bought locally. The tape recorder had not only never been reconditioned, but it had been used to death and then either dropped from a great height or stomped on by an elephant. It was a miracle, he said, that we had been able to get any result out of it at all. The one partial tape we had made was surely all we were ever going to have from this machine. He would not undertake to repair the tape recorder; he and his mechanic had taken it apart, and they would now put it back together again the way they found it, but they would not try to repair it. He suggested that since it had clearly been sent out by the New York store in error—at least, he hoped it was an error, although if I had gotten a tape recorder from him I would have been *sure* that if he said it was reconditioned that *meant* it was reconditioned—since, then, it was some kind of mistake, I must send it back to New York and let them take care of it.

I drove into town and the man in the music store and his mechanic carried the tape recorder out and put it into the car and I brought it home and my husband and our older son carried it into the house and put it on the dining room table. When I told my husband what the man in the music store had said about the tape recorder he was highly indignant and said I must certainly send it back and write in a complaint besides.

We had dinner on the kitchen table because the tape recorder was on the dining room table, and after the dinner dishes were done I sat down and wrote a letter to Fairchild's, explaining all that had happened, and stressing the conviction of the man in the music store that the machine had been sent out by mistake. I said that naturally we intended to send the tape recorder back, and what did Fairchild's suggest? I received an immediate answer, signed S. B. Fairchild. He said that I must put the tape recorder back into the crate, and send it to them express prepaid, and he was sorry that we had not decided whether or not we really wanted a tape recorder before we ordered it, because constant return of merchandise was a nuisance to the purchaser and to the store. I wrote S. B. Fairchild and said that the tape recorder was broken, that I had already paid the express charges for the tape recorder coming, and that anyway I could not possibly get the tape recorder back into the original wooden crate because it had been wholly dismantled when we took the tape recorder out and the children had used the pieces of wood for a lion cage. S. B. Fairchild wrote back and said it was a standing policy of Fairchild's not to pay express charges on return merchandise and if the tape recorder were not crated it could not be sent back. If I had thoughtlessly broken the original crate I must get a new crate. Fairchild's, S. B. Fairchild pointed out, did not encourage customers who ordered merchandise wantonly and returned it heedlessly; this caused expense to both the customer and the store.

I wrote back that in our town handicraft is at a premium and the only way I could get a new crate was by paying to have one made, and that would cost me several dollars. S. B. Fairchild wrote back suggesting that I keep the tape recorder, then, since I had wanted it enough to order it in the first place.

S. B. Fairchild's obvious conviction, that my eyes were bigger than my stomach, irritated me so much that I wrote back a fairly tart letter saying that the tape recorder was Fairchild's responsibility and not

mine, and that I personally no longer shared the sanguine opinion of the man in the music store, but felt that Fairchild's had deliberately sent me a faulty tape recorder, figuring to make a profit on what they could rake off on crating and express charges. S. B. Fairchild, clearly misreading my letter from beginning to end, wrote back that the policy of a small profit on many items had been a foundation of the Fairchild Organization since 1863.

I was trying to think of a way to answer Fairchild's letter, when a friend of ours called to say that they were driving down to New York at the end of the week, and could they do any errands for us? I said well, yes, they certainly could; would they mind taking a tape recorder back to Fairchild's for us? After some hesitation my friend said well, she guessed they could and I said I would bring the tape recorder right over. My husband and our older son carried the tape recorder out to the car and I drove it over to my friend's house and we got two men who were sanding the driveway to come and carry the tape recorder and put it in the luggage compartment of my friend's car. I gave the two men who were sanding the driveway a dollar. By way of thanks to our friends for taking the tape recorder down to New York, I got their young son an electric clock-making set, which cost four ninety-five, and he made a nice electric clock and put it in his bedroom. We were able to give up the kitchen table and start having dinner in the dining room again.

Our friends were in New York for a week, and when they came back they brought me a receipt from Fairchild's for the tape recorder. They had not been able to carry it any farther than a desk on the main floor of Fairchild's, they said, although the department where articles were to be returned was on the ninth floor. They had not been, they said, equal to carrying the tape recorder up nine escalators. Consequently, they had left the tape recorder in charge of a floorwalker on the main floor, and had gotten a receipt from him for its return. The receipt said that the tape recorder had been returned to the repair shop, and when I said it was to have been returned for ever and ever, they explained that the only counters on the main floor where you could put anything down at all were the repair counter and the wrapping desk. They had not thought I would like having the tape recorder left at the wrapping desk, and in order to accept the tape recorder at all the floorwalker had had to give them a repair receipt, unless they could figure a way to get the tape recorder up the nine escalators to the desk on the ninth floor where things were returned. The floorwalker explained that as long as the tape recorder was just being carried aimlessly around the store by people with no official standing at Fairchild's, it could be transported only by escalator, but as soon as he had formally accepted the tape recorder in Fairchild's name he could put it right on the freight elevator. They said that the floorwalker said that all I needed to do was write to the store explaining the situation and everyone, the floorwalker said, would be satisfied.

I thanked our friends and read over the receipt, which said that a tape recorder had been accepted for repair. Then I wrote Fairchild's a long and civil letter, recounting the scene of the return of the tape recorder, and stressing the floorwalker's acceptance of full responsibility. I carefully copied out all the numbers on the receipt, and filed the receipt itself away in the box where I keep recipes and guarantees and the instructions for using the electric mixer.

Because we had in the meantime ordered from Fairchild's a party dress for our younger daughter and a kitchen stool, our next monthly bill was for a hundred and thirty-two dollars and sixty-one cents. I was puzzled, and wrote Fairchild's, asking why the returned tape recorder was still on our bill. I pointed out that I had written them two weeks before, explaining about the return of the tape recorder, and had naturally assumed that since I received no answer to my letter I would find the price of the tape recorder deducted from my bill.

Under pressure from the children, who wanted to hear themselves singing again, my husband and I bought a new tape recorder, considerably more expensive, from the man in the music store. It worked beautifully. We recorded our older son playing "Royal Garden Blues" on the trumpet, our younger daughter singing a fairly one-dimensional song about tulips and sunshine, our older daughter doing something called "Who Strangled Old Man Gratton (with a Wire)?" which she learned from her grandfather, and the baby singing "Riding with an Engineer."

I ordered three boxes of initialed stationery and a box of expensive bath powder from Fairchild's, and our next month's bill was a hundred and sixty dollars and four cents. I wrote Fairchild's asking why the tape recorder—returned, I pointed out, two months ago—was still not deducted from our bill, and received no answer. My husband, who had not been able to decide what to do the month before, concluded that ignoring the tape recorder was the best idea, and he sent Fairchild's a check for sixty dollars and five cents, deducting the ninety-nine dollars and ninety-nine cents for the tape recorder.

Fairchild's sent us a receipted bill, pointing out that there was a balance of ninety-nine dollars and ninety-nine cents still due. Would we clear this off their books, they asked, or at least pay them part of it? I wrote back a letter saying "See Enclosed" and enclosing a copy of the letter I had written them before.

By now we had begun to perceive that the receipt signed by the floorwalker was a very precious paper, and I took it out of the box of recipes and gave it to my husband and he put it into his desk in the envelope where he kept the copy of our mortgage and the preliminary listings for his income tax statements. I wrote another department store in New York, one just as big as Fairchild's, and opened an account *there,* ordering a toy train for the baby's birthday and a new kind of pencil sharpener, so our next monthly bills included a bill for eight dollars and forty cents from the new department store, and a bill from Fairchild's for ninety-nine dollars and ninety-nine cents, with a little slip pasted on the bottom of the bill asking if we would PLEASE ignore the above account no longer. My husband wrote a check to pay the bill of the second department store and threw away the bill from Fairchild's.

About three weeks later my husband and I went out one evening to play bridge and when we got home the baby-sitter told us, blushing, that there had been a telegram phoned in; she had taken a copy of it; the message, she said, edging toward the door, was on my husband's desk. The telegram said that unless we paid our long overdue account at Fairchild's Department Store the store would start legal proceedings, and it was signed S. B. Fairchild. The baby-sitter said nervously that it was *perfectly* all right, we didn't need to pay her for tonight, because she knew what it was to run short of money and she hoped that everything was going to be all right. My husband, who was beginning to get a little purple in the face, took out his wallet with his hands shaking and insisted upon paying her double. I said it was fantastic, that we didn't owe that store a cent, and she said of *course* we didn't, and it was a shame that people like that would never even give you a little time to get the money together.

The next morning the baby-sitter's mother called me to say sympathetically that under the circumstances she supposed I would want to cut down a little on my usual contribution to the School Band Booster Drive. When I went down to the store that afternoon the grocer said that he supposed I knew by now that some people were always thinking about money they had due them, but he wasn't one of them, and if I wanted to let my bill go this month he wouldn't say a word. The boy who delivers the afternoon paper wheeled his bike around and raced off before I could pay him his weekly thirty cents, calling back over his shoulder that it was all right, pay him when it was convenient.

Our mail the next morning included a letter from the baby-sitter's uncle. I knew it was from her uncle because his picture was in the upper left-hand corner, smiling broadly and pointing a finger at the legend across the top of the page, which said "YES! I am a fellow who WANTS to lend you money! Your FINANCIAL worries are OVER, and I mean *OVER*!" Among our bills, which came a day or so later, were a bill from Fairchild's for ninety-nine dollars and ninety-nine cents and a bill from the telephone company with an item for one dollar and sixty-nine cents for a collect telegram from Fairchild's. I called the telephone company and got the night supervisor and asked what on earth gave her the notion that the telephone company could charge me for a collect telegram from Fairchild's, particularly when the telegram had been delivered without my authority to my baby-sitter. The night supervisor agreed that there was a certain injustice in expecting me to pay for such an offensive telegram, but said regretfully that she had no authority to take it off the bill; I must write to the credit manager, she said, and explain it to *him*. I asked why couldn't I telephone him? and she said that they were not allowed to use the telephone to discuss company business.

The next month I got another letter from S. B. Fairchild saying that they had been patient long enough and I must pay my long overdue account ($99.99) by return mail or suffer the consequences. I wrote Fairchild another letter saying "See Enclosed," enclosing a copy of my letter to the credit manager of the telephone company, refusing to pay charges of one dollar sixty-nine cents for a collect telegram incorrectly delivered. The next month we received a bill from Fairchild's for ninety-nine dollars and ninety-nine cents and a letter saying that my credit everywhere would be permanently impaired so long as I neglected this outstanding account, particularly if Fairchild's had to send a collection agency after me. I also got another letter from the baby-sitter's uncle asking me to "BRING your TROUBLES to SOMEONE who can *HELP*!"

The next month Fairchild's went back to the beginning and started all over again; we got the little slip of paper pasted on the bill, asking us please no longer to ignore the above account, and the month after that we got the collect telegram again; this time, fortunately, I answered the phone and refused the telegram peremptorily, since I was still corresponding with the credit manager of the telephone company over the dollar and sixty-nine cents for the first collect telegram. The following month S. B. Fairchild sent us the suffer-the-consequences letter again, and the month after that was the collection-agency one.

For our sixteenth anniversary I bought my husband a nice wallet from the second department store. The children were tired of listening to their own voices on tape, and were bothering us to get a color television set. Fairchild's had an ad in the Sunday paper one week offering color television sets at almost thirty percent off. We told the children that they had to be patient, that color television sets did not grow on trees.

About two months later—we were in the suffer-the-consequences month again—I saw in the paper that Fairchild's was closing out a particular line of garden chairs, which I wanted very much to buy. I wrote to them ordering three plaid-seated garden chairs, and a set of nesting wastebaskets, which had been in the same ad, and an ornamental pewter tray that I thought would be nice for my mother-in-law's birthday, and a few days later I got a letter from S. B. Fairchild. All of the Fairchild Organization, he told me, was shocked, grieved, and revolted at my double-dealing and deceptive tactics. Was I, after all this time, unaware that I had an outstanding debit of ninety-nine dollars and ninety-nine cents ($99.99) owing to Fairchild's Department Store? Did I think I might cavalierly overlook this obligation, sacking the noble counter of Fairchild's Department Store for merchandise for which I did not intend to pay? Indeed, no such wool was to be pulled over the eyes of S. B. Fairchild. Old and valued customer as I was, I had gone too far. My order had been cancelled by the hand of S. B. Fairchild himself; my account was closed. No nesting wastebaskets, no pewter tray, not one plaid-seated garden chair would be forthcoming from Fairchild's until I was prepared to meet my natural obligations and remit in full the sum ($99.99) long overdue to Fairchild Department Stores.

I read the letter twice and then, in an exaltation of pure fury, went to the phone and put through a call, person to person, to Mr. S. B. Fairchild, of the Fairchild Department Store in New York. I waited, gripping the phone, while the phone rang at Fairchild's, and then through the series of connections that took my call from the main switchboard to the switchboard on the eleventh floor, to the credit office line, to the telephone of the secretary, to the credit office, to the office of Mr. S. B. Fairchild, to the secretary of Mr. S. B. Fairchild, to the confidential assistant to Mr. S. B. Fairchild, to the confidential secretary of Mr. S. B. Fairchild. For a while it looked as if we were stopped dead at the confidential secretary to Mr. S. B. Fairchild, but then I said if I did not get Mr. S. B. Fairchild on my long-distance person-to-person call I would put the call through every ten minutes for the rest of the day, making every attempt to tie up all telephone lines to Fairchild's Department Store. After a minute a busy-sounding man's voice got on the phone and said, "Well? Well?"

I told him who I was and said that I was calling about my bill.

"If you're calling about your bill you should be talking to Accounts Due," Mr. Fairchild said. "I'm a very busy man."

"I'm calling because you wrote me a letter," I said.

"The Business Office—"

"I ordered a pewter tray and some nesting wastebaskets and three plaid-seated garden chairs and you said—"

"If you want to place an order you should be talking to Telephone Service," Mr. Fairchild said. "I cannot be expected to personally handle all—"

"I want my pewter tray and my plaid-seated garden chairs."

"Or else Personal Shoppers down on the main floor."

"I refuse, I flatly and absolutely refuse, to pay my bill."

"Why don't I connect you with Complaints?" Mr. Fairchild said hopefully. "I'm a *very* busy man."

"I answered an ad for a tape recorder—"

"All of that material goes to Ad Response. That is not *this* office."

"But the tape recorder was broken."

"Then you want Repairs, on the main floor near the Avenue entrance."

"No. The tape recorder was no good. I didn't want it."

"Then why didn't you send it back?"

"I *did* send it back. I sent it back nearly two years—"

"Then it's Returns you want, on the ninth floor. I can*not* see why all these petty problems are pushed up to *me;* I have enough to do without—"

"I have written you nineteen letters, and it has cost me, altogether, counting an electric clock-making set, nearly forty-five dollars not to get that tape recorder. Do you think there is any merchandise in your store worth forty-five dollars *not* to get?"

"Office Equipment," said Mr. Fairchild, confused. "Eighth floor."

"I insist on satisfaction," I said.

"I am sorry," he said with dignity. "Are you sure you have the right store?"

I hung up and sat down to write, once more, to Mr. Fairchild. I wrote—since it was the last time—a complete and detailed account of the entire transaction of the tape recorder. I enclosed a copy of the receipt, drawn to scale, and a note signed by the man in the music store stating that the tape recorder I had brought him to repair had clearly been sent out by mistake. I reordered the pewter tray, the nesting wastebaskets, and the plaid-seated garden chairs. I included the name and address of the friends who had brought the tape recorder to Fairchild's, and finished with a paragraph telling about how my husband and I wanted to sit quietly in years to come and listen to the voices of our children. My letter covered three pages, and when I sealed it I felt that there was nothing that needed to be added to give Mr. Fairchild the whole picture on the tape recorder. I took the letter to the post office, and said that I wanted to send it by registered mail, to ensure that it should be delivered *only* to Mr. S. B. Fairchild, at the Fairchild Department Store. The postmaster suggested that I ask for a receipt on the letter, which must be signed by the person addressed and then returned to me, so I could be sure that only the person addressed had received the letter. I paid seventy-seven cents postage.

Two days later I got back my postal receipt. In the line reading Signature of Addressee someone had written in Fairchild Department Stores. In the line underneath, which my postmaster had crossed out, there was a signature reading Jane Kelly, sec'y. At the top of the receipt was stamped DELIVER TO ADDRESSEE ONLY and at the bottom of the receipt was stamped DELIVER TO ADDRESSEE ONLY. I took the receipt over to the postmaster and showed it to him, and he was surprised.

"That's no way to run a post office," he said.

"What should I do?" I asked him.

"Well." He thought. "I guess we can't get the letter back *now*," he said. "This secretary, whatever her name is, the one who signed it down here, *she's* got your letter now."

"And Mr. Fairchild won't get it?"

"Tell you what to do," he said. "You got to turn in a complaint on this, see? So you write a letter to *me*, postmaster here, and I'll send it on. Then you write another letter to this here Fairchild, and I think when they get your complaint in the post office department, well, they'll let you send the second letter for nothing."

I went home and wrote a letter explaining what had happened, and I addressed it to our local postmaster and then I took it down to the post office and put a three-cent stamp on it and handed it to him through the window, and he cancelled the stamp and opened the letter and read it and said that was fine, he would send it right on.

One week later—not quite two years since we had first ordered the tape recorder, since our seventeenth anniversary was still nearly a month off and I was getting my husband a sword cane—I went down to pick up the mail.

There was a letter from Fairchild's, signed S. B. Fairchild, saying that my credit everywhere would suffer if they had to turn my account over to a collection agency. There was a letter from the United States Postal Department enclosing three forms to be filled out explaining misdelivery of registered mail. There was a letter from the manager of the telephone company saying that it was against their policy to continue carrying unpaid bills, and unless charges of one dollar and sixty-nine cents were remitted, telephone service would be discontinued. There was a letter in a plain envelope from the baby-sitter's uncle asking "Money troubles got YOU down? Because I'm WAITING to HELP!" There was a letter from the repair department of Fairchild's Department Store. They were extremely sorry that repairing my tape recorder had taken a little longer than their original estimate. There had been a slight delay in getting parts. The machine was put in order now, however, and waiting for me; would I please pick it up right away? Because after ten days they would not be responsible.

DECK THE HALLS

🎶

IT WAS EIGHT O'CLOCK in the evening, Christmas Eve, and Mr. and Mrs. Williams were decorating their Christmas tree. It was the first Christmas tree they had had since they were married, but this year their little girl was two years old, and Mrs. Williams had thought that it was time they started making a real Christmas for her to remember when she grew up. Mrs. Williams had bought some ornaments at the five and ten, and a lot of little toys to hang on the tree, and Mr. Williams had brought out a kitchen chair and was standing on it, hanging things on the top branches. All of the baby's relatives and friends had sent lovely things, which Mrs. Williams intended to pile lavishly under the tree, and Mr. and Mrs. Williams had bought an enormous teddy bear, taller by a head than the baby herself, which would be the first thing she would see in the morning.

When the tree was finished, with the packages and the teddy bear underneath, Mrs. Williams stood back and looked at it, holding her breath with pleasure. "Bob," she said, "it looks lovely. Like a *dream* of Christmas."

Mr. Williams eased himself off the chair gingerly. "Looks good," he admitted.

Mrs. Williams went over and moved an ornament to a higher branch. "She'll come running into the room and we'll have it all lighted up," she said happily, "and it will be something for her to remember all year round."

"We used to have fine Christmases when I was a kid," Mr. Williams said, "all the family together, and a turkey and everything."

The doorbell rang, and Mrs. Williams went to open it. "I could only get a goose for tomorrow," she said over her shoulder, "not many turkeys this year." When she opened the door there were two little girls standing on the porch, snow in their hair and on their shoulders, and both looking up at her. The taller of the two was holding a folded piece of paper, which she held out to Mrs. Williams.

"My mother said to give you this," she said to Mrs. Williams.

Mrs. Williams frowned, puzzled, looking down at the children, wondering if they lived in the neighborhood. "Come in," she said, "don't stand out there in the cold." She closed the door behind the little girls, and they stood expectantly in the hall, their eyes on the Christmas tree beyond the archway into the living room. Mrs. Williams, still puzzled, opened the paper and started to read it aloud.

"Dear neighbor," she read, "these are my two little girls. The oldest is eight years of age and the little one is five . . ." Mrs. Williams suddenly stopped reading aloud and shut her lips tight, reading on to herself: "If you do not want to give them anything please don't bother, but if you do Jeanie wears a size four shoe children's size and Helen needs something to wear to school this winter. Even if you do not give them anything, a Merry Christmas." Mrs. Williams finished reading and looked at the children for a minute. "Bob," she said.

Mr. Williams came out from the living room, and Mrs. Williams handed him the note and turned again to the children. "You sit down there for a minute," she said, indicating the leather bench in the hall, "and I'm going to get you something hot to drink to warm you up, and then we'll see what we can do about this letter of your mother's." She turned to the littler child. "You're Jeanie?" The girl nodded solemnly. "Well, you just let me take your muffler off and sit you up here on this bench, and then we'll have some lovely hot cocoa . . ." While she talked, Mrs. Williams had put the little girl on the bench and taken off her coat, and the older girl, watching, finally took off her coat and sat beside her sister. Mrs. Williams turned around to Mr. Williams, who was standing helplessly, holding the letter. "You amuse these youngsters," she said, "while I run out and make some cocoa."

The children sat on the bench looking at the Christmas tree, and Mr. Williams squatted on the floor beside them. "Well," he said, "you're a little bigger than my little girl, so I hardly know what to say to you . . ."

Mrs. Williams went out into the kitchen and put some milk on to heat while she arranged a dish of oatmeal cookies and two cups and saucers on a tray. When she had made the cocoa, she put the pot on the tray and carried it out into the hall. The littler girl was laughing at Mr. Williams, and the older girl was watching with a smile. Mr. Williams was telling them a story and Mrs. Williams waited with the cocoa while he put a quick ending on it and stood up. She handed each little girl a cup and filled it with cocoa, and then gave them each a cookie. "*That* will make you nice and warm," she said. "Believe I'll have some, too," Mr. Williams said.

Mrs. Williams went back into the kitchen and got two more cups, and brought them out and filled them, and she and Mr. Williams sat on the floor drinking, and Mr. Williams made faces that made little Jeanie laugh so that she could hardly hold her cup. When she had finished her cocoa, Mrs. Williams went upstairs and got out an old coat of her own, and a couple of sweaters and a warm bathrobe. She put them in an old suitcase so the children could carry them, and tore off a page from the telephone pad and scribbled on it: "I have nothing that will fit the children, but maybe you can use these. Or you can make them over." She slipped the note in with the clothes and came back downstairs to the children, who had begun to talk to Mr. Williams.

"The second grade," the older one was saying shyly.

"Well, isn't that fine," Mr. Williams said. "I bet you're lots smarter than Helen, though," he said to the smaller girl.

"*I'm* smarter than *her,*" Helen said.

The smaller girl giggled. "Old Helen has to go to school every day," she said.

When Mrs. Williams came back into the hall, Mr. Williams stood up and turned away from the children. He took out his wallet, selected a five-dollar bill, and held it up to Mrs. Williams, who nodded. Mr. Williams went over and slipped it into the older girl's hand. "Don't you lose that, now," he said. "Tell your mother that's for a Christmas present for all of you."

"Can they carry the suitcase?" Mrs. Williams asked anxiously. The older girl slipped off the bench and picked up the suitcase. Even with the coat in it, it wasn't very heavy, and she would manage it all right, Mrs. Williams thought. Mrs. Williams helped the smaller girl down off the bench and began putting her coat on again.

"Thank you very much," the older girl said to Mr. Williams.

"Nonsense," Mr. Williams said, "it's Christmastime, isn't it?" The older girl smiled and reached for the suitcase.

"Wait a minute," Mrs. Williams said. She ran in to the Christmas tree and took off a couple of candy canes, and brought them back to the children.

They accepted them silently, but suddenly Jeanie began to cry, taking her sister's hand and pointing.

The older girl looked up apologetically. "It's the teddy bear," she said. "She just saw it this minute and she's always wanted one." She tried to pull her sister to the front door, but the little girl refused to move, standing and crying.

"Poor little kid," Mr. Williams said. Mrs. Williams kneeled down beside the little girl.

"Jeanie, honey," she said, "just listen to me for a minute. The teddy bear is pretty, but it's for *my* little girl," she finished.

Jeanie stopped crying, looking up at Mrs. Williams. "Wait," Mrs. Williams said. She went back to the Christmas tree, Jeanie watching her eagerly, and took two little toys off the branches. It spoiled the whole balance of the tree, having them gone, but Mrs. Williams thought quickly that she could fix that later. One of the toys was a little doll, and the other was a folded piece of blanket with three very tiny dolls in it. Mrs. Williams gave the three tiny dolls to Jeanie and the larger doll to Helen. "These are for you," she said. Jeanie held the blanket with the little dolls, looking beyond Mrs. Williams at the teddy bear.

"Thank you very much," Helen said. "We better be going." She hesitated, and finally said to Mrs. Williams, "Please may I have the piece of paper back now?"

Mr. Williams handed her the folded note and Helen put it in her pocket and took Jeanie's hand.

"Merry Christmas," she said. She picked up the suitcase in her free hand and led Jeanie to the door, which Mr. Williams opened for her. On the porch she stopped again, and turned around. "We're going to sing a Christmas carol for you," she said, "I learned it in school." She began, and after a minute Jeanie joined in weakly: "Deck the hall with boughs of holly, tra la la la la . . ."

Mr. and Mrs. Williams stood on the porch and watched them going down the walk, singing carefully together. When they reached the street Mr. Williams stepped back inside. "Coming?" he asked.

"Merry Christmas," Mrs. Williams called out after the children, but even to her, her voice sounded inadequate.

LORD OF THE CASTLE

$\mathcal{D}$

I T WAS A BLACK winter's day when I watched my father hanged. I stood, fifteen years old but too proud to show my fear before the villagers who crowded around, and watched the man I adored ascend the scaffold and take his last look at the sky and the trees and the mountains he loved.

In that ignorant little village the punishment for witchcraft was death, and not even the lord in the castle on the mountaintop was great enough to stand against the law of superstition and dread. And so my father stood today before the hatred in the eyes of the villagers and went gallantly to his death.

As I stood there, alone, I could feel the secret glances that followed me, and I could almost hear the whispers—"That's his son"—"That's the young one"—"Yonder goes the boy who inherits the devil's lore"—and I hated them all for their ignorance and fear. And when they brought my father out to walk the steps to his death, I came forward to stand beside him before he mounted the scaffold. I looked deep into his black eyes, haunted by the sight of things no mortal had ever seen before him, and I stood as straight as I could, and said to him clearly: "I know you are unjustly accused, Father, and those who have done it will suffer at my hand."

But he looked at me, and smiled, and said: "It is not well to return death for death, my son. Rather hope that I shall rest quietly, and leave you in peace." And he touched his hand to my head, and took his great signet ring from his finger and put it on mine. Then I stood watching him climb up to the platform, and as one man close by me cried out against my father: "Go back to the devil, your master!" I cried "Quiet!" and lashed out at him with the whip I carried. And the crowd moved slowly backward, sullen and murmuring, while I stood alone beside the scaffold. But I could not turn my eyes away while my father died, for I would rather have died myself than show myself, before the eyes of that crowd, a coward.

And, afterward, I rode alone, back up the hill to the tall, dark castle, mine now, my home and the home of my vengeance. At fifteen I was the lord on the hill, and possessor of such wealth, in gold and land and antique treasures, as would make me a success in any world's capital I chose to frequent. I chose none, however, for my heart and my passion and the wild, long history of my name held me to my home and the home in which my father had lived and died. I wished never to lose sight of that long black line against the sky that meant my castle on the hill, and, too, my promise to revenge my father's death held me to this place.

Many days and nights I spent there alone, reading my father's books and studying his knowledge, with only an old dumb man moving quietly (who moves more quietly than those who cannot speak?) about the darkness, bringing me what I needed and turning the world from the door. It was vengeance I was studying, and a means of it, for I was bound by that very devil lore that had killed my father, to turn it to bringing his murderers to justice. And soon it was almost a year, and I still knew nothing, and was no closer to my heart's desire.

And it was a year to the day later that I sat in the garden, hidden below the crest of the hill by a heavy stone wall, safe, I thought, from any watcher. I was reading, and no footfall disturbed my work, but a voice spoke at my elbow.

"Is this not part my garden?" it spoke, and I leaped to my feet, the book fallen to the ground, seeing before me a tall and slim young man, ragged and tired, but with a hint of my family in his half-closed eyes.

"Who are you?" I demanded of the stranger, and he laughed.

"I am your half brother," he said.

Then I laughed, but I fell back before the look in his eyes, so much my father that I feared him.

"Your father had more than one son," he said, and touched the signet ring on my hand with the tip of his finger, and when I moved my hand away he laughed once more.

Then he was sober again, and his eyes were kind as he watched me. "Our father," he said, "gave you his ring, because I am afraid that I had no legal right to it . . . yet."

Then I understood. "You are the son of some poor country woman whom my father . . ." It was delicacy made me pause, but he laughed still more.

"I am," he said.

I felt a great kindness growing in me toward this poor unfortunate. "I owe you something, then," I said, and he nodded idly.

I offered him sanctuary in the castle for a day or two, until we could decide what I should do for him by way of reparation for my father's unfortunate legacy to him. And together, almost arm in arm, we walked into the castle from the garden, and through the dark hallways, I the lord of the castle, he the beggar hoping for assistance, and we passed down the long hall from whose sides great dark portraits looked down, portraits of those who had borne us and cherished us and given us our common life.

Then, in the chamber where old Joseph had kindled a fire and set out supper, I turned to my companion to bid him be seated and eat with me.

"First, tell me," I said. "What do they call you?"

For a long moment he stared at me from under his lids, and the firelight made his eyes sparkle. "Nicholas," he said.

"Good." And I waved him to bring his chair nearer the fire.

As we dined for the first time together he told me strange tales of wandering and seekings, of far lands and places that existed, I was certain, in no country but that of his moving mind. He talked of wonders he had seen, of princes he had met, and queens, and I let him talk, half listening, and half wondering what part this queer half brother of mine could play in the plans I was making. For I needed help, of that there was no doubt, and perhaps this was my help, sent to me, as it were, from my dead father himself.

So, when at last the fire was growing dim, and he had silenced himself with talking, I said to him: "Do you know how our father died?"

"He was hanged."

"Were you there?"

"I saw it." As he spoke, he looked long into the fire, as though seeing it again.

"I have committed myself to vengeance upon my father's murderers," I said. "I promised him as he died that they would suffer."

Nicholas looked at me suddenly. "But he bade you forget his death so that he might leave you in peace."

I shook my head, gazing in my turn into the fire. What secret faiths it held for us that night! "By my father's death his work was broken and destroyed. By revenging him I shall recreate that work, and follow my father's dearest dreams."

Nicholas frowned. "But you cannot help your father's work by harming a few blind villagers, or even by wiping out the village itself."

"I could have put the village in flames, and the villagers into the ground, a year ago, had I wished that. They did not murder my father. It was the forces of evil and darkness and fear who gave my father into the hands of the villagers, and gave the villagers a scaffold upon which to hang him."

Then Nicholas put back his head and laughed longer and louder than ever before. "Do you want, then, to destroy the forces of evil?"

I rose. "I *will* destroy the forces of evil, and for that I require your help."

"You will require the help of the devil himself," said Nicholas.

And so Nicholas remained in the castle with me, and there were two of us who walked the dark halls, and read the old books. But it was Nicholas who led me onto the trail of the vengeance which I sought.

"Do you know what the villagers fear?" he asked of me one day.

"They believe that a demon haunts the castle, and makes the land dark and blood-thickened, and that so long as the lord is under this demon's claw, there will be death and destruction along the land. My father was good and kind, but he sought this demon on the hill to defeat it, and was defeated himself."

"And you?"

"When I myself have found and destroyed this demon, then shall my father be revenged."

"And what is your plan?" asked Nicholas.

"To seek and destroy."

"And who will revenge you?" asked Nicholas. "If you should perish, the demon will hold sway, and his evil will be turned loose upon the land, to bring harm as he wishes."

"Then I must marry," I said firmly, but Nicholas laughed. "You will really go to any length to achieve your object," he said.

Then, for the first time since my father's death, I rode down to the village. From the sunny windows of the houses women watched me ride by, and the men in the streets narrowed their eyes and spat in my path. On the farther outskirts of the village I dismounted, for here was the family that had brought my father's death. There had been a man to this family, a great motionless beast, and it had been he who stopped before my father and challenged the demon of the hill. When my father's sword had taken the man's life, it was witchcraft that helped him, they cried; not all the strength of my father's arm nor the power of his voice could avail against their cries. And here was the cottage where the man had lived, and here the very path upon which he had awaited my father, and the dirt on which he had died. I stood, not knowing what I sought, and then a clear, cool laugh reached me, from the cottage garden.

It was a girl, young and golden-haired, and she stood watching me through the rosebushes.

"Are you counting pebbles," she cried, "that you stand so silent and careful?"

I frowned. "Come here," I said. She made an insolent curtsy, and with no hurrying of her steps came lazily through the garden gate to me.

"Who are you?" I said.

"Elizabeth," she said demurely.

"And why do you live here?" I gestured at the cottage of the man who had killed my father.

"Please, sir," she said, dimpling, "it is my father's home, and my mother's, I have no place else to live."

"Your father?"

"He's dead now, sir."

"Are you the daughter of the man who died before the old lord of the hill?"

"I am, sir."

"Do you know who I am?"

She glanced up at me from beneath her eyelashes. "You are the young lord, sir," she said, "and a fine figure of a man, at that," and, laughing, she turned and ran away.

I stood for a moment looking after her, and then I mounted my horse and rode back through the village and up the hill. There I found Nicholas, and I told him of Elizabeth.

And: "Bring her here," I said.

Nicholas laughed.

"I have certainly made up my mind to marry," I said, and then we both laughed.

And so Elizabeth came to the castle on the hill. How Nicholas brought her there I never asked, nor did he tell me what he had done. I know only that one day the door of the great study fell open, and Elizabeth stood before me, not laughing now, but proud and stubborn and lovely.

"So you came after all?" I said, genuinely pleased with my triumph.

"I had little choice," she said.

"You make a charming addition to our family circle here," I said.

Then, furiously angry, she cried out at me: "I am here because your devil's hands brought me, and yet I am not afraid of you. Your devil's hands killed my father, and he was not afraid, and I saw your father hanged and I was glad, do you hear me? And I wanted nothing more than to see your whole foul line perish, and yet I was a poor woman and could never revenge myself on you and your evil blood. But now—I am here, and I think I will see you die because of it. And I defy you and your castle and your devil, too!"

"At any rate the lady's prayers should help you in your task," Nicholas said, coming softly into the room, "for, if I know your devil at all, nothing will bring him more quickly than the defiance of a beautiful woman."

And so I called Joseph and bade him keep Elizabeth prisoner in a high tower of the castle until such time as she should be more inclined to be courteous to her host.

And now suddenly Nicholas and I were feverish and hopeful of our search, for the time had come when the books my father had followed were beginning to be intelligible to me, and I could read easily the secrets they held. And one night I determined to be at this business of the devil and his will. I had caused Elizabeth to be brought to dinner, where she sat sullen and silent, and so I ordered her removed, to hide her tears in her tower prison.

The incident had left me in an evil humor, and I was ready, that night, for anything the devil might bring with him.

When Nicholas and I had finished dinner, we sat together quietly, until I said: "Nicholas, I mean to try the devil tonight."

Nicholas laughed, as always. "Go carefully," he said. "Our father's ghost will be watching."

"Will you try with me?" I asked.

Nicholas shook his head. "Sometimes, half brother," he said, "these things are better done alone. I will be waiting to hear of your success."

And so I sat alone in the study that had been my father's, with one of his great books open on the table in front of me, and I drew the awful diagrams the books ordered, and mixed my secret potions, and spoke the dreadful words that were to call the devil to my side.

"In nomino lutheris, sathanus, et spiritus acherontis . . ."

These words the book had ordered me to speak, and as my lips formed the unholy syllables, the room rocked and a great thundering roll came from the walls and the ceiling, and from a cloud before the fire where lay my deadly potion stepped the most beautiful woman I have ever seen.

Aghast, I let my hand fall from the book, and I stared at this image in wonder and delight. Elizabeth? She was forgotten, and my father, and my vengeance, and the devil himself, for I had found a way to greater joy than either vengeance or love could bring. I felt myself drawn forward to the figure that stood so silently, regarding me, and I took a half step toward her. Then she held up her hand warningly.

"Walk carefully," she said. "Come not too close to *me*."

Recklessly I ran to her, and seized her hand. "Is there any danger in you that I would not willingly embrace?" I demanded, and came ever closer to her. With this, however, she laughed, and leaned her head back to look at me. "You are brave indeed . . ." she said.

No more than that shall I say of my lady of the fire. Let it be enough to add that for many nights, while Nicholas laughed at my anxiety, I locked myself again in the great study and from my father's book repeated the spell that had brought her to me at first. I cannot say how the love of a being such as this will affect a man; I know only that I was mad, and, being mad, knew my madness and deliberately sought it out. No word of my father passed, those days, between Nicholas and me—everything was forgotten before the dreams of the image which came to me from the fire. Ardently as I implored her not to leave me, to stay or to take me with her, she would always reply, half smiling: "You will be with me soon enough, and we shall never be parted then."

Such things, I know, lead to desperate deeds in a man, and yet it was Elizabeth, weary of her prison, who led me to my last disaster. For one golden afternoon, as I lay in the garden dreaming of my love, Nicholas came to me, and spoke softly and quickly: "I have given orders, half brother, that Elizabeth be released from the tower."

Angrily, I half rose. "Who are you to be giving orders in my home?" I demanded first, and then: "And Elizabeth? Has she repented?"

"I give orders because I, too, am lord here," Nicholas said quietly, "and Elizabeth—has repented."

I could not speak before the mockery in his eyes. What would I have to do with Elizabeth, who was nothing before my lady from the flames? And Nicholas—he would be driven away, half brother or no, and I would have no rivals in my home.

But Nicholas said: "Elizabeth has repented, and yet, despairing of your love, she has turned her heart another way . . . to one not, perhaps, as wealthy, but of as noble blood." And he made a gallant bow.

Then I was on my feet, hating him and seeing how surely he had stolen my life while I had lain idly under the curse of my spells. And I reached for my sword, but it lay in the study, by the fire, where I had cast it off and forgotten it, to kneel at the feet of my lady.

Then, afraid, I saw that I had been tricked, and that while Nicholas had stolen my life, my fair lady had held me bound in witchcraft. And I turned from Nicholas and went to the study, and, for the last time, spoke the words that brought my lady to me. And then, when she came, I did not go to her, but stood safely within the compass of my charmed circle, knowing now that to leave it was death, and I watched her, standing lovely before the fire, and I said:

"Did you, then, betray me?"

She laughed. "Are you afraid to come closer to me and ask that?"

I nearly went over to the fire when she spoke, because the enchantment in her voice was enough to turn any man's head, except if he had in him, as I did, the warm memory of betrayal.

"I want to come no closer to you than I now know I can stand with safety," I said.

"You will be with me soon enough."

"And you and Nicholas . . ." I said. "What have I left now?"

She laughed again. "Even as I betrayed your father," she said.

And now I knew that I could still be revenged.

"He bade you stay in peace," she added, "and leave him in his grave!"

And then I thought, and, crying aloud to her, I made the sign of the cross, again and again, and watched her stand untouched before me. "You have no contact with the powers of good now," she said. "Why do you invoke them against me?"

And I fell on my knees and covered my head, and she whispered: "You will be with me soon, my love, for I will be here. I will be waiting for you to come." And when I looked up she had gone.

Then, indeed, I came out from my charmed circle, and raged as a madman at the walls and the fire, seeking her to destroy her. All the curses and invocations I could find in my mind I employed against her, and still found myself only raging against stone. And then I remember my crying: "Then I shall destroy you, if you are here, if I must destroy the whole world around you!"

And I ran into the darkness of the night outside, and knew only that there was a flaming torch in my hand, but the castle was old and the trees were dry, and there was more wood than stone that had gone to make up my home. . . .

And as I ran down the road crying aloud, with the flames from the hill close on my heels, I thought I heard a voice crying from the tower, and I thought of Elizabeth and nearly turned back. But then, seeing the castle where it stood, a thing of flame, I fell instead on my knees and thought of Elizabeth, and called her name, and tried to return again from the powers of darkness and ask a kinder Lord to forgive me. And it was there that they found me, the villagers, and dragged me away, still crying out among themselves at my madness.

And so I die, as did my father, for the crimes of witchcraft and murder, for Elizabeth lay in the ruins of the castle. And for a day only I lay in my jail, watching the scaffold outside, and I wondered long about the madness that will take a man.

And then, with day, and as I stood (like my father so long ago; like my father!) at the foot of the scaffold and heard the crowd cry out against me, the ranks of them parted, and Nicholas came up to me where I stood.

"Ah, half brother!" he cried gaily. "You have made a pretty revenge for your father!"

But I asked him only: "How did you escape the flames in the castle?"

"My mother brought me out safely," Nicholas said.

"Your mother?"

"Yes," said Nicholas. "She whom you saw each night in the fire—she who betrayed our father, half brother!"

And he started away, laughing, but then he turned and came to me, and his deep eyes were serious. "Half brother," he said, "I have one further thing to give you." He lifted my hand as he spoke, and held it tight between his own. A wild, desperate hope leaped up within me, and I cried, thinking I might yet save myself from death: "Nicholas, help me now! What will you give me?"

"Oh, half brother," Nicholas sighed mockingly, "how eager you are!" And he lifted my helpless hand and slipped my ring, and my father's ring, the signet ring of our house, off my finger. "I give you your freedom, brother of my house," he said, and he gestured at the gallows.

Then, laughing still, he turned again and went through the crowd, as I cried after him, and raged at my bonds to escape and be on him, but the crowd roared me back and the jailers forced me up the steps of the scaffold. And from the height, I saw one thing. I saw Nicholas, on his way home, as he turned and waved at me; and then, as I saw him ride alone, up the long road to the smoldering embers of my house, I buried my head in my hands and knew cruelly that now, indeed, the devil held the hill.

WHAT A THOUGHT

D INNER HAD BEEN GOOD; Margaret sat with her book on her lap and watched her husband digesting, an operation to which he always gave much time and thought. As she watched he put his cigar down without looking and used his free hand to turn the page of his paper. Margaret found herself thinking with some pride that unlike many men she had heard about, her husband did not fall asleep after a particularly good dinner.

She flipped the pages of her book idly; it was not interesting. She knew that if she asked her husband to take her to a movie, or out for a ride, or to play gin rummy, he would smile at her and agree; he was always willing to do things to please her, still, after ten years of marriage. An odd thought crossed her mind: She would pick up the heavy glass ashtray and smash her husband over the head with it.

"Like to go to a movie?" her husband asked.

"I don't think so, thanks," Margaret said. "Why?"

"You look sort of bored," her husband said.

"Were you watching me?" Margaret asked. "I thought you were reading."

"Just looked at you for a minute." He smiled at her, the smile of a man who is still, after ten years of marriage, very fond of his wife.

The idea of smashing the glass ashtray over her husband's head had never before occurred to Margaret, but now it would not leave her mind. She stirred uneasily in her chair, thinking: what a terrible thought to have, whatever made me think of such a thing? Probably a perverted affectionate gesture, and she laughed.

"Funny?" her husband asked.

"Nothing," Margaret said.

She stood up and crossed the room to the hall door, without purpose. She was very uneasy, and looking at her husband did not help. The cord that held the curtains back made her think: strangle him. She told herself: it's not that I don't love him, I just feel morbid tonight. As though something bad were going to happen. A telegram coming, or the refrigerator breaking down. Drown him, the goldfish bowl suggested.

Look, Margaret told herself severely, standing just outside the hall door so that her husband would not see her if he looked up from his paper, look, this is perfectly ridiculous. The idea of a grown woman troubling herself with silly fears like that—it's like being afraid of ghosts, or something. *Nothing* is going to happen to him, Margaret, she said almost aloud; *nothing* can happen to hurt either you or your husband or anyone you love. You are perfectly safe.

"Margaret?" her husband called.

"Yes?"

"Is something wrong?"

"No, dear," Margaret said. "Just getting a drink of water."

Poison him? Push him in front of a car? A train?

I don't *want* to kill my husband, Margaret said to herself. I never *dreamed* of killing him. I want him to live. Stop it, stop it.

She got her drink of water, a little formality she played out with herself because she had told him she was going to do it, and then wandered back into the living room and sat down. He looked up as she entered.

"You seem very restless tonight," he said.

"It's the weather, I guess," Margaret said. "Heat always bothers me."

"Sure you wouldn't like to go to a movie?" he said. "Or we could go for a ride, cool off."

"No, thanks," she said. "I'll go to bed early."

"Good idea," he said.

What would I do without him? she wondered. How would I live, who would ever marry me, where would I go? What would I do with all the furniture, crying when I saw his picture, burning his old letters. I could give his suits away, but what would I do with the house? Who would take care of the income tax? I love my husband, Margaret told herself emphatically; I *must* stop thinking like this. It's like an idiot tune running through my head.

She got up again to turn the radio on; the flat voice of the announcer offended her and she turned the radio off again, passing beyond it to the bookcase. She took down a book and then another, leafing through them without seeing the pages, thinking: It isn't as though I had a motive; they'd never catch me. Why would I kill my husband? She could see herself saying tearfully to an imaginary police lieutenant: "But I loved him—I can't *stand* his being dead!"

"Margaret," her husband said. "Are you worried about something?"

"No, dear," she said. "Why?"

"You really seem terribly upset tonight. Are you feverish?"

"No," she said. "A chill, if anything."

"Come over here and let me feel your forehead."

She came obediently, and bent down for him to put his hand on her forehead. At his cool touch she thought, Oh, the dear, good man; and wanted to cry at what she had been thinking.

"You're right," he said. "Your head feels cold. Better go on off to bed."

"In a little while," she said. "I'm not tired yet."

"Shall I make you a drink?" he asked. "Or something like lemonade?"

"Thank you very much, dear," she said. "But no thanks."

They say if you soak a cigarette in water overnight the water will be almost pure nicotine by morning, and deadly poisonous. You can put it in coffee and it won't taste.

"Shall I make *you* some coffee?" she asked, surprising herself.

He looked up again, frowning. "I just had two cups for dinner," he said. "But thanks just the same."

I'm brave enough to go through with it, Margaret thought; what will it all matter a hundred years from now? I'll be dead, too, by then, and who cares about the furniture?

She began to think concretely. A burglar. First call a doctor, then the police, then her brother-in-law and her own sister. Tell them all the same thing, her voice broken with tears. It would not be necessary to worry about preparations; the more elaborately these things were planned, the better chance of making a mistake. She could get out of it without being caught if she thought of it in a broad perspective and not as a matter of small details. Once she started worrying about things like fingerprints she was lost. Whatever you worry about catches you, every time.

"Have you any enemies?" she asked her husband, not meaning to.

"Enemies," he said. For a moment he took her seriously, and then he smiled and said, "I suppose I have hundreds. Secret ones."

"I didn't mean to ask you that," she said, surprising herself again.

"Why would I have enemies?" he asked, suddenly serious again, and setting down his paper. "What makes you think I have enemies, Margaret?"

"It was silly of me," she said. "A silly thought." She smiled and after a minute he smiled again.

"I suppose the milkman hates me," he said. "I always forget to leave the bottles out."

The milkman would hardly do; he knew it, and he would not help her. Her glance rested on the glass ashtray, glittering and colored in the light from the reading lamp; she had washed the ashtray that morning and nothing had occurred to her about it then. Now she thought: It ought to be the ashtray; the first idea is always the best.

She rose for the third time and came around to lean on the back of his chair; the ashtray was on the table to her right, now, and she bent down and kissed the top of his head.

"I never loved you more," she said, and he reached up without looking to touch her hair affectionately.

Carefully she took his cigar out of the ashtray and set it on the table. For a minute he did not notice and then, as he reached for his cigar, he saw that it was on the table and picked it up quickly, touching the table underneath to see if it had burned. "Set fire to the house," he said casually. When he was looking at the paper again she picked up the ashtray silently.

"I don't want to," she said as she struck him.

When Barry
Was Seven

℈

BARRY: Eight hundred and nine pages. That's the biggest book I ever owned.

SHIRLEY: You ought to take a while reading that.

BARRY: But I'm not going to start it until I go to bed. Because I don't want to finish too soon.

SHIRLEY: Look, Mr. Untermeyer has autographed it to you.

BARRY: Yes, I saw that already. Now *(complacently)* I have two books with the writer's name written on.

SHIRLEY: Two?

BARRY: Yes. This book, and *Louis Pasteur*. Because on the outside of my *Louis Pasteur* book it has "Louis Pasteur" in gold handwriting, and it would be senseless to use his name in handwriting unless he really wrote it. It's senseless. Because why would somebody else write his name? So now I have two books. Mr. Untermeyer and Louis Pasteur.

SALLY: I have books from Jay Williams with his signature.

BARRY: *(reasonably)* Well, you are older than I am.

(later, Barry still carrying his book with him everywhere)
BARRY: This is the heaviest book I ever owned.

SHIRLEY: You have done everything with that book except read it. Stop carrying it around and look inside, for heaven's sake.

BARRY: I have already read the story about Louis Pasteur.

SHIRLEY: *(nervously)* Well? Is it all right? Does he know what he's talking about?

BARRY: Yes. He knows very well. He knows all the facts. Of course I do not know the facts about some of the other people he has written about—*(mispronouncing)*—Leo Tolstoi, or Winston Churchill, but about Louis Pasteur, I think he has gotten all the facts.

SHIRLEY: Will you write to him and tell him you think so?

BARRY: *(considering)* Yes. When I have read a little more. First, though, I have to weigh it.

SHIRLEY: Weigh it? The book?

BARRY: Yes. It is the heaviest book I ever owned. Also it costs six dollars and ninety-five cents and that is almost seven dollars. I think Mr. Untermeyer would like me to find out how much it weighs.

SHIRLEY: And how much *does* it weigh?

BARRY: *(over the bathroom scales)* Twelve pounds? No, that is with my foot. Three pounds. That is really a pretty heavy book. Pretty heavy for a young boy like me to carry.

SHIRLEY: Look, creep. You aren't *supposed* to carry it, you're supposed to *read* it.

BARRY: All right. I will read *Mark Twain*.

(later, Barry reading in a big study chair, vis-à-vis *Stanley, also reading)*

BARRY: Dad, what are *you* reading?

STANLEY: *Moby Dick*.

BARRY: How many pages does it have?

STANLEY: Oh, God, five hundred or so. Too many.

BARRY: *(with enormous satisfaction)* My book is larger.

STANLEY: *(defensively)* But I have to read footnotes and then Melville's correspondence and then more books about—

BARRY: Who wrote your book?

STANLEY: Herman Melville.

BARRY: *(superior)* I don't think that *he* is in *my* book. *I* have a writer named Leo Tolstoi.

STANLEY: Well, Melville—

BARRY: You may read my book when I have finished. There are some pages about Darwin you can read. Probably you would like them.

BEFORE AUTUMN

ALL THAT SUMMER SHE had been increasingly aware of the growing turbulence among the trees, and in the grasses, and around the hills; in the vegetable garden each morning there had been vague markings of snails, and the trees were less certain of their birds, somehow, she thought, and more noisy in the wind. That the paints had something to do with it she was certain; before the sudden violence of green in the paint box the grass flattened and grew bladed and pale, and the hills plunged mistily ahead of a purple so carefully compounded of blue, and red, and white, and sometimes, in the late afternoons, yellow. Even Daniel became less of a husband, less of a reddish-brown certainty, and more of a careful blend of plum and ochre, with brush strokes to simulate tweeds . . . "Possibly," she would think, "if I paint more carefully . . . since everything but Daniel seems to stay such a long time . . ."

But what of this new irresistible impulse to draw the curtains against the trees, to read by lamplight in the mornings, to move carefully into a room to Daniel, saying, "My dear, could you arrange to look less ruddy, for my sake . . . ?" And that incredible question, at dinner, over the candles, to his open mouth—"Daniel, do you do everything the way you chew your food?"

As certainly it was not the coming of fall, always frightening, for the month was only . . . she would stop and think . . . July, in the middle, and the days long and hot.

Narrowing it down, finally, to the colors in her room, she determined on a change from pale yellow to lavender and pink, but, surrounded by curtain material, she found that her paint box could duplicate exactly (blue, touched with pink, and much white; red, watered into rose) and she folded and boxed her cloths to wait until September, when she had intended to change anyway. Then, to Daniel's mild questions ("What if I should rush in ardently and shriek: 'Daniel, for sweet heaven's sake, will you go kill something . . . ?'!'"):

"Curtains all tacked together, honey?"

"Quite finished, Daniel, thank you."

"Like them better, now you've got them?"

"Much better, thank you, Daniel."

"Why thank me, I only paid for them."

And he would smile at her, because that was a joke.

It was not until the coming of Jimmie Wilson that she made any effort to break away from Daniel. And Jimmie was only fifteen, and still vague and blurred; no tweeds, she thought, and no tan. Jimmie moved next door, so easily, and played ball against the fence, and moved about his house, and became friends with Daniel, and Jimmie's mother expected to be called upon. Jimmie, sitting on the porch, pale against the trees and the hills and the grass, first gave her the idea, and then there was the preparation, so careful, so cautious:

"Jimmie, you should learn to paint; you should try to paint the hills and the trees around here."

"As a matter of fact, ma'am, I don't have much time for things like painting. There's school, and scouts, and then my homework, you know."

"You have a painter's hands, Jimmie."

Long afternoons; frequent, warm afternoons. ("Jimmie, can you help me cut the roses today? The thorns are so bad, and I have no gloves . . ." "Do you have a minute, Jimmie? Come and talk to me while I do my nails here in the sun . . . isn't it warm?" "When shall I give you a painting lesson, Jimmie?")

Nothing obvious, nothing daring. Jimmie's mother was called upon, learned to use the back gate, called in return. ("Jimmie, pass your mother her tea, like a nice boy.")

A very careful, very cautious, easy and lazy preparation.

"Jimmie, my husband is going to teach you to shoot, he says."

"I know, he promised me a long time ago. We have to wait until deer season, though."

"Why for the deer season, Jimmie?"

"Why, to kill anything."

"I see. You won't kill each other, then?" (Too sudden? Too daring?)

"You can't kill anyone with those guns!"

"I'm so glad to hear that, Jimmie. I must confess that I had been worried. But why can't you kill anyone with those guns?"

"Oh, you learn to be too careful. No one wants to get hurt."

"I wouldn't want you to get hurt, Jimmie. But I'm sure my husband's very careful."

"Of course he is. They wouldn't let him have a gun if he weren't."

"Do you want a gun, Jimmie? I'll buy you one if you like."

"Why, thanks very much . . . Gee . . ." (too soon; he was surprised) "but of course you couldn't; it's too much, and my mother . . ."

"Well, we'll see. But I'm sure you'll need one."

"I'll see what my mother says."

"Don't let yourself get hurt with it, Jimmie. But then, of course he's very careful. I can't describe how careful he is."

There, it had been started; it would work of itself from now on. Jimmie knew, she was sure, and sympathized, and would help; she was sure because she could paint him so well. She was there in her room, painting, that day after talking to Jimmie, when Daniel came home.

"Painting again, honey? And by lamplight?"

"The sun hurts my eyes, Daniel."

"Better see an oculist, then. Got to take care of your eyes."

"I shall, thank you, Daniel."

"Don't thank me, honey, I only pay for it."

THE STORY WE
USED TO TELL

ᗧ

THIS IS THE STORY that Y and I used to tell, used to tell in the quiet of the night, in the hours of the quiet of the night, and the moonlight would come, moving forward, moving close; used to whisper to each other in the night . . .

And I, Y would say, had to go first. With the moonlight making white patterns in her hair, she would shake her head and say: I had to go first. Remember, she would say. In this very house. That night. Remember? And the picture, and the moonlight, and the way we laughed.

We had sat on the foot of the bed, the way we used to when we roomed together in school, talking together and laughing sometimes in spite of the grief that filled Y's great house. It was only a month or so after her husband's funeral, I remember, and yet being together again, just the two of us, was somehow enough to make Y smile sometimes, and even occasionally laugh again. I had been wise enough not to remark on the fact that Y had closed off the rooms of the house in which she had lived with her husband, and had moved into an entire new wing of the old place. But I liked her little bedroom, quiet and bare, with no room for books, and only the one picture on the wall.

"It's a picture of the house . . ." Y said to me. "See, you can barely see the windows of this very room. It's before my grandfather-in-law remodeled it, which is why the new wing isn't there."

"It's a beautiful old place," I said. "I almost wish he hadn't changed it so much."

"Plumbing," Y said. "There's nothing wrong with plumbing."

"No," I said, "but I'm glad you've reopened the old wing . . . it must have been a gorgeous place in—say—your grandfather-in-law's time."

And we looked at the picture of the old old house, standing dark and tall against the sky, with the windows of this very room shining faintly through the trees, and the steep winding road coming through the gates and down to the very edge of the picture.

"I'm glad the glass is there," I said, giggling. "I'd hate to have a landslide start on that mountain and come down into our laps!"

"Into my bed, you mean," Y said. "I don't know if I'll be able to sleep, with the old place overhead."

"Grandpop's probably still in it, too," I said. "He's wandering around in a nightcap with a candle in the old barn."

"Plotting improvements." Y pulled the covers up over her head.

I told her, "God save us from all reformers," and went across the hall to my own room, pulled the heavy curtains to shut out the moonlight, and went to bed.

And the next morning Y was gone.

I woke up late, had breakfast downstairs with a first assistant footman or something of the sort presiding (even Y, married for four years into a butler-keeping establishment, had never found out which one to send for to bring tea in the afternoons, and had finally given up completely and taken to serving sherry, which she could pour herself from a decanter on the sideboard), and finally settled down to read, believing that Y would sleep late and come down in her own sweet time.

One o'clock was a little late, however, and when the menagerie began announcing lunch to me, I went after Y.

She wasn't in her room, the bed had been slept in, and none of the menagerie knew where she was. More than that, no one had seen or heard of her since I had left her the night before; everyone else had thought, as I did, that she was sleeping late.

By late afternoon I had decided to call Y's family lawyer, John, who lived on an adjoining estate and had been a close friend of Y's husband, and a kind advisor to Y. And by evening Y's lawyer had decided to call the police.

At the end of a week, nothing had been heard from or of Y, and the police had changed their theory of kidnapping to one of suicide. The lawyer came to me one of those afternoons with a project for closing up the house.

"I dread saying it, Katharine, but—" He shook his head. "I'm afraid she's dead."

"How can she be?" I kept crying out, I remember. "I tell you I was with her all that evening. We talked, and she was happier than she has been for weeks—since her husband died . . ."

"That's why I think she's dead," he said. "She was heartbroken. She had nothing to keep her alive."

"She had plans . . . she was going to sell this house, and travel! She was going to live abroad for a while—meet people, try to start life over again—why, I was going with her! We talked about it that night . . . and we laughed about the house . . . she said the picture would fall on her bed!!" My voice trailed off. It was, I know certainly, the first time I had thought of the picture since I had left Y in her room, with the moonlight coming in and shining on her pale hair on the pillow. And I began to think.

"Wait until tomorrow," I begged him. "Don't do anything for a day or two. Why . . . she might come back tonight!"

He shook his head at me despairingly, but he went away and left me alone in the house. I called the menagerie, and ordered my things moved into Y's room.

The full moon had turned into a lopsided creature, but there was still moonlight enough to fill the room with a haunted light when I lay down in Y's bed, looking into the empty windows in the picture of a house. I fell asleep thinking miserably of Y's cheerful conviction that the old man was loose in the picture, plotting improvements.

The moonlight was still there when I woke up, and so was the old woman. She was hanging on the inside of the glass of the picture, gibbering out at me, and she looked twenty feet high, standing in front of that picture of the house. I sat up in bed and backed as far away from the picture as I could, realizing, in the one lucid moment I had before the cold terror of that thing hit me, that she was on the inside of the glass, and couldn't get out.

Then suddenly she moved aside and I could see the road leading down from the house, and, while I watched, Y came through the gates, running, and waving desperately at me. I could feel my eyes getting wider and wider and the back of my neck getting colder and colder, and then I knew that I had been right and that Y had been caught in some malevolence of the old house, and I began sobbing in thankfulness that I had found her in time.

I picked up my slipper and smashed the glass of the picture and held out my hands to Y to hurry her on toward me. And then I saw that the old woman, no longer hanging on to the inside of the glass, was now free, and in the room with me, and I could hear her laughing. I fell back on the bed in a wild attempt to shove the old woman back into the picture and I could just see Y, dropping her hands in helpless grief, turn around and start slowly back up the road to the house. Then the room went out from under me, and the glass on the picture closed around me.

"I was waving at you to go away," Y was saying over and over. "You should have left me here and gone away. We can't ever get out now—either of us. You should have gone away."

I opened my eyes and looked around. I was in the dining room of the house, but so changed and gloomy! It was dark, and there was no furniture, no ornamentation. The place was still, and damp.

"No plumbing, either," Y said dryly, noticing the bewilderment on my face. "This picture was painted before the improvements were put in."

"But—" I said.

"Hide!" Y whispered. She pushed me into a corner, out of the light of the one candle on the floor.

"Oh my God," I said, and grabbed Y's hands.

Through the doorway came the old man, giggling and pulling at his beard. He was followed by the old woman, silent now, but with glittering grin, and half waltzing.

"Young ladies!" the old man called in a shrill, cracked voice, looking eagerly about the room. He picked up the candle and began going to the corners with it. "Young ladies," he cried, "come out! We are going to celebrate! Tonight there is to be a ball!"

"Y!" I said. He was coming toward us.

"There you are, there you are. Lovely young ladies, shy over their first ball! Come ahead, young ladies!"

Y gave me one look, and then moved slowly forward. The old man waved the candle at me, calling, "Come along, don't be too demure, no partners then, you know!" and I followed Y into the room. The old man waved at the woman then, saying, "Let the musicians start now," and our first ball began. The music did not materialize, but the old man danced solemnly, first with Y and then with me, while the old crone sat dreamily in the corner, swinging the candle in time.

While the old man was dancing with Y, he would wave at me roguishly as they passed, calling out, "Wallflower!" and something that was very like a grin would come over Y. And once when he was dancing with me and we passed Y, sitting on the floor in abject misery, he cried out sternly: "Come now, look gay! Honey catches more flies than vinegar, you know!" And Y actually began to laugh.

No one could possibly say that I enjoyed myself at my first ball. But, you see, I still thought I was lying on Y's bed, dreaming of the picture. Later, when the old man had limped off to bed, after kissing our hands gallantly, Y and I sat on the dining room floor and talked about it. In spite of the icy touch of the old man's fingers which lingered on our hands, in spite of the chill of the stone floor and the memory of the old crone's cackling, we sat there in the dark together and told each other that it was all a horrible dream.

Y said: "I've been here for a long time. I don't know how long. But every night there's been a ball."

I shivered. "He's a lovely dancer," I said.

"Isn't he though," Y agreed. "I know who he is," she said after a few minutes. "He's grandpop-in-law. He died in this house, crazy."

"You might have told me before I came to visit you," I said.

"I thought he'd stay dead," Y said.

We sat there, not talking, until finally the room began to grow lighter, and the dusk in the house was brightened with sunlight. I ran to the window, but Y laughed. "Wait," she said gloomily.

Outside the window I could see the trees that surrounded the old house, and the road down to the gates. Beyond the gates the trees prevented my seeing much, but I did manage to make out light, and color, and . . . the outlines of Y's bed.

Y came over to the window and stood beside me. "Now do you know why I keep saying I'm dreaming?" she demanded.

"But . . ." I turned around and looked at her. "But you aren't," I said.

"No," Y replied after a minute. "I'm not."

We stood close together then, looking out over the trees and the gate, and beyond them, ridiculously, maddeningly, to the room that would mean freedom.

"Y," I said finally, "this isn't true. It's—" I began to laugh, at last. "It's outrageous!" I shouted. And Y began to laugh, too.

And for a time Y and I, hidden away among the trees around the house, planned an escape. "We're completely helpless unless someone comes into the room," Y said, "and we're completely helpless as long as these two old wrecks wander around loose."

"Remember how I thought you were waving me on when I couldn't hear you through the glass," I said.

"But if the old woman hadn't been there . . ."

We looked at each other. "Why is she here?" I said finally. Y shook her head. "It's not as though she wasn't already dead," I began, and finished weakly—"probably . . ."

And that night, while the old man prepared the room for the ball, Y asked him who the woman was. And, "One of your aunts, my dear," he chuckled, pinching Y's cheek, and, "And I never saw a prettier girl, at that." He shook his head sadly. "She's aged a good deal since we've lived here, though. Not so pretty nowadays, are you, old hag!" he screamed suddenly, and ran over to the old woman to give her a shove that sent her rocking back and forth, giggling wildly and nodding her head.

"Has she been here long?" Y asked timidly, but the old man skipped back and forth, pirouetting with exaggerated grace. "No questions, young ladies, no questions! Pretty heads should be empty, you know!"

That was what decided Y and me. The next day our plans were made, and it all had to be done fast. I do not like to remember what we did, and Y swears now that it is all gone from her mind, but I know as well as she does that we stuffed a pillow over the old man's face while he slept, and hanged him to a tree afterward, in an ecstasy of hatred which spent itself on him, and left us little eagerness for the old woman. But we finished it, and never went back to the forest behind the castle, where the two bodies still hang, for all I know. It's as Y said, then: "We don't know if we can kill them, but we do know that if they're not dead, they're still tied up . . ."

And then, weak and happy and laughing, we lay all day in the sun near the gates, waiting for someone to come into the room.

"How long has it been, Y, that we've been held here?"

"A year, I guess—" This muffled, from Y's face hidden in her arms. "Or maybe more."

"It hasn't been more than a week," I said.

"It's been years," Y said again.

And how much longer was it that we waited? The room, which we could see from the gates, had been dismantled. How bitterly we repented of the time spent away from the view of the room, the time lost while someone had taken up the carpets in the room, had taken away the linen and the mattress from the bed, had taken down the curtains and stripped the room bare of everything but dust! Where had we been, and who would come now to an empty and forsaken room? But it was Y, as always, who thought of it first.

"Why didn't they take the picture down, then?" she said. "They've emptied the room and left the picture still hanging!"

"They must know something! They must believe that the picture has something to do with us!"

"They'd know the room was haunted, since two of us disappeared from there . . ." Y began.

"And no one will ever come into it for that reason," I finished.

We were there long enough for the ivy on the house to grow a quarter inch before someone came to rescue us.

We had often speculated as to who would come. Both of us had believed that it would be a stranger, come to see for himself if he could solve the secret of the room, but when our rescuer finally arrived one evening, it was John. I saw him first, while Y slept, and when I woke her to tell her it was John, she cried for the first time since we had given up hope. We lay in the grass before the gates, waiting for the moon to rise so John could see us and let us out.

We watched him put down a blanket on the empty bed, and lie down to stare directly into the picture. In the half-darkness that meant the moon was rising, we saw him lying there, watching for us. And as the moon rose slowly, coming toward the picture, we stood by the gates, clinging to each other and trembling with excitement.

Even before the full light was upon us, we were racing down the road to him, to the glass that he must break. I remember falling once, and stumbling to my feet to run on, with blood on my face and hands, crying out to John, and I believe now that it was during that moment wasted in getting to my feet that I knew exactly, because I heard Y's voice calling, "Come, John, come on, John, come on!" And I knew that I was screaming, too, and shrieking at the top of my lungs.

And John was sitting up in the bed, and screaming, too, and he put up his foot and kicked at the glass and broke it—at last.

. . .

And that is how we tell it, Y and I, in the quiet of the night, in the hours of the quiet of the night, with the moonlight moving close, while we wait in the secret of the night, and John runs constantly about the house, screaming and beating the walls. For I have no partner, now in the evenings, and Y and John do not like to dance alone.

My Uncle in
the Garden

🐦

I HAVE ALWAYS TAKEN presents when I go to visit my uncle Oliver and my uncle Peter: a fruit cake, certainly, and a dozen oranges, and toys, a little jumping rabbit that winds with a key for Uncle Oliver, and a chocolate bone for Uncle Peter's cat. I get on the ferry at San Francisco, stopping in the ferry building for identical boxes of candied cherries, and run at Sausalito for the train that will take me into San Rafael. Then, carrying my packages and my suitcases and my book, I must walk slowly up the long country road in the sun, waiting for Uncle Peter to catch the first sight of me, or Uncle Oliver to look up from the wicker chair on the porch and come running down to meet me. Their cottage is halfway up a steep little country hill, with flowers growing down to the road on both sides, and orchards beyond, and Uncle Oliver will be out of breath walking up with me, eyeing the packages and saying: "Peter will be pleased to see what you have brought him." Both Uncle Oliver and I know that Peter will be pleased to see what I have brought, but Uncle Oliver will carry the presents away, to be disposed of carefully and doled out slowly.

When I reach the cottage, I must stop for a moment in the road, looking at the roof low enough to touch from the garden, the roses going up the walls and leaning over the doorway, the two flat stone steps, and the orchard and the vegetable garden creeping around the sides of the house, not content with their position in the backyard, and I must stand there for a moment and then say: "Nothing has been changed since last year, Uncle Oliver; how do you and Uncle Peter stay so young, and keep your home so pretty?"

And then Uncle Oliver, twisting his hands with delight, will say, as he always does: "I never get any older; Peter ages for both of us, and for the house, too." Then I may go inside to be graciously received by Uncle Peter.

I call them my uncles only because it is so difficult to address both of them as Mr. Duff; some fifty years ago, when Uncle Oliver was courting my grandmother, she is said to have declared that they would be satisfactory only as bachelor brothers who would take her future grandchildren to the zoo, and so Uncles Peter and Oliver did, and her children, too, and probably my children someday as well. Aside from the one incredible year Uncle Oliver spent married to a lady known as Mrs. Duff, they have lived together, at first in a little flat in San Francisco, and finally in this rose-covered cottage, which the semi-mythical Mrs. Duff planned and arranged as a suitable bower for her husband. Neither Uncle Peter nor Uncle Oliver has ever tried to work at anything; some farsighted relative left them a small mutual income, which, augmented by the presents of oranges and fruitcake that they receive from the children whom they took to the zoo, keeps them excellently, with their several cats. Uncle Peter is lean and tired; he cares for the house and watches over the garden and the three or four trees in the orchard and the one cat that is especially his own; Uncle Oliver is rounder and lazier; he does the cooking and watches the vegetable garden and the five other cats. Uncle Peter's gray cat, Sandra Williamson, is the only one distinguished by a name; the others, all white cats left in the house by Mrs. Duff, operate as a unit and come and go to the name of Kitty.

"They all had names once," Uncle Oliver explains mournfully, "Mrs. Duff used to call them pretty things. One was Rosebud, as I remember, and all the others were pretty things, too."

"Someday we will name them all again," Uncle Peter adds, "and I will make little leather collars for them, each with his own name around his neck on a leather collar."

The white cats will all be sitting on the front porch when I come, washing one another and playing with the sunlight. Uncle Oliver will stop and touch one or two of them on the head; "Pretty little things," he will say. "Nice kitty." I do not believe that the white cats understand Uncle Oliver the way Sandra Williamson understands Uncle Peter; wherever Uncle Peter goes, Sandra Williamson will follow him, sometimes so far forgetting her dignity as to touch at a dangling shoelace. And when I come, she will be standing next to Uncle Peter in the little living room, waiting to receive me.

"Peter," Uncle Oliver will say joyously, including Sandra Williamson in his expansive loving gesture, "here is such a nice child, such a nice child, and I walked up the hill with her, and she has brought you presents."

And then Uncle Peter, who always remembers my name and will take Uncle Oliver aside later and tell him what to call me, will come forward and kiss me on the forehead while Sandra Williamson rubs against my ankles, and Uncle Oliver will pull at my sleeve and point to the packages, winking and giggling, and, with Peter on one side and Oliver on the other, and Sandra Williamson perched on the windowsill above the sofa, I will open the packages.

"Oranges," Uncle Peter will say with pleasure, and he will take one and offer it solemnly to Sandra Williamson, who will touch it with her gray paw.

"Look, Peter, what Sandra Williamson may have for her own, instead of an orange which we will eat ourselves, look at what this dear pretty child has brought Sandra Williamson," Uncle Oliver will say, with the chocolate bone. Peter must offer the bone to Sandra himself, and she will sit cheerfully with it under her paw until Uncle Peter moves to another room and requires her to bring it along.

Finally, when all of us have watched Uncle Oliver's mechanical toy move about the room, crashing into the furniture and even moving out to the front porch to startle the white cats, Uncle Oliver will gather together all the presents except Sandra Williamson's bone and an orange apiece for his and Uncle Peter's dinner, and hide them away in the back of a kitchen cabinet, to be taken out at a less exciting time. Then Uncle Oliver will remove himself to the stove, and dinner, and Uncle Peter will show me his garden, Sandra Williamson following and the white cats moving about under the trees in the dusk.

I do not think that there is any possibility that Uncle Peter and Uncle Oliver and the cats and the cottage will change or go away with time. Every year, when spring has irrevocably asserted itself, I begin to wonder about Uncle Oliver and Uncle Peter, and every year I gather together the fruitcake and the oranges, the toys and the candied cherries, and take the ferry to Sausalito. They are as apt not to be there as San Rafael is apt to have moved to Florida.

Always, during the two or three days I spend with Uncle Peter and Uncle Oliver, some minor domestic crisis arrives, brought on principally by the strain of having company. One year Sandra Williamson was ill from too much company food, one year the strain of baking a chicken pie brought Uncle Oliver into a hysterical temper, and one year Uncle Peter and Uncle Oliver quarreled. That is the visit I remember most clearly; the quarrel first made itself evident at the dinner table the evening of my arrival, and over the tomatoes, or rather the lack of them.

"Don't we always have tomatoes?" Uncle Oliver asked me angrily, indicating the table with the creamed beef on toast and the plain lettuce salad. "Don't we usually have tomatoes when you come?"

"I seem to remember that you do," I said placatingly, "but everything is so delicious . . ."

"We have always had tomatoes up until this year," Uncle Oliver persisted, "and we have always grown them in our own vegetable garden, too. My particular care," he added bitterly in Uncle Peter's direction.

"Possibly something got into the vines this year," I said. "They very often die off just when you expect them to be the best."

"We *would* have had tomatoes this year," Uncle Oliver said.

"I always thought the tomatoes were the least important," Uncle Peter said suddenly. "I prefer the radishes myself, and the squash."

"I notice nothing happened to the apples," Uncle Oliver said pointedly. There was a long moment of silence, and then Uncle Peter excused himself and left the table. Sandra Williamson followed him, and they went out into the garden.

"I think you hurt Uncle Peter's feelings," I said to Oliver.

"I intended to," he answered, staring at his plate. "He has been very wicked, and the tomatoes were mine by rights."

"What could he do to the tomatoes?" I was bewildered. "Surely he isn't directly responsible if the tomato vine doesn't bear tomatoes."

"Ah," said Uncle Oliver. "That is just it. Heaven only knows what the tomato vine *will* bear now. He has been consorting with the devil."

"Surely, Uncle Oliver," I began, "surely you cannot say that just because there are no tomatoes—"

"Ah," said Uncle Oliver, "but in the garden at night, in only his nightshirt, and dancing. And with Sandra Williamson dancing along behind him, the garden at night, and both of them going among the trees and over the vegetable garden. Is it any wonder," he cried out despairingly, "that the tomato vine refuses to bear tomatoes!"

"I should, in its place," I agreed, suppressing the picture of Uncle Peter dancing in his nightshirt.

"The devil has no place in San Rafael, and no business with Peter or with Sandra Williamson, and certainly no traffic with my tomatoes! Perhaps you can put a stop to it?" he asked me.

"What makes you think it's the devil?"

Uncle Oliver waved his hands. "Peter brought him to lunch one day. He smiled at me, his pointed little nose right at me, and said, 'You cook admirably, Oliver Duff,' and I said, 'I'll have no thanks from you, evil sir,' and he smiled at me still."

"Couldn't it be a neighbor?"

"It could not," Uncle Oliver said absolutely, "and I'll thank you not to suggest it."

"I'll speak to Uncle Peter," I said.

"Speak, better, to my tomato vine," Uncle Oliver said sullenly. Uncle Peter was coming in the door, followed by Sandra Williamson. He came over to Oliver and said, "It's been so long since we quarreled. What do we say to each other now?" They both looked at me.

"Uncle Oliver," I instructed, "you will say that you regret being ugly about the tomato vine, and Uncle Peter, you will say that you will make every effort to console Uncle Oliver for its loss."

"Regret ugly," Uncle Oliver muttered to Uncle Peter.

"Make every effort," Uncle Peter said. They smiled at each other.

"Now," I said, "I will go out into the garden with Uncle Peter."

Uncle Peter held the back door open for me, and we went out into the dark garden. The fruit trees were silent in the night, and the vegetable garden lay in heavy masses against the fence. Sandra Williamson preceded us down between the trees to the foot of the garden, where the grass was tall against the fence.

"Is this where he comes?" I asked Uncle Peter.

"To the other side of the fence," Uncle Peter said. "He seldom comes over. He lives in the woods on the hill."

"Are you sure it isn't a neighbor?" I said.

"Quite sure," Uncle Peter answered in surprise. "I have been consorting with the devil."

"Tell me about him."

"He comes down from the hill and stands on the other side of the fence. He came first some weeks ago, and Sandra Williamson saw him and came over to talk to him and I came over, too, and we talked to him."

"What about the tomatoes?"

Uncle Peter shrugged. "He asked me what in the garden I would give him for tribute; he said he would protect the fruit trees and the rest if I gave him something and I said he could have the tomato vine, because Oliver likes tomatoes least. He said that would do splendidly; I didn't know that Oliver would mind."

"Possibly if you talked to him," I said, "and asked him what else he would accept . . ."

"I had thought of giving him the apple tree," Peter said. "He will come later tonight, and I had thought of asking him then."

"Wait," I said. I ran back through the garden and into the house. Uncle Oliver was standing miserably by the sink, washing dishes.

"If you could have the tomatoes back," I said, "would you mind losing the apple tree?"

"The pretty little apples?" Uncle Oliver gasped. "Your uncle Peter likes them boiled with a little cinnamon and just a fragment of a sugar lump."

I thought. "If I were to promise to send you another fruitcake when I got back to town . . ." I suggested. Uncle Oliver sighed, but he dried his hands and opened the cupboard. Carefully he took out the bag with the oranges, the two boxes of candied cherries, the mechanical rabbit, and, finally, the fruitcake.

He looked up at me. "Do you suppose one orange . . . or perhaps two?"

"I think the fruitcake," I said.

He sighed again, and handed me the fruitcake. While he was storing the rest back in the cupboard I hurried out with the fruitcake and down through the garden to Uncle Peter. "Here," I said. "Try this." Uncle Peter brightened.

"Do you suppose it will work?" he asked. "I was thinking about the apple tree. You see, Oliver likes apples, and the white cats eat them."

"Try the fruitcake first," I said.

Uncle Oliver and I sat in the living room until very late, watching the white cats settle to sleep, and Uncle Peter stayed in the garden. When I finally went to bed I glanced out of my window and thought I saw, far down among the trees, a white shape moving and Sandra Williamson capering along behind.

The next morning I woke very early and went into the garden before Peter and Oliver were awake. There was no sign of the fruitcake near the fence, but the white cats were walking about, stretching in the morning and unafraid. When I came in to breakfast there were tomatoes on the table, ripe and red and sitting on a green plate, with Uncle Oliver crowing over them.

"See, how pretty," he said. "Pretty tomatoes. A little boy brought them."

Peter came into the doorway, smiling. "He was so pleased with the fruitcake," he said. "Perhaps next time you come you will bring two?"

All during breakfast Peter and Oliver were smiling at each other, making quick little gestures of friendship. Oliver insisted on my having a tomato with my coffee, and asked if it were not the prettiest I had ever tasted, while Peter sat back and watched admiringly.

Finally, when the dishes had been cleared off, Uncle Oliver sat down beside Peter and they smiled again at each other. "Perhaps soon we will go to the city for a visit," Peter said to me. Neither of them had ever come into the city since they left it to live in San Rafael, and neither of them ever expected to come; it was enough to know that they could if they wanted to. Next to the death of Mrs. Duff, it was their favorite mutual whimsy, and mention of it meant that everything was friendly again between them.

And Oliver took up the conversation from there:

"I remember so clearly the morning she died," he said to me. "Mrs. Duff, in the house here, and so pleasant a morning. And all the white cats one after another going over the fence and away."

"It was over a week before they came back at all," Uncle Peter added, "and then, just over the fence one after another, with never an explanation."

"She had pretty little names for them all," Uncle Oliver said.

"They should all have little leather collars with their names on. You could name them, Oliver, and I would make each one a little leather collar with its name on." Uncle Peter stroked Sandra Williamson's head. "All with little leather collars," he said.

When I left they walked down to the bottom of the hill with me, standing to wave goodbye, with Sandra Williamson sitting behind them, while I went along down the dirt road, carrying my suitcase.

But ever since then, when I go back each spring, I take oranges, the fruitcakes, and three toys, and three boxes of candied cherries, and Oliver puts them all away, some to be given out to himself and Peter in less exciting times, and some to be doled out carefully and exactly over the back fence at the foot of the garden.

PART TWO

ON THE HOUSE

The New Yorker, *October 30, 1943*

ARTIE WATSON SAT ON a folding chair behind the
counter of the liquor store and read his paper. Business was
slow these rainy nights, and Steve, his partner, had run down to the
all-night delicatessen to get some sandwiches and milk. Artie sighed
and reached under the counter for his pencil to do the crossword
puzzle. Might as well close up, he thought. If no one comes in by the
time Steve comes back I'll tell him we ought to close up early and go
home.

A customer came in before Steve came back, a man who came
slowly in through the door, not quickly from the rain, but slowly. It
took Artie a minute to realize that he was blind and another minute
to see the woman following him.

"Evening," Artie said.

"Good evening," the blind man said, and the woman echoed,
"Good evening." She walked over to the rows of bottles against the
wall and walked along, reading the labels. "How about brandy?" she
asked. "That's supposed to be good, isn't it?"

"I want to get bourbon," the blind man said. He turned in Artie's
direction. "Do you have any bourbon?" he asked.

Artie nodded, and then said, "Some. Not as much as we used to
have, of course. Pretty hard to get good liquor these days."

"Really?" the blind man said. "Can you pick me out a nice kind of
bourbon, not too expensive?"

The woman came over to the counter. "I think we ought to get brandy," she said, "but he says bourbon."

"If it's for a party or something," Artie said, "you'd do better with bourbon."

The woman giggled. "We just got married," she said. "That's what it's for."

"Congratulations," Artie said warmly. "Going to have a celebration, then?"

"Man doesn't get married every day," the blind man said. He laughed and reached out for the woman's hand, which she immediately put into his. "I guess I did pretty well, too," he said.

Artie looked at the woman. She was small and dark and wearing a corsage of gardenias. She looked about ten years older than the blind man. "You sure did all right," Artie said. "Looks like she's a good cook, too."

"She's a fine cook," the blind man said. "Aren't you, Rosalie?"

"I'm a pretty good cook," the woman said, "but what about this brandy?" When she spoke to the blind man, her voice was low and lovely, but Artie, looking at her again, figured that she could raise her voice if she wanted. And plenty high, too, he thought.

"You'd do better with the bourbon," Artie said again.

"How do they compare in price?" the blind man asked.

"The brandy's a little more," Artie said. "I can give you a pretty good bourbon for four sixty-two. And the brandy"—he squinted at the bottles across the store—"I guess the cheapest brandy I can give you is four ninety-seven."

"Four sixty-two?" the blind man said.

"Tell you, folks," Artie said. "You're just married and all, I'll let you have either one for, say, four. Sort of a wedding present."

"That's very nice of you," the woman said.

"We may as well get the brandy, then," the blind man said. "Being as this gentleman is giving it to us for the same price."

"Sure," Artie said. He was sorry already that he had offered to lower the price, that he would have to tell Steve when Steve came back, that the blind man had taken the brandy because it was more of a bargain.

"Then we'll take the brandy," the blind man said, "and thanks."

"All right," Artie said. "Many happy returns."

He took the bottle of brandy the woman brought over to him and began to roll it in brown paper. "You'll like this brandy," he said.

"You said four dollars?" the blind man asked. He had taken his wallet out of his pocket and was thumbing over his money. "Four dollars," he said, and held out four bills.

Artie looked down at the bills, and then at the woman, who had gone back across the store and was looking at the bottles on the shelf. "Missus," Artie said.

"What's the matter?" the blind man said. "Here's the money."

The woman came back over and stood next to the blind man and looked at Artie, shaking her head no. Artie looked down at the five-dollar bill and the three one-dollar bills the man was holding out and said, "But, mister, look, you've—"

"What's the matter?" the woman said. "You think he can't tell a one-dollar bill? He knows one bill from another." She shook her head again at Artie.

The blind man laughed. "Don't try any jokes with me," he said. "It doesn't work anymore. I know what money I've got here."

"Right," Artie said. He took the five and the three ones and went to the cash register and rang up four dollars. He put in the five and took out one dollar and brought it back with the three ones. Before he could say anything, the woman held out her hand insistently. The blind man had found the wrapped bottle on the counter and was turning toward the door. Artie put the money in the woman's hand, nodded reassuringly, and said, "Well, folks, hope you'll be very happy. And have a nice celebration."

"Thanks," the blind man said as the woman took his arm and led him to the door. "Good night."

"Good night," Artie said. He was still sore about giving them the brandy at that price.

"Blind man like that has no business drinking liquor," Steve said when Artie told him. "First thing you know he has one too many and loses control of himself and gets in real trouble."

"He probably had to work a long time for that money he tried to give me," Artie said. "A guy like that couldn't earn much, could he?"

"Hard to tell," Steve said. "Might be one of these precision workers who doesn't need to see what he's doing."

"Wonder how come a woman would marry a blind man? I'd hate to be . . ." Artie's voice trailed off as he saw the door open and the blind man come slowly in, followed, after a minute, by the woman.

"Hello again," Artie said. "You back for more brandy?"

The blind man walked up to the counter without assistance, felt for the surface with his free hand, and then put the bottle of brandy, still wrapped, down in front of Artie. "I came for my money," he said.

Artie stared. "Something wrong?" he asked finally. Steve came over and stood next to him.

"Yeah," Steve said, "something wrong?"

"There's plenty wrong," the blind man said. "When people steal from a guy that doesn't know what's going on, there's plenty wrong."

Artie looked at the woman, who was standing in the doorway. "What's the matter with him?"

"Look," the blind man said, "you took plenty advantage because I didn't know, that's all. I thought I was giving you four ones, and you wouldn't say a word, just stood there and took advantage."

"You think you're so smart," the woman said. "A blind man."

"I can get along without your help," the blind man said, turning in the woman's direction. "This guy steals my money, I can take care of him." He turned back to Artie. "You better give me back that money," he said, "or I'll really make you some trouble."

"I gave it to your wife," Artie said, knowing already it was no use.

The woman laughed. "Now he's taking advantage of me," she said.

Artie looked at Steve. He knew Steve was thinking the same thing: a blind man telling the cops he had been robbed. Steve shrugged.

Artie went to the cash register and opened it. "O.K.," he said, "so I robbed you. You gave me three ones and a five and I thought it was four ones."

"That's a little better," the woman said.

Artie took four one-dollar bills out of the cash register and walked over and put them in the blind man's hand. "These four ones?" the blind man asked.

"Four ones," Artie said.

"These four ones?" the blind man asked, turning to the woman. She came forward, peering.

"Yes, they are," she said.

"See," the blind man said, "I got down to the corner and I remembered I had a five and three ones instead of four ones. I guess next time you won't try anything with a guy like me."

"That's right," Artie said, watching the woman come forward and take the blind man's arm. The blind man felt around on the counter for the bottle of brandy and put it under his other arm.

Artie and Steve stood watching them go out, and when the door had closed behind them Artie went over and closed the drawer of the cash register.

LITTLE OLD LADY

IN GREAT NEED

❦

Mademoiselle, *September 1944*

IT WAS LATE IN the afternoon, but even though she was tired from shopping all day, Kitty forced herself to alternate a grave skip with her hurried walk after Great-Grandmother. Great-Grandmother liked to see little girls active, and she herself was as spry now as she had been in the morning when they started out to buy Kitty a new coat. If Kitty lagged behind, Great-Grandmother was apt to stop and, tapping severely with her cane, say to Kitty: "A laggard step, a faltering mind." With so many people on the street, someone was sure to turn and smile when Great-Grandmother said something like that, so Kitty rushed her steps along, sometimes clinging to Great-Grandmother's arm and sometimes getting a little ahead, so that she could slow down a minute until Great-Grandmother caught up.

"I think the plaid coat was very nice on you, Katharine," Great-Grandmother was saying for the thousandth time. "I think you were wise to choose that one instead of the brown."

"Everyone else has a brown coat, though," Kitty said.

"Never try to look like everyone else, my dear," Great-Grandmother said placidly. "It doesn't pay to be like everyone else. Did I ever tell you that I was the first woman—lady, that is—to smoke a cigarette in San Francisco?"

"Grandma! What a cute little dog!" Kitty ran ahead, and stopped to pet the dog while the lady who held it on a leash stood patiently, smiling as Great-Grandmother came slowly toward them. "Grandma," Kitty said. "I wish I had a dog like this, Grandma."

"Never intrude yourself upon a stranger," Great-Grandmother said, bowing slightly to the lady with the dog. "Never intrude yourself on any pretext whatever, Katharine."

Kitty blew a kiss to the dog behind Great-Grandmother's back, and ran to catch up. Great-Grandmother was saying: "A very fine animal, my dear, pedigreed, no doubt. Perhaps we should have a dog, Katharine."

"I would like a white one, like that one," Kitty said. "Did you ever have a dog?"

"We used to have a mastiff when I was a girl in England," Great-Grandmother said. She laughed. "Your great-grandfather bought me a lap dog when we married."

"What happened to those dogs?"

Great-Grandmother laughed again. "I believe the lapdog was given away," she said. "Perhaps the mastiff died. It was long before we came to the United States. Then we were in San Francisco, and I was the first real lady to smoke a cigarette there in public."

"Can I wear my plaid coat to school next week, Grandma?"

"If the weather accommodates, my dear."

"I think it will be cold. If I had a dog like that one I would make him a little red coat and he could wear it when he came to school with me. Can we have dinner in a restaurant tonight, Grandma?"

Great-Grandmother looked at Kitty and hesitated. Then she turned aside and into a doorway, gesturing for Kitty to follow. She handed her packages to Kitty and took out her pocketbook, saying: "A lady never examines her pocketbook nor inquires into the state of her finances in public, Katharine." Great-Grandmother counted the change in her hand, her weak old eyes squinting. "One dollar and thirty-one cents, Katharine. When is our pension check due?"

"It comes on Saturday, Grandma."

"I was afraid so." Great-Grandmother sighed. "We had better plan to stay at home until then, my dear. We will stop and buy something for dinner on our way home, Katharine. What would you like?"

"If I had that dog I would have to get him a bone," Kitty said. "I would like to have a great big roast turkey for dinner."

"We will stop at the butcher's," Great-Grandmother said. "I hope he has something tender. Young meat for old teeth."

The butcher had turkeys and chickens in his window, and ham and frankfurters. Kitty pressed her nose against the glass, saying: "Grandma, he has more things in his window than any other butcher had today."

"Come inside, my dear," Great-Grandmother said. "A lady makes no display of herself on the street."

Inside, the butcher's counter was empty. The butcher, a thin, red-faced man in a bloodied white apron, stood watching Kitty and Great-Grandmother as they entered.

"Not much to offer today, ladies," he said.

"Turkeys?" Kitty said eagerly.

"Well, I got one or two turkeys, fine ones," the butcher said.

"Let me see." Great-Grandmother stood, her fingers at her lips, regarding the empty counter. "How about a steak?"

"No steak," the butcher said.

"Sirloin?" Great-Grandmother asked amiably.

"No steak, lady."

Great-Grandmother looked at him. "Something tender," she said.

"I have some nice franks," the butcher said. "Nice little frying chickens. A few hams."

"Let me see," Great-Grandmother said. "I think I prefer steak."

"No, lady," the butcher said desperately.

Great-Grandmother smiled. "Why do you refuse to sell me meat?" she asked. "Must I take my patronage elsewhere?"

"Lady," the butcher said, "we got shortages. We don't get no meat, we can't sell any. Earlier, you came in, I coulda sold you a fine sirloin. Now—I got nothing left."

"Sir." Great-Grandmother stepped up closer to the counter and gestured the butcher to her. "I am an old lady. My great-granddaughter here could, I have no doubt, tell you exactly how old. I was not bred, sir, for dealing with tradespeople. Until my great-granddaughter and I were left alone in the world, there were always others to take care of business dealings for us. I am not able, therefore, to discuss your business with you, and, equally, I am unable to go from store to store to make purchases."

"Lady," the butcher said unhappily, "would you take one and a half pounds of sirloin?"

Great-Grandmother considered. "I would," she said gravely.

The butcher held up his finger, and turned to go into the ice room. "Wait," he said. He returned after a minute or two with a piece of sirloin steak, which he put on the counter in front of Great-Grandmother. "It's my own piece of meat, and you couldn't ask for a better. My wife told me I should bring home a little meat, and I saved this."

Great-Grandmother drew herself up. "I would not take your food, young man."

"Take it," the butcher said. "I don't want to see you and the kid here without anything for your supper tonight. My wife—she can fix something outta nothing."

"I cannot accept this as a gift, you understand," Great-Grandmother said. "You must let me give you something, at any rate, in exchange for this kindness."

The butcher looked surprised. "But I'll sell—" he began.

"No," Great-Grandmother said. "I cannot permit it. I was brought up a lady, sir, and a lady does not permit herself to accept favors from tradesmen. You must let me give you something, in addition to my ration stamps, even if it is only a few pennies." She took out her pocketbook and searched in it. "Fifty cents," she said, putting the coin with the stamp book on the counter. "You must accept it. It is what I intended to pay for our dinner tonight."

The butcher counted and tore off the stamps, slid the steak into a brown paper bag and handed it silently to Great-Grandmother. "Thank you," she said. "You are a fine man, sir. A gentleman." She moved to the doorway. "Come, Katharine," she said.

"I love steak," Kitty said excitedly.

"One and a half pounds is hardly enough for two," Great-Grandmother said. "Still, he did the best he could."

"He was a nice man," Kitty said.

Great-Grandmother smiled. "It was in the Mark Hopkins Hotel, Katharine, I believe. Did I ever tell you? Perhaps it was another hotel. Perhaps it was a restaurant. At any rate, I had become accustomed to smoking in England, where all ladies had taken it up. And the manager, such a polite man, and so elegant, came to me and said: 'Madam, I must request that you retire to the smoking room if you intend to indulge.' Of course your great-grandfather would never permit that; it was a men's smoking room. Then, of course, American ladies took up smoking. But I was the first in San Francisco."

"I bet that man's wife's going to be mad," Kitty said, "not bringing home any meat."

"Nonsense," Great-Grandmother said. "He'll tell her, that's all.

He'll say that a child and a little old lady with a cane came in and he'll tell her he had to give it to us."

"I bet his wife'll be mad anyway."

"A lady does not permit herself to show anger in public," Great-Grandmother said.

When Things
Get Dark

The New Yorker, *December 30, 1944*

Mrs. Garden was sitting in the overstuffed chair in her furnished room, smoking. She was a young woman, not more than twenty-three or four. She was small and thin and she was wearing a light blue corduroy housecoat and had her hair in curlers. It was eleven in the morning. She was finishing her third cup of coffee from the pot on the electric plate. Beside her on the small table was a letter. When she put her cup down, she took up the single sheet of ruled letter paper and read it again. "Dear Mrs. Garden," it said, "I can't help feeling that right now you are in need of a friend. You seemed to be so strong and courageous when I met you, in spite of your great trouble, that I am sure your young heart will be equal to any burden. When things get dark, remember there are always friends thinking of you and wishing you well." The letter was signed "A.H." After a minute Mrs. Garden put it down on the table and went over to the dresser. She took her pocketbook out of it and, rummaging through it, found a match folder. On the inside of the folder was written "Mrs. Amelia Hope, 111 Mortimer Street, Brooklyn Hgts."

Mrs. Garden stood in front of the dresser for a minute, looking at herself in the glass. I won't show at all for a while, she thought. No one would know unless I told them. She turned, holding her arms high, to look at herself in profile. After a minute she walked across the room and got the letter and put it and the match folder in her pocketbook. She went to the closet and took down a dark blue suit and a white blouse, thinking, My clothes still fit me—all the nice things I bought and won't be able to wear. She dressed carefully, pinning the tiny infantry insignia to her lapel, and took a dark blue hat out of the closet. When she was dressed she glanced around the room before she locked the door. She looked quiet and decent and worried. Out in the hall, she put the key in her pocketbook and went down the stairs.

All the way in the subway, Mrs. Garden held the pocketbook quietly in her lap, looking out the windows into the darkness. When she reached the station where the subway guard had told her to get off, she got up and went out into the street, where she went to a newsstand and asked the way to the address. Then, still holding her pocketbook close to her, she walked to 111 Mortimer Street. It was an old house, clearly a rooming house, and it looked ugly and decayed. Mrs. Garden went up the steps and rang the bell. When the landlady opened the door, Mrs. Garden said, "I want to see Mrs. Amelia Hope, please."

The landlady stood back and said, "Second floor, in the back."

Mrs. Garden went up the wide staircase, the sort of staircase you would find in an old, beautiful house, to a second floor with a high-ceilinged hall and white plaster ornamental molding. There was one door toward the back, at the end of the long hall, and Mrs. Garden knocked on it.

"Come in, please," an old lady's voice said. Mrs. Garden opened the door and stood just inside. For a minute it was hard for her to see, because she was facing a high, narrow window with long brown drapes down each side of it. Then she saw a small, old-fashioned desk with carved spindle legs in front of the window, and Mrs. Hope sitting at it.

"I'm Mrs. Garden. Do you remember me?"

Mrs. Hope rose and came a step or two forward. "Mrs. Garden?" she said.

Mrs. Garden opened her pocketbook and took out the letter. She held it out to Mrs. Hope and said, "I wanted to ask you about this."

Mrs. Hope looked at the letter and then at Mrs. Garden. "Won't you sit down?" she said. She gestured at a little gilt chair near the desk. "You find me in a good deal of confusion," she said. "It seems that they clean my room later each day. You know," she said, leaning forward to touch Mrs. Garden on the knee, "I pay a small sum extra each week to have my room cleaned *well*—really well, you know—

and I think I'm going to have to speak to them about it. They don't do it at all as they should."

Mrs. Garden looked around. The narrow bed in one corner looked, at first, hardly disturbed, and then she saw that it had not been made up yet that morning. A cup with a tea bag in the saucer sat on the desk, and beside it a pad of ruled writing paper, like the paper Mrs. Garden's letter was written on.

"I hope I didn't interrupt you at anything," Mrs. Garden said.

"Indeed not," Mrs. Hope said. She stood up and Mrs. Garden realized that she was incredibly small. She was wearing a plain black dress with a red belt, and around her neck was a long rope of aromatic cedar beads. "Will you have some candy?" she asked. She went over to the table by her bed and brought back a small glass dish of candy corn, which she set on the desk where Mrs. Garden could reach it. "I was just writing my letters," she said.

"It's funny," Mrs. Garden said. "I never expected to meet you again."

"I'm sure I know you," Mrs. Hope said, "but I can't quite remember where we met." She was leaning forward, pleased and attentive.

Mrs. Garden looked up, surprised. "Why, on the bus. You were so nice to me."

Mrs. Hope glanced down at the letter on the desk. "Certainly I remember now," she said. "You're the young lady with the child."

"No," Mrs. Garden said. "My husband had just left to be sent overseas. Mrs. Hope, I need advice very badly."

"It wasn't a child, come to think of it," Mrs. Hope said. "It was a sick mother. We women are terrible when we're sick."

"I thought maybe when I got your letter," Mrs. Garden said awkwardly, "I thought I might come in and talk to you. We haven't been married very long, Jim and I, and now when he comes back we're going to be saddled with a baby, and instead of starting out again together and going dancing and having a good time together, we're going to have responsibilities and everything. And I thought maybe you could tell me something to do."

"Of course you did," Mrs. Hope said. "I meet so many people," she added, looking down at the desk. "I don't think anyone has ever come to see me before, though."

"They say, 'Gain one, lose one,'" Mrs. Garden said. "I don't know what I'd do if anything happened to Jim."

"Love is a very important thing," Mrs. Hope said.

"I haven't even told him yet," Mrs. Garden went on. "Every time I write him I mean to put it in, about the baby, and then I think how awful he'll feel."

Mrs. Hope leaned back in her chair and picked up the string of beads. "My dear," she said, "you would really be surprised how much trouble there is in the world. If I can do anything to make the skies brighter for any of the poor people I meet, I have served my purpose in life."

"I thought you might just give me some advice," Mrs. Garden said. "You were so kind that day, and I'm afraid I don't know anyone else. Not in New York, anyway, and I wanted to talk to someone."

"And my little note comforted you?" Mrs. Hope said. She smiled wistfully. "This is the first time I have been allowed to see that I am doing some good. I talk to people everywhere and ask them for their names and addresses, and then when I feel that they need a friendly word, I send them a little note telling them to be of good heart."

"I know," Mrs. Garden said. "You told me, that day on the bus."

"On buses and everywhere," Mrs. Hope said. "I meet people wherever I go."

"But you can help me," Mrs. Garden said, "can't you?"

Mrs. Hope smiled and put her hand on Mrs. Garden's. "Let me show you," she said. She got up again and went over to the table by the bed. From a drawer in it she took a big scrapbook. "I make copies of all my letters," she said, "so I can send more to the same people if I think they need it." She handed the big book to Mrs. Garden. Then she took the desk chair and brought it over. "Wait till you see," she said, taking half of the book in her lap. On the first page a slip of paper was pasted with "A word to the wise is sufficient" written on it in Mrs. Hope's careful hand. "Here is my first letter—to a boy who wanted to change his job," she said. "See, here, I tell him to be careful in his decision."

"Don't think I'm the type of person who's always complaining," Mrs. Garden said, turning to look at Mrs. Hope. "But we had so many plans for our life together."

"This is odd," Mrs. Hope said, turning the page. "You ought to look at this one. Here was a girl with your same situation. Let me see, what did I say to her?" She leaned forward to read the letter.

"I write to him every other day," Mrs. Garden said, "and I have to write today. I want to have my mind made up."

"Of course you do," Mrs. Hope said. "This is one I wrote to Mr. Adolf Hitler. When he first started killing and rampaging, that was.

I said for him to look into his heart and find love." She touched the letter pasted on the page. "I don't very often write like that, but some people are so much in need of a thoughtful word."

Mrs. Garden's lips trembled and she put her hand up to her mouth. "I suppose everyone gets desperate sometimes," she said.

"Everyone does, my dear." Mrs. Hope waited a minute, then closed the scrapbook and went over and put it carefully away in the drawer. "You haven't eaten any candy," she said. She took the plate and passed it to Mrs. Garden, who shook her head. "I wish I could ask you to stay for lunch," Mrs. Hope said, "but I only have a sandwich and a cup of tea here in my room."

"I just had breakfast," Mrs. Garden said. She stood up and picked up her pocketbook. "It's been very nice," she said.

"I've enjoyed seeing you again," Mrs. Hope said. "Maybe we'll meet again on a bus sometime."

"I hope so," Mrs. Garden said. She went toward the door.

Mrs. Hope followed her. "I can't tell you how comforting it's been," she said, "knowing how much good my little letters bring."

Mrs. Garden opened the door. "I'm sure they do," she said. "Well, goodbye."

"Wait a minute," Mrs. Hope said. She ran over, picked up Mrs. Garden's letter from the desk, and brought it to her. "You don't want to forget this," she said. "Keep it near you, to read when things get dark. Goodbye, my dear." She stood courteously by the door until Mrs. Garden closed it behind her.

Outside the door, Mrs. Garden waited a minute, fumbling in her pocketbook for her gloves. She heard Mrs. Hope cross the room, humming softly. Then there was the movement of a chair across the floor. Straightening the room, Mrs. Garden thought, pulling on a glove absentmindedly. She heard the click of the cedar beads brushing against something; probably the desk. There was silence for a minute; then Mrs. Garden heard the faint scratching of Mrs. Hope's pen. With only one glove on and her pocketbook flying wildly behind her, Mrs. Garden turned and ran down the stairs and out into the warm noon sun.

WHISTLER'S

GRANDMOTHER

✵

The New Yorker, *May 5, 1945*

THE LITTLE OLD LADY on the train obviously wanted to talk. She had got on at Albany and she was sitting in the seat next to the aisle. She looked rather charming, in a neat black coat and an old lady's hat, and she watched the woman next to her, who was reading a mystery, smiled at the children who constantly hurried up and down the aisle of the crowded car, and looked affectionately at the two sailors in the seat across the aisle.

At last she turned to the woman beside her and said, "I'm sorry to interrupt you, but how soon do we get to New York?"

The younger woman smiled politely. "At six o'clock, I think."

"Thank you," the old lady said. "I can hardly wait. I haven't been to New York in nearly fifteen years."

"It must be exciting."

"I'm going to see my grandson," the old lady said. "He's home on leave."

The younger woman hesitated, then closed her book and leaned back. "Really?" she said. "Where has he been?"

The old lady waved her hand vaguely. "In the Pacific."

"How wonderful," the younger woman said. "You'll certainly be glad to see him."

"I'm all the family he has left."

"I guess he'll be glad to see you, too," the younger woman said.

"Let me show you his picture." The old lady opened her pocketbook and took out a folding cardboard picture frame, with spaces for two pictures facing one another. One side had the picture of a soldier standing in front of a barracks; he looked very young. On the other side was the same soldier in front of the same barracks, but he had his arm around a pretty girl in a flowered dress. "He's very handsome," the younger woman said. "Is this his wife?"

The man in the seat in front of them, who looked as if he might be a prosperous businessman, was half listening. He had on a light gray suit. The paper he had been reading sagged in his hands. The old lady leaned forward and touched his shoulder. The man turned around. "Let me show you a picture of my grandson," she said. "He's coming home on furlough."

The man took the picture and nodded solemnly. "Fine-looking young man."

"It's the first time he's been near home in two years," the old lady said. "He couldn't come upstate to me, so I'm going to New York to him."

"I've got two sons in the army," the man said. "Sure glad to see those rascals when they come home."

"Are they in the Pacific?" the old lady asked.

"In Mississippi. Both together, so far. They enlisted together."

"How proud you must have been," she said.

The old lady turned to the two sailors across the aisle. "I haven't been to New York in fifteen years," she said, leaning forward and raising her voice. "And now I'm going to meet my grandson. He's on a furlough."

When she held out the picture the two sailors rose and came across the aisle to look at it. "Are you on *your* way home?" the old lady asked them.

"No, ma'am," one of the sailors said, "we're on our way back."

"Pretty lively time the last few days?" the man in the gray suit asked.

The sailors laughed, and the old lady said quickly, "I hope my grandson is cheerful like you boys. It's been pretty hard for him."

There was a silence, and then the man said reverently, "Guess they've all had a tough time, those boys."

"This your grandson's wife?" one of the sailors asked, passing the picture back to the old lady. "Mighty pretty girl."

"Depend on a sailor to notice a thing like that," the man said, and he and the sailors laughed again.

"That's his wife, all right," the old lady said with a trace of bitterness in her voice.

"She looks like a very nice girl," the younger woman said.

"Very nice girl," the old lady repeated scornfully. She leaned over and tapped the younger woman's arm. "The way that girl's been acting!" Her voice trembled slightly. "She hasn't been fair to my grandson when he was fighting overseas."

"That's not very nice of her," one of the sailors said.

"Coming up to visit me," the old lady said, "with her fur coat and her indecent shoes. Talking all the time about how dead it was up where I live."

"Where does she live?" the man in the gray suit asked.

"She lives in New York. My grandson, now, he has to stay in New York when he comes back."

"Maybe you're mistaken about her," the younger woman said. "It's so easy to make a mistake about people."

"True is true," the old lady said. "My grandson's wife, she stayed with me awhile upstate. She used to get letters from men."

The younger woman started to say something and then stopped, and the man said, "How do you know?"

"Don't you think I can tell a man's handwriting when I see it?" the old lady asked. "I know when a woman like that, with her clothes and the way she talked, when she gets letters every day they're from men. It's time my grandson heard."

"You mean you're going to tell him?" the man said. The sailors looked at the old lady, and the younger woman stared at her book.

"You wouldn't want to do a thing like that," one of the sailors said.

The old lady nodded emphatically. "All the way to New York," she said, "to see she gets what's coming to her."

"Maybe you're being too hard on her," the man said. "Maybe she can explain everything."

"True is true," the old lady repeated. "I don't have to listen to anything *she* has to say."

"Is your grandson's wife meeting you at the train?" the younger woman asked.

"She didn't even ask me down to see my grandson," the old lady replied. "She doesn't know I'm coming, anyway."

"Listen," the younger woman said, "why don't you sit down with her and have a long talk about the whole thing? Maybe you could clear it all up without saying anything to your grandson."

"I'm not making a long trip like this to listen to her stories," the old woman said.

"You ought to give that girl a chance to speak up for herself," the man said.

"It's not that we don't think you're doing right," one of the sailors said. "It's just that it seems sort of hard on everybody, him coming home after so long."

"I'll thank none of you to interfere," the old lady said. "I can take care of my own affairs."

After a minute the sailors slipped quietly back to their seat and the man returned to his paper. The younger woman said softly to the old lady, "You know, you're not being very charitable."

"I asked her to stay on and live with me in my own house," the old lady said, "and she told me no, right to my face."

The younger woman waited for a minute and then went back to her book.

When the train plunged into the tunnel to Grand Central, the old lady gathered her packages together, ready to get off. The younger woman stepped out into the aisle to put on her coat and found herself standing between the sailors and the man in the gray suit. When the old lady rose, she dropped one of her bundles and the man picked it up and handed it to her. She took it carefully and slipped her hand through the string around it. "It's homemade doughnuts," she said, smiling at them amiably, "for my grandson."

"I hope you have a pleasant visit," the younger woman said when the train came to a stop.

"Thank you," the old lady said. "Will you excuse me, please?"

As the younger woman stepped back, she realized that for a moment she and the sailors and the man had been standing in front of the old lady, as though trying to block her way.

She followed the old lady out of the car, and had a brief picture of the sweet, grandmotherly old face as it turned to look at the people on the platform. Then the fragile black figure disappeared into the crowd.

FAMILY MAGICIAN

☞

Woman's Home Companion,
September 1949

NATURALLY I REMEMBER THE summer Mallie was with us. That was the time I got to be captain of the Crocodile team and we beat the Nine-Man Wonders from Acacia Street. It was only three summers ago and we had moved to town the first of that year, so we were still pretty new. Mother was working herself nearly crazy trying to make the house and everything go smoothly for us kids. While Dad was alive she'd had a maid, but doing her own housework again was too much for her, I guess. And Dottie didn't help much. She'd left forty or fifty boyfriends back in the town we moved away from, and when she wasn't writing them letters she was upstairs bawling over their pictures, and worrying Mother about how they didn't write. And I hadn't got my pitching arm limbered up and the fellows around weren't sure they'd even let me on the team. So there we were.

Anyway, one Saturday morning about the middle of May—it was a month or so before summer vacation started, too early for swimming and the fishing not much good—I came in from the backyard and there was a little old woman sitting in the kitchen. She was round and she had a pink face and she smiled up at me when I came in.

I said, "Hi," just to be polite.

There was a row of what looked like cherry pies on the table, something smelled good on the stove, and the table was set, so I sort of smiled back at her and said, "When's lunch?"

I found out later that the smile I thought she had on just for me was permanent—she never stopped smiling, far as I knew. She said, "Sit right down, son. You're Jerry, aren't you?"

"Yes," I said. I sat down in my place and she got up and took my plate and brought it back from the stove filled with a kind of stew that tasted fine.

"This is good," I said. "Is that pie?"

"Cherry pie," she said. "How many can you eat?"

"Two," I said. Just then Mother and Dottie came into the kitchen. Mother looked even more worried than usual and Dottie looked as though she had been crying again.

"What's the matter?" I asked Dottie, still being polite. "No letter from Dickie again today?"

"How *can* you?" Dottie said. All the time in those days when she talked to me she would raise her eyes and sigh, as though I were getting to be too much for her to bear.

Mother looked at me and at the strange little woman and said, "Dorothy, sit down and eat your lunch."

"It's pretty good," I said. When the little woman brought Mother's plate she said, "Now, Mrs. Livingston, I got everything for today figured out. You run along downtown this afternoon and go to a movie, maybe, or do some shopping. I do like to see a boy eat," and she pulled my hair when she went around to get Dottie's plate.

"I can't eat a thing, thank you very much," Dottie said. She sighed and looked out the window. "I'm really not hungry at all, thank you very much."

"Nonsense," the little woman said, which is just what I was thinking. She filled Dottie's plate and after a minute, when no one seemed to be looking, Dottie took a tiny taste. Pretty soon she was eating as well as I was.

"How about some pie, pal?" I said to the little woman, and Mother said, "Really, Jerry!" like she always does, but the little woman said, "You call me Mallie, son, and keep a civil tongue in your head, you hear?" and she laughed and I laughed and the pie was swell.

"Reason I want you to run along early this afternoon," Mallie said to Mother, "Jerry here has a practice game on."

"Baseball team," I explained.

"And Missy here," Mallie said, waving at Dottie, "she's going to have company."

"Me?" Dottie said. She looked up with a forkful of stew halfway to her mouth. "Really, I can't imagine . . ."

Mallie winked at me. "You think I give away secrets?" she said. "If I told you who he is, you wouldn't be surprised."

"He?" Dottie said. She put her fork down.

"He?" I said in a squeaky voice. "You don't want to see any boys, Dottie. You run along to the movies and Mallie can send him home again when he comes."

Dottie started to fold her napkin but Mallie said, "You have plenty of time, Missy. He can't get here before three. You run upstairs and get your blue linen dress and I'll iron it for you. And *you* get along," she said to me, and gave me a swift spank as I reached over to pick up my mitt. She was pretty fresh, all this spanking and hair pulling and stuff, but I figured that was mighty good pie and I gave her a poke in the ribs as I went by and all the way out of the yard I could hear her laughing and Mother saying, "Jerry, really!"

Anyway, I got home about five. A couple of the fellows on the team were walking along with me and when we got to my house Mallie stuck her head out of the kitchen window and called us. She told us to be ready to catch, and started throwing fresh hot dough-nuts out of the window. I made a neat high catch on the first one, and while we sat on the fence eating, they said they thought I ought to be on the team, a substitute at first, of course, but on the team anyway.

After a while I went inside. Mother had just come home and Dottie was following her upstairs saying, "And it's the biggest dance of the year and I *can't* wear that old white . . ."

"Listen to her," I told Mallie.

"You keep your mouth still," she said to me. "All I want *you* to do is run right out in the yard and catch me a ladybug."

"What?" I said, gawking at her.

"A ladybug," Mallie said. "You just lift your big feet and march out in that yard and catch me a ladybug."

"A ladybug?" I said, and she aimed a wallop at me that would have knocked me through the wall if she hadn't pulled it short. I ran but I put my head through the back door and said, "A ladybug?" and she said, "And some dandelions, if you can find any."

I figured she was crazy but I hunted around until I found a couple of dandelions. One of them had a ladybug on it so I took them both in to Mallie and she said, "Fine. Now get me the box of starch in the pantry and if you see any wax bring it along."

By this time I knew she was crazy. When I came back with the starch and a bottle of floor wax, Dottie and my mother were standing in the kitchen and Mallie was saying, "So we can fix up a party dress in no time."

"But how?" Mother asked. Dottie was still all dressed up from the afternoon and every time anyone looked at her she giggled.

"I'm going to the spring dance," she told me with a sweet smile. "Robert Dennison came by this afternoon and asked me to go."

"He must be crazy," I said.

I sat on the kitchen table and watched while Mallie sent Dottie upstairs for a bed sheet and Mother into the attic to dig out the blue taffeta curtains we had in the living room of our other house. While they were gone I asked Mallie, "Are you going to make a dress for Dottie?"

"That's right," she said. She had the starch and the wax and the dandelions and the ladybug on the table next to me and she was looking at them, figuring them out.

"Out of this stuff?" I said. "How?"

"Like making a pie," she explained. "You just get all the things it's made of and then you stir them together right."

Dottie came back with the bed sheet as Mother came in with the curtains.

"*Now* then," Mallie said. She made Dottie take off her dress and stand there in her slip. Then she took the bed sheet and draped it around Dottie's waist, so that it made a sort of skirt down to the floor in all directions. Not *much* like a skirt, though—it looked a lot like a sheet. Dottie stood there looking at Mother as though she didn't know what to do. Mother was worried, too, and finally she said, "Really, Mallie, it's not necessary—we can probably afford a new dress for Dorothy."

"You just stop worrying," Mallie said. "We can't buy Dottie a dress and still have new slipcovers in the living room and that furniture looks pretty shabby. You leave things to me." She took the curtains and fastened them around Dottie, so that soon all of them except one made an overskirt over the sheet, and the one left she pulled around Dottie's shoulders to make a top for the dress. "There now," she said. She stood back and stared at Dottie and poor Dottie certainly looked silly. She looked as if she were dressed up for Halloween. But she stood there, being a good sport the way she can, sometimes, and Mother and I just watched.

Mallie took the dandelions and fastened them on the neck of the dress. She sprinkled some of the floor wax on the skirt and a little starch on the bed sheet underneath that was like a petticoat. Finally she set the ladybug carefully on the bed sheet. Then she stood back and smiled and said, "You'll look real nice in that."

Mother couldn't stand it any longer. She said, "Oh, *Mallie,*" and almost cried. And I thought it was pretty mean to take a girl who wanted a new dress and pin her up in curtains and then say she looked nice.

"My chicken in the oven!" Mallie said suddenly, and opened the oven door. "Thank goodness," she said, lifting it out. "Missy, you take off all that stuff and get ready for dinner."

Well, Mother just looked at Dottie and me hard, meaning we weren't to say anything more, and Dottie got out of the curtains and sheets as fast as she could and we sat down to dinner. Even though the chicken was fine, we didn't eat very much—we were all watching Mallie, who went along with her affairs singing to herself as though she had forgotten all about Dottie's dress.

Mallie went home after dinner without saying any more about the dress. When we were sitting in the living room Mother said to Dottie, "Dear, please don't worry about the dress. I think Mallie really thought she was helping, making a joke, perhaps."

"Where did she come from?" I asked. "I just walked in at lunchtime and there she was."

"That's about the way she came," Mother said. "I was waxing the living room floor this morning and I turned around and saw Mallie standing there in the doorway watching me. I was scared for a minute, but she *does* look harmless."

I thought of Mallie's round pink face and laughed.

"Anyway," Mother said, "she wouldn't answer any questions, but just said she had come to help. And she took the mop away from me. Have you noticed," Mother asked, "that when Mallie says to do something you *do* it, without asking any questions?"

"Golly," I said, thinking about the ladybug.

"*Honestly,*" Dottie said, "I couldn't even *move* to take off that stuff she kept putting on me. *Honestly,* I was *shaking.*"

"She's a good cook, though," I put in.

"She seems to be a very kind and generous person," Mother said. "It's so hard to get anyone to help around a house these days that even if she is a bit eccentric . . ."

"It seems to me," I said very thoughtfully, "that if Mallie has decided to keep on coming to help us, we can't stop her. Not if she's made up her mind, that is."

"Stop her?" Dottie said. "Not likely."

"What troubles me," Mother said slowly, "is how she made those pies we had for lunch. When she came in and took the mop away from me I went upstairs to tell Dottie about her and it was only about fifteen minutes later that she called us down for lunch."

"And there were the pies," Dottie said.

"I'm not worrying about where they came from," I said, "just as long as there are some more."

Well, that was the situation when we went to bed that night. The next day was Sunday. About eight o'clock in the morning the doorbell rang and I answered it. It was a big box, special delivery, for Dottie, so I left it outside her door and went back to bed. Dottie woke me up about an hour later. I could hear Mother saying, "Good heavens," over and over again. Dottie had opened the box and found a dress. It gave me a jolt when I saw it—it was a dress with a blue taffeta skirt and top, and around the neck were little gold buttons like dandelions, and under the skirt was a stiff white ruffled petticoat. And what really took my breath away was that all over the white petticoat were printed thousands of little red ladybugs.

Well, Dottie put it on and it looked pretty good, for a dress, and we all went tearing down to the kitchen. Dottie ran up and kissed Mallie. While Dottie and Mother were both talking at once and poking and pulling at the dress I asked Mallie, "How'd you do it?"

"Magic," she said, and winked at me.

That was the only answer she'd give, no matter what we asked her about the dress. That was the only answer we *ever* got. There was no question about Mallie herself, though. She came back every day and about twice a week she made doughnuts and at least once a week she made pies—sometimes cherry, sometimes lemon meringue, sometimes apple. Dottie went off to her dance in her new dress and woke everybody up trying to tiptoe upstairs when she came in. And then she kept me awake all night, sitting on the foot of Mother's bed in the next room, the two of them giggling like dopes.

I got on the team that week, first as a substitute, and then the Hammond boy moved away and I got a chance at being regular pitcher. After a while Mallie started making Mother have breakfast in bed, and the house began filling up weekends with Dottie's boy-friends, and twice they finished all the pie.

Somehow Mallie did everything so fast that it seemed as though she could straighten a room just by standing in the doorway and looking around hard. She used to get the dishes done so fast, Dottie and I never had time to get in and help her. I used to ask her how she did it, even after Mother and Dottie got tired of asking questions that were never answered, but Mallie only laughed at me and said, "Magic."

I think it *was* magic, too. Sometimes I'd bring the team home with me—there were about fifteen of us, counting substitutes—and we'd sneak over the fence as quietly as we could and tiptoe up to the back porch and by the time we got there Mallie would have lemonade and cookies ready for us, even if she'd been somewhere in the front of the house all the time and couldn't have seen us.

Once Dottie, who had turned sweet-tempered and polite all of a sudden, came out into the kitchen and said, "I wish you'd teach *me* some of that magic, Mallie."

Mallie was making a salad but she looked at Dottie and said, "What do you need magic for, Missy? You're doing all right without any."

"*You* know," Dottie said. She sat down at the table next to me and Mallie just went on making the salad around us. "Look at all you can do—making dresses and doing housework without lifting a finger, and all that."

"I only do work fast so's I'll have more time to do other things," Mallie said. "Like trying to get dinner with two good-for-nothing lazy kids sitting smack in the middle of my salad. I'm real busy and busy people don't have time for everything they want to do. So I make time."

"That's it," Dottie said. "I'm real busy, too. I want to learn some magic."

Mallie laughed. "Tell you what I'll do, honey. I'll teach you how to make a pie. That's all the magic *you'll* ever need."

And golly if she didn't teach Dottie right then and there how to make a pie; just pushed the salad off to one side and went to work. I could have laughed myself silly watching Dottie. It was the first time she had cooked anything in her life, I guess, and Mallie stood over her and really made her learn. It was a pretty good pie, too—apple. And after that Mallie taught Dottie a lot of other things—and she told Dottie over and over again, "That's all the magic *you'll* ever need."

. . .

Then again, about a month later, when it was only a couple of days to the end of school and the weather was already hot, I came home from swimming with the fellows to find Mother out in the kitchen with a telegram. She was saying anxiously to Mallie, "It's just *got* to be nice, that's all. If we'd only known in time . . ."

It seems that the telegram had been misdirected and had reached Mother at five in the afternoon instead of in the morning as it should. It wouldn't have done much good to know earlier anyway, because it was Sunday and we still wouldn't have been prepared. The telegram said that Uncle Ralph and Aunt Gertrude were coming that evening on the six o'clock train and would stay over till Monday. They were an aunt and uncle of my dad's and everyone tried to be nice to them because they were always nice to everybody in spite of being sort of fussy. Mother wanted to have a fancy dinner for them but all the stores were closed for Sunday. Mallie was thinking hard and Mother went on. "It means dinner tonight and fixing up the guest room and I don't know *what* else."

"Things will be all right," Mallie said. "No use worrying."

"Isn't there some grocery open?" Mother said. "Jerry could run out and get *some*thing."

"There's Spencer's," I said. "I could get there and back in time but he doesn't have much."

"Just let me think," Mallie said. Mother and I were both quiet while Mallie sat and figured. "I'll tell you," she said at last. "You just give me a little time. It ought to take you a good fifteen minutes to get to the station and another fifteen back. There's a half hour. Then you sit your aunt and uncle down in the living room and give them a glass of that sherry we have in the pantry. That ought to make it about seven. If I can't do anything by then we might's well give up."

"I'll go to Spencer's—" I suggested again, but she waved her hand at me.

"I can manage, thanks, son," she said. "I just remembered that hat of yours, Mrs. Livingston, the one with the birds. I don't like hats trimmed with birds but I guess I can stand it for once. You bring that right downstairs and, Jerry, you run and get me a handful of down out of a pillow and swipe your sister's cotton dress with the pattern of cherries on it. Now, hurry."

Well, I sneaked the dress out of Dottie's closet and ripped open a pillow and got a handful of the stuffing, and tore down to the kitchen with it. Mother had brought in her hat with the two birds on it. It looked funny there on the kitchen table with the pillow down and Dottie's dress.

"Get me some gravel," Mallie said, and I brought her a handful from the driveway. So there they were—dress, hat, down, and gravel. I looked at her sort of cross-eyed and she said, "You march upstairs and change to some decent clothes. Thank goodness you've been swimming today—at least you're clean."

Dottie came in just as Mother and I were ready to go to the station, so we all three piled into a taxi and went to meet Uncle Ralph and Aunt Gertrude. And I was glad I had changed my shirt because they brought me a football and they brought some fancy girl's stuff for Dottie, and Aunt Gertrude had embroidered an apron for Mother.

We sat in the living room and they had sherry until Mallie said dinner was ready. Mother sat at the head of the table and tried to look serious while we were eating, but she kept starting to laugh and so did I and it made everything cheerful. Because we had broiled squab with a cherry sauce, and once when Mother meant to tell me I was listening too much instead of eating, she slipped and said, "Jerry, eat your hat." That made me choke and then all I could do was pass her the dish of wild rice and say very solemnly, "Have some gravel, Mother?"

We also had lettuce and tomato salad. When Mallie passed it I whispered to her, "Where did you get *this*?" and she said, "I picked it in the garden," which shut *me* up.

And when Mallie brought the dessert I thought for a minute it was the down from the pillow but it turned out to be baked Alaska. Uncle Ralph stood up and bowed to Mallie at the end of dinner and said it was the finest meal he had ever tasted.

After dinner we sat around and talked for a while and then we all took Uncle Ralph and Aunt Gertrude up to the guest room. Mallie had done one of her fastest jobs on the room, and it was as neat and clean as anything you ever saw. There were fresh curtains, which looked suspiciously like the veil from Mother's hat, and a big bunch of flowers in a bowl. I was the only one who noticed how much they looked like the flowers on the wallpaper in my room, although Aunt Gertrude asked what kind they were and no one knew. I said something to Mallie about it the next day and she laughed and took a swing at me, which I ducked, as usual.

Things went on like that all summer. Dottie started wearing a college fraternity pin but she gave it back before high school opened. Mother had something done to her hair and bought a lot of new clothes. And, as I said, I got to be captain of the team and a pretty good pitcher after all. And then one day while we were all having lunch together in the kitchen Mallie said, "Mrs. Livingston, I've got to be thinking about leaving one of these days."

We all tried to argue with her but no one could convince her. All I could say, finally, was "Will you come back and see us sometime?" and she said, "Not unless you need me for something." Then she winked the way she always did and said, "But you'll be hearing from me sooner or later."

She wouldn't say where she was going, or why, but she did say that she was getting old. She looked about sixty then, but she said she was really old.

"I find these days," she said to Mother, "that instead of going upstairs to make the beds, I'd rather just sit in the kitchen and *wish* them done. And that's not good." She shook her head. "I've got to get off by myself and think myself younger."

"You can make yourself *younger*?" Mother said real fast, but Mallie just laughed and said, "Only by thinking so, Mrs. Livingston. *You* wouldn't be happy any younger than you are, not with two grown children. And you'd be surprised what's coming along for you."

Mallie added that she would go in a week and then Dottie, who was, as I say, getting politer but not any smarter, said, "Listen, Dopey, before Mallie goes, why don't you ask her to do something for that football team of yours?"

"Baseball, fathead," I said.

"Get her to fix it for you," Dottie said, "so you'll win all the time."

Well, *there* was a silly idea. Trust a girl to think of it. "Listen," I told her very slowly and clearly so she could understand, "with me pitching, magic is *not* necessary."

Mallie winked at me and pulled my hair. "Can't use magic on boys, anyway," she said. "Just wears away on their tough hides."

Well, she left the next week and then school started again and summer ended. After a while we sort of stopped talking about Mallie, because so much was happening all the time. I used to think about her sometimes during baseball season or when I was eating a cherry pie that didn't have much taste, and once in a while Mother would say how much she missed Mallie's being so cheerful around the house. Then when Dottie was packing to go away to college she took out the blue dress with the dandelions on it and tried it on once more before she put it in her trunk.

"This was always one of my favorite dresses," she said, looking dreamy. "I wore it to the spring dance with that boy—remember him?" she asked Mother and Mother nodded.

"You know," Mother said slowly, looking at Dottie, "that dress is just as fresh now as it was when it came. I don't believe it's ever going to wear out."

"It's magic," Dottie said. "I wore it to the spring dance and to the country club dance last summer and then the senior ball and I guess dozens of other times."

"Remember dinner with Uncle Ralph and Aunt Gertrude?" I said. "Remember the gravel?"

"And my hat!" Mother said. We all laughed.

"I'll never forget Dottie standing there all hung with curtains," I said.

"Or your face when you saw the dress," Dottie said. "Everyone asks me where I got it."

"I guess Mallie ought to be a family secret," Mother said. "Imagine trying to tell people that your dress—and that dinner—and the housework—and—"

"Dottie's cooking," I said.

"And Jerry's ball team," Dottie said.

"No!" I put in, but Mother went on quickly, "Anyway, imagine trying to tell anyone all of that was *magic*."

"Well," I said, "magic or no magic, she was sure some cook."

Mother and I saw Dottie off on the train. Mother got sort of tearful and it was strange even to me to have Dottie gone. But then the time kept going on and Dottie came home for Christmas and she and Mother made the blue dress over so Dottie could wear it to some fancy party. I was sorry when they took the dandelions off; somehow they reminded me of Mallie as much as anything else I knew.

Then in the spring Mother pulled her big surprise, getting married again. Dottie came home from college specially, and things were pretty exciting for a while. We heard from Mallie at last on the morning of the day Mother was getting married. Mother was all dressed and ready for the wedding to start, and she and Dottie and I were sitting there together sort of having one last family talk, when someone brought up a package that had just arrived. I think we all guessed who it was from right away, just from the sudden way it arrived. Mother took out the card and read: "With love, from Mallie." Then she looked at Dottie and me and said, "Imagine her remembering us after all this time!"

"I figured she would," I said.

"So did I," said Dottie, and that surprised me a little.

Inside the package was a mirror with blue flowers painted around the edge and funny old-fashioned cupid faces on the corners. Mother liked it the minute she saw it, and set it up on her dresser. And when she looked in it, she looked sort of surprised, and then she smiled and began to touch her hair, the way women do. She called Dottie and Dottie looked in the mirror and *she* began to smile and fiddle with her hair, and the two of them were laughing and fooling around with the mirror and I sat there and got more and more nervous because I had to walk down the aisle with Mother and I was sure I'd trip.

Someone finally called them from downstairs and they went down together, looking all excited and pretty. Before I followed them I sneaked a look in the mirror for myself. It was funny; I looked different. My face was thinner, somehow, without that awful pink look you have when you're what they call a healthy boy. And there was a shadow across the mirror that made it look almost as though I had a mustache, like a big-league pitcher, maybe, or an explorer. I looked really grown up, so I went downstairs, all set for the wedding.

All day they kept going upstairs, Mother and Dottie and all the other women who were there, and they'd all take a look in the mirror and come downstairs again all smiles. I even took another couple of looks myself, when there was no one else around.

After the wedding Mother put the mirror in the hall downstairs so that everyone coming in or going out of the house could look in it. You'd be surprised at how it seems to make people feel pleased with themselves. I keep thinking what Mallie would have said if I asked her why the mirror made people feel so much handsomer and smarter. She'd wink at me, as always, and say, "Magic."

I guess it *was* magic, all of it—though I wouldn't like to say for sure. All of it, that is, except that game when my team beat the Nine-Man Wonders. *I* pitched that game and I *know*.

THE WISHING DIME

🜍

Good Housekeeping, *September 1949*

M̲R. H̲O̲W̲A̲R̲D̲ J̲. K̲E̲N̲N̲E̲Y̲, trudging disconsolately, noticed the bright shine of a coin in the gutter and for a minute regarded it cynically, without attempting to pick it up. It was a dime, and Mr. Howard J. Kenney felt with some justice that one dime more or less would make very little difference in his life at present; this was the end of his second week of job-hunting. The two weeks' salary with which he had been discharged had dwindled to an alarmingly small sum; his wife no longer tried to cover her worry with a brave smile; the whole world—or so it seemed to Mr. Kenney—saw them with a suspicious, no-credit eye. And so fate offered Mr. Kenney a dime, glittering brightly in the late afternoon sunlight. After a minute, Mr. Kenney shrugged, leaned over, and took up the dime. It felt light in his hand, and solid, but very small indeed. Mr. Kenney started to drop it into his pocket and then he thought suddenly: Always give away found money; brings luck. I could use some luck. He held the dime in his hand as he walked toward his home.

There were two little girls ahead of him, about half a block away. They were the only people on the street, and they were playing together solemnly. They were about eight years old, Mr. Kenney decided as he came nearer to them, and he thought drearily what a pleasant age eight must be—no responsibilities, no thought for the future, nothing but sunlight and games. When he came close to the little girls, they both looked up at him, watching him approach with grave, unselfconscious interest. One of them was wearing a pink dress, the other, a blue blouse and yellow skirt. They looked like pleasant, agreeable little girls, and Mr. Kenney smiled tentatively at them.

"Hello," he said.

"Hello," said the little girl in pink.

"Here," Mr. Kenney said. He held out the hand with the dime in it and took the hand of the little girl in pink. He put the dime into her hand, closed her fingers over it, and smiled again. "For luck," he said, and walked on quickly.

For a minute, the girls were silent with surprise; Mr. Kenney felt them watching him walk away. Then, after a minute, one of them— probably the one in pink—called, "Thank you. Thank you very much for the dime."

Mr. Kenney waved without looking around and walked on toward his home.

Behind him, the two little girls bent their heads over the dime, shining in the hand of the little girl in pink.

"Why'd he give it to us, do you think?" the little girl in pink, whose name was Nancy, asked the little girl in blue and yellow, whose name was Jill.

"I don't know," Jill said. "He just gave it to us."

"He said it was for luck, though."

"I wonder why he didn't keep it if it was so lucky," Jill said. She turned all the way around to stare down the street at Mr. Kenney, now far distant. "Ten cents," she said. "That's a lot of money."

"What'll we do with it?" Nancy asked.

"We could get two Popsicles for ten cents," Jill said.

"Or two chocolate bars."

"Or ice cream."

Nancy was looking intently at the dime. "It doesn't look like a regular dime, somehow," she said. "Somehow it doesn't look like a regular dime at *all*."

Jill leaned over and looked at it. "It's different, all right," she said. "I don't know *how,* but it's most certainly different from a regular dime."

"A regular dime's thinner, maybe," Nancy said. She bent her head far down, next to Jill's, and the two of them looked wonderingly at the dime.

"Or maybe this is more silvery," Jill said. "Anyway, it's most certainly not a *regular* dime."

They lifted their heads suddenly and stared at each other for a minute with lovely, credulous speculation. Then Jill said softly, "Nancy, do you suppose—"

"I'm almost *sure* of it," Nancy said firmly. "It's a *magic* dime."

"A wishing dime," Jill added. "For wishes."

"*That's* why he said, 'For luck,' " Nancy said.

"Three wishes," Jill said.

Nancy closed her fingers tight around the dime. "Jill," she said, "we've got to be very, very careful with this wishing dime. We've got to be *very* careful."

"It's not like ordinary wishing," Jill agreed, "where you go on wishing and wishing and you know nothing's going to happen because you don't have something like a wishing dime." She stopped for breath and then added, "This is very, very different."

"We can't just go around wishing for anything," Nancy said.

Jill sat down abruptly on the sidewalk, putting her chin into her hands and setting her small mouth; she was thinking. "We could wish for a million dollars," she said finally.

"We don't need any more money," Nancy pointed out. "We have a dime already."

"A pony?"

"Where would we keep it?" Nancy objected. "There's not room in your house, and I asked Mother to get us a baby brother and I'm pretty sure she wouldn't let me have a pony, *too*."

"We could wish for all the candy in the world," Jill said, "but then we'd be sick."

They both thought soberly for a few minutes, sitting together on the sidewalk, Nancy with her fingers carefully closed over the dime.

"Christmas?" Jill suggested, but Nancy only shook her head. "Coming anyway," she said briefly.

"Listen," Jill said suddenly. "What we've got to do is let someone *else* make the first wish. Then we'll find out how to do it."

"We've got three wishes, after all," Nancy said in agreement, "and we wouldn't need more than one for ourselves. If we could even think of anything for one wish."

"Besides," Jill said, "there might be someone around who's been looking and *looking* for a wishing dime because they had a terribly important wish to make."

"We ought to go home, then," Nancy said. "Maybe there's someone in your family or someone in my family with a wish to make."

They stood up and carefully brushed off their skirts. Then, moving busily along side by side, they went to the house where Jill lived with her mother and father and two older brothers.

"I don't know who would be best to ask at my house," Jill said uncertainly. "My brother George is out back painting the steps, but he's so mean these days."

Nancy looked at the house next door, where she lived with her mother and father and sister. "Sally's on the porch," she said. "You think we could ask *her*?"

"Will she do it?" Jill asked.

"Sometimes she's sort of funny," Nancy said. "But we can ask her."

They went up the walk to Nancy's front gate and then to the porch steps. Nancy's older sister Sally was swinging in the porch swing, holding a book; but when Nancy and Jill arrived, Sally was staring at Jill's house next door.

"Sally," Nancy said, and Sally jumped.

"You scare a person to death," she said. She glanced once, nervously, at Jill's house, and then said hastily, "I was just wondering when Mother was coming home."

"She's not at my house," Jill said.

"I wasn't looking at *your* house," Sally said. "I was looking to see if I could see Mother coming down the street."

Both Jill and Nancy had agreed that Sally was the prettiest girl they had ever seen. She was seventeen, and in high school, and she had curly hair that fell to her shoulders in pretty waves. Sally had brown eyes, and she crinkled up her nose whenever she smiled. Right now, however, she was frowning, and her nice mouth was twisted in discontent.

"I wonder when Mother's coming home," she said aimlessly. "Nothing to do around here."

"Why don't you go talk to my brother George?" Jill asked. "He's out back, painting the steps."

"I don't really care to talk to George, thank you," Sally said. She lifted her chin a little higher and shrugged her shoulders. "I'm not really interested in anything George has to say."

"Mother said he had to paint the steps because he was so grouchy all day."

"I'm not surprised," Sally said. "I'm not at *all* surprised that your mother thinks George is grouchy. George is one of the grouchiest—"

"Listen, Sally," Nancy said. "Will you make a wish for us on our magic dime?"

"He is *really* unbearable," Sally said. "What's a magic dime?"

Nancy showed Sally the magic dime, and she and Jill explained to Sally that there were three wishes attached to it, and it had been given them for luck, and Sally was to try the first wish.

"Heavens," Sally said. "What on earth would I wish for?" Because she was really a very kind and charming girl, she smiled at Jill and Nancy and said with interest, "I couldn't think of a thing to wish for."

"That was our trouble, too," Nancy said sadly.

"Well, let me see," said Sally. She stared into space and tapped her fingers thoughtfully on the edge of the book.

"You could wish for George to finish painting and come over to see you," Jill suggested.

"Well, *really,*" Sally said. Her smile disappeared and again she looked very haughty indeed. "If you think I'd waste a wish on something like *that*—"

"Maybe we better ask someone else," Nancy said.

"Well," Sally said hesitantly, "if you really want me to wish for something. How do I do it?"

"I suppose," Nancy said, "I *suppose* you just hold it in your hand."

"And count to ten," Jill said.

"And make my wish," said Sally. She smiled again. "Do I have to tell what I wish?"

Jill and Nancy consulted each other with their eyes. "I think you can say it to yourself if you want to," Nancy said.

"All right, then," Sally said. She held out her hand, and Nancy put the dime into it.

"One, two, three, four," Sally counted while Jill and Nancy watched her breathlessly. "Five, six, seven, eight, nine, ten." Then, eyes shut and a half smile on her face, she made her wish to herself. "There," she said. She handed the dime to Nancy.

"Has anything happened?" Jill asked curiously.

"It hasn't come true yet, if that's what you mean," Sally said. She glanced again, as if involuntarily, at Jill's house next door. "We ought to give it a while, anyway."

"You going to tell us what you wished?" Nancy asked.

Sally leaned against the pillows and sighed deeply. "Someday," she said. "If it comes true."

"It'll come true," Nancy said confidently. "It's a wishing dime, isn't it?"

"We ought to find someone else," Jill said. "There are two more wishes left, and we've got to be careful with them."

As the little girls started down the steps, Sally sighed again deeply. "Who you going to ask next?" she said.

"I don't know," Nancy said. "George, I guess."

"Of all the people in the world!" Sally said. "Heaven only knows what *George* might wish for." She sighed again and leaned her head on her hand.

"We'll ask him anyway," Jill said to Nancy as they went down the walk. "He might *want* to make a wish."

George was at the back of Jill's house. The can of paint he had been using stood on the top step, only half of which was painted. George sat on the unpainted bottom step, his fingers holding the brush idly and his handsome mouth set in a grim line.

"Hi," he said gloomily as the little girls came around the corner of the house.

"He looks worse than Sally," Jill said critically. "Doesn't he, Nancy?"

"Sally looks pretty bad," Nancy said. "But George looks pretty bad, too."

"You're a great pair to brighten a dreary afternoon," George said. "Did you just come to cheer me up?"

"We want you to make a wish," Jill said. "Sally did."

"I don't care what Sally—" George began, but Jill interrupted him.

"We got a wishing dime from a man going down the street," she said. "He just gave it to us for luck, and Sally made a wish and we want you to make a wish, too."

George asked, as if not able to stop himself in time, "What did Sally wish?"

"She wished you would come over and see her," Jill said promptly.

"Right away this afternoon," Nancy added.

"So we want you to make a wish, too," Jill said.

"Wish?" George said. He stared at them vaguely. Then he stood up and put down the paintbrush. "Wish?" he said.

"Yes," Jill said patiently. "Like Sally did. We want you to make a wish."

"You wish for me," George said. Suddenly, without warning, he began to run. With one leap he cleared the low hedge between Jill's backyard and Nancy's backyard, and Jill and Nancy could see him racing for the front porch, where Sally was sitting.

"They sure act funny, those two," Jill said.

"Now we've got to find someone else," Nancy said.

They went through Jill's house, but no one was around. Then, outside again, they sat down to wait for someone to come along.

"It's wonderful to have a wishing dime," Jill said.

"And to be able to wish for anything you want," Nancy said. "Suppose we wanted a fire engine all our own, we could wish for it."

"It's lucky we *don't* want a fire engine," Jill pointed out. "We couldn't drive it."

"Same with something like a doll as big as we are," Nancy said. "We couldn't play with it. It would be too big and too heavy for us to carry."

"Or going to the movies every night," Jill said.

They were quiet, sitting comfortably side by side with the dime still in Nancy's hand. Then Nancy's mother came around the corner from the bus stop and started toward them. She was carrying packages and walking slowly.

Both Jill and Nancy got up and ran. Nancy reached her mother and hugged her enthusiastically. Mrs. Waite drew back, saying irritably, "Nancy dear, *please* watch what you're doing. You'll knock everything out of my hands."

Nancy and Jill began telling her about the magic dime, about the man who had given it to them for luck, about Sally's wishing and George's not wishing.

"How do you children *think* of such things?" Mrs. Waite said.

When they came to Nancy's porch there was no sign of Sally on the swing, except for the book lying where it had fallen on the porch floor. Mrs. Waite went inside, closely followed by Nancy and Jill, still talking, and she put her packages on the table in the hall. "There," she said. "I'm glad to get rid of *those*." She stretched her arms wearily.

Before she had taken off her hat, Nancy pressed the dime into her hand. "Please," Nancy said. "Wish right away." She held her breath, and so did Jill. "It's the second wish," Nancy said.

"Oh, dear," Mrs. Waite frowned. "Really," she said, "I wish you girls would save your games for some time when I'm not so busy, and so tired." She tried to make her voice gentle, but it was sharp in spite of her. "I've been shopping all day," she said. "I'm really *very* tired, girls, and I've got a lot to do. Can't it wait?"

When she saw Nancy's and Jill's disappointment, she sighed impatiently and said in a resigned voice, "All right, then. What do you want me to wish for?"

"Anything," Nancy said eagerly. "That's what it does—it gives you anything you wish for."

"I could wish dinner was all made," Mrs. Waite said.

"Dinner couldn't be all made," Jill said reasonably. "The dime wouldn't know what to cook, for one thing. And anyway, it's too early."

"I suppose," Mrs. Waite said. She stood frowning while her hands absently busied themselves with the packages on the table. "I know," she said. "How do I do it?"

"Take the dime in your hand," Nancy told her carefully. "Count to ten, and then make your wish."

"All right," Mrs. Waite said. She held out her hand, and Nancy put the dime into it. Slowly Mrs. Waite counted to ten, and then she said, "I wish the dishes I left in the sink when I went out this afternoon were all washed and put away."

"Do you think that's all right, for a real wish?" Nancy asked Jill anxiously.

"It's too late, anyway," Jill pointed out. "She's already wished it."

"It's the best I can do," Mrs. Waite said. She turned back to her packages. "I hope your magic dime works, because I'd like nothing better than to be saved doing those dishes." She had taken off her hat and coat, and now, selecting the packages that went to the kitchen, she went down the hall and opened the kitchen's swinging door, while Nancy and Jill, who felt a certain justifiable anxiety about the powers of their wishing dime, followed her.

A burst of laughter met them when Mrs. Waite pushed open the door. Sally and George, each wearing an apron, were racing around the kitchen table, George flicking at Sally's feet with the dish towel. The dishes were washed, and most of them were dried and stacked on the table.

"Be fresh to me, will you," George was shouting.

The kitchen table, with its load of dishes, trembled perilously as George and Sally frolicked around it. Sally saw her mother and, with a wild scream, fled behind Mrs. Waite for protection. George, unable to stop in time, crashed against Mrs. Waite and sent her, with Sally, Nancy, and Jill behind her, sprawling into the hall, while the door swung after them and then gently back into George's face.

For a minute Mrs. Waite sat where she had fallen. "A magic dime," she said to herself. "Me still in my best shoes." She looked up at Nancy and Jill, who, with Sally, were hovering over her solicitously. "I see your dime got my dishes washed," Mrs. Waite said ironically.

"I *told* you," Nancy said. "It's a real wishing dime."

"Mrs. Waite," George said weakly, peering red-faced around the edge of the swinging door, "Mrs. Waite, I'm *terribly* sorry—"

"Never mind, George," Mrs. Waite said, accepting Sally's hand to help herself up. "I wished for it."

"He was chasing me, Mother," Sally said helpfully.

"*Don't* those two act funny, though?" Nancy said to Jill.

"Chasing each other," Jill said disgustedly.

"Mrs. Waite," George said, "I can't tell you how sorry—"

"We were doing the dishes for you," Sally said eagerly. She and George had been carefully not looking at each other, but now Sally looked at him accidentally, and they both began to giggle.

"We thought we'd wash the dishes for you," George explained, and then he and Sally began to laugh again. "We were sort of washing the dishes," he went on feebly, "and I got to chasing—we got to fooling around—I guess I ran into you."

Mrs. Waite looked at Nancy solemnly clutching the dime in her hand, at Jill standing close to her, at Sally and George with their red faces; and she began to laugh helplessly.

"She wished the dishes would get washed," Nancy said to Sally.

"*My* wish came true," Sally said, surprised. "I hadn't thought of it till now."

"We figured it came true," Jill said. "Didn't we, Nancy?"

Nancy nodded. "There's one left," she said. She pulled Jill to one side and whispered in her ear.

Jill, nodding, said, "That's right. I think so, too."

Sally and Mrs. Waite began to put the dishes away, and George backed carefully into a corner, apologizing violently whenever he got in Mrs. Waite's way.

Finally Nancy went over to her mother and said, "This is very, very important, everybody. We're going to make our last wish."

Mrs. Waite paused, both hands full of silverware, to look with suspicion on her younger daughter. Sally and George watched, full of curiosity, as Nancy and Jill, with great ceremony, put their hands together with the dime between.

"This is the last wish on this dime," Nancy said, turning to explain to her mother more fully. "Because this is our very own wishing dime, Jill and I are going to make the last wish. You all had a chance to wish on it, and now it's our turn."

"And we're going to wish now," Jill said.

"One, two, three, four, five," Nancy said with great dramatic emphasis.

"Six, seven, eight, nine, ten," Jill said.

"With this magic dime, we wish for two Popsicles."

Later, when they were working on their Popsicles—Jill had orange, and Nancy's was cherry—Nancy said, "The nicest thing about wishing dimes is that they're about something special."

"Suppose we had one every day," Jill suggested. "They wouldn't be *half* so much fun."

"There aren't that many things to wish for," Nancy said wisely.

"The nicest thing about wishing dimes," Jill said, "is that after you're all through wishing with them, you can use them to spend."

And what about Mr. Howard J. Kenney, who had given the dime away for luck? Mr. Kenney arrived home about fifteen minutes after he had given away the dime, and he was met at the doorway by a hysterical wife and a group of chattering neighbors. Mr. Kenney's wife, with great presence of mind, had remembered the correct name of a song she had heard when the man from the radio station called her; she was expecting immediate delivery on a new car, a new refrigerator, an astronomical sum of money, a new fur coat, and a complete wardrobe of new clothes.

About Two Nice People

Ladies' Home Journal, *July 1951*

A PROBLEM OF SOME importance, certainly, these days, is that of anger. When one half of the world is angry at the other half, or one half of a nation is angry at the rest, or one side of town feuds with the other side, it is hardly surprising, when you stop to think about it, that so many people lose their tempers with so many other people. Even if, as in this case, they are two people not usually angry, two people whose lives are obscure and whose emotions are gentle, whose smiles are amiable and whose voices are more apt to be cheerful than raised in fury. Two people, in other words, who would much rather be friends than not and who yet, for some reason, perhaps chemical or sociological or environmental, enter upon a mutual feeling of dislike so intense that only a very drastic means can bring them out of it.

Take two such people:

Ellen Webster was what was referred to among her friends as a "sweet" girl. She had pretty, soft hair and dark, soft eyes, and she dressed in soft colors and wore frequently a lovely old-fashioned brooch that had belonged to her grandmother. Ellen thought of herself as a very happy and very lucky person because she had a good job, and was able to buy herself a fair number of soft-colored dresses and skirts and sweaters and coats and hats; she had, by working hard at it evenings, transformed her one-room apartment from a bare, neat place into a charming little refuge with her sewing basket on the table and a canary at the window; she had a reasonable conviction that someday, perhaps soon, she would fall in love with a nice young man and they would be married and Ellen would devote herself wholeheartedly to children and baking cakes and mending socks. This not-very-unusual situation, with its perfectly ordinary state of mind, was a source of great happiness to Ellen. She was, in a word, not one of those who rail against their fate, who live in sullen hatred of the world. She was—her friends were right—a sweet girl.

On the other hand, even if you would not have called Walter Nesmith sweet, you would very readily have thought of him as a "nice" fellow, or an "agreeable" person, or even—if you happened to be a little old white-haired lady—a "dear boy." There was a subtle resemblance between Ellen Webster and Walter Nesmith. Both of them were the first resort of their friends in trouble, for instance. Walter's ambitions, which included the rest of his life, were refreshingly similar to Ellen's: Walter thought that someday he might meet some sweet girl, and would then devote himself wholeheartedly to coming home of an evening to read his paper, and perhaps work in the garden on Sundays.

Walter thought that he would like to have two children, a boy and a girl. Ellen thought that she would like to have three children, a boy and two girls. Walter was very fond of cherry pie, Ellen preferred Boston cream. Ellen enjoyed romantic movies. Walter preferred westerns. They read almost exactly the same books.

In the ordinary course of events, the friction between Ellen and Walter would have been very slight. But—and what could cause a thing like this?—the ordinary course of events was shattered by a trifle like a telephone call.

Ellen's telephone number was 3-4126. Walter's telephone number was 3-4216. Ellen lived in apartment 3-A and Walter lived in apartment 3-B; these apartments were across the hall from each other, and very often Ellen, opening her door at precisely quarter of nine in the morning and going toward the elevator, met Walter, who opened *his* door at precisely quarter of nine in the morning and went toward the elevator. On these occasions Ellen customarily said, "Good morning," and looked steadfastly the other way. Walter usually answered, "Good morning," and avoided looking in her direction. Ellen thought that a girl who allowed herself to be informal with strangers created a bad impression, and Walter thought that a man who took advantage of living in the same building to strike up an acquaintance with a girl was a man of little principle. One particularly fine morning he said to Ellen in the elevator, "Lovely day," and she replied,

"Yes, isn't it?" and both of them felt secretly that they had been bold. How this mutual respect for each other's dignity could have degenerated into fury is a mystery not easily understood.

It happened that one evening—and, to do her strict justice, Ellen had had a hard day: she was coming down with a cold, it had rained steadily for a week, her stockings were unwashed, and she had broken a fingernail—the phone which had the number 3-4126 rang. Ellen had been opening a can of chicken soup in the kitchenette, and she had her hands full; she said, "Darn," and managed to drop and break a cup in her hurry to answer the phone.

"Hello?" she said, thinking, *This is going to be something cheerful.*

"Hello, is Walter there?"

"Walter?"

"Walter Nesmith. I want to speak to Walter, please."

"This is the wrong number," Ellen said, thinking with the self-pity that comes with the first stages of a head cold, that *no* one ever called *her.*

"Is this three-four two one six?"

"This is three-four one two six," Ellen said, and hung up.

At that time, although she knew that the person in the apartment across the hall was named Walter Nesmith, she could not have told the color of his hair or even of the outside of his apartment door. She went back to her soup and had a match in her hand to light the stove, when the phone rang again.

"Hello?" Ellen said without enthusiasm; this *could* be someone cheerful, she was thinking.

"Hello, is Walter there?"

"This is the wrong number again," Ellen said; if she had not been such a very sweet girl she might have let more irritation show in her voice.

"I *want* to *speak* to Walter Nesmith, *please.*"

"This is three-four one two six again," Ellen said patiently. "You want three-four two one six."

"What?" said the voice.

"This," said Ellen, "is number three-four one two six. The number you want is three-four two one six." Like anyone who has tried to say a series of numbers several times, she found her anger growing. Surely anyone of *normal* intelligence, she was thinking, surely anyone *ought* to be able to dial a phone, anyone who can't dial a phone shouldn't be allowed to have a nickel.

She had got all the way back into the kitchenette and was reaching out for the can of soup before the phone rang again. This time when she answered she said, "Hello?" rather sharply for Ellen, and with no illusions about who it was going to be.

"Hello, may I please speak to Walter?"

At that point it started. Ellen had a headache and it was raining and she was tired and she was apparently not going to get any chicken soup until this annoyance was stopped.

"Just a minute," she said into the phone.

She put the phone down with an understandable bang on the table, and marched, without taking time to think, out of her apartment and up to the door across the hall. "Walter Nesmith" said a small card at the doorbell. Ellen rang the doorbell with what was, for her, a vicious poke. When the door opened she said immediately, without looking at him:

"Are you Walter Nesmith?"

Now, Walter had had a hard day, too, and *he* was coming down with a cold, and *he* had been trying ineffectually to make himself a cup of hot tea in which he intended to put a spoonful of honey to ease his throat, that being a remedy his aunt had always recommended for the first onslaught of a cold. If there had been one fraction less irritation in Ellen's voice, or if Walter had not taken off his shoes when he came home that night, it might very probably have turned out to be a pleasant introduction, with Walter and Ellen dining together on chicken soup and hot tea, and perhaps even sharing a bottle of cough medicine. But when Walter opened the door and heard Ellen's voice, he was unable to answer her cordially, and so he said briefly:

"I am. Why?"

"Will you please come and answer my phone?" said Ellen, too annoyed to realize that this request might perhaps bewilder Walter.

"Answer your phone?" said Walter stupidly.

"Answer my phone," said Ellen firmly. She turned and went back across the hall, and Walter stood in his doorway in his stocking feet and watched her numbly. "Come *on*," she said sharply as she went into her own apartment, and Walter, wondering briefly if they allowed harmless lunatics to live alone as though they were just like other people, hesitated for an instant and then followed her, on the theory that it would be wise to do what she said when she seemed so cross, and reassuring himself that he could leave the door open and yell for help if necessary. Ellen stamped into her apartment and pointed at the phone where it lay on the table. "There. Answer it."

Eyeing her sideways, Walter edged over to the phone and picked it up. "Hello," he said nervously. Then, "Hello? Hello?" Looking at her over the top of the phone, he said, "What do you want me to do now?"

"Do you mean to say," said Ellen ominously, "that that terrible terrible person has hung up?"

"I guess so," said Walter, and fled back to his own apartment.

The door had only just closed behind him, when the phone rang again, and Ellen, answering it, heard, "May I speak to Walter, please?"

Not a very serious mischance, surely. But the next morning Walter pointedly avoided going down in the elevator with Ellen, and sometime during that day the deliveryman left a package addressed to Ellen at Walter's door.

When Walter found the package he took it manfully under his arm and went boldly across the hall and rang Ellen's doorbell. When Ellen opened her door she thought at first—and she may have been justified—that Walter had come to apologize for the phone call the evening before, and she even thought that the package under his arm might contain something delightfully unexpected, like a box of candy. They lost another chance then; if Walter had not held out the package and said, "Here," Ellen would not have gone on thinking that he was trying to apologize in his own shy way, and she would certainly not have smiled warmly, and said, "You *shouldn't* have bothered."

Walter, who regarded transporting a misdelivered parcel across the hall as relatively little bother, said blankly, "No bother at all," and Ellen, still deceived, said, "But it really wasn't *that* important."

Walter went back into his own apartment convinced that this was a very odd girl indeed, and Ellen, finding that the package had been mailed to her and contained a wool scarf knitted by a cousin, was as much angry as embarrassed because, once having imagined that an apology is forthcoming, it is very annoying not to have one after all, and particularly to have a wool scarf instead of a box of candy.

How this situation disintegrated into the white-hot fury that rose between these two is a puzzle, except for the basic fact that when once a series of misadventures has begun between two people, every-thing tends to contribute further to a state of misunderstanding. Thus, Ellen opened a letter of Walter's by mistake, and Walter dropped a bottle of milk—he was still trying to cure his cold, and thought that perhaps milk toast was the thing—directly outside Ellen's door, so that even after his nervous attempts to clean it up, the floor was still littered with fragments of glass, and puddled with milk.

Then Ellen—who believed by now that Walter had thrown the bottle of milk against her door—allowed herself to become so far confused by this succession of small annoyances that she actually wrote and mailed a letter to Walter, asking politely that he try to turn down his radio a little in the late evenings. Walter replied with a frigid letter to the effect that certainly if he had known that she was bothered by his radio, he would surely never have dreamed—

That evening, perhaps by accident, his radio was so loud that Ellen's canary woke up and chirped hysterically, and Ellen, pacing her floor in incoherent fury, might have been heard—if there had been anyone to hear her, and if Walter's radio had not been so loud—to say, "I'll get even with him!" A phrase, it must be said, which Ellen had never used before in her life.

Ellen made her preparations with a sort of loving care that might well have been lavished on some more worthy object. When the alarm went off she turned in her sleep and smiled before quite wak-ing up, and, once awake and the alarm turned off, she almost laughed out loud. In her slippers and gown, the clock in her hand, she went across her small apartment to the phone; the number was one she was not soon apt to forget. The dial tone sounded amazingly loud, and for a minute she was almost frightened out of her resolu-tion. Then, setting her teeth, she dialed the number, her hand steady. After a second's interminable wait, the ringing began. The phone at the other end rang three times, four times, with what seemed inter-minable waits between, as though even the mechanical phone system hesitated at this act. Then, at last, there was an irritable crash at the other end of the line, and a voice said, "Wah?"

"*Good* morning," said Ellen brightly. "I'm so terribly sorry to disturb you at this hour."

"Wah?"

"This is Ellen Webster," said Ellen, still brightly. "I called to tell you that my clock has stopped—"

"Wah?"

"—and I wonder if you could tell me what time it is?"

There was a short pause at the other end of the line. Then, after a minute, his voice came back: "Tenny minna fah."

"I beg your pardon?"

There was another short pause at the other end of the line, as of someone opening his eyes with a shock. "Twenty minutes after four," he said. *"Twenty minutes after four."*

"The reason I thought of asking you," Ellen said sweetly, "was that you were so *very* obliging before. About the radio, I mean."

"—calling a person at—"

"Thanks so much," said Ellen. "Goodbye."

She felt fairly certain that he would not call her back, but she sat on her bed and giggled a little before she went back to sleep.

Walter's response to this was miserably weak: He contacted a neighboring delicatessen a day or so later, and had an assortment of evil-smelling cheeses left in Ellen's apartment while she was out. This, which required persuading the superintendent to open Ellen's apartment so that the package might be left inside, was a poor revenge but a monstrous exercise of imagination upon Walter's part, so that, in one sense, Ellen was already bringing out in him qualities he never knew he had. The cheese, it turned out, more than evened the score: The apartment was small, the day was warm, and Ellen did not get home until late, and long after most of the other tenants on the floor had gone to the superintendent with their complaints about something dead in the woodwork.

Since breaking and entering had thus become one of the rules of their game, Ellen felt privileged to retaliate in kind upon Walter. It was with great joy, some evenings later, that Ellen, sitting in her odorous apartment, heard Walter's scream of pure terror when he put his feet into his slippers and found a raw egg in each.

Walter had another weapon, however, which he had been so far reluctant to use; it was a howitzer of such proportions that Walter felt its use would end warfare utterly. After the raw eggs he felt no compunction whatever in bringing out his heavy artillery.

It seemed to Ellen, at first, as though peace had been declared. For almost a week things went along smoothly; Walter kept his radio turned down almost to inaudibility, so that Ellen got plenty of sleep.

She was over her cold, the sun had come out, and on Saturday morning she spent three hours shopping, and found exactly the dress she wanted at less than she expected to pay.

About Saturday noon she stepped out of the elevator, her packages under her arm, and walked briskly down the hall to her apartment, making, as usual, a wide half circle to avoid coming into contact with the area around Walter's door.

Her apartment door, to her surprise, was open, but before she had time to phrase a question in her own mind, she had stepped inside and come face-to-face with a lady who—not to make any more mysteries—was Walter Nesmith's aunt, and a wicked old lady in her own way, possessing none of Walter's timidity and none of his tact.

"Who?" said Ellen weakly, standing in the doorway.

"Come in and close the door," said the old lady darkly. "I don't think you'll want your neighbors to hear what I have to say. I," she continued as Ellen obeyed mechanically, "am Mrs. Harold Vongarten Nesmith. Walter Nesmith, young woman, is my nephew."

"Then you are in the wrong apartment," said Ellen quite politely, considering the reaction which Walter Nesmith's name was beginning by now to arouse in her. "You want Apartment Three-B, across the hall."

"I do *not*," said the old lady firmly. "I came here to see the designing young woman who has been shamelessly pursuing my nephew, and to warn her"—the old lady shook her gloves menacingly—"to warn her that *not one cent* shall she have from me if she marries Walter Nesmith."

"Marries?" said Ellen, thoughts too great for words in her heart.

"It has long been my opinion that some young woman would be after Walter Nesmith for his money," said Walter's aunt with satisfaction.

"Believe me," said Ellen wholeheartedly, "there is not that much money in the world."

"You deny it?" The old lady leaned back and smiled triumphantly. "I expected something of the sort. Walter," she called suddenly, and then, putting her head back and howling, "Walllllter."

"Shhh," said Ellen fearfully. "They'll hear you all over."

"I expect them to," said the old lady. "Walllll—oh, there you are."

Ellen turned, and saw Walter Nesmith, with triumph in his eyes, peering around the edge of the door. "Did it work?" he asked.

"She denies everything," said his aunt.

"About the eggs?" Walter said, confused. "You mean, she denies about the eggs and the phone call and—"

"Look," Ellen said to Walter, stamping across the floor to look at him straight in the eye, "of all the insufferable, conceited, rude, self-satisfied—"

"What?" said Walter.

"I wouldn't want to marry you," said Ellen, "if—if—" She stopped for a word, helpless.

"If he were the last man on earth," Walter's aunt supplied obligingly. "I think she's really after your *money,* Walter."

Walter stared at his aunt. "I didn't tell you to tell her—" he began. He gasped, and tried again. "I mean," he said, "I never thought—" He appealed to Ellen. "I don't want to marry you, either," he said, and then gasped again, and said, "I mean, I told my aunt to come and tell you—"

"If this is a proposal," Ellen said coldly, "I decline."

"All I wanted her to do was scare you," Walter said finally.

"It's a good way," his aunt said complacently. "Turned out to be the only way with your uncle Charles and a Hungarian adventuress."

"I mean," Walter said desperately to Ellen, "she owns this building. I mean, I wanted her to tell you that if you didn't stop—I mean, I wanted her to scare you—"

"Apartments are too hard to get these days," his aunt said. "That would have been *too* unkind."

"That's how I got my apartment at all, you see," Walter said to Ellen, still under the impression he was explaining something Ellen wanted to understand.

"Since you *have* got an apartment," Ellen said with restraint, "may I suggest that you take your aunt and the both of you—"

The phone rang.

"Excuse me," said Ellen mechanically, moving to answer it. "Hello?" she said.

"Hello, may I speak to Walter, please?"

Ellen smiled rather in the manner that Lady Macbeth might have smiled if she found a run in her stocking.

"It's for you," she said, holding the phone out to Walter.

"For me?" he said, surprised. "Who is it?"

"I really could not say," said Ellen sweetly. "Since you have so many friends that one phone is not adequate to answer all their calls—"

Since Walter made no move to take the phone, she put it gently back on the hook.

"They'll call again," she assured him, still smiling in that terrible fashion.

"I ought to turn you both out," said Walter's aunt. She turned to Ellen. "Young woman," she said, "do you deny that all this nonsense with eggs and telephone calls is an attempt to entangle my nephew into matrimony?"

"Certainly not," Ellen said. "I mean, I *do* deny it."

"Walter Nesmith," said his aunt, "do you admit that all your finagling with cheeses and radios is an attempt to strike up an acquaintance with this young woman?"

"Certainly," said Walter. "I mean, I do *not* admit it."

"Good," said Walter's aunt. "You are precisely the pair of silly fools I would have picked out for each other." She rose with great dignity, motioned Walter away from her, and started for the door. "Remember," she said, shaking her gloves again at Ellen, "not one cent."

She opened the door and started down the hall, her handkerchief over her eyes, and—a surprising thing in such an old lady—laughing until she had to stop and lean against the wall near the elevator.

"I'm sorry," Walter was saying to Ellen, almost babbling. "I'm *really* sorry this time—please believe me, I had *no* idea—I wouldn't for the world—nothing but the most profound respect—a joke, you know—hope you didn't really think—"

"I understand perfectly," Ellen said icily. "It is all perfectly clear. It only goes to show what I have always believed about young men who think that all they have to do is—"

The phone rang.

Ellen waited a minute before she spoke. Then she said, "You might as well answer it."

"I'm *terribly* sorry," Walter said, not moving toward the phone. "I mean, I'm *terribly* sorry." He waved his hands in the air. "About what she said about what she thought about what you wanted me to do—" His voice trailed off miserably.

Suddenly Ellen began to giggle.

Anger is certainly a problem that will bear much analysis. It is hardly surprising that one person may be angry at another, particularly if these are two people who are gentle, usually, and rarely angry, whose emotions tend to be mild and who would rather be friends with everyone than be enemies with anyone. Such an anger argues a situation so acute that only the most drastic readjustment can remedy it.

Either Walter Nesmith or Ellen Webster could have moved, of course. But, as Walter's aunt had pointed out, apartments are not that easy to come by, and their motives and their telephone numbers were by now so inextricably mixed that on the whole it seemed more reasonable not to bother.

Moreover, Walter's aunt, who still snickers when her nephew's name is mentioned, did not keep them long in suspense, after all. She was not lavish, certainly, but she wrote them a letter that both of them found completely confusing, and enclosed a check adequate for a down payment on the extremely modest house in the country they decided upon without disagreement. They even compromised and had four children—two boys and two girls.

MRS. MELVILLE
MAKES A PURCHASE

Charm, *October 1951*

MRS. RANDOLPH HENRY MELVILLE was not accustomed to being kept waiting by a salesgirl. Mrs. Melville believed that salesgirls who were not at the moment waiting upon herself were standing at the other end of the counter gossiping with other salesgirls about the private life of the floorwalker, or engaged in secret transactions with other customers, no doubt involving special and unusually unobtainable merchandise. Now, ordinarily, it was adequate for Mrs. Melville to rap sharply upon the counter and say "Miss!" Sometimes it was necessary, however, for Mrs. Melville to go up to the salesgirl and interrupt her private conversation with some cutting remark such as "How long do I have to wait for service here?," emphasizing the *service* so that the salesgirl understood clearly, if she had not before, that she was there to serve Mrs. Melville, to obey her, to follow abjectly her orders, and not to stand around and gossip.

This time—and it is to Mrs. Melville's everlasting glory that she was not angrier, even, than she was—Mrs. Melville had rapped and said "Miss!," had marched down the counter and said with heavy accent, "How long do I have to wait for *service* here?," had stood first on one foot and then on the other, had sighed, tapped her fingers, looked around irritably, had made, for no one's benefit, a great display of impatience, fingering and tossing away blouses, and finally, and with great emphasis, had said aloud to the store in general, "Well, *really*!" And all the while, all the blessed while that

Mrs. Melville waited, the salesgirl stood at the other end of the counter, gossiping and smiling and presumably not selling a blouse at all to the timid woman in the gray coat who could not make up her mind.

When Mrs. Melville had said "Miss!" the salesgirl had turned and smiled at her, and nodded; when Mrs. Melville had asked how long she had to wait, the salesgirl had said politely that she would be with Mrs. Melville in a minute; when Mrs. Melville had said "Well, *really!*" the salesgirl had said in a voice almost as sharp as Mrs. Melville's now, "Madam, I cannot help you until I am finished with my customer." Mrs. Melville had reported employees, and probably had had them discharged, for less than this. She would at least have gone to the floorwalker to describe the salesgirl's insolence if she had not wanted this blouse so very much. It was precisely the style for her black faille suit, for one thing. It had the rare, the almost-despaired-of, neckline, the half sleeve, the buttoned back, the curved collar. No other store in town—and Mrs. Melville was positive that she had tried them all—had this blouse. It was Mrs. Melville's blouse, if—and she tried not to think of this—they had it in her size.

She could see the blouses stacked neatly on the shelves behind the counter. One precious stack contained *her* blouse. She could not see the sizes, but she could see that the blouse came in shocking pink, which Mrs. Melville secretly adored, and which tempted her very much; in chartreuse, which she thought she would take as a second choice; in a sort of palish blue, which she was convinced made her complexion look sallow; in white, which was impractical in her eyes; in black, which would be odd with a black suit; and in several plaids, which Mrs. Melville had regretfully abandoned when her age turned forty overnight and her size passed almost imperceptibly from a thirty-eight into something more than her age. If the shocking pink came in her size . . . or the chartreuse . . .

"May I help you?"

Mrs. Melville jumped; she had been lost in dreams of herself in the black faille suit with the shocking pink (or the chartreuse?) blouse. ("I hunted all over town," she was telling some unidentified friend with whom she was lunching in a terribly smart restaurant, "and I simply couldn't find the blouse I wanted. Until one day—I don't know why I was there, it was just by chance, I never *thought* of looking at blouses—anyway, I said to myself that it wouldn't do any harm just to run in here and . . .") "I've been waiting here for half an hour," Mrs. Melville said. "Is there any *reason* why I should wait half an hour for service?"

"I'm sorry," said the salesgirl, obviously refraining with an effort from telling Mrs. Melville that she had been there no more than four minutes. "I had a customer."

"Well, are you the only person here? Aren't there more sales-girls?"

"The other girl is out to lunch, madam. What was it you wished to see?"

"Lunch?" said Mrs. Melville crossly.

The salesgirl sighed, hesitated, and said, "May I show you anything?"

Mrs. Melville decided to secure her blouse first and be angry afterward. "Well," she said reluctantly, "I might just like to look at the blouse on this figure."

"What size, please?"

Mrs. Melville glanced at her nervously. "Fairly large, I think," she said. "I always like to get my blouses good and large." The salesgirl waited. "Forty-four," Mrs. Melville said softly.

"Forty-four," repeated the salesgirl loudly. "What color?"

"The pink," said Mrs. Melville, "or the chartreuse."

"I'm not sure I have it in your size, madam," said the salesgirl. Her voice still seemed overloud for the circumstances. She turned without enthusiasm and began to leaf through the blouses in the stack. "Forty," she said. "Forty-two. I don't think *any* of these come in forty-four."

"Not even the pink?" said Mrs. Melville. "Are you sure you're looking in the right place?"

"I have the black," said the salesgirl. "Most large figures prefer the black."

"Young lady," said Mrs. Melville, "I am buying a *blouse,* not your *opinions.*"

The salesgirl looked at Mrs. Melville over her shoulder. "I can't give you what I haven't got," she said.

"The chartreuse?" said Mrs. Melville. "Don't I see a chartreuse in there?"

The girl pulled it out of the stack rudely. "Does that look like a forty-four?" she said.

"Forty-two," said Mrs. Melville, consulting the tag. "I *could* wear a forty-two," she said earnestly to the girl. "I just like to get my blouses large."

The girl shrugged. "I have the pink *and* the green in forty-two," she said. "That is, if you think you can wear a forty-two. That blouse is twelve ninety-five."

"That's very expensive," said Mrs. Melville immediately.

"It's what it says on the tag," said the girl. "I don't set the prices."

"I'm not at *all* sure about that pink," said Mrs. Melville.

"I have that blouse in pink, chartreuse, blue, black, and white," said the girl wearily.

"Well," said Mrs. Melville, "I *can't* take black, and white just isn't right for me. I need color near my face."

The girl looked up at Mrs. Melville and said without interest, "It comes in black, white, blue, pink, or chartreuse."

"The pink is very nice," said Mrs. Melville, considering. She held it up against herself and looked at herself in the mirror over the counter. Then she put it down and held up the chartreuse. "I really think the pink does more for me," she said.

The girl yawned, covering her mouth politely, and said, "They're both very good numbers."

"But, on the other hand," said Mrs. Melville, "the chartreuse . . . somehow, it's more sophisticated. Don't you think so?"

"The chartreuse is a very good number," said the girl. "So is the pink."

"Which one do *you* think?" said Mrs. Melville.

"I really couldn't say," said the girl.

Mrs. Melville looked at her sharply; this girl was really being very annoying. "I'll take *this* one," Mrs. Melville said abruptly. The girl nodded without interest, not glancing at the blouse Mrs. Melville held out. She took the blouse indifferently, with Mrs. Melville's money, and went off. Mrs. Melville had to wait again.

By the time the girl came back with Mrs. Melville's blouse in a bag and her change, Mrs. Melville was angry again. "Before I leave," she said to the girl in a voice that implied that the quality of service Mrs. Melville had been vouchsafed in this store was very low indeed, "will you please give me your name and number?"

"It's on the sales slip," said the girl. "In the bag."

"You may as well know," said Mrs. Melville, "that I intend to report you for insolence. I think that your attitude toward this sale has been perfectly dreadful, and I shall make every effort to—"

"Excuse me," said the girl. "I have to go and wait on another customer."

She was smiling as she went off, and then she turned and came back. "The complaint department," she said. "Report your complaints to the complaint department. On the ninth floor, near the elevator."

Mrs. Melville turned with anger and marched away.

She was on the second floor. She knew from past experience that it would do her no good at all to report the insolent girl to the floor-walker or to the elevator operator. With her jaw set and her package under her arm, Mrs. Melville headed for the escalator and the ninth floor, thinking as she went that in any well-regulated store the complaint department would be more accessible. When she came to the escalator she stepped on as one who goes toward a duty not entirely unpleasant.

The third floor was to Mrs. Melville nothing more than a brief display of bathing suits, all obviously size nine, and, Mrs. Melville thought righteously, all far too shocking to be seen on a public beach. The fourth floor was suits, extravagantly cut, overdecorated, and seeming to come no larger than about a fourteen. The fifth floor was china and glassware and Mrs. Melville thought, as she passed, that they must lose a lot of sales because they had placed their tables full of china displays so close together that no one but a very slim person could pass between them without danger of upsetting something.

On the sixth floor was the restaurant. It was called Ye Olde Taverne, and was heavily decorated in dark red and old oak. The walls were paneled and tapestried, with small leaded windows looking out onto the rug and credit departments on one side, facing a blank wall on the other.

Mrs. Melville was not able to pass by a restaurant. Restaurant, her mind ran, food, sit down, menu, eat. The complaint department, it occurred to her, would be there as well in an hour. The salesgirl, kept in suspense that much longer, would probably learn a more severe lesson. With no more resistance than a glance at the escalator, Mrs. Melville passed through the ornamental wooden portals and into Ye Olde Taverne. She sat down at a table comfortably near the back, and stretched her feet out with a sigh.

A waitress in a full, starched yellow skirt came over to take her order, and when Mrs. Melville looked at the menu, she was whole-heartedly glad she had stopped. By some extraordinarily lucky chance, she had hit the exact moment when the Shopper's Lunch gives way before the Shopper's Tea, and so, if she wished, she might choose from either. Her eye was caught by the tuna fish salad on the Shopper's Lunch, and by the cinnamon toast on the Shopper's Tea. Hot roast beef sandwich? Mrs. Melville—who had lunched two hours before on chicken croquettes and French fried potatoes and chocolate cream pie—wondered if the beef was lean. Or the assorted tea sandwiches? Mrs. Melville dwelt lovingly on the thought of tiny crustless delicacies, filled perhaps with cream cheese and jelly, or a rich salmon filling, or peanut butter and bacon, and sighed again. She read the Fountain Suggestions, the lists of possible beverages, the desserts, and hesitated long over the butterscotch nut sundae. Perhaps a deviled egg? An English muffin? Mrs. Melville tapped the menu against her cheek in a long moment of indecision.

Finally, with the waitress standing impatiently over her, Mrs. Melville hesitated one last time, and chose the tuna fish salad. With another sigh, this time a sigh of pure satisfaction, Mrs. Melville carefully set her package on the chair beside her and slipped her coat from her shoulders. Easing her tired feet under the table, she leaned back and closed her eyes for a minute. Shopping was tiring, particularly with everything so hard to find and salesgirls so impudent and the complaint department so far away.

Her tuna fish salad, when it arrived, was not quite all that Mrs. Melville could have wished. The tuna fish was scanty, with little mayonnaise and much celery, the lettuce was wilted, and the waitress had, for some reason, decided to serve Mrs. Melville Ry-Krisp instead of the hot muffins promised by the menu. Finger upraised, Mrs. Melville summoned the waitress.

"I thought I was supposed to have hot muffins?" she said.

"Sorry," said the waitress. "All out of muffins."

"Rolls?"

"All gone."

"Bread?" said Mrs. Melville, her voice rising slightly.

The waitress indicated the Ry-Krisp. "That's all we got," she said shortly.

"That woman over there has muffins," Mrs. Melville pointed out.

"She was here before you."

"This is disgraceful," said Mrs. Melville. "I certainly would *not* have ordered the salad if I had known there were no more muffins. Don't you *tell* customers these things?"

Without answering, the waitress began to move slowly away toward another table. "Miss!" Mrs. Melville said sharply. The waitress turned. "Bring me more mayonnaise," Mrs. Melville directed, "another pat of butter, and coffee without cream or sugar at once."

The waitress glanced at Mrs. Melville and moved away again. Mrs. Melville began her salad. She would report the girl in the blouse department and stand there until she was assured the girl was fired. She would report the waitress and insist upon a formal apology.

Someone sat down in the chair across the table from her.

Now, Mrs. Melville at all times hated to have anyone watch her eat, and she detested having to ask for more butter under the eye of an unknown person, particularly if, as it seemed in this case, the unknown person was small and quick-moving and a woman. To indicate her extreme disapproval, Mrs. Melville did not once glance up at the woman, but she could see from under her lashes that this was a woman in a dark suit or coat, and certainly someone very small, since she had gone into the narrow seat between the table and the wall without squeezing and without stirring the table or asking Mrs. Melville to move. When the waitress came, the other woman said, briefly, "Tea with lemon," and further infuriated Mrs. Melville. Anyone who came into a restaurant, where the serving and eating of food was an obligation, and ordered only a cup of tea with lemon, was automatically in Mrs. Melville's bad graces. More annoyed than she had been all day, Mrs. Melville abandoned the vestiges of her salad and said, "Check, please," to the waitress.

Without comment, the waitress wrote on the check and handed it to Mrs. Melville. Mrs. Melville, with an effort, began to edge into her coat, carefully avoiding looking at the woman across the table; Mrs. Melville did not like being watched while getting into her coat. Ye Olde Taverne was beginning to fill up with shoppers taking Shopper's Tea, and the passage of people back and forth behind Mrs. Melville's chair made her effort to don her coat more violent; as she gave the lapels a last pull together across the front, the waitress returned, set down a cup of tea in front of the woman across the table, and a tiny paper cup in front of Mrs. Melville. "Your mayonnaise," said the waitress, and grinned.

•   •   •

Mrs. Melville indignantly forbore leaving any tip, but got up with vast dignity and made her way to the cashier.

"I wish to report this waitress for impertinence," she said. "The one over there in the yellow skirt."

"What'd she do?" asked the cashier without interest.

"She refused to give me what I had ordered," Mrs. Melville said. "She spoke rudely, and when I asked for more—"

"Complaint department," said the cashier unenthusiastically. "I can't do nothing about that here, miss."

She looked up at Mrs. Melville without interest and said, "Complaint department" again wearily as she took Mrs. Melville's money. "Ninth floor," she said. *"I think."*

With one final furious glance at the waitress, Mrs. Melville snatched up her change and made purposefully for the escalator. The salesgirl, the waitress, the cashier—what sort of a store could this be? Mrs. Melville, setting her shoulders firmly as she stood on the escalator, thought with satisfaction that she was certainly glad no one she knew ever came here to shop; how could anything be purchased in a store where the salesgirls criticized one's figure, the waitress kidnapped one's muffins, the cashiers had no sympathy for one's feelings?

She stepped off the escalator at the eighth floor, started for her final escalator, and stopped dead. Her package. Her package, her bag with her precious blouse in it, was down in the restaurant.

"Now, why do you think no one *reminded* me?" Mrs. Melville said aloud, so that a woman passing her on the way to the next escalator looked at her disagreeably. Irritated beyond further words, Mrs. Melville turned silently and made her way across the store to the down escalator. Back she went, the way she had come, and back through the wooden portals of Ye Olde Taverne. There were people at the table she had used—indeed, almost all the tables were filled now— two young women, obviously suburban matrons, in neat pretty hats and neat pretty coats, sitting where Mrs. Melville and the unknown woman had sat so shortly before. Although one of the two young suburban matrons wore a dark green coat with a mink collar and a green straw hat and the other one wore a brown wool suit with a fur scarf and a tan straw hat, they looked somehow subtly, unbelievably alike, and both raised calm, assured eyes to Mrs. Melville as she came up to the table and said, restraining her voice:

"I beg your pardon, but I left a package here on the chair." She indicated the chair in which the young woman in dark green was sitting. "Have you seen it?"

The two young women glanced at one another. "A bag, was it?" said the one in brown; she was, Mrs. Melville noticed, having tea with cinnamon toast. "A bag from this store?"

"Yes, certainly," said Mrs. Melville, growing impatient again. "Where is it?"

"Good heavens," the one in green said to the one in brown. She was having a ham and cheese sandwich on whole wheat; a good choice, Mrs. Melville thought.

"I *know*," said the one in brown, nodding. She turned to Mrs. Melville. "I think we did a *terrible* thing," she said. "There was a woman here drinking tea when we came and she left just as we came and we found the package on the chair and I called her back and gave it to her."

"Gave her *my* package?" said Mrs. Melville, mystified.

"We thought it was hers," the one in green explained. "It was here on the chair, you see. Now that I think of it," she said to the one in brown, "she *did* act sort of funny."

"Sort of funny," the one in brown agreed. "*Very* funny. When I gave her the package she sort of *looked* at me."

"Yes," the one in green agreed. "Why don't you ask at the Lost and Found?" she inquired brightly of Mrs. Melville.

"What did she look like, this woman?" said Mrs. Melville.

"Well," said the one in green, "she was small and dark. And sort of funny."

"*I* thought she was definitely funny," said the one in brown decisively. "Sort of dark, and small, she was."

Mrs. Melville turned abruptly, without thanking them, and found the waitress who had been so rude to her. Marching up to the girl, Mrs. Melville said, "Did you see the other woman who sat at my table?"

The girl stared. "No," she said. Mrs. Melville remembered that she had left no tip. When the girl continued to stare at her blankly, Mrs. Melville said persuasively, "She stole a package that belonged to me. I want to get my package back."

"What was in the package?" said the waitress.

"A blouse," said Mrs. Melville tensely. "Did you see her?"

The waitress looked sweetly at Mrs. Melville. "Try the complaint department," she said. "It's up on the ninth floor."

Mrs. Melville tightened her lips, and then decided not to bandy words with this impolite girl; she hurried over to the cashier, who turned her blond head tiredly. "Did you see a small, dark woman come out of here with a package?"

"I seen a million," said the cashier.

"This one had a cup of tea, that's all she had," Mrs. Melville said.

"A thousand of them had a cup of tea," the cashier said. "You was here before."

"I lost a package," Mrs. Melville said. "She stole it."

The cashier shook her head. "Never seen it," she said.

Irritably, Mrs. Melville stamped out of Ye Olde Taverne. Near the escalator to the seventh floor, and beyond it, on the way to the ninth floor, she stopped again. Her blouse had been stolen, certainly, but by a very small woman. Now, Mrs. Melville was very well aware that her blouse was a size forty-two, and, whatever else she knew about the small woman who had stolen it, she knew perfectly well that the small woman would not wear a blouse size forty-two; she had, after all, squeezed without complaint into the narrow space between the table and the wall; she had ordered only a spartan cup of tea. Furthermore, anyone who had taken illegally a blouse bought in the store would be in immediate terror of being found out. Now, Mrs. Melville reasoned, if *she* (perish the thought!) had stolen a package and, taking it to the nearest ladies' room, had found that it contained a blouse several sizes too large, *and* the sales slip for the blouse, what would she do? Why, Mrs. Melville told herself triumphantly, she would hurry with the blouse to the department where it had been purchased, and, with some credible story, return it for a smaller size before any fuss could be raised about its loss. Obviously, Mrs. Melville deduced, the woman with the blouse was perhaps even now exchanging it.

Mrs. Melville doggedly got back onto the escalator again, this time going down. She went as quickly as possible back to the blouse department, looking as she went for a small, dark, suspicious size ten.

The blouse department was deserted. The salesgirl whom Mrs. Melville was still on her way to report lounged on the counter. Mrs. Melville headed for her.

"Miss," she said loudly, even before she had reached the counter. "Do you remember me buying a blouse here?"

The girl nodded. She remembered.

Mrs. Melville said emphatically, "Someone *stole* that blouse."

The salesgirl took a deep breath. "What am *I* supposed to do about it?" she said. "Give you another?"

"Now, listen here," Mrs. Melville began, and then stopped herself, and said instead, "What I want to know is this: has anyone come here to return that blouse for another size?"

"Let me see," said the girl. "It was a size forty-two, wasn't it? Or a forty-four?"

"A forty-two," said Mrs. Melville.

"Well," said the girl, "not very many people wear blouses that *large*. So if anyone came to return a blouse of that *size*, I'd surely notice it."

Mrs. Melville clenched her hands around her pocketbook. "Someone in this store stole that blouse," she said.

"You might try the complaint department," the girl said innocently.

As Mrs. Melville was opening her mouth to answer, a woman came up beside her at the counter. "Miss?" she said softly.

Mrs. Melville turned slowly. The woman was small, and wearing a dark coat and hat. Moreover, she was carrying a package that looked suspiciously like Mrs. Melville's package, and she was saying to the salesgirl:

"Earlier today I bought a blouse here. I think I bought it from the other girl, because I'm pretty sure *you* didn't sell it to me." She laughed embarrassedly. "Anyway," she said, "when I bought it I told her I wanted to take it upstairs and try it on with a suit and perhaps exchange it for another color if it didn't match the suit. . . ." Her voice trailed off as she saw the salesgirl nod politely.

"Wrong color?" said the salesgirl professionally, beginning to open the bag.

"Oh, *no*," said the woman. "I mean, the color is *perfect*. I *love* it. No, it's the size. She must have got it mixed up, somehow."

The salesgirl took the blouse out of the bag and spread it on the counter. Mrs. Melville looked at it and began to breathe more quickly; a deep happiness filled her.

"It's just the right shade of pink," the small woman said timidly. "But I mean, it's a size forty-two. She must have given it to me by mistake." The small woman laughed. "You can *see* I don't wear a forty-two," she said.

It was the laugh which decided Mrs. Melville on her future course of action. She looked briefly at the salesgirl, who looked back at her without expression, and then stepped back a few feet. The small woman looked at her nervously. "I didn't mean to push in here," the small woman said, smiling shyly at Mrs. Melville. "I was so upset, I mean, and I'm in such a hurry . . ."

"That's perfectly all right," said Mrs. Melville. "Go right ahead." She had never said this before in her life.

"Well," said the small woman to the salesgirl, "you can see, it must have been some kind of a mistake. I wanted the pink blouse, size ten, and somehow she picked up the pink blouse, size forty-two, and put it in the bag by mistake. I mean, she must have made a mistake."

"Size ten?" said the salesgirl. She turned to the stacks of blouses behind her. "The pink, size ten." Without looking at Mrs. Melville, she said clearly, "I can use the forty-two back. Had a call for a size forty-two blouse this morning."

"Really?" said the small woman. "You wouldn't think anyone that large would wear this pink."

"You'd be surprised what people think they can wear," said the salesgirl, not looking at Mrs. Melville. "I had a lady in here this morning looking at that pink blouse size forty-two."

The small woman shuddered. "I didn't know they made *any*thing that large," she said. "Not in any colors except maybe black or brown."

"Oh, yes," said the salesgirl. She was folding the blouse to put it into the bag. "I don't think some of these women ever think what they're going to look like. They figure they're going to look like anyone else in that blouse."

The small woman took the bag. "Thanks *very* much," she said. "I appreciate all your trouble."

"No trouble at all," said the salesgirl.

The small woman smiled again at Mrs. Melville. "I hope I didn't delay *you*."

"Not at all," said Mrs. Melville.

The small woman moved off quickly and Mrs. Melville, giving the salesgirl one last ominous glance, followed her.

The small woman had several packages, but the bag containing the blouse was the one Mrs. Melville was watching; it was being carried under one of the thin, black-covered arms, and as the woman walked hurriedly toward the down escalator, Mrs. Melville was able to see her dark hat and the package under her arm.

The store was not crowded, so it was not difficult for Mrs. Melville to keep the woman in sight without coming recognizably close, and she let the woman step onto the escalator and go nearly halfway down before stepping on herself. When the woman reached the bottom she turned to the right, heading for one of the big avenue entrances of the store, and then Mrs. Melville realized that she must hurry, because the woman was planning to leave the store and, once out on the street, would be practically uncatchable. Closing in on her quarry, Mrs. Melville debated the possibilities: Could she corner the woman, accuse her, between handkerchiefs and stockings? Bring her to bay in cosmetics? Face her down before the interested shoppers at the glove counter? Force her to give up the blouse under the eyes of the information clerk?

Then, mercifully, the woman ahead hesitated, glanced at the clock, at a counter, at the clock again, and then paused and turned to the counter. Mrs. Melville came up behind her purposefully and saw that she was hastily turning over a pile of sweaters that lay on the counter, with a sign above reading "Reduced—$1.98." Moving up beside the woman, Mrs. Melville also began turning over sweaters. They were hideous, she thought, brightly colored small things, not fit for any female over the age of ten. The woman next to her pulled one sweater from the pile, shifting all her packages to one arm to use the other hand to spread the sweater out.

"Miss," she said shyly to the salesgirl, "how much is this?"

Mrs. Melville moved closer.

"All one ninety-eight," the salesgirl said. "All the same price."

The woman looked at the sweater. "Is it my size?" the woman asked the salesgirl. "I can't seem to find a tag."

The salesgirl regarded the sweater with cynicism. "These people pull the tags off of everything just because it's on sale," she said. "About a ten."

The woman nodded briskly, and set her packages down on the counter next to Mrs. Melville in order to lift the sweater and hold it against her. "It's a pretty color," she said to the salesgirl. "Much prettier than a blouse I just bought upstairs, and I paid . . ."

But Mrs. Melville did not hear what the small woman had paid for the blouse; she already knew, in any case, and she was heading rapidly for the escalator with the package containing the expensive blouse clutched tightly in front of her. She tried to lose herself immediately among the crowds of shoppers, and went onto the escalator with a group of people, pushing herself without apology ahead of them. On the escalator she walked quickly, almost running up the moving steps, and then, on the second floor, walked as rapidly as she had ever walked in her life, toward the blouse department. The same girl, as bored and dreamy as ever, stood at the counter. Mrs. Melville slammed the bag containing the blouse down on the counter and said loudly, "There."

The salesgirl recognized her; by now Mrs. Melville's must have been as familiar a face to her as her own mother's, or the floor-walker's, because, looking once at Mrs. Melville, she closed her eyes briefly and said, "Yes?"

"Give me back my blouse," Mrs. Melville said; she was frankly trying too hard to breathe slowly to speak much. "I want you to give my own blouse back to me."

The salesgirl opened the bag and took out the pink size ten blouse. "You want," she said deliberately, "to exchange this blouse for another size?"

"I do," Mrs. Melville said. "You know perfectly well what I want."

"And what size did you want?"

"Give it to me," said Mrs. Melville through her teeth. "You know which one it is. Give it to me."

The salesgirl shrugged, turned, and took down the pink blouse, glanced at the tag, said, "Size forty-two" in a loud voice, and put it in the bag.

"The next time . . ." Mrs. Melville began, and then for the life of her could not conceive of a next time; there was no statement crushing enough. "The next time . . ." Mrs. Melville said again futilely. She turned and stamped away.

"Complaint department, ninth floor," the girl called after her, and giggled.

Mrs. Melville, her blouse tightly held under her arm—although she did not really believe that the small woman was now following *her*—went on her way deep in thought. She had triumphed, she thought, over this store with its discourtesy and inefficiency, this store where people were allowed to steal from harmless customers. Where would this store be, Mrs. Melville asked herself indignantly, if people like herself did not shop here? It had just been pure chance that she had come into the store at all, and did they think for a minute that the way she had been treated would encourage her to come *back*? Mrs. Melville remembered clearly her initial irritation, when she had bought the blouse in the first place. The girl, so rude about the shocking pink and the chartreuse . . .

Mrs. Melville stopped dead in the middle of the shoe department.

She remembered herself buying the blouse, debating over the color, deciding that the chartreuse was more sophisticated, and—she realized it suddenly and irresistibly—buying the chartreuse blouse. She had definitely considered the pink, worried about it, and then decided that the chartreuse blouse was more sophisticated, it was the very thing she had told herself, it was the very word she had used. She had most emphatically bought the chartreuse blouse the first time. And the blouse in the bag now under her arm was shocking pink.

Hesitation was not one of Mrs. Melville's vices. For a moment, she stood still in the middle of the shoe department and then, shifting the bag to hold it more firmly, she set her shoulders back and with goodwill toward the world, marched heartily down to where the sign for the up escalator showed her the way toward the small suits, the glassware, Ye Olde Taverne, and—Mrs. Melville knew she would make it this time—the complaint department.

JOURNEY WITH

A LADY

Harper's, *July 1952*

H ONEY,'' MRS. WILSON SAID uneasily, "are you *sure* you'll be all *right?*" "Sure," said Joseph. He backed away quickly as she bent to kiss him again. "Listen, *Mother*," he said. "Everybody's *looking*."

"I'm still not sure but what someone ought to go with him," said his mother. "Are you *sure* he'll be all right?" she said to her husband.

"Who, Joe?" said Mr. Wilson. "He'll be fine, won't you, son?"

"Sure," said Joseph.

"A boy nine years old ought to be able to travel by himself," said Mr. Wilson in the patient tone of one who has been saying these same words over and over for several days to a nervous mother.

Mrs. Wilson looked up at the train as one who estimates the probable strength of an enemy. "But suppose something should *happen?*" she asked.

"Look, Helen," her husband said, "the train's going to leave in about four minutes. His bag is already on the train, Helen. It's on the seat where he's going to be sitting from now until he gets to Merrytown. I have spoken to the porter and I have given the porter a couple of dollars, and the porter has promised to keep an eye on him and see that he gets off the train with his bag when the train stops at Merrytown. He is nine years old, Helen, and he knows his name and where he's going and where he's supposed to get off, and Grandpop is going to meet him and will telephone you the minute they get to Grandpop's house, and the porter—"

"I know," said Mrs. Wilson, "but are you sure he'll be all *right?*"

Mr. Wilson and Joseph looked at one another briefly and then away.

Mrs. Wilson took advantage of Joseph's momentary lapse of awareness to put her arm around his shoulders and kiss him again, although he managed to move almost in time and her kiss landed somewhere on the top of his head. "*Mother,*" Joseph said ominously.

"Don't want anything to happen to my little boy," Mrs. Wilson said with a brave smile.

"Mother, for heaven's *sake,*" said Joseph. "I better get on the train," he said to his father. "Good idea," said his father.

"Bye, Mother," Joseph said, backing toward the train door; he took a swift look up and down the platform, and then reached up to his mother and gave her a rapid kiss on the cheek. "Take care of yourself," he said.

"Don't forget to telephone the minute you get there," his mother said. "Write me every day, and tell Grandma you're supposed to brush your teeth every night and if the weather turns cool—"

"Sure," Joseph said. "Sure, Mother."

"So long, son," said his father.

"So long, Dad," Joseph said; solemnly they shook hands. "Take care of yourself," Joseph said.

"Have a good time," his father said.

As Joseph climbed up the steps to the train he could hear his mother saying, "And telephone us when you get there and be careful—"

"Goodbye, goodbye," he said, and went into the train. He had been located by his father in a double seat at the end of the car and, once settled, he turned as a matter of duty to the window. His father, with an unmanly look of concern, waved to him and nodded violently, as though to indicate that everything was going to be all right, that they had pulled it off beautifully, but his mother, twisting her fingers nervously, came close to the window of the train, and, fortunately unheard by the people within, but probably clearly audible to everyone for miles without, gave him at what appeared to be some length an account of how she had changed her mind and was probably going to come with him after all. Joseph nodded and smiled and waved and shrugged his shoulders to indicate that he could not hear, but his mother went on talking, now and then glancing nervously at the front of the train, as though afraid that the engine might start and take Joseph away before she had made herself absolutely sure that he was going to be all right. Joseph, who felt with some justice that in the past few days his mother had told him every conceivable pertinent fact about his traveling alone to his grandfather's, and her worries about same, was able to make out such statements as "Be careful," and "Telephone us the minute you get there," and "Don't forget to write." Then the train stirred, and hesitated, and moved slightly again, and Joseph backed away from the window, still waving and smiling. He was positive that what his mother was saying as the train pulled out was "Are you *sure* you'll be all right?" She blew a kiss to him as the train started, and he ducked.

Surveying his prospects as the train took him slowly away from his mother and father, he was pleased. The journey should take only a little over three hours, and he knew the name of the station and had his ticket safely in his jacket pocket; although he had been reluctant to yield in any fashion to his mother's misgivings, he had checked several times, secretly, to make sure the ticket was safe. He had half a dozen comic books—a luxury he was not ordinarily allowed—and a chocolate bar; he had his suitcase and his cap, and he had seen personally to the packing of his first baseman's mitt. He had a dollar bill in the pocket of his pants, because his mother thought he should have some money in case—possibilities which had concretely occurred to her—of a train wreck (although his father had pointed out that in the case of a major disaster the victims were not expected to pay their own expenses, at least not before their families had been notified) or perhaps in the case of some vital expense to which his grandfather's income would not be adequate. His father had thought that Joe ought to have a little money by him in case he wanted to buy anything, and because a man ought not to travel unless he had money in his pocket. "Might pick up a girl on the train and want to buy her lunch," his father had said jovially and his mother, regarding her husband thoughtfully, had remarked, "Let's hope *Joseph* doesn't do things like that," and Joe and his father had winked at one another. So, regarding his comic books and his suitcase and his ticket and his chocolate bar, and feeling the imperceptible but emphatic presence of the dollar bill in his pocket, Joe leaned back against the soft seat, looked briefly out the window at the houses now moving steadily past, and said to himself, "This is the life, boy."

Before indulging in the several glories of comic books and chocolate, he spent a moment or so watching the houses of his hometown disappear beyond the train; ahead of him, at his grandfather's farm, lay a summer of cows and horses and probable wrestling matches in the grass; behind him lay school and its infinite irritations, and his mother and father. He wondered briefly if his mother was still looking after the train and telling him to write, and then largely he forgot her. With a sigh of pure pleasure he leaned back and selected a comic book, one that dealt with the completely realistic adventures of a powerful magician among hostile African tribes. This *is* the life, boy, he told himself again, and glanced again out the window to see a boy about his own age sitting on a fence watching the train go by. For a minute Joseph thought of waving down to the boy, but decided that it was beneath his dignity as a traveler; moreover, the boy on the fence was wearing a dirty sweatshirt, which made Joe move uneasily under his stiff collar and suit jacket, and he thought longingly of the comfortable old shirt with the insignia "Brooklyn Dodger," which was in his suitcase. Then, just as the traitorous idea of changing on the train occurred to him, and of arriving at his grandfather's not in his good suit became a possibility, all sensible thought was driven from his mind by a cruel and unnecessary blow. Someone sat down next to him, breathing heavily, and from the quick flash of perfume and the movement of cloth that could only be a dress rustling Joe realized with a strong sense of injustice that his paradise had been invaded by some woman.

"Is this seat taken?" she asked.

Joe refused to recognize her existence by turning his head to look at her, but he told her sullenly, "No, it's not." Not taken, he was thinking, what did she think *I* was sitting here for? Aren't there enough old seats in the train she could go and sit in without taking mine?

He seemed to lose himself in contemplation of the scenery beyond the train window, but secretly he was wishing direly that the woman would suddenly discover she had forgotten her suitcase or find out she had no ticket or remember that she had left the bathtub running at home—anything, to get her off the train at the first station, and out of Joe's way.

"You going far?"

Talking, too, Joe thought, she has to take my seat and then she goes and talks my ear off, darn old pest. "Yeah," he said. "Merrytown."

"What's your name?"

Joe, from long experience, could have answered all her questions in one sentence, he was so familiar with the series—I'm nine years old, he could have told her, and I'm in the fifth grade, and, no, I don't like school, and if you want to know what I learn in school it's nothing because I don't like school and I do like movies, and I'm going to my grandfather's house, and more than anything else I hate women who come and sit beside me and ask me silly questions and if my mother didn't keep after me all the time about my manners I would probably gather my things together and move to another seat and if you don't stop asking me—

"What's your name, little boy?"

Little boy, Joe told himself bitterly, on top of everything else, little boy.

"Joe," he said.

"How old are you?"

He lifted his eyes wearily and regarded the conductor entering the car; it was surely too much to hope that this female plague had forgotten her ticket, but could it be remotely possible that she was on the wrong train?

"Got your ticket, Joe?" the woman asked.

"Sure," said Joe. "Have you?"

She laughed and said—apparently addressing the conductor, since her voice was not at this moment the voice women use in addressing a little boy, but the voice that goes with speaking to conductors and taxi drivers and salesclerks—"I'm afraid I haven't got a ticket. I had no time to get one."

"Where are you going?" said the conductor.

Would they put her off the train? For the first time, Joe turned and looked at her, eagerly and with hope. Would they possibly, hopefully, desperately, put her off the train? "I'm going to Merrytown," she said, and Joe's convictions about the generally weak-minded attitudes of the adult world were all confirmed: The conductor tore a slip from a pad he carried, punched a hole in it, and told the woman, "Two seventy-three." While she was searching her pocketbook for her money—if she knew she was going to have to buy a ticket, Joe thought disgustedly, whyn't she have her money ready?—the conductor took Joe's ticket and grinned at him. "Your boy got *his* ticket all right," he pointed out.

The woman smiled. "He got to the station ahead of me," she said.

The conductor gave her her change, and went on down the car.

"That was funny, when he thought you were my little boy," the woman said.

"Yeah," said Joe.

"What're you reading?"

Wearily, Joe put his comic book down.

"Comic," he said.

"Interesting?"

"Yeah," said Joe.

"Say, look at the policeman," the woman said.

Joe looked where she was pointing and saw—he would not have believed this, since he knew perfectly well that most women cannot tell the difference between a policeman and a mailman—that it was undeniably a policeman, and that he was regarding the occupants of the car very much as though there might be a murderer or an international jewel thief riding calmly along on the train. Then, after surveying the car for a moment, he came a few steps forward to the last seat, where Joe and the woman were sitting.

"Name?" he said sternly to the woman.

"Mrs. John Aldridge, Officer," said the woman promptly. "And this is my little boy, Joseph."

"Hi, Joe," said the policeman.

Joe, speechless, stared at the policeman and nodded dumbly.

"Where'd you get on?" the policeman asked the woman.

"Ashville," she said.

"See anything of a woman about your height and build, wearing a fur jacket, getting on the train at Ashville?"

"I don't think so," said the woman. "Why?"

"Wanted," said the policeman tersely.

"Keep your eyes open," he told Joe. "Might get a reward."

He passed on down the car, and stopped occasionally to speak to women who seemed to be alone. Then the door at the far end of the car closed behind him and Joe turned and took a deep look at the woman sitting beside him. "What'd you do?" he asked.

"Stole some money," said the woman, and grinned.

Joe grinned back. If he had been sorely pressed, he might in all his experience until now have been able to identify only his mother as a woman both pretty and lovable; in this case, however—and perhaps it was enhanced by a sort of outlaw glory—he found the woman sitting next to him much more attractive than he had before supposed. She looked nice, she had soft hair, she had a pleasant smile and not a lot of lipstick and stuff on, and her fur jacket was rich and soft against Joe's hand. Moreover, Joe knew absolutely when she grinned at him that there were not going to be any more questions about nonsense like people's ages and whether they liked school, and he found himself grinning back at her in quite a friendly manner.

"They gonna catch you?" he asked.

"Sure," said the woman. "Pretty soon now. But it was worth it."

"Why?" Joe asked; crime, he well knew, did not pay.

"See," said the woman, "I wanted to spend about two weeks having a good time there in Ashville. I wanted this coat, see? And I wanted just to buy a lot of clothes and things."

"So?" said Joe.

"So I took the money from the old tightwad I worked for and I went off to Ashville and bought some clothes and went to a lot of movies and things and had a fine time."

"Sort of a vacation," Joe said.

"Sure," the woman said. "Knew all the time they'd catch me, of course. For one thing, I always knew I had to come home again. But it was worth it!"

"How much?" said Joe.

"Two thousand dollars," said the woman.

"Boy!" said Joe.

They settled back comfortably. Joe, without more than a moment's pause to think, offered the woman his comic book about the African headhunters, and when the policeman came back through the car, eyeing them sharply, they were leaning back shoulder to shoulder, the woman apparently deep in African adventure, Joe engrossed in the adventures of a flying newspaper reporter who solved vicious gang murders.

"How is your book, Ma?" Joe said loudly as the policeman passed, and the woman laughed and said, "Fine, fine."

As the door closed behind the policeman the woman said softly, "You know, I like to see how long I can keep out of their way."

"Can't keep it up forever," Joe pointed out.

"No," said the woman, "but I'd like to go back by myself and just give them what's left of the money. I had my good time."

"Seems to me," Joe said, "that if it's the first time you did anything like this they probably wouldn't punish you so much."

"I'm not ever going to do it again," the woman said. "I mean, you sort of build up all your life for one real good time like this, and then you can take your punishment and not mind it so much."

"I don't know," Joe said reluctantly, various small sins of his own with regard to matches and his father's cigars and other people's lunch boxes crossing his mind; "seems to me that even if you do think *now* that you'll never do it again, sometimes—well, sometimes, you do it anyway." He thought. "I always *say* I'll never do it again, though."

"Well, if you do it again," the woman pointed out, "you get punished twice as bad the next time."

Joe grinned. "I took a dime out of my mother's pocketbook once," he said. "But I'll never do *that* again."

"Same thing I did," said the woman.

Joe shook his head. "If the policemen plan to spank you the way my father spanked me . . ." he said.

They were companionably silent for a while, and then the woman said, "Say, Joe, you hungry? Let's go into the dining car."

"I'm supposed to stay here," Joe said.

"But I can't go without you," the woman said. "They think I'm all right because the woman they want wouldn't be traveling with her little boy."

"Stop calling me your little boy," Joe said.

"Why?"

"Call me your son or something," Joe said. "No more little-boy stuff."

"Right," said the woman. "Anyway, I'm sure your mother wouldn't mind if you went into the dining car with *me*."

"I bet," Joe said, but he got up and followed the woman out of the car and down through the next car; people glanced up at them as they passed and then away again, and Joe thought triumphantly that they would sure stare harder if they knew that this innocent-looking woman and her son were outsmarting the cops every step they took.

They found a table in the dining car and sat down. The woman took up the menu and said, "What'll you have, Joe?"

Blissfully, Joe regarded the woman, the waiters moving quickly back and forth, the shining silverware, the white tablecloth and napkins. "Hard to say right off," he said.

"Hamburger?" said the woman. "Spaghetti? Or would you rather just have two or three desserts?"

Joe stared. "You mean, like, just blueberry pie with ice cream and a hot fudge sundae?" he asked. "Like that?"

"Sure," said the woman. "Might as well celebrate one last time."

"When I took that dime out of my mother's pocketbook," Joe told her, "I spent a nickel on gum and a nickel on candy."

"Tell me," said the woman, leaning forward earnestly, "the candy and gum—was it all right? I mean, the same as usual?"

Joe shook his head. "I was so afraid someone would see me," he said, "I ate all the candy in two mouthfuls standing on the street and I was scared to open the gum at all."

The woman nodded. "That's why I'm going back so soon, I guess," she said, and sighed.

"Well," said Joe practically, "might as well have blueberry pie first, anyway."

They ate their lunch peacefully, discussing baseball and television and what Joe wanted to be when he grew up; once the policeman passed through the car and nodded to them cheerfully, and the waiter opened his eyes wide and laughed when Joe decided to polish off his lunch with a piece of watermelon. When they had finished and the woman had paid the check, they found that they were due in Merrytown in fifteen minutes, and they hurried back to their seat to gather together Joe's comic books and suitcase.

"Thank you very much for the nice lunch," Joe said to the woman as they sat down again, and congratulated himself upon remembering to say it.

"Nothing at all," the woman said. "Aren't you my little boy?"

"Watch that little-boy stuff," Joe said warningly, and she said, "I mean, aren't you my son?"

The porter who had been delegated to keep an eye on Joe opened the car door and put his head in. He smiled reassuringly at Joe and said, "Five minutes to your station, boy."

"Thanks," said Joe. He turned to the woman. "Maybe," he said urgently, "if you tell them you're *really* sorry—"

"Wouldn't do at all," said the woman. "I really had a fine time."

"I guess so," Joe said. "But you won't do it again."

"Well, I knew when I started I'd be punished sooner or later," the woman said.

"Yeah," Joe said. "Can't get out of it now."

The train pulled slowly to a stop and Joe leaned toward the window to see if his grandfather was waiting.

"We better not get off together," the woman said; "might worry your grandpa to see you with a stranger."

"Guess so," said Joe. He stood up, and took hold of his suitcase. "Goodbye, then," he said reluctantly.

"Goodbye, Joe," said the woman. "Thanks."

"Right," said Joe, and as the train stopped he opened the door and went out onto the steps. The porter helped him to get down with his suitcase and Joe turned to see his grandfather coming down the platform.

"Hello, fellow," said his grandfather. "So you made it."

"Sure," said Joe. "No trick at all."

"Never thought you wouldn't," said his grandfather. "Your mother wants you to—"

"Telephone as soon as I get here," Joe said. "I know."

"Come along, then," his grandfather said. "Grandma's waiting at home."

He led Joe to the parking lot and helped him and his suitcase into the car. As his grandfather got into the front seat beside him, Joe turned and looked back at the train and saw the woman walking down the platform with the policeman holding her arm. Joe leaned out of the car and waved violently. "So long," he called.

"So long, Joe," the woman called back, waving.

"It's a shame the cops had to get her after all," Joe remarked to his grandfather.

His grandfather laughed. "You read too many comic books, fellow," he said. "Everyone with a policeman isn't being arrested—he's probably her brother or something."

"Yeah," said Joe.

"Have a good trip?" his grandfather asked. "Anything happen?"

Joe thought. "Saw a boy sitting on a fence," he said. "I didn't wave to him, though."

THE MOST
WONDERFUL THING

Good Housekeeping, *June 1952*

YOUNG MRS. HARTLEY, WHO could still remember most clearly the pain and bitterness and injustice she had known so recently, lay absolutely flat on the hospital bed, trying to count to a thousand by sevens, or to recite from memory as many recipes as she could. When a nurse (young Rose, who came singing down the halls) glanced quickly in through the doorway, Mrs. Hartley smiled and lifted a hand to wave to her, and the nurse smiled back and went on. They're so sure I'm all right, Mrs. Hartley thought. When she lost count at four hundred and twenty, or could not remember a half teaspoonful of rosemary, Mrs. Hartley raised herself on her elbow to sip water through the glass straw, or she counted the squares in the ceiling—such clean, perfect squares, so sanitary and neat, like the beds, and the food, and even Mrs. Hartley herself—or she did crossword puzzles, worrying irritably over a ten-letter word meaning "hopeless." Today, her pencil well within reach on the bed table, she took up her watch instead. It was just after three: an hour and a half to washing-for-supper, six hours to bed-time, fifteen hours to waking-tomorrow-morning. She glanced at the stack of mystery stories conveniently close on the table, and sighed. Only an hour and a half to washing-for-supper, she told herself as though it were a kind of magic, only six hours to—

"*Now,* then," said Mac, and Mrs. Hartley said without turning, "I'm all *right,* Mac." Mac was the nurse who took care of Mrs. Hartley and heaven only knew how many others; who had probably not been called Miss MacIntyre since she first shook a thermometer; who prided herself on her natural talents with the enema bag and the hypodermic needle; who brought daily bulletins about whether or not the sun was warm outside the hospital. "*Now,* then," said Mac.

Mrs. Hartley turned, frowning. "Mac," she began, "I said—" She interrupted herself to stare. "Look," she went on after a minute, "this is supposed to be a private room, Mac. I'm *paying* for a private room."

"So?" said Mac amiably. "*I'm* the one will be getting into trouble for it, I suppose. But be quiet, please; this lady is sleeping."

"But she can't come in here," Mrs. Hartley said. "This is a *mistake,* Mac."

Mac grinned, and Mrs. Hartley had to smile back, even though Mac continued to maneuver the wheeled stretcher past Mrs. Hartley's bed and toward the other bed in the room.

"You'll only have to move her right out again," Mrs. Hartley said.

Mac left the front of the stretcher and came over to shake a warning finger under Mrs. Hartley's nose. "Just scream," she said. "Raise your voice and get everyone in here and tell them I brought a sick lady into a hospital room. But *unless* you're going to scream, you keep quiet and let me get her into bed."

"What's wrong with her?" Mrs. Hartley asked suspiciously.

Mac scowled, then laughed. "She's got a baby she didn't have before," Mac said. "What else would be wrong with her?"

Silently Mrs. Hartley watched, raised on one elbow, while Mac and another nurse lifted the slight body from the stretcher and onto the other bed, left vacant for so long because Mrs. Hartley had insisted on a private room. The girl's blond head lay quietly on the pillow, and she seemed to be scarcely breathing, but now and then in the silence she stirred a little and murmured.

"She'll be awake soon," Mac said. "Let me know, will you?" She pinched Mrs. Hartley's toe under the covers, and wheeled the stretcher through the door.

"Mac, listen," Mrs. Hartley began, and then fell silent as the girl on the other bed stirred. What if she tried to get out of bed? Mrs. Hartley thought nervously, what could *I* do? It wasn't fair of Mac to do this; I could even complain about her—Mrs. Hartley took a firm hold of the small button that turned on the light outside the door and summoned Mac, and then, ready, she told herself firmly that tomorrow morning, first thing, this girl was leaving her private room. Was the girl's breathing weaker? Her finger hovering over the light button, Mrs. Hartley watched, looking from the door to the other bed and back again.

"Jimmie?" the girl on the other bed said clearly. "Jimmie?"

Mrs. Hartley stared for a minute, but when the girl said again, insistently, "Jimmie?" Mrs. Hartley said, "He'll be here soon."

"Mother?"

Mrs. Hartley cleared her throat nervously. "Right here, dear," she said.

"Jimmie?" said the girl. She turned her head. Horrified, Mrs. Hartley saw that her eyes were open.

"What happened?" asked the girl. Her voice was suddenly different, conscious instead of unaware, firm instead of wavering. "Where am I now?"

"In the hospital. Everything's fine."

The girl frowned. "I don't understand," she said fretfully. "First you're on a bus and everything's fine, and then you're in a hospital and everything's fine, and what's happened? I mean, why am I here?" She turned and looked accusingly at Mrs. Hartley. "Who are *you*?"

"My name's Beth Hartley. You're not supposed to move." The girl on the other bed tried to sit up, and Mrs. Hartley put her finger down hard on the nurse button. "Please lie still," she said.

"I want to get out of here," the girl said.

"So do I," Mrs. Hartley said wryly. And I want *you* out of here, too, she thought; you couldn't be more anxious to leave than I am to have you. "I tell you, you'd better lie still," she said, her voice more gentle because of what she was thinking.

Briskly, Mac swept into the room. "Well, well," she said, "are we awake? So soon?" She glanced professionally at Mrs. Hartley. "Any trouble?"

"*I'm* not the nurse," Mrs. Hartley said sulkily.

"Why am I here?" the girl demanded, her voice rising. "I wake up all of a sudden and find myself in a strange room with a strange woman and no one will take the least bit of trouble to explain to me—"

"This lady is Mrs. Hartley," Mac said. "And you're here because not five minutes ago I personally wheeled you in on a stretcher. My name's Mac." She smiled engagingly, then turned to Mrs. Hartley.

"This lady," she said, "is Mrs. Williams, Mrs. Molly Williams. And now we've all been introduced."

The blue eyes moved over to Mrs. Hartley and then away again. "What do I say?" the girl demanded. "How do you do?"

Mrs. Hartley tried to smile, but could only grin unenthusiastically. "I'm so glad you're in here with me," she said, looking squarely at Mac.

"How long do I have to stay here?" the girl asked.

"As long as it takes to get you feeling fine again," Mac said, and moved toward the door. "Supper soon," she said, and pinched Mrs. Hartley's toe before she went out.

"I'm sorry you don't like it here," Mrs. Hartley said after a minute.

"Why don't they leave me alone?" said the girl.

Mrs. Hartley laughed. "They can't, very well," she said. "You're sick."

"I am *not*," said the girl. She moved again, stirring irritably under the bedclothes, and Mrs. Hartley again reached apprehensively for the light button. But the girl only said, "You sick, too?"

"I am," said Mrs. Hartley shortly, hoping to discourage other questions.

The girl continued the conversation. "What's the matter with *you*? You look all right."

"I'm nearly all right," Mrs. Hartley said evasively. "I ought to be going home in a few days."

"Me, too," said the girl. "They're not going to keep *me* here."

"How did you happen to come? I mean," Mrs. Hartley went on, embarrassed, "what made you pick this hospital if you didn't like it?"

"I wish I knew," said the girl; her voice was emphatic. "It must have been that busybody on the bus. I wasn't feeling very well and she chafed my hands; and then the bus stopped and she helped me off and she was going to get me some coffee and then—well, I guess then they must have brought me here, because I don't remember any more."

She hasn't even *asked* about her baby, Mrs. Hartley thought suddenly, appalled; could anyone be that callous? "What were you doing on a bus, for heaven's sake?" she asked, and added gracefully, "in your condition?"

"My condition!" said the girl, and laughed. "Who cared about my condition?—me?" She thought for a minute. "Maybe that woman on the bus," she conceded. "I was going home, you know. My father lives upstate and I was going there, only he didn't even know I was coming."

Mrs. Hartley hesitated, debated with herself for a minute, started to speak, and then hesitated again. What do I care? she thought; it's not *my* worry. Finally, she said, "Isn't there anyone else who might care?"

"No," said the girl.

Mrs. Hartley plunged. "What about your husband?"

There was a short silence, and then the girl said, as though she clearly recognized Mrs. Hartley's hesitation and wanted the subject closed at once, "He's in the army, overseas. Somewhere." She raised her hands and let them fall helplessly, and spoke louder because Mrs. Hartley tried to interrupt. "We never figured on having any children," she said. "We don't either of us *like* kids, and he certainly wasn't planning on coming back to find a whole family waiting for him . . ." Her voice trailed off, bitterly, and Mrs. Hartley could not find anything to say. "He'd be better off if he never found either of us again," the girl said with finality.

"Mrs. Williams," Mrs. Hartley began, and then stopped. I'm not a welfare society, she thought; I don't care if this disagreeable girl and her disagreeable husband never see each other again. I'm sorry about the baby, it's too bad about the baby, but what business is it of mine? No one worries about *me*. "It's none of my business," Mrs. Hartley began again, "but—"

"That's right," the girl said. "It's not."

They were lying silent, separated by four feet of space and a world of animosity, when Mac's step, heavier because she was carrying a bowl of warm water in each hand, forced them both to stir and smile slightly. I'll catch Mac after this girl is asleep, Mrs. Hartley was telling herself; she's *got* to get her out of here tomorrow. A great feeling of self-pity had filled Mrs. Hartley; it seemed just too much that after all she had been through, and the long days she had spent alone in this room, she should now be forced to endure this flat and insolent company. I am really really annoyed with Mac, Mrs. Hartley thought.

"Wash for supper, girls," Mac said cheerfully. "Can't have any supper till your hands are clean."

"Suppose I don't want any supper?" the girl asked sourly.

"Then you don't have to eat it. But you'll be clean anyway."

Mrs. Hartley, who was allowed to have the head of her bed slightly raised, had learned to wash her face inadequately with a damp washcloth, and to scrub her hands almost without being able to see them; the bed table was raised enough above eye level to make normal gestures impossible. Her favorite joke with Mac was a remembrance of the evening when supper had been spaghetti and Mrs. Hartley had tried to eat it lying down. Tonight, she glanced across at the other bed, where Mrs. Williams, lying flat on her back, was irritably struggling to wash her hands. "Careful not to tip the bowl," Mrs. Hartley said.

"How do they expect *any*body—"

"Wait till you try to eat," Mrs. Hartley said. "You know, the first night I was here they served spaghetti, and—"

"I'll bet the food is terrible," Mrs. Williams said. She gave a disgusted little shove to her bed table, and the water in the bowl spilled a little. "I hate this place," she said.

"They always serve supper," Mac said, sweeping wildly into the room and scooping up the bowls, "before my ladies are clean. Always, always—you washed?" she demanded severely of Mrs. Williams as she darted outside for the trays.

"I don't want any supper," Mrs. Williams said.

"Too bad," said Mac, reappearing. "Chicken soup, veal cutlet, mashed potatoes, asparagus, chocolate pudding."

"I don't want any," Mrs. Williams said sullenly. "I hate this place."

"Suppose I just set the tray down anyway," Mac said. "No place else to put it." She put the tray down on the table in front of Mrs. Williams, and came over to stand by the foot of Mrs. Hartley's bed. "How is it tonight?" she asked softly. "You doing any better?"

"Fine," Mrs. Hartley said, avoiding looking at Mac. "I'm doing beautifully."

"It's a shame, sometimes," Mac said. "If they could only fix it so we all could stop thinking altogether."

Mrs. Hartley laughed. "I don't believe you have time to think," she said.

Mac glanced cautiously at Mrs. Williams, who was now taking quick mouthfuls of her chocolate pudding. "Sometimes I manage to get an idea," she said.

·   ·   ·

After the supper trays had been taken away, Mrs. Williams asked suddenly, "How long have you been here?"

"Six days."

"Why so long?"

Mrs. Hartley sighed. "I'm leaving soon," she said. "I'll be walking around tomorrow, maybe, or the day after."

"How soon do you think they'll let me out? A couple of days, maybe?"

"That depends on the doctor."

"*I'm* getting up right away," Mrs. Williams said with finality.

"You ready for your baby?" Mac said, putting her head around the door.

"Me?" said Mrs. Williams. She turned to Mrs. Hartley. "Does she mean me?"

"I certainly do," Mac said. "Coming now."

She moved aside as another nurse, looking, if possible, even cleaner and more starched than Mac, came in the door, smiled at Mrs. Hartley, and said, "Mrs. Williams? Here's your baby."

"I don't want it," Mrs. Williams said. "Take it away."

The nurse hesitated and glanced at Mac, who shrugged. "Well, someone's got to see that she gets this bottle," the nurse said.

"You could leave her on a doorstep somewhere," Mac said.

"I don't want her," Mrs. Williams said, her voice muffled by the pillow.

"You take her?" Mac said to Mrs. Hartley. "Just this once?"

Mrs. Hartley stared at Mac, wanting to push the baby away, yet finding that instead she held out her arms. Mac pinched Mrs. Hartley's toe under the covers. "Good girl," she said.

Mrs. Hartley, looking down at the small, unthinking face, the clenched hands and tiny head of the baby, thought, *I* started like this, and half smiled. "It's a pretty baby," she said tentatively.

"Wipe your fingers on the gauze pad," the nurse said mechanically. "Remember to support the head."

Ushering Mac ahead of her, she went out, leaving Mrs. Hartley alone with Mrs. Williams and the baby. "It's a pretty baby," Mrs. Hartley said again, suddenly appalled at the concentrated desire for food in this very small creature. Every part of it, even the toes she could feel curling under the blankets, the hands, the neck, seemed bent on nothing but nourishment. "Such small hands," Mrs. Hartley said inadequately.

"Who cares?" said the muffled voice from the other bed.

Perhaps I will be able to do this right, Mrs. Hartley thought, and she said carefully, "My baby died, you know."

"What?"

Perhaps, Mrs. Hartley thought—I might just as well learn to say these things without thinking too much about them. "It would have been a girl," she said. "That's why I've been here so long." Don't *keep* talking about it, she thought; everyone has troubles.

There was a sudden movement from the other bed, and then the blond head turned toward Mrs. Hartley. "That's really too bad," Mrs. Williams said.

"It's not as though we didn't *know*," Mrs. Hartley said carefully. "I mean, if you know ahead of time that things are not going all right, then somehow it's not as great a shock when—I was going to name her Elizabeth. That's my name, even though everyone calls me Beth. I have two boys, you see," she added, knowing that she was talking on and on but thinking, It's the first person I've talked to about it, even Mac won't listen, and I ought to say it all first before she asks me any more questions, and anyway she'd have to know later on. She said insistently, "You see, it isn't as though I won't try again. I have two fine boys, but this one would have been a girl. We were going to name her Elizabeth, after me."

There was a short pause. Then Mrs. Williams said, "It's funny, you wanted your baby and all, and me—"

"You've got a pretty baby," Mrs. Hartley said, looking down at the baby again. "She's almost finished her bottle."

"*Most* people," said Mac, putting her head around the door, "are hanging over their babies and saying 'Didums want its bottle?' or 'Was it a tweet 'ittle sing,' and here you two ladies sit with a baby and you talk to each other. It's not human, that it isn't." She came and stood over Mrs. Hartley and the baby. "Nice baby," she said. "What're you going to name her?"

"Me?" said Mrs. Williams.

"Well," Mac said consideringly, "the poor child is going to have an awful time of it *without* a name. Suppose she gets to be six or seven years old, and she's in school, and people are still calling her 'Hey!' or 'Miss X.'"

"I want to call her Elizabeth," Mrs. Williams said.

Mac glanced quickly at Mrs. Hartley and then away. "Pretty name," she said. "You could call her Betty, or Lizzie, or Betsy."

"I want to call her just Elizabeth," Mrs. Williams said. She lifted her head and smiled for the first time, directly at Mrs. Hartley. "Elizabeth," she said again.

Mrs. Hartley smiled back. "*I* always liked the name," she said.

"Do you suppose I could hold her for a minute before you take her back?" Mrs. Williams said to Mac.

Later that night, after Mac had straightened the beds, and taken out Mrs. Hartley's flowers, and opened the window, and after Mrs. Hartley and Mrs. Williams had both protested violently—and been overruled—about the little paper cups of milk of magnesia, Mrs. Williams, who had been lying back staring at the ceiling, asked suddenly, "You got any writing paper?"

"Here somewhere." Mrs. Hartley put down her mystery story and searched on her bed table. "In a box; I'll toss it over. Pen inside."

"Thanks," said Mrs. Williams.

Mrs. Hartley leaned her head back against the pillow and thought, Nine hours to waking-tomorrow-morning. I could be back here in a year, and I'd know all the routine when I came. There's nothing wrong with *me;* if she can do it, I can. . . . Nine hours to waking-tomorrow-morning, maybe ten months and I'll be back. She glanced across at the other bed and saw that Mrs. Williams was looking at her.

"Tired?" Mrs. Hartley asked.

"Sort of," Mrs. Williams said. "All right if I keep your stuff and finish my letter tomorrow?"

"Of course," Mrs. Hartley said. "You'd better get to sleep—they bring your baby back again a little after six in the morning."

"Golly," Mrs. Williams said. "I guess she's going to keep me pretty busy."

There was a minute's silence, and then Mrs. Williams said softly, "Good night, Elizabeth."

"Good night, Molly," Mrs. Hartley said.

Mrs. Hartley lay awake a long time, watching Mrs. Williams, counting the hours. Then, when she was almost asleep, the door opened softly and Mac came in. Mac stood looking down at Mrs. Williams, and Mrs. Hartley thought, She thinks I'm asleep, too. And then, How tired Mac looks; she isn't smiling now that no one can see her. It was too much to see Mac not smiling, and Mrs. Hartley said softly, "Good night, Mac."

Mac turned quickly, and she was smiling again. "You still awake?" she said. "Look at this." She went across to Mrs. Hartley's bed and held out a sheet of paper.

Mrs. Hartley realized that it was the letter Mrs. Williams had been writing when she fell asleep. "You want me to *read* it?" she asked.

"I do indeed," Mac said. "It isn't addressed to you and me, but I think it's partly meant for us."

Looking up at Mac and then across at the other bed, Mrs. Hartley took the letter and read it in the dim light of her bed lamp.

"Dearest Jimmie," it began. "The most wonderful thing in the world has happened. Little Elizabeth—"

THE FRIENDS

⚅

Charm, *November 1953*

E LLEN L ANSDOWNE HAD SURELY never considered herself a cruel, or an unkind, or a vicious woman. She still retained a tiny sense of sick shame at vaguely remembered schoolgirl injustices (that poor child, so long ago, the one who had that dreadful mother), and whenever possible Ellen Lansdowne made a clear and conscious effort to exhibit generosity and thoughtfulness. When there was literally no one who would volunteer to run the community concerts this year, or *someone* had to collect the articles for the white elephant sale, or the laundress's poor children were going to have an inadequate Christmas, dear Mrs. Lansdowne could always be counted on, cheerful and accommodating, sympathetic.

"I have so *much,*" she told herself often. "I've been so *lucky.*" The rich fur of her coat, she might remind herself with quiet happiness, the good health and intelligence of her two young sons, her pleasant home, the near probability of a glittering birthday present from Arthur . . . Ellen Lansdowne could point to a world of treasures to show that she had indeed been greatly favored by life.

Much more so, indeed, than most of her friends; certainly much more so than her dear friend Marjorie, with whom she had gone to school and to luncheons, to church to be married, and to concerts. Marjorie had always been weak, Ellen thought sometimes when she was counting her blessings; Marjorie never had quite enough of anything or the best of what she did have. It was a source of deep satisfaction to Ellen that dear Marjorie, too, had a fur coat—not quite so expensive a fur, certainly, as Ellen's—and an affectionate husband, and children—only little Joan, of course—and a nice home. Perhaps Arthur patronized the Actons a little, understandably, because Charles Acton *was* a bit on the pompous side and hadn't done nearly so well as he might, and Marjorie *did* whine a little about almost everything—well, Ellen would think, sighing, I have been *so* lucky. Arthur, and the boys, and everything I ever wanted. Poor Marjorie, she thought constantly and unwillingly, poor, lovely Marjorie, always so much prettier than the rest of us, poor Marjorie. And from reflections like this Ellen Lansdowne would usually step briskly out to do some good deed—invite someone's aunt to lunch, perhaps, or volunteer to drive the high school cheering section to the basketball game.

Poor Marjorie, Ellen always thought, poor Marjorie—up to the night of the country club dance when, running upstairs to gather her fur jacket, she absentmindedly opened the door of the cloakroom and then, stunned, backed out into the hall again, her hands trembling and her mind saying over and over, "Why, that was Marjorie, Marjorie and John Forrest. *Marjorie.*" For a minute she stood, bewildered, her hand still shaking against the doorknob, and then she turned and ran back downstairs, thinking only of getting away. A few couples were still dancing, and Arthur came across the dance floor, looking surprised. "Thought you went to get your coat," he said. "Changed your mind?"

No, no, Ellen wanted to say, I just couldn't go in while Marjorie and John—while John and Marjorie—I could hardly just walk right in and say . . . "I stopped to talk to someone," she said, surprised at the quiet of her own voice. "I'll get it now."

This is silly, she thought, holding up her long dress as she went back up the stairs, making two trips to get my jacket—they should have more sense. The door of the cloakroom was open, and Marjorie, inside, was touching up her lipstick at the mirror. Ellen refused to meet Marjorie's eyes in the mirror, and hoped she was not reddening as she crossed the room quickly to the rack where her jacket hung. "Nearly everyone's leaving," she said, addressing her jacket.

"Did you see us?" Marjorie asked.

"Arthur's waiting for me," Ellen said, and fled. Of course I saw you, you crazy fool, she thought, of course. "Ready?" she said, smiling, to her husband: It must have been going on for a long time, she thought, remembering slight oddnesses of behavior, sudden glances, almost unnoticed disappearances at dances and parties; could anyone else know? Not *her* husband, surely; not mine. Not John's wife.

"Nice party, wasn't it?" Arthur asked, and after a minute she said, "Lovely. But I'm tired."

"Poor Ellen," he said. "You worked so hard arranging every-thing."

I would like, she thought with the great clarity of weariness, to arrange Marjorie Acton right out of this town. And then she thought, how perfectly *beastly* of her, how foul.

Half a dozen times, during the ride home and after Arthur had come back from taking the sitter home and while they were having a glass of milk companionably together in the cool kitchen and then when they were getting ready for bed, Ellen came close to saying, bluntly and without warning, "Dear, Marjorie and John Forrest—I only *knew,* tonight, but I think I've felt it for a long time—Marjorie and John Forrest—" Each time she deliberately stopped herself from speaking, thinking that she had to be loyal to Marjorie, that Marjorie was her friend, that there was no imaginable word she could bring herself to use to her husband that would describe what she thought about Marjorie.

She did not realize how clearly she knew all the truth of it until the next morning when she met Marjorie in the grocery, and, saying, "Good morning, Marjorie," and hearing Marjorie say, "Ellen, hello," she found herself strongly wanting not to remember, and then saw last night's speculative fear still in Marjorie's eyes.

"How are you this morning?" Marjorie asked, and the words had a special weight, as though they should be translated ("I suppose you told Arthur?") before they could be entirely understood.

"Very well. And you?" ("No, of course not; how could I tell any-one?")

"See you soon," Marjorie said as they separated.

It was, however, a day or two before the complete destructiveness of her knowledge came to Ellen. Here we were, she realized sud-denly, sitting one morning at her kitchen table with the coffeepot and the morning paper waiting for her, here we were, a little group of friends, playing bridge, dancing, dining, swimming together, and then two among us fall out of step and introduce a new pattern, frightening and dreadful, into our well-filled lives. Good Lord, Ellen thought. I've known Marjorie for twenty-two years. Always so much prettier than the rest of us, we thought she'd do so well for herself, but *I* got Arthur. I *have* been lucky. Sitting peacefully at her kitchen table in the morning sunlight, she thought, without warning, but could I be wrong? Am I, perhaps, the only one who *hasn't* been in step; is everyone like Marjorie, like John, perhaps laughing at innocent Ellen: has Arthur . . . ? "No, *no*," she said aloud, pushing violently at her coffee cup, "this business has me all upset."

Although she tried to avoid seeing Marjorie, and succeeded, she believed, in largely forgetting that there had been any noticeable break in the deepest foundations of all their lives, she found that she had become an unwilling observer; it was almost as though Marjorie and John, reconciled to her awareness, felt a kind of relief at having one person they need not trouble to deceive. There was an evening not more than a week after the country club dance when Ellen, turning to light a cigarette at a cocktail party, saw John Forrest rise and walk casually out onto the terrace; after a minute Marjorie, meeting Ellen's eyes and even smiling a little, went quietly and without other notice after him. "I enjoyed his first play much more," Ellen said easily without more than a second's pause in the conversation in which she had been engaged. "I think this one is somehow too—pretentious."

"And did you see—" someone went on, and Ellen was thinking, it's as though *I* were doing it; *I* feel guilty. They ought to be punished, she thought.

Then there was a moment when, sitting quietly across a bridge table from her husband, with Charles Acton on her left and Marjorie on her right, safe with her own home around her, Ellen turned politely to Charles, waiting for him to bid, and he said, arranging his cards, "You girls enjoy your lunch today?"

"Lunch?" Ellen said, comprehending almost at once, and angry; she had lunched alone and not agreeably on a bowl of vegetable soup at home. The king of hearts winked at her from her hand; irrepressibly she thought of some private little restaurant, where the waiter was quiet and unobtrusive and perhaps recognized them (the handsome young lovers, they came every week), and Marjorie speaking softly, leaning forward, and music, perhaps, in the background, and the conversation of romance, of undying devotion. "Of course," she said half to herself, and Marjorie at the same time cut in swiftly, speaking ostensibly to Arthur, "Ellen and I went out to lunch together in town today. As though we were a couple of debutantes."

"Two spades," Charles said.

"As though we had no responsibilities at all," Ellen said, looking at Marjorie.

"Good idea," Arthur said, nodding. "Ellen ought to get around more. Always doing something for other people," he told Charles, "all this planning bazaars, and concerts, and whatnot."

"Marjorie, too," Charles said vaguely. "I bid two spades."

"Ellen," Marjorie said with all appearance of sincerity, "you look *so* pretty tonight."

No, no, oh, no, Ellen thought, she can't pay off like that, and, almost without thinking of what she was saying, she said to her husband, "Marjorie has offered to take the boys this weekend so we can go skiing. I thought we might go back to that nice place by the lake."

"But I—" Marjorie began, and Ellen cut in smoothly, "I saw John Forrest for a minute today in the bank," she said to Arthur. "That's what made me think of skiing, actually—he was talking about it. And then when Marjorie offered to take the boys . . ." She smiled affectionately on Marjorie.

"Two no trump," Marjorie said, her voice sullen, and Charles glanced up reprovingly and said, "Not your turn to bid, dear."

Skiing at the lake was wonderful, and Ellen, who had at the last moment decided to borrow Marjorie's new scarlet snowsuit, had never enjoyed herself more; for two days she successfully forgot the precarious defense she and Marjorie held against catastrophe. Driving home from the lake, luxuriously tired and warm in her fur coat, she leaned her head back against the seat, thinking, I *have* been taking this too seriously, and asked, "Arthur, did you ever love anyone but me?"

"Millions of girls," he said obligingly. "Movie stars, and Oriental princesses, and beautiful international spies, and—"

"What would you do if I fell madly in love with some other man?"

"Make him pay for your birthday present," Arthur said without hesitation. "Why, have you got an offer?"

Ellen laughed happily, and fell asleep.

The boys welcomed them with enthusiasm, and Ellen, thanking Marjorie, found herself speaking and laughing with almost the old friendship. "It was *marvelous,*" she said. "You've simply got to—"

"I want to hear all about it," Marjorie said, "at lunch tomorrow."

And she glanced briefly past Ellen to Charles, and then back at Ellen again.

Ellen, holding on to a hand of each of her sons, turned toward the door at once and said flatly, "Of course, I'll see you tomorrow."

She was weak with anger and helplessness, seeing how this small fiction had been eased past her; she and Marjorie now lunched together regularly in town because dear Ellen needed more gadding about, and she recognized that her lonely lunch at home might give her more discomfort in deception and guilt than Marjorie's clandestine appointment. She is asking too much of loyalty, Ellen thought; she is charging right ahead and expecting to sweep me before her: she thinks I can be handled easily. "Marjorie," she said on the phone the next morning, "I've decided that you can manage the flower show this year. I've done it for three years and I'm tired of it."

"But I can't manage *anything*—you know I'm not any—"

"But of course you'll do it," Ellen said lightly. "Unless it interferes with your various social entanglements?"

"Ellen, look—"

"Shall we discuss it today at lunch?" Ellen said, and hung up. The flower show would be abominable under Marjorie's management, but then, she thought wryly, Marjorie managed *everything* so badly.

It was more difficult to persuade Marjorie to give up little Joan's dancing class in order to take Ellen's boys into town to a matinee, but Ellen, who disliked unpleasant words and avoided unpleasant scenes, found that by now she and Marjorie had developed a private language where comparatively harmless words substituted for the disagreeable ones the rest of the world was required to use: "Cloakroom," for instance, was a word of such threatening import to Marjorie that it might easily have meant "exposure" or "scandal," and even such a trivial phrase as "lunch in town" had come to mean something close to "liar" or "hypocrite." And yet, even though it was Marjorie whose world was endangered, it was Ellen who seemed to suffer for it; when Marjorie and John, driving together to the Golfers' Dinner at the club, arrived half an hour late, only Ellen came, worried, to meet them at the door. "Did you get lost?" she asked, "Don't tell me the two of you lost your way?"

"We had to stop for gas," John said easily, moving already toward their party in the dining room.

"By the way," Ellen said to Marjorie, "I want you to take me to that auction tomorrow, over in East Sundale."

"But tomorrow—" Marjorie began, glancing after John.

"Are you busy tomorrow? Something you can't break?"

"No, of course not," Marjorie said, and turned to follow John, pulling away from Ellen's hand on her arm.

Ellen came up to the long table with them, saying loudly, "Well, here they are, everybody; made it at last."

She slid into her own place next to Charles Acton, and said, "Honestly, how they could get *lost* around *here*," and smiled down the table at Marjorie.

It was not always difficult for Ellen. "I'm going into town to the theater," she told Marjorie one morning over the phone. "With my *own* husband, of course. And I'd like to borrow the pearls Charles gave you last Christmas; will you run over with them later?" Or, lightly at the meat counter in the mornings, "Marjorie, I've such a headache today; suppose *you* could bake the cakes for the club luncheon?" And always, if Marjorie protested, or refused, or looked sulky, Ellen could say with affectionate solicitude, "Poor Marjorie, you *do* look worn out. I'm really tempted to speak to Charles about you—you're doing too much. I'm going to tell that husband of yours that he has to keep more of an eye on you." And, with a gentle laugh, "Why don't you just run over to the florist's for me this afternoon? The flowers for the school, you know. I've got so much else to do . . . unless *you're* too busy?"

It was finally with a kind of amusement that Ellen recognized Marjorie's decision to give up the humiliating affair. It's a shame, Ellen thought, regarding Marjorie amiably over a cup of tea, always the weakest way; poor Marjorie, she was always so much prettier than the rest of us. "You *do* look exhausted these days," Ellen said, setting down her cup.

Marjorie looked up at her, and then down again. She's afraid of me, Ellen thought, leaning back comfortably, and we've been friends for twenty-two years. They were in Marjorie's living room, alone together of an afternoon for an intimate cup of tea. Unpleasantly, it occurred to Ellen that John Forrest must often have come here, secretly, afraid of the neighbors, and she made a little face of disgust and sat up, drawing away from the back and arms of the chair. "How beastly you are," she said, and it was the first time since she had known that she had mentioned, directly, her knowledge.

Marjorie looked up again, steadily this time. "I think you're jealous of me," she said.

"Good *Lord*." Ellen laughed, a little shocked laugh. "After all," she said with a gesture of distaste, "don't try to drag *me* down *with* you."

"That's what John says—he says you're only jealous." A little thrill of fury went up Ellen's back at the light, familiar naming of John. "I'd really rather not talk about it, I think," she said.

"There's just one thing you ought to know, though," Marjorie said. "There's not going to be any more. It's all through. Over with."

"Marjorie, my dear." Ellen got up and came across the room to sit down next to her friend. "I'm really glad; you've no idea how *worried* I've been."

"So I'll tell Charles myself," Marjorie said. "You needn't bother."

Ellen gasped. "Marjorie!" she said, almost crying. "Did you think I would tell *Charles*? *I*? Why, I'm your oldest friend and I—"

"How lucky I am," Marjorie said evenly, "that it was my oldest friend who found out and not," she went on, smiling at Ellen, "one of my enemies."

"Margie," Ellen said, her voice tender, "you *are* taking this hard. Look—put it this way. You got yourself caught up in a kind of romantic adolescent dream, and it just wasn't till you began to see it through my eyes that you realized that it wasn't a great rosy love at all, but just something kind of cheap and nasty. After all," she added, touching Marjorie's cheek gently with one finger, "we've always been pretty honest, you and I."

"More tea?" Marjorie asked. She moved away from Ellen and lifted the teapot.

"Thanks, no," Ellen said, and then, after a minute, "I must rush. Million things to do."

"Incidentally," Marjorie said, rising, "I won't be able to pick up your groceries for you this afternoon. I'll be busy."

The coward, Ellen thought, stamping homeward through the snow: *I* would have fought tooth and nail, and she laughed, walking by herself, at the thought of poor Marjorie scratching and biting. Oh, *poor* Marjorie, she thought, and John thinks I'm jealous.

It was like an entirely new kind of freedom, somehow, knowing that she need no longer watch Marjorie. The sun the next day was bright on the snow, and the thought of spring coming inevitably was exhilarating.

"John," she said, sitting in his banker's office looking up at him prettily, "I've done a *dreadful* thing," and then laughed without being able to help it at the panic that showed immediately in his eyes. "No, no," she said, laughing, "not *that* bad." The man's poor conscience, she thought; outside the broad window of the bank the snow seemed cleaner with the sun on it, and Ellen knew that people passing in the street might look in and see her, a pretty woman, talking and laughing with Mr. Forrest in his private office, her furs thrown back over her chair and her head bent charmingly forward to accept a light for her cigarette. "If you're going to jump at every word I say . . ." she said, and shook her head sadly. "All I've *really* done is overdraw my account."

He smiled, relieved. "New dress?" he asked.

"Hardly. I'm not as wicked as you *think* I am. No, it's some things I got for my boys—clothes, and a bicycle for Jimmie—and I just didn't realize how it mounted up, and then when I came to figure it out—" She stopped, and made a face. "The thing is, I don't dare tell Arthur," she said. "You know all wives keep *some* things from their husbands."

"How much does it come to?" John asked.

Ellen thought. "Not more than forty dollars, I'm *sure*. Probably even less than that. But say fifty to be sure."

"I see," said John.

"If you could . . ." She was embarrassed, but she went on bravely. "Well . . . sort of *cover* it for me, and I could get it to you the first of the month."

"Yes," John said without expression. "Of course."

"I don't usually ask men to lend me money," Ellen said, laughing, "but of course with *you* it's different. That is, I never mind borrowing from a banker."

"It's part of the business of a bank," John said, "lending money."

"Is it part of the business of a banker," she asked, almost flirtatiously, "to take his clients to lunch? I've been waiting for you to ask me."

He looked at her, perplexed, and she went on mockingly. "I wouldn't want to force you into it: perhaps you—"

"Not at all," John said, "I've been waiting for *you* to ask *me*."

They laughed together then, and she said, "But I want you to be sure to figure out the right interest on my loan. This is an honest business transaction."

"Of course," John said, still laughing.

"And," she went on, rising and taking up her gloves and her furs. "I'll surely get it to you on the first of the month. Or, at the very *latest,* the month after." Then, aware that she was a pretty woman and that her half smile made her look even prettier, she turned toward the door and waited for him to open it for her.

Alone in a
Den of Cubs

Woman's Day, *December 1953*

Although I know perfectly well that I am by nature trustworthy, loyal, helpful, friendly, courteous, kind, obedient, cheerful, thrifty, brave, clean, and reverent, I do not flatter myself that I am therefore true-steel material for a Cub Scout Den Mother. Up until the time my older son Laurie became a Cub Scout, I had always pictured a Den Mother as a woman of iron, with a clear head and a strong right arm, and I still do, I still do.

And yet, although Den Four had no relief maps, knot displays, model villages, homemade fudge, or amateur radio sets to show at the annual meeting, I congratulate myself secretly on having introduced a revolutionary disciplinary technique into the movement, which had a marked effect on the six Cub Scouts with whom I came in contact, and may indeed influence the whole future course of American manhood.

When Laurie asked me if I would be a Den Mother for the group of Cub Scouts he belonged to, I did not have to pause for any reflection before I said no. "I'm too busy," I told him. "Much too busy."

"At what?" Laurie wanted to know.

"At all sorts of things," I said firmly. "Learning to pitch horseshoes with your father, and all sorts of things."

"You'll never learn to pitch horseshoes," Laurie said. "Not as long as you throw with both hands, you won't. So why—"

"Why don't you ask Mrs. Oliver?" I suggested magnanimously.

"Or Mrs. Roberts? Or Mrs. Stuart? I'm sure they'd be glad to do it. But I'm too busy."

"They're all too busy, too," Laurie said. "If we could get anyone else, we wouldn't ask you, for heaven's sake."

"Or Mrs. Williams," I said with enthusiasm. "I'm sure Mrs. Williams would love to be your Den Mother."

"You think we didn't ask?" Laurie said. He looked at me wearily. "She told us she couldn't. You're the only one left," he said.

"But I'm too *busy*," I insisted.

"At what?"

And so I became official Den Mother of Den Four. Since I have no illusions about my own abilities at climbing a greased pole or laying a trail over ten miles of rough country or tying a cow-hitch, I found myself forced to consider the few talents I do possess. My bridge game, although fairly good, would not do for Cub Scouts, I felt, although I also feel—as I believe every bridge player has at one time or another—that the young might really be taught to play a decent game now, instead of waiting to learn until they sit down at the table with me.

At any rate, bridge would not do, and neither would the composing of limericks, another talent upon which I pride myself and which I gave up reluctantly as Den Four's project for the fall season; the art form is really too difficult for the minds of young boys, for one thing.

The whole tone of my Den Mothership was finally set by a lucky inspiration, and once the disciplinary setup was arranged, our meetings went smoothly: I supplied two bottles of soda and four doughnuts for each Cub at each meeting, we had a brief parliamentary discussion, and then everybody went quietly about his business. The boys tied their knots and painted the attic walls—of their own volition and with great energy—while I peeled potatoes for dinner and sang old camp songs to myself. And every Cub came to every meeting every week.

I confess to some nervousness at our first meeting. I gathered up my six Den Fours at the school on Wednesday afternoon. I knew most of them slightly, and apparently they all knew me, since conversation in the car was devoted exclusively to speculation on what kind of Den Mother Laurie's old lady was going to be. I had anticipated some difficulty with my son's feeling arrogant and superior because his mother was the Den Mother and the meetings were to be in his house; but it turned out that my fears were as nothing compared to his.

When we got out of the car, he took me aside and said nervously, "Look, don't try anything you can't *finish*."

"Nonsense," I told him. "We're all going to have a lovely time."

"Listen," he asked, "did you remember to get food?"

At ten minutes past three, when all the doughnuts had been consumed and all the empty soda bottles had been put back neatly in the case, my six Cub Scouts folded their hands, sat dutifully in a row on the playroom floor, and turned expectant, and in one case cynical, looks upon me. "Well?" said my son.

"Boys," I said brightly, "I think we ought to elect officers." There was a long silence. "Like a Den president," I continued weakly, "and a treasurer." I looked around at the silent faces. "To collect dues, you know," I said, remembering unhappily that Election of Officers, on my rough schedule, was supposed to take us until four o'clock and was supposed, also, to be an enthusiastic, although gentlemanly, sporting event, approximating movies I had seen of the British House of Commons. "Officers," I finished, smiling at the blank faces.

"She means like a president and stuff," Laurie said with desperate urgency.

"No, I don't," I said, suddenly getting my inspiration. "I mean, for instance, an Official Whiner. So that all the whining about everything"—I looked at my son—"can be done by one person, and the rest of you won't have to bother."

"Hey," said one of the boys, interested, "that would do for Harry, here, I bet." He shoved the boy next to him violently, and the other Cubs said, "Cut it out," and, "Shuddup," and, "*Will* ya?"

"I nominate George," said the Cub who had been pushed. "George for Official Whiner."

"Sure," said someone I took to be George. He sounded flattered. "And I betcha Billy could be the Giggler and laugh for all of us."

"And whaddya say we make Artie Old Know-It-All?"

I caught a respectful glance from my son and sat back, grinning smugly. Elections went on until I had to herd the boys into the car to take them home. We elected Laurie the Big Talker, and Artie got to be the General Expert Who Knows the Best Way to Do Everything, and Michael, who is able to crow like a rooster, got the rooster-crowing job, but was confined by bylaws to one crow per meeting. (I did not know at the time, although I do now, why the other Cubs insisted on putting that in about only one crow per meeting; they were, of course, more farsighted than I was.) By unanimous consent, Peter was elected Guy Who Always Says He Isn't Coming to Cub Scouts but Then Always Comes Anyway, and I got an honorary post—Utility Outfielder. Toby, our dog, was elected President, and Laurie's year-old brother, Barry, got to be Sergeant at Arms, with a salary of one doughnut a meeting.

I discovered, too, that something I believed peculiar to Laurie was actually true of all ten-year-old boys; they feel an extreme sentimentality toward babies, kittens, and little girls under four. Jannie, our seven-year-old daughter, was just old enough to be regarded as an intruder. She wanted to participate as a full member and was told, "G'way. We don't want no *girls*." But Barry and Sally—who is only just four—were regarded instantly as Den pets, and Sally was voted in as Bat Girl and Mascot. When I insisted that it wasn't fair to leave out Jannie, she was elected Waitress, to hand out the soda at meetings, with one dissenting vote—her older brother's.

My contribution to the world of discipline came during the voting for Rooster-Crower, when silence became imperative. I had thought to use the method of insuring silence that has always been most practical with my own four children when general roughhouse prevails; I usually yell *Quiet!* at the top of my lungs, and since I can yell louder than four children, of whom two are still pretty small, I frequently get quiet. If my own voice cannot prevail, I can always get their father to come and yell with me. I do not suppose that this is the ideal method of silencing children who are knocking each other around and stamping and pulling and shoving and screaming and howling; but it is the only way I have ever found that works, and so I assumed that it would work with six Cub Scouts.

The first time I yelled *Quiet!* at my Cub Scouts, however, the effect was so shocking, they were immediately silenced. The second time I yelled *Quiet!* nobody heard me. When I had yelled *Quiet!* about six times and gotten no results, I reached without conscious intention (I sincerely maintain) into my box of groceries, which sat on the floor behind me, and in which I vaguely hoped I might uncover a forgotten box of doughnuts or a bunch of bananas or some such, and in which I found, instead, an egg.

I took little thought, but good aim. Assuming that my own son was the most reasonable target, since I had to wash his shirts myself, I fired. Silence was instant and profound. Five potential roosters, halted in mid-crow, regarded Laurie dripping eggshell and yolk, and when I remarked that that was better, and set the box of eggs meaningfully on the floor next to me, our meeting resumed in a manner almost subdued.

Later that year, when eggs went way up in price, I fell back on marshmallows as ammunition; these had the additional advantage of being edible (edible, that is, by Cub Scouts), and although they did not carry the impact of a raw egg, I found that by then all I had to do to bring a dead silence was to raise my right arm.

Except for the improvement in my throwing arm, a new technique of discipline, and our painted attic walls, we had, as I say, nothing to show for our work at the annual meeting. We had been laboriously working out a haphazard and hilarious skit to present, although at the last minute Michael got chicken pox and Jannie had to fill in as the Tree. Suddenly, as I sat there, eyes shut and teeth clenched in the despairing hope that the Lion would not forget his lines and the Cake would not stumble again over the Crocodile's tail, a staggering and frightening thought came to me. Someday—and not very long off, either—Laurie will be a Boy Scout, Jannie will be a Girl Scout, Sally will be a Brownie, and Barry will be a Cub Scout. All at once. I hope the price of eggs comes down again before then.

THE ORDER OF
CHARLOTTE'S GOING

𝕯

I ALWAYS USED TO love June, and the roses, and the heat; I used to sit at the breakfast table and feel the warm, rich air coming in from the garden, and linger over my coffee just because it seemed somehow to make the days longer, and everything, all day, was easier when the weather was warm. I can remember that Charlotte felt the same way; sometimes at the breakfast table we would catch each other smiling. "I wish I could sleep all winter," I said once, "and only wake up for June."

"You're wishing your life away," Charlotte said.

That must have been early in the summer of Charlotte's death; I cannot remember a time during her illness when that remark was not at the back of my mind. Wishing my life away, I might think, the roses heavy in the window beside me, and Charlotte just faintly more pale than the morning before; "You look well this morning," I would say.

Charlotte would look over at me, and smile, and say, "Thanks so much, dear. And please either stop telling me or make it sound true." Then we would both laugh, because neither of us took the notion of Charlotte's dying very seriously; no one, I think we both felt, could just *die,* not in June with the roses out. We tried making a joke of it—only at first, of course—"Coffee?" I would say, giving the coffee-pot a little shove in her direction, "It may be your last cup, you know." Or she might remark, eyeing the pastries, "I feel that I have a right to the larger, since I shall so soon be deprived of earthly joys." I believed then that if Charlotte ever did think she was dying, she rather enjoyed the idea—it was all but painless, at first, and more than anything else like a schoolgirl dream of Camille, you know; she felt reasonably well, sometimes better than others, but she knew she was dying only because Doctor West and Doctor Nathan said so, and it seemed so silly, after all, to let *them* decide.

Actually, she had all the pleasures of dying for that whole summer. Everyone knew about it, and they gave her the best of everything, and always found a chair for her at the garden parties, and someone was always sure to be there to fetch poor Charlotte a drink or to talk to poor Charlotte or to play up to poor Charlotte's gallant attempts to tone down her part; she used to wink at me across the room and I might wander over and say amiably, "Well, Charlotte dear, dead yet?" and everyone would gasp and say "Shhh" and "Good *Lord*," and Charlotte wouldn't be able to keep from laughing, and of course *that* made everyone tell everyone else how courageous poor Charlotte was, and wasn't it lucky she was taking it so well, when of course all the time she was just enjoying herself right up to the hilt, more than she ever did before she was dying.

Charlotte was, of course, several years older than I; she was my older cousin, and I was the one always left out when she and my sisters used to gather together at parties and whisper and giggle, but then, the way things turned out, Charlotte and I ended up together, after all. There was I, no money and no place to go, just out of college and a little bit frightened, and there was Charlotte, all the money in the family, and tired of paid companions and being alone, and we ran into each other one day in town, and had lunch together, and decided we'd try putting up with each other for a while, with the understanding, of course, that we could always quit if we couldn't stand each other. Well, it was fourteen years now, and we'd fought our way through most of it, spending our winters quarreling in town and our summers quarreling out at the cottage, and both of us livelier and happier than we would have been any other way. Charlotte always wanted to die at the cottage, anyway, so we came out early that year, after she'd seen Nathan, in town, and he'd told her about her heart, and her blood pressure, and everyone had looked gravely at everyone else, and Nathan said to me, "Take very good care of her, Miss Baxter—she's always taken good care of *you*." Charlotte of course began to laugh when he said that, and that made poor old Nathan the first person to pat Charlotte on the shoulder and say she was taking it courageously. So we came out to the cottage early that summer, and I began wishing my life away, and then around the middle of June Charlotte got the first communication. We started right away calling them communications, right with that first one, because there wasn't much else to call them without taking them too seriously.

The first one was in the morning mail, and addressed to Charlotte, of course. I used to be complacent about how all the mail I got meant something; Charlotte was the one who got all the bills and all the ads and all the begging letters, and anything I got was either a letter from someone or an invitation. Anyway, this first communication made Charlotte laugh. "Look at this thing," she said, tossing it across the table to me, "someone's gotten *some* wire crossed."

It was an ordinary congratulatory card, and very ordinary indeed—vulgar, *I* would have called it, actually. It was full of painted pink roses and cupids and was sticky with sequins: "Best Wishes on Your Plighted Troth," it read in pink letters, and there was a white satin bow.

"Golly," I said, "you suppose it's meant for Martha?"

"If Martha's getting married, I want to know about it," Charlotte said grimly, and she put her head back and yelled, "Martha!"

"Hon, cut it out," I said. "You know you're supposed to be an invalid. Let me do the yelling, if you won't let me go and get her."

"Martha?" Charlotte said over my shoulder. "You getting married?"

"Me?" Martha was a good solid country woman; she was the greatest glory of our summer life, and thinking about it, Martha—who had already tried it twice, anyway—would as soon think of getting married again as she would of putting tomatoes in a chowder. "You think I'm crazy?" Martha said.

"Look," Charlotte said, holding out the card. "*I'm* not getting married, and neither is Anne."

"Me neither," Martha said. "So I guess that's none of us." She looked down at the card disdainfully, holding it far away so she could read it. "Look at that card," she said, and handed it back delicately. "My," she said, and made a face. "Could use it to trim a cake," Martha said.

"I believe I'll put it on the mantel," Charlotte said.

"I'll do it," I said as Charlotte started to get up, and Martha winked at me. "Might as well let her," Martha said to me, "neither of us can stop her doing *any*thing."

"She's supposed to be sick," I said. "I'm supposed to be taking care of her, Doctor Nathan said so."

"Hah," said Martha. "You feel like coconut cake for lunch? That card put it in my mind."

"Sure," I said. "Plenty of frosting."

The card stayed there on the mantel for about a week, but I don't think Charlotte kept on finding it as funny as she thought she would. In the first place, just about all the jokes you could think of to make to an unmarried lady of forty-eight about her getting congratulations on her engagement either were made in the first twenty-four hours or were too indelicate to make, anyway, and in the second place, Charlotte and I had gotten sort of used to being spinsters, and never gave it much thought, and even talked about it sometimes, between ourselves, but having the card up there on the mantel sort of brought it to mind, somehow, and even made people think we *did* wonder a little about ourselves. Anyway, Charlotte took the card down and I imagine she burned it, because it wasn't there by the time the second one came.

"This isn't funny," Charlotte said, passing it across the breakfast table to me. "You think it's funny?"

It was covered with sequins, like the first one, and cupids and roses, only this one had a white satin heart in the center, and *it* said "Blessings on Your Nuptials." It was like the first one also in that it was not signed; this time we both looked at the envelope and wondered where it had come from. "Two can't be an accident," Charlotte said. "Someone's doing it on purpose."

"Some kind of a misguided practical joke," I said.

"Trying to cheer me up in my last hours?" Charlotte said. "Not quite the way to do it, *I* think."

"Mailed locally, too," I said. "Put down that cigarette. You've had one," I added. "You're not allowed *any*."

"It's not worth it," Charlotte said, "I'd even rather live."

"You can't, now," I told her. "All arrangements have been made. Mrs. Austin's planning a luncheon for after the funeral."

"You suppose Mrs. Austin . . . ?" Charlotte wondered, regarding the envelope.

"Why on earth? It's some fool who got caught in a joke in bad taste and won't ever admit it now."

The third card was done in pink ribbons, and read "Love to the New Arrival." It amused no one very much. We decided that the envelopes had been addressed left-handed, and got everyone we knew trying left-handed stabs at writing Charlotte's name, although we were sure by then we'd never know who sent them, because anyone who thought they were funny would have come out with it by that time, and in any case it's easy to make a mess of trying to write left-handed. The next card, which I thought was probably the least happily chosen, was bright yellow, with puppies looking dolefully at one another, and on the front it said, "Sorry for Your Aches and Pains," and inside there was a verse about being sorry she was sick, and hoping she'd be real well soon and back at play with the other boys and girls. "I don't *like* these," Charlotte said, handing me this last one, "they are beginning to frighten me."

"Suppose I open the mail?" I said. "I know the writing by now, and I'll just sort out any of these things and throw them away."

Charlotte shrugged, and laughed a little. "I guess I'm curious," she said, "I want to know what they'll think of next."

Well, then, of course, the next one did it. We both recognized the handwriting on the envelope and I came around the table to watch Charlotte open it and she tore open the flap and two live spiders skidded out and one ran along her hand and up her arm. I thought she was going right then—and I think it was the first time I ever took the doctor seriously—because she screamed and jumped up and kicked over her chair and slapped at her arm and said, "Get it away, get it *away*." I stepped on one of the spiders and took the second one off her arm and squeezed it between my fingers; I've never done such a thing in my life, but for some reason this particular spider just made me sick.

I had to call Doctor West from the village, and he put Charlotte to bed and I told him about the cards and the spiders and he looked as sick as I felt and said, "I can only believe that someone thinks it's funny. Horrible thing to do, though."

"He probably didn't know how she loathes insects," I said. "They horrify her."

He nodded. "She ought to take it a lot easier, though, Miss Baxter," he said. "I tell you, I don't know what your doctor in town saw fit to warn you against, but I'm not going to try to confuse you or make you feel better by hiding it in a lot of medical phrases; Miss Allison is in a dangerous condition, and it's not going to take much—" He had to stop because Charlotte was calling me, and then even so he held my arm long enough to say, "Watch out for Martha's cooking; those rich cakes and fried chicken are no good at all for Miss Allison. And of course see that she doesn't get any more spiders in the mail."

"I'll open everything," I told him. "Even if it's a man-eating tiger in an envelope."

"Good girl," he said.

Well, of course Martha thought the only thing she could do to show how mad she was at whoever sent those spiders was to get to work and make brown-sugar pie and shrimp casserole for lunch, and when I sat there with my plate full and saw Charlotte's tray with the cup of vegetable soup and glass of buttermilk, what could I do?

"This once, *only*," I said, passing her over my shrimp casserole. "I won't tell the doc. But from now on it's whole wheat bread and beet greens."

"Certainly," she said, diving into the shrimp.

"And no cigarettes."

"I don't smoke," she said virtuously. "Doctor's orders."

I told Martha not to put her homemade strawberry preserves on the breakfast table anymore, and to butter the toast in the kitchen, and to use one slim pat of butter for four slices of toast, and not to serve *more* than four slices of toast. I began ordering a coffee without caffeine, but Charlotte raised such a fuss, I had to go back to our regular brand, but I made Martha serve only hot water and lemon juice at dinner. I broke Martha's heart by ruling out absolutely all baked goods and all fried foods and all spices, which, since it eliminated fried chicken and blueberry pie and lamb curry, got Martha's cooking down to a kind of basic boiled codfish, with now and then a lamb chop for variety. Charlotte began losing weight, and I began dropping in to the kitchen after dinner to take a little of whatever Martha had prepared for herself. "If I didn't know it was doing her good," I told Martha, my mouth full of kidney stew, "I'd give it up right now. It's making her suffer."

"Not right for a person not to eat," Martha said.

"My God," I said, "*I* can't live on it."

"You're not sick," Martha said reasonably. "After she's gone, after all, *you'll* still be eating good meals."

"Doesn't seem fair, does it? You and me eating kidney stew, and Charlotte . . ." I looked at Martha and she looked at me. "Why not?" I said.

"Shouldn't do it," Martha said.

"I don't care." I fixed a tray with a generous serving of kidney stew, threw on a couple of Martha's hot yeast rolls, and a cup of coffee with plenty of cream and sugar. Then I stuck my tongue out at Martha and took the tray upstairs.

After that, whenever Martha made anything particularly nice, I took Charlotte along a tray; it was always done as a special treat, and Martha and I always pretended it was something unusual for Charlotte, and Charlotte and I always pretended it was a trick on Martha, and then after a while it seemed silly and Martha went back to making her regular meals and Charlotte and I got strawberry preserves for breakfast again.

The cards stopped coming, but Charlotte began finding little boxes of candy everywhere. Now, candy, and especially chocolate, was one thing she was absolutely *not* supposed to have, and leaving it around was about the cruelest practical joke anyone could try, because Charlotte was one of those people who just can't turn her back on a piece of candy. Not the way you and I eat candy, you see—if there was a dish of candy on the table, Charlotte couldn't sit still until she'd polished it off, just keep coming back and coming back and knowing all the time she shouldn't. I like candy well enough, and I used to keep some in my room until once Charlotte found out about it and made me give it to her, but as far as the house in general was concerned, I kept it out. Cooking chocolate in the pantry and not even Charlotte could eat *that*—but no sweets of any kind around where anyone could get at them. Even Charlotte hadn't the nerve to go dipping sugar out of the sugar bowl, so we were all right until this joker started getting little boxes of candy to Charlotte. First it came in the mail, a small sample box of sweet chocolate, and naturally I couldn't stop Charlotte from going right at it, even in the middle of breakfast. Then one day I found a box of chocolates on the living room table, and I knew Martha hadn't put them there, and I didn't dare ask Charlotte, so I gave them to Martha to take home, but Charlotte wandered into the kitchen and saw them. Then it got worse. Little wax paper packages, two or three pieces, would turn up on her dresser—homemade fudge, sometimes, or caramels, or orange creams, or plain chocolate—and sometimes I found them and of course sometimes I didn't. I remember once I found a package in the pocket of her dressing gown, and one in the drawer of her desk, next to her checkbook. I knew I wasn't finding them all because she was always asking Martha for soda for indigestion or heartburn, and of course that was no good for her either. Then one day I came into her room without knocking, just to catch her, and there she was eating candy and with a cigarette in her hand, and of course I was just as mad as could be. I threw the candy into the wastebasket and took away the cigarette—and the pack of cigarettes in her pocket, too, by the way—and said, "Now, look, hon, this is really getting out of hand. What on *earth* do you think you're *doing*?"

It was the first time she was ever sullen with me. As I say, we did a good deal of fighting, back and forth, but always giving as good as we got, and here she was now, acting like a child caught stealing a nickel out of its mother's pocketbook, and I felt awful. "I've got a right to do as I please," she said.

"Not if you deliberately harm yourself. You *know* this is all bad for you. Smoking, and eating rich candy, and trying to keep it all a secret."

"I don't care," she said. "I can enjoy myself if I want to."

"Don't be silly," I said, and then something occurred to me, because that didn't sound at all like Charlotte, and I went and put my hand into her bathrobe pocket and took out a note, written the way the cards had been addressed—left-handed, and in purple ink—and the note said, "You got a right to enjoy yourself."

"Where did you get *this*?" I asked, disgusted.

"It was with the cigarettes," she said, and then she smiled up at me, like my old Charlotte. "*Don't* I have a right?" she wanted to know.

"Look," I said, "what I want is that you'll still be enjoying yourself next year at this time. You've gotten into a state of mind where you think fooling me is enjoying yourself. Go ahead and fool me all you like—send me spiders in the mail if it gives you any pleasure—but just keep off the cigarettes and the candy and stuff."

I shouldn't have reminded her of the spiders; her face got all sick again and she turned away from me and wouldn't talk anymore. And I suppose the candy and stuff kept coming because she kept talking about indigestion and she began to look frightened, as though she couldn't stop herself anymore and knew just the same that she was getting worse. We weren't making our little jokes anymore; somehow people had stopped thinking of her as being so courageous, I suppose because she looked so terrible, and had started talking about how long she could last, and where she had left the money. I was pretty sure she had left the money to me, but I was getting more and more worried about how long she could last, so I went and had a talk with Doctor West in the village about the secret candy and cigarettes.

"There's no controlling her," I said to him, and he shook his head.

"I don't know of any cruelty like it," he said. "You might better give her a dose of arsenic on the spot, and get it over with fast. This way, she's not only pushing herself into the grave, she feels guilty about it besides. *I* can't do anything except warn her."

"*I* can't even do that," I said. "She's stopped listening to me at all and if I try to keep an eye on her she just laughs at me."

"Keep after her as much as you can," he said. "All you *can* do."

Well, the roses bloomed and kept their blossoms and got heavier and richer as the summer went on, and by the end of August our garden was so lovely, I would have liked to die there myself. Charlotte was tired and lethargic all the time; she might come downstairs for an hour or so in the morning, but she spent most of her time in her room, looking down at the roses from her window and I suppose stuffing herself with the lavish gifts from her unknown friend. It was all I could do to coax her out into the air for five minutes, and of course in the end that was what finally did it.

We had had breakfast together, eating buckwheat cakes and country sausage and toast and Martha's strawberry preserves, and the mail had been good—one invitation for me, to a dance; one subscription renewal and one dividend check for Charlotte—and I asked her if she'd like to spend half an hour in the garden, after being indoors so much.

"I don't think so." Charlotte shook her head. "I believe I'll just go back to bed."

"You haven't seen the rock garden. You can't see it from your window. And you're not sick enough to stay in bed and pamper yourself; you've *got* to get outdoors more."

Charlotte sighed. "I'm so tired," she said. "I hate walking around or standing up."

"Half an hour?" I asked.

She shrugged. "These days," she said wearily, "it's more trouble to resist. Ten minutes."

I took her arm, because she had trouble walking, and we went together out into the garden, among the roses. I knew I was right, when she stopped at once and just touched a rose with one finger. "They're lovely this year," she said.

"Each summer they're lovelier than the last. That's one of the things about roses."

She laughed. "You thinking that next summer they'll be just as lovely without me?"

"I'll plant some on your grave," I said amiably. "Come and see the rock garden."

We went slowly down the path beside the cottage, between the rows of roses, past Martha's kitchen window, and she leaned out to say, "Good to see *you* outdoors at last," and then we went around past the house down to the back, to the rock garden that Charlotte and I had built together, and which I had tended alone this summer. "You've been spending too much time on *me*," Charlotte said critically. "Look at those weeds."

"I've been more concerned about you." I gave her a little hug. "Next year—" I said.

"Anne," she said as though she hadn't expected to be saying anything, and was a little bit surprised, and even shocked, to hear her own voice saying this, "Anne, you know I've left you all of it?"

"Have you, Charlotte?"

"The house, and the money, and everything. I thought you knew."

"I just think it's silly to talk about it."

"I suppose it is. I've been wondering if maybe they weren't wrong, Nathan and this other fellow. If maybe I'm not going to—"

"Look out," I shouted, "*snake,* Charlotte, look *out!*" I jumped away from her, screaming, "Martha, Martha, help, *snake!*"

Martha ran out, gasping, and killed the snake with a shovel, and Doctor West told me afterward that of course it was not a rattler, but only a milk snake.

"I feel so awful," I told him, "I keep thinking of how we were standing there talking quietly, and if I had only kept my head . . ."

"You couldn't know, of course," he said.

"I guess I'm about as afraid of snakes as she was of spiders. But still . . . it was my job to take care of *her*. If I had only thought in time . . ."

"It was bound to happen sometime," Doctor West said.

About the worst job Martha and I had was going over Charlotte's clothes. There was still chocolate in some of the pockets, and in one pocket, in the sweater she was wearing that morning, I found another note, saying, "They're just trying to leave you out. You better show them you can still be in the center of things." It was the only one of those things that I hadn't written left-handed, and I burned it.

One Ordinary Day, with Peanuts

Fantasy and Science Fiction,
January 1955

Mr. John Philip Johnson shut his front door behind him and went down his front steps into the bright morning with a feeling that all was well with the world on this best of all days, and wasn't the sun warm and good, and didn't his shoes feel comfortable after the resoling, and he knew that he had undoubtedly chosen the very precise tie that belonged with the day and the sun and his comfortable feet, and, after all, wasn't the world just a wonderful place? In spite of the fact that he was a small man, and though the tie was perhaps a shade vivid, Mr. Johnson radiated a feeling of well-being as he went down the steps and onto the dirty sidewalk, and he smiled at people who passed him, and some of them even smiled back. He stopped at the newsstand on the corner and bought his paper, saying, "*Good* morning" with real conviction to the man who sold him the paper and the two or three other people who were lucky enough to be buying papers when Mr. Johnson skipped up. He remembered to fill his pockets with candy and peanuts, and then he set out to get himself uptown. He stopped in a flower shop and bought a carnation for his buttonhole, and stopped almost immediately afterward to give the carnation to a small child in a carriage, who looked at him dumbly, and then smiled, and Mr. Johnson smiled, and the child's mother looked at Mr. Johnson for a minute and then smiled, too.

When he had gone several blocks uptown, Mr. Johnson cut across the avenue and went along a side street, chosen at random; he did not follow the same route every morning, but preferred to pursue his eventful way in wide detours, more like a puppy than a man intent upon business. It happened this morning that halfway down the block a moving van was parked, and the furniture from an upstairs apartment stood half on the sidewalk, half on the steps, while an amused group of people loitered, examining the scratches on the tables and the worn spots on the chairs, and a harassed woman, trying to watch a young child and the movers and the furniture all at the same time, gave the clear impression of endeavoring to shelter her private life from the people staring at her belongings. Mr. Johnson stopped, and for a moment joined the crowd, then he came forward and, touching his hat civilly, said, "Perhaps I can keep an eye on your little boy for you?"

The woman turned and glared at him distrustfully, and Mr. Johnson added hastily, "We'll sit right here on the steps." He beckoned to the little boy, who hesitated and then responded agreeably to Mr. Johnson's genial smile. Mr. Johnson took out a handful of peanuts from his pocket and sat on the steps with the boy, who at first refused the peanuts on the grounds that his mother did not allow him to accept food from strangers; Mr. Johnson said that probably his mother had not intended peanuts to be included, since elephants at the circus ate them, and the boy considered, and then agreed solemnly. They sat on the steps cracking peanuts in a comradely fashion, and Mr. Johnson said, "So you're moving?"

"Yep," said the boy.

"Where you going?"

"Vermont."

"Nice place. Plenty of snow there. Maple sugar, too; you like maple sugar?"

"Sure."

"Plenty of maple sugar in Vermont. You going to live on a farm?"

"Going to live with Grandpa."

"Grandpa like peanuts?"

"Sure."

"Ought to take him some," said Mr. Johnson, reaching into his pocket. "Just you and Mommy going?"

"Yep."

"Tell you what," Mr. Johnson said. "You take some peanuts to eat on the train."

The boy's mother, after glancing at them frequently, had seemingly decided that Mr. Johnson was trustworthy, because she had devoted herself wholeheartedly to seeing that the movers did not—what movers rarely do, but every housewife believes they will—crack a leg from her good table, or set a kitchen chair down on a lamp. Most of the furniture was loaded by now, and she was deep in that nervous stage when she knew there was something she had forgotten to pack—hidden away in the back of a closet somewhere, or left at a neighbor's and forgotten, or on the clothesline—and was trying to remember under stress what it was.

"This all, lady?" the chief mover said, completing her dismay.

Uncertainly, she nodded.

"Want to go on the truck with the furniture, sonny?" the mover asked the boy, and laughed. The boy laughed, too, and said to Mr. Johnson, "I guess I'll have a good time at Vermont."

"Fine time," said Mr. Johnson, and stood up. "Have one more peanut before you go," he said to the boy.

The boy's mother said to Mr. Johnson, "Thank you so much; it was a great help to me."

"Nothing at all," said Mr. Johnson gallantly. "Where in Vermont are you going?"

The mother looked at the little boy accusingly, as though he had given away a secret of some importance, and said unwillingly, "Greenwich."

"Lovely town," said Mr. Johnson. He took out a card, and wrote a name on the back. "Very good friend of mine lives in Greenwich," he said. "Call on him for anything you need. His wife makes the best doughnuts in town," he added soberly to the little boy.

"Swell," said the little boy.

"Goodbye," said Mr. Johnson.

He went on, stepping happily with his new-shod feet, feeling the warm sun on his back and on the top of his head. Halfway down the block he met a stray dog and fed him a peanut.

At the corner, where another wide avenue faced him, Mr. Johnson decided to go on uptown again. Moving with comparative laziness, he was passed on either side by people hurrying and frowning, and people brushed past him going the other way, clattering along to get somewhere quickly. Mr. Johnson stopped on every corner and waited patiently for the light to change, and he stepped out of the way of anyone who seemed to be in any particular hurry, but one young lady came too fast for him, and crashed wildly into him when he stooped to pat a kitten, which had run out onto the sidewalk from an apartment house and was now unable to get back through the rushing feet.

"Excuse me," said the young lady, trying frantically to pick up Mr. Johnson and hurry on at the same time, "terribly sorry."

The kitten, regardless now of danger, raced back to its home. "Perfectly all right," said Mr. Johnson, adjusting himself carefully. "You seem to be in a hurry."

"Of course I'm in a hurry," said the young lady. "I'm late."

She was extremely cross, and the frown between her eyes seemed well on its way to becoming permanent. She had obviously awakened late, because she had not spent any extra time in making herself look pretty, and her dress was plain and unadorned with collar or brooch, and her lipstick was noticeably crooked. She tried to brush past Mr. Johnson, but, risking her suspicious displeasure, he took her arm and said, "Please wait."

"Look," she said ominously, "I ran into you, and your lawyer can see my lawyer and I will gladly pay all damages and all inconveniences suffered therefrom, but please this minute let me go because *I am late*."

"Late for what?" said Mr. Johnson; he tried his winning smile on her but it did no more than keep her, he suspected, from knocking him down again.

"Late for work," she said between her teeth. "Late for my employment. I have a job, and if I am late I lose exactly so much an hour and I cannot really afford what your pleasant conversation is costing me, be it *ever* so pleasant."

"I'll pay for it," said Mr. Johnson. Now, these were magic words, not necessarily because they were true, or because she seriously expected Mr. Johnson to pay for anything, but because Mr. Johnson's flat statement, obviously innocent of irony, could not be, coming from Mr. Johnson, anything but the statement of a responsible and truthful and respectable man.

"What *do* you mean?" she asked.

"I said that since I am obviously responsible for your being late, I shall certainly pay for it."

"Don't be silly," she said, and for the first time the frown disappeared. "*I* wouldn't expect you to pay for anything—a few minutes ago I was offering to pay *you*. Anyway," she added, almost smiling, "it *was* my fault."

"What happens if you don't go to work?"

She stared. "I don't get paid."

"Precisely," said Mr. Johnson.

"What do you mean, precisely? If I don't show up at the office exactly twenty minutes ago I lose a dollar and twenty cents an hour, or two cents a minute or"—she thought—"almost a dime for the time I've spent talking to you."

Mr. Johnson laughed, and finally she laughed, too. "You're late already," he pointed out. "Will you give me another four cents' worth?"

"I don't understand why."

"You'll see," Mr. Johnson promised. He led her over to the side of the walk, next to the buildings, and said, "Stand here," and went out into the rush of people going both ways. Selecting and considering, as one who must make a choice involving perhaps whole years of lives, he estimated the people going by. Once he almost moved, and then at the last minute thought better of it and drew back. Finally, from half a block away, he saw what he wanted, and moved out into the center of the traffic to intercept a young man, who was hurrying, and dressed as though he had awakened late, and frowning.

"Oof," said the young man, because Mr. Johnson had thought of no better way to intercept anyone than the one the young woman had unwittingly used upon him. "Where do you think you're going?" the young man demanded from the sidewalk.

"I want to speak to you," said Mr. Johnson ominously.

The young man got up nervously, dusting himself and eyeing Mr. Johnson. "What for?" he said. "What'd I do?"

"That's what bothers me most about people nowadays," Mr. Johnson complained broadly to the people passing. "No matter whether they've done anything or not, they always figure someone's after them. About what you're going to do," he told the young man.

"Listen," said the young man, trying to brush past him, "I'm late, and I don't have any time to listen. Here's a dime, now get going."

"Thank you," said Mr. Johnson, pocketing the dime. "Look," he said, "what happens if you stop running?"

"I'm late," said the young man, still trying to get past Mr. Johnson, who was unexpectedly clinging.

"How much you make an hour?" Mr. Johnson demanded.

"A Communist, are you?" said the young man. "Now will you please let me—"

"No," said Mr. Johnson insistently, "*how* much?"

"Dollar fifty," said the young man. "And *now* will you—"

"You like adventure?"

The young man stared, and, staring, found himself caught and held by Mr. Johnson's genial smile; he almost smiled back and then repressed it and made an effort to tear away. "I got to *hurry*," he said.

"Mystery? You like surprises? Unusual and exciting events?"

"You selling something?"

"Sure," said Mr. Johnson. "You want to take a chance?"

The young man hesitated, looking longingly up the avenue toward what might have been his destination and then, when Mr. Johnson said, "I'll pay for it" with his own peculiar convincing emphasis, turned and said, "Well, okay. But I got to *see* it first, what I'm buying."

Mr. Johnson, breathing hard, led the young man over to the side, where the girl was standing; she had been watching with interest Mr. Johnson's capture of the young man and now, smiling timidly, she looked at Mr. Johnson as though prepared to be surprised at nothing.

Mr. Johnson reached into his pocket and took out his wallet. "Here," he said, and handed a bill to the girl. "This about equals your day's pay."

"But no," she said, surprised in spite of herself. "I mean, I *couldn't*."

"Please do not interrupt," Mr. Johnson told her. "And *here*," he said to the young man, "this will take care of *you*." The young man accepted the bill dazedly, but said, "Probably counterfeit" to the young woman out of the side of his mouth. "Now," Mr. Johnson went on, disregarding the young man, "what is your name, miss?"

"Kent," she said helplessly. "Mildred Kent."

"Fine," said Mr. Johnson. "And you, sir?"

"Arthur Adams," said the young man stiffly.

"Splendid," said Mr. Johnson. "Now, Miss Kent, I would like you to meet Mr. Adams. Mr. Adams, Miss Kent."

Miss Kent stared, wet her lips nervously, made a gesture as though she might run, and said, "How do you do?"

Mr. Adams straightened his shoulders, scowled at Mr. Johnson, made a gesture as though *he* might run, and said, "How do you do?"

"Now, *this*," said Mr. Johnson, taking several bills from his wallet, "should be enough for the day for both of you. I would suggest, perhaps, Coney Island—although I personally am not fond of the place—or perhaps a nice lunch somewhere, and dancing, or a matinee, or even a movie, although take care to choose a really *good* one; there are *so* many bad movies these days. You might," he said, struck with an inspiration, "visit the Bronx Zoo, or the Planetarium. Anywhere, as a matter of fact," he concluded, "that you would like to go. Have a nice time."

As he started to move away, Arthur Adams, breaking from his dumbfounded stare, said, "But see here, mister, you *can't* do this. Why—how do you know—I mean, *we* don't even know—I mean, how do you know we won't just take the money and not do what you said?"

"You've taken the money," Mr. Johnson said. "You don't have to follow any of my suggestions. You may know something you prefer to do—perhaps a museum, or something."

"But suppose I just run away with it and leave her here?"

"I know you won't," said Mr. Johnson gently, "because you remembered to ask *me* that. Goodbye," he added, and went on.

As he stepped up the street, conscious of the sun on his head and his good shoes, he heard from somewhere behind him the young man saying, "Look, you know you don't *have* to if you don't want to," and the girl saying, "But unless *you* don't want to . . ." Mr. Johnson smiled to himself and then thought that he had better hurry along; when he wanted to he could move very quickly, and before the young woman had gotten around to saying, "Well, *I* will if *you* will," Mr. Johnson was several blocks away and had already stopped twice, once to help a lady lift several large packages into a taxi, and once to hand a peanut to a sea gull. By this time he was in an area of large stores and many more people, and he was buffeted constantly from either side by people hurrying and cross and late and sullen. Once he offered a peanut to a man who asked him for a dime, and once he offered a peanut to a bus driver who had stopped his bus at an intersection and had opened the window next to his seat and put out his head as though longing for fresh air and the comparative quiet of the traffic. The man wanting a dime took the peanut because Mr. Johnson had wrapped a dollar bill around it, but the bus driver took the peanut and asked ironically, "You want a transfer, Jack?"

On a busy corner Mr. Johnson encountered two young people— for one minute he thought they might be Mildred Kent and Arthur Adams—who were eagerly scanning a newspaper, their backs pressed against a storefront to avoid the people passing, their heads bent together. Mr. Johnson, whose curiosity was insatiable, leaned onto the storefront next to them and peeked over the man's shoulder; they were scanning the Apartments Vacant columns.

Mr. Johnson remembered the street where the woman and her

little boy were going to Vermont and he tapped the man on the shoulder and said amiably, "Try down on West Seventeen. About the middle of the block, people moved out this morning."

"Say, what do you—" said the man, and then, seeing Mr. Johnson clearly, "Well, thanks. Where did you say?"

"West Seventeen," said Mr. Johnson. "About the middle of the block." He smiled again and said, "Good luck."

"Thanks," said the man.

"Thanks," said the girl as they moved off.

"Goodbye," said Mr. Johnson.

He lunched alone in a pleasant restaurant, where the food was rich, and only Mr. Johnson's excellent digestion could encompass two of their whipped-cream-and-chocolate-and-rum-cake pastries for dessert. He had three cups of coffee, tipped the waiter largely, and went out into the street again into the wonderful sunlight, his shoes still comfortable and fresh on his feet. Outside he found a beggar staring into the windows of the restaurant he had left and, carefully looking through the money in his pocket, Mr. Johnson approached the beggar and pressed some coins and a couple of bills into his hand. "It's the price of the veal cutlet lunch plus tip," said Mr. Johnson. "Goodbye."

After his lunch he rested; he walked into the nearest park and fed peanuts to the pigeons. It was late afternoon by the time he was ready to start back downtown, and he had refereed two checker games, and watched a small boy and girl whose mother had fallen asleep and awakened with surprise and fear that turned to amusement when she saw Mr. Johnson. He had given away almost all of his candy, and had fed all the rest of his peanuts to the pigeons, and it was time to go home. Although the late afternoon sun was pleasant, and his shoes were still entirely comfortable, he decided to take a taxi downtown.

He had a difficult time catching a taxi, because he gave up the first three or four empty ones to people who seemed to need them more; finally, however, he stood alone on the corner and—almost like netting a frisky fish—he hailed desperately until he succeeded in catching a cab that had been proceeding with haste uptown, and seemed to draw in toward Mr. Johnson against its own will.

"Mister," the cabdriver said as Mr. Johnson climbed in, "I figured you was an omen, like. I wasn't going to pick you up at all."

"Kind of you," said Mr. Johnson ambiguously.

"If I'd of let you go it would of cost me ten bucks," said the driver.

"Really?" said Mr. Johnson.

"Yeah," said the driver. "Guy just got out of the cab, he turned around and give me ten bucks, said take this and bet it in a hurry on a horse named Vulcan, right away."

"Vulcan?" said Mr. Johnson, horrified. "A fire sign on a Wednesday?"

"What?" said the driver. "Anyway, I said to myself, if I got no fare between here and there I'd bet the ten, but if anyone looked like they needed a cab I'd take it as an omen and I'd take the ten home to the wife."

"You were very right," said Mr. Johnson heartily. "This is Wednesday, you would have lost your money. Monday, yes, or even Saturday. But never never never a fire sign on a Wednesday. Sunday would have been good, now."

"Vulcan don't run on Sunday," said the driver.

"You wait till another day," said Mr. Johnson. "Down this street, please, driver. I'll get off on the next corner."

"He *told* me Vulcan, though," said the driver.

"I'll tell you," said Mr. Johnson, hesitating with the door of the cab half open. "You take that ten dollars and I'll give you another ten dollars to go with it, and you go right ahead and bet that money on any Thursday on any horse that has a name indicating . . . let me see, Thursday . . . well, grain. Or any growing food."

"Grain?" said the driver. "You mean a horse named, like, Wheat or something?"

"Certainly," said Mr. Johnson. "Or, as a matter of fact, to make it even easier, any horse whose name includes the letters C, R, L. Perfectly simple."

"Tall Corn?" said the driver, a light in his eye. "You mean a horse named, like, Tall Corn?"

"Absolutely," said Mr. Johnson. "Here's your money."

"Tall Corn," said the driver. "Thank *you,* mister."

"Goodbye," said Mr. Johnson.

He was on his own corner, and went straight up to his apartment. He let himself in and called, "Hello?" and Mrs. Johnson answered from the kitchen, "Hello, dear, aren't you early?"

"Took a taxi home," Mr. Johnson said. "I remembered the cheesecake, too. What's for dinner?"

Mrs. Johnson came out of the kitchen and kissed him; she was a comfortable woman, and smiling as Mr. Johnson smiled. "Hard day?" she asked.

"Not very," said Mr. Johnson, hanging his coat in the closet. "How about you?"

"So-so," she said. She stood in the kitchen doorway while he settled into his easy chair and took off his good shoes and took out the paper he had bought that morning. "Here and there," she said.

"I didn't do so badly," Mr. Johnson said. "Couple young people."

"Fine," she said. "I had a little nap this afternoon, took it easy most of the day. Went into a department store this morning and accused the woman next to me of shoplifting, and had the store detective pick her up. Sent three dogs to the pound—*you* know, the usual thing. Oh, and listen," she added, remembering.

"What?" asked Mr. Johnson.

"Well," she said, "I got onto a bus and asked the driver for a transfer, and when he helped someone else first I said that he was impertinent, and quarreled with him. And then I said why wasn't he in the army, and I said it loud enough for everyone to hear, and I took his number and I turned in a complaint. Probably got him fired."

"Fine," said Mr. Johnson. "But you do look tired. Want to change over tomorrow?"

"I *would* like to," she said. "I could do with a change."

"Right," said Mr. Johnson. "What's for dinner?"

"Veal cutlet."

"Had it for lunch," said Mr. Johnson.

THE MISSING GIRL

Fantasy and Science Fiction,
December 1957

S HE WAS HUMMING, TUNELESSLY, moving around somewhere in the room stirring things gently, and always humming. Betsy tightened her shoulders over the desk and bent her head emphatically over her book, hoping that her appearance of concentration would somehow communicate a desire for silence, but the humming went on. Debating a dramatic gesture, a wild throwing of the book to the floor, a shout of annoyance, Betsy thought as she had so often before, but you *can't* be cross with her, you just *can't,* and she bent farther over her book.

"Betsy?"

"Um?" Betsy, still trying to look as though she were studying, realized that she could have described every movement in the room until now.

"Listen, I'm going out."

"Where? At this time of night?"

"I'm going out anyway. I've got something to do."

"Go ahead," Betsy said; just because one could not be cross, one need not necessarily be interested.

"See you later."

The door slammed and Betsy, with relief and a feeling of freshness, went back to her book.

It was not, as a matter of fact, until the next night that anyone asked Betsy where her roommate had gone. Even then it was casual, and hardly provoked Betsy to thought: "You all alone tonight?" someone asked. "She out?"

"Haven't seen her all day," Betsy said.

The day after that, Betsy began to wonder a little, mostly because the other bed in the room had still not been slept in. The monstrous thought of going to the Camp Mother occurred to her ("Did you *hear* about Betsy? Went tearing off to old Auntie Jane to say her room-mate was missing, and here all the time the poor girl was . . .") and she spoke to several other people, wondering and curious, phrasing it each time as a sort of casual question; no one, it turned out, had seen her roommate since the Monday night when she had told Betsy, "See you later," and left.

"You think I ought to go tell Old Jane?" Betsy asked someone on the third day.

"Well . . ." consideringly. "You know, it might mean trouble for *you* if she's really missing."

The Camp Mother, comfortable and tolerant and humorous, old enough to be the mother of any of the counselors, wise enough to give the strong impression of experience, listened carefully and asked, "And you say she's been gone since Monday night? And here it is Thursday?"

"I didn't know what to do," Betsy explained candidly; "she could have gone home, or . . ."

"Or . . . ?" said the Camp Mother.

"She said she had something to do," Betsy said.

Old Jane pulled her phone over and asked, "What was her name again? Albert?"

"Alexander. Martha Alexander."

"Get me the home of Martha Alexander," Old Jane said into her phone, and from the room beyond, in the handsomely paneled building that served as the camp office and, at the other end, as kitchen, dining room, and general recreation room, Old Jane and Betsy could hear the voice of Miss Mills, Old Jane's assistant, saying irritably, "Alexander, Alexander," as she turned pages and opened filing drawers. "Jane?" she called out suddenly, "Martha Alexander from . . . ?"

"New York," Betsy said. "I *think*."

"New York," Old Jane said into her phone.

"Righto," Miss Mills said from the other room.

"Missing since Monday," Old Jane reminded herself, consulting the notes she had made on her desk pad. "Said she had something to do. Picture?"

"I don't think so," Betsy said uncertainly. "I may have a snapshot somewhere."

"Year?"

"Woodsprite, I *think*," Betsy said. "I'm a woodsprite, I mean, and they usually put woodsprites in with woodsprites and goblins in with goblins and senior huntsmen in with—" She stopped as the phone on Old Jane's desk rang and Old Jane picked it up and said briskly, "Hello? Is this Mrs. Alexander? This is Miss Nicholas calling from the Phillips Education Camp for Girls Twelve to Sixteen. Yes, that's right. . . . Fine, Mrs. Alexander, and how are *you*? . . . Glad to hear it. Mrs. Alexander, I'm calling to check on your daughter. . . . Your *daughter*, Martha. . . . Yes, that's right, Martha." She raised her eyebrows at Betsy and continued. "We're checking to make sure that she's come home or that you know where she is . . . yes, where she is. She left the camp very suddenly last Monday night and neglected to sign out at the main desk and of course our responsibility for our girls requires that even if she has only gone home we must—" She stopped, and her eyes focused, suddenly, on the far wall. "She is not?" Old Jane asked. "Do you know where she is, then? . . . How about friends? . . . Is there anyone who might know?"

The camp nurse, whose name was Hilda Scarlett and who was known as Will, had no record of Martha Alexander in the camp infirmary. She sat on the other side of Old Jane's desk, twisting her hands nervously and insisting that the only girls in the infirmary at that moment were a goblin with poison oak and a woodsprite with hysterics. "I suppose you *know*," she told Betsy, her voice rising, "that if you had come to one of us the *minute* she *left* . . ."

"But I didn't *know*," Betsy said helplessly. "*I* didn't know she was gone."

"I am afraid," said Old Jane ponderously, turning to regard Betsy with the air of one on whom an unnecessary and unkind burden has been thrust, "I am very much afraid that we must notify the police."

It was the first time the chief of police, a kindly family man whose name was Hook, had ever been required to visit a girls' camp; his daughters had not gone in much for that sort of thing, and Mrs. Hook distrusted night air; it was also the first time that Chief Hook had ever been required to determine facts. He had been allowed to continue in office this long because his family was popular in town and the young men at the local bar liked him, and because his record for twenty years, of drunks locked up and petty thieves apprehended upon confession, had been immaculate. In a small town such as the one lying close to the Phillips Education Camp for Girls Twelve to Sixteen, crime is apt to take its form from the characters of the inhabitants, and a stolen dog or broken nose is about the maximum to be achieved ordinarily in the sensational line. No one doubted Chief Hook's complete inability to cope with the disappearance of a girl from the camp.

"You say she was going somewhere?" he asked Betsy, having put out his cigar in deference to the camp nurse, and visibly afraid that his questions would sound foolish to Old Jane; since Chief Hook was accustomed to speaking around his cigar, his voice without it was malformed, almost quavering.

"She said she had something to do," Betsy told him.

"How did she say it? As though she meant it? Or do you think she was lying?"

"She just *said* it," said Betsy, who had reached that point of stubbornness most thirteen-year-old girls have, when it seems that adult obscurity has passed beyond necessity. "I *told* you eight times."

Chief Hook blinked and cleared his throat. "She sound happy?" he asked.

"Very happy," said Betsy. "She was singing all evening while I was trying to write in my Nature Book, is how I remember."

"Singing?" said Chief Hook; it was not possible to him that a girl upon the very edge of disappearance had anything to sing about.

"Singing?" said Old Jane.

"Singing?" said Will Scarlett. "You never told *us*."

"Just sort of humming," Betsy said.

"What tune?" said Chief Hook.

"Just *humming*," Betsy said. "I *told* you already, just *humming*. I nearly went crazy with my Nature Book."

"Any idea where she was going?"

"No."

An idea came to Chief Hook. "What was she interested in?" he asked suddenly. "You know, like sports, or boys, or anything."

"There are no boys at the Phillips Educational Camp for Girls," Old Jane said stiffly.

"She could have been *interested* in boys, though," Chief Hook said. "Or—like, well, books? Reading, you know? Or baseball, maybe?"

"We have not been able to find her Activity Chart," the camp nurse said. "Betsy, what recreational activity group was she in?"

"Golly." Betsy thought deeply, and said, "Dramatics? I think she went to Dramatics."

"Which nature study group? Little John? Eeyore?"

"Little John," said Betsy uncertainly. "I *think*. I'm pretty sure she was in Dramatics because I think I remember her talking about *Six Who Pass While the Lentils Boil*."

"That would be Dramatics," Old Jane said. "Surely."

Chief Hook, who had begun to feel that this was all unnecessarily confusing, said, "What about this singing?"

"There's singing in *Six Who Pass While the Lentils Boil*," Will Scarlett said.

"How about boys?" said Chief Hook.

Betsy thought again, remembering as well as she could the sleeping figure in the other bed, the soiled laundry on the floor, the open suitcase, the tin boxes of cookies, the towels, the face cloths, the soap, the pencils . . . "She had her own clock," Betsy volunteered.

"How long have you roomed together?" Old Jane asked, and her voice was faintly sardonic, as though in deference to Chief Hook she were forced to restrain the saltier half of her remark.

"Last year and this year," Betsy said. "I mean, we both put in for rooms at the same time and so they put us together again. I mean, most of my friends are senior huntsmen and of course I can't room with them because they only put senior huntsmen with—"

"We know." Old Jane was beginning to sound shrill. "Any mail?"

"I don't know about that," Betsy said. "I was always reading my own mail."

"What was she wearing?" Chief Hook asked.

"I don't know," Betsy said. "I didn't turn around when she left." She looked from Chief Hook to Will Scarlett to Old Jane with a trace of impatience. "I was doing my *Nature* Book."

A search of the room, from which Betsy abstained and which was carried on with enthusiasm by Old Jane and Will Scarlett and with some embarrassment by Chief Hook, showed that after Betsy's possessions had been subtracted from the medley, what was left was astonishingly little. There was a typed script of *Six Who Pass While the Lentils Boil*, and a poorly done painting of Echo Lake, which was part of the camp. There was a notebook, labeled, like Betsy's, "Nature Book," but it was unused, lacking the pressed wildflowers and blue jay feathers; there was a copy of *Gulliver's Travels* from the camp library, which Old Jane felt might be significant. No one was able to tell certainly what she had been wearing, because the clothes in the closet were mostly Betsy's, and jackets or overshoes left in the room by Betsy's friends. In the drawers of the second dresser were a few scraps of underwear, a pair of heavy socks, and a red sweater which Betsy was fairly sure belonged to a woodsprite on the other side of camp.

A careful checkup of Recreational Activity lists showed that while she was listed for dramatics and nature study and swimming, her attendance at any of them was dubious; most of the counselors kept slipshod attendance records, and none of them could remember whether any such girl could have come on any given day.

"I'm almost sure I remember *her,* though," Little John, an ardent girl of twenty-seven who wore horn-rimmed glasses and tossed her hair back from her face with a pretty gesture that somehow indicated that winters she wore it decently pinned up, told Chief Hook. "I have an awfully good memory for faces, and I think I remember her as one of Rabbit's friends and relations. Yes, I'm sure I remember her, I have a good memory for faces."

"Ah," said the librarian, who was called Miss Mills when she was secretary to Old Jane, and the Snark when she was in the library, "one girl is much like another, at *this* age. Their unformed minds, their unformed bodies, their little mistakes; we, too, were young once, Captain Hook."

"Hell," said the muscular young woman who was known as Tarzan because she taught swimming, "did you ever look at fifty girls all in white bathing caps?"

"Elm?" said the nature study counselor, whose name was Blue-bird. "I mean, wasn't she an elm girl? Did a nice paper on blight? Or was it the other girl, Michaels? Anyway, whichever one it might have *been,* it was a nice job. Out of the ordinary for *us,* you know; remember it particularly. Hadn't noticed either of the girls to speak of—but if she's really gone, she might be up on Smoky Trail looking for fern; want the girls to make a special topic of fern and mushroom." She stopped and blinked, presumably taking in a new supply of chlorophyll. "Fern," she said. "Pays to know plenty about fern."

"Few of them have any talent, anyway," the painting counselor said. "In any of the progressive schools *this* sort of thing—" She gestured tiredly at the canvases propped up against tree stumps or stacked upon a rock, and moved her shoulders nervously under her brand-new blue and yellow checked shirt. "Interested *psychologically,* of course," she added quickly. "If I remember this girl, she did sort of vague stuff, almost *unwilling.* Rejection, almost—if I can find a picture you'll see right away what I mean." She poked unenthusiastically among the canvases stacked on the rock, pulled her hand back and said, "Why did I ever—" wiping wet paint off on her blue jeans. "Funny," she said, "I could have taken an oath she had a canvas around here somewhere. Sort of vague stuff, though—no sense of design, no eye."

"Did she *ever,*" Chief Hook asked Betsy, "ever ever *ever* mention anyplace she might want to go? Some foreign country, maybe?"

Old Jane's voice had an odd tone. "The parents are arriving tomorrow."

Chief Hook rubbed his forehead nervously. "Lost a hunter last fall on Bad Mountain," he suggested.

It was decided to search Bad Mountain, and then, unexpectedly, a house-to-house canvass along the road leading to Bad Mountain uncovered an honest clue. A housewife, glancing out her window to see if her husband was coming home from a poker game, had seen, she thought, the figure of a girl moving along the road, lighted occasionally by the headlights of passing cars.

"I couldn't *swear* it was a girl, though," the housewife persisted nervously. "That is, nights when Jim is out playing, I go to bed, and this night I was only up on account we had fried clams for supper, and I like clams but they don't—"

"What was she wearing?" Chief Hook demanded.

The woman thought. "Well," she said finally, "the reason I figured she was one of those girls from the camp was she was wearing pants. But then, it could have been a man, you see, or a boy. Only somehow I sort of figured it was a girl."

"Did she have on a coat? Hat?"

"A coat, I think," the woman said, "leastways, one of those short jackets. She was going up the road toward Jones Pass."

Jones Pass led to Bad Mountain. It was not possible to get a picture of the girl; the picture on her camp application blank was so blurred that it resembled a hundred other girls in the camp; it was assumed, however, from the picture, that she had dark hair. A man was discovered who had given a ride to a girl hitchhiking on the road to Jones Pass; she had dark hair and was wearing blue jeans and a short tan leather jacket.

"I don't think she was a *camp* girl, though," the man added earnestly, "not the way she talked, she wasn't any girl from Phillips Camp, not *her*," he said, and looked at Chief Hook, "Bill, you remember that youngest girl over to Ben Hart's?"

Chief Hook sighed. "You see anyone else driving down the road?" he asked. The man shook his head emphatically.

One of the junior counselors at the camp, who went by the name of Piglet, had been driving home late from town that night and at one point in the road near Jones Pass had had the clear impression of someone ducking behind a tree into the shadows. She was unable to say whether or not it had been a girl, or even whether it had been a person, but Chief Hook questioned her remorselessly.

"Can you face this girl's parents and honestly tell them you never lifted a finger to save her?" he demanded of Piglet. "That innocent girl?"

Will Scarlett had shut herself into the infirmary and refused to let go of the phenobarbital; it was announced that she could not be disturbed. The press agent for the camp was taking all calls and managing the general search. Newspaper reporters were encouraged, but the seventeen-year-old son of the owner of the local paper was given first chance at all new developments; it occurred to this young man to ensure that a search be made over Bad Mountain by helicopter, and the camp went to tremendous expense to import one, although its six-day tour of the mountains showed nothing, and the son of the newspaper owner subsequently informed his father that he preferred having a plane to inheriting the paper, which went to a distant cousin. It was said that the girl had turned up in a town seventy-five miles away, dead drunk and trying to get a job in a shoe store, but the proprietor of the shoe store was unable to identify her picture, and it was later proven that the girl in question was actually the daughter of the mayor of that town. The widowed mother of the missing girl was prostrate with grief and under the care of a physician, but her uncle arrived at the camp and took personal charge of the search. The girls from the camp, led by the counselor in nature study and the senior huntsmen, had already gone over the mountain, looking for bent twigs and rock signs, but without success, although they had the assistance of chosen boy and girl scouts from the town. It was afterward told that Old Jane, indefatigable in leather puttees and a striped bandana and known to be extraordinarily susceptible to cold, had fallen down dead drunk in front of Chief Hook and had had to be carried home on a stretcher hastily improvised by the boy scouts, leading many people to believe that the girl's body had been found.

In the town it was generally believed that the girl had been killed and *"You* know," and her body buried in a shallow grave somewhere east of Jones Pass, where the woods were deepest and ran downhill and for miles along the edge of Muddy River; knowing folk in town who had hunted the pass and Bad Mountain were quoted as saying that it would be mighty easy for anyone to miss a body in them woods; go ten feet off the path and you're lost, and the mud that deep already; it was generally conceded in the town that the girl had been followed in the darkness by a counselor from the camp, preferably one of the quiet ones, until she was out of sight or sound of help. The townspeople remembered their grandfathers had known of people disposed of in just that way, and no one had ever heard about it, either.

In the camp it was generally believed that one of the low bloods around the town—and try to match them for general vulgarity and insolence, and the generations of inbreeding that had led to idiocy in half the families and just plain filth in the rest—had enticed the girl off into an assignation on the mountain, and there outraged and murdered her and buried her body. The camp people believed that it was possible to dispose of a body by covering it with lime—heaven knew these country farmhands had enough lime in a barn to dispose of a dozen bodies—and that by the time the search started there wasn't enough left of the body to find. The camp people further believed that it was no more than you might expect of a retarded village in an isolated corner of the world, and they thought you might go far before you met up with a lower and a stupider group of clods; they pointed with triumph to the unusual lack of success of the Camp Talent Show early in the summer, to which the townspeople had been invited.

On the eleventh day of the search, Chief Hook, who perceived clearly that he might very well lose his job, sat down quietly for a conference with the girl's uncle, Old Jane, and Will Scarlett, who had emerged from the infirmary on the ninth day, to announce that she had for a long time been renowned as a minor necromancer and seer, and would gladly volunteer her services in any possible psychic way.

"I think," said Chief Hook despondently, "that we might as well give it up. The boy scouts quit a week ago, and today the girl scouts went."

The girl's uncle nodded. He had gained weight on Mrs. Hook's cooking and he had taken to keeping his belt as loose as Chief Hook's. "We haven't made any progress, certainly," he said.

"I told you to look under the fourth covered bridge from the blasted oak," said Will Scarlett sullenly. "I *told* you."

"Miss Scarlett, *we* couldn't find no blasted oak," Chief Hook said, "and we looked and looked— No oaks in this part of the country at all," he told the girl's uncle.

"Well, I told you to keep looking," said the seer. "I told you also look on the left-hand side of the road to Exeter."

"We looked there, too," Chief Hook said. "Nothing."

"You know," said the girl's uncle, as though it were a complete statement. He passed his hand tiredly across his forehead and looked long and soberly at Chief Hook, and then long and soberly at Old Jane, who sat quietly at her desk with papers in her hands. "You know," he said again. Then, addressing himself to Old Jane and speaking rapidly, he went on. "My sister wrote to me today, and she's very upset. Naturally," he added, and looked around at Old Jane, at Will Scarlett, at Chief Hook, all of whom nodded appreciatively, "but listen," he went on, "what she says is that of course she loves Martha and all that, and of course *no* one would want to say anything about a girl like this that's missing, and probably had something horrible done to her . . ." He looked around again, and again everyone nodded. "But she says," he went on, "that in spite of all that . . . well . . . she's pretty sure, what I mean, that she decided against Phillips Educational Camp for Girls. What I *mean*," he said, looking around again, "she has three girls and a boy, my sister, and of course we both feel *terribly* sorry and of course we'll still keep in our end of the reward and all that, but what I *mean* is . . ." He brushed his hand across his forehead again. ". . . What I mean is this. The oldest girl, that's Helen, she's married and out in San Francisco, so that's *her*. And—I'll show you my sister's letter—the second girl, that's Jane, well, *she's* married and *she* lives in Texas somewhere, has a little boy about two years old. And then the third girl—well, *that's* Mabel, and she's right at home with her mother, around the house and whatnot. Well—you see what I mean?"

No one nodded this time, and the girl's uncle went on nervously. "The boy, *he's* in Denver, and his name is—"

"Never mind," said Chief Hook. He rose wearily and reached into his pocket for a cigar. "Nearly suppertime," he said to no one in particular.

Old Jane nodded and shuffled the papers in her hand. "I have all the records here," she said. "Although a girl named Martha Alexander applied for admission to the Phillips Educational Camp for Girls Twelve to Sixteen, her application was put into the file marked 'possibly undesirable' and there is no record of her ever having come to the camp. Although her name has been entered upon various class lists, she is not noted as having participated personally in any activity; she has not, so far as we know, used any of her dining room tickets or her privileges with regard to laundry and bus services, not to mention country dancing. She has not used the golf course nor the tennis courts, nor has she taken out any riding horses. She has never, to our knowledge, and our records are fairly complete, sir, attended any local church—"

"She hasn't taken advantage of the infirmary," said Will Scarlett, "or psychiatric services."

"You see?" said the girl's uncle to Chief Hook.

"Nor," finished Old Jane quietly, "nor has she been vaccinated or tested for any vitamin deficiency whatsoever."

A body that might have been Martha Alexander's was found, of course, something over a year later, in the late fall when the first light snow was drifting down. The body had been stuffed away among some thorn bushes, which none of the searchers had cared to tackle, until two small boys looking for a cowboy hideout had wormed their way through the thorns. It was impossible to say, of course, how the girl had been killed—at least Chief Hook, who still had his job, found it impossible to say—but it was ascertained that she had been wearing a black corduroy skirt, a reversible raincoat, and a blue scarf.

She was buried quietly in the local cemetery; Betsy, a senior huntsman the past summer but rooming alone, stood for a moment by the grave, but was unable to recognize any aspect of the clothes or the body. Old Jane attended the funeral, as befitted the head of the camp, and she and Betsy stood alone in the cemetery by the grave. Although she did not cry over her lost girl, Old Jane touched her eyes occasionally with a plain white handkerchief, since she had come up from New York particularly for the services.

THE OMEN

❧

Fantasy and Science Fiction,
March 1958

IT WOULD BE PUSHING truth too far to say that Grandma Williams was the finest person in the world to live with. As her daughter said sometimes, but only after the greatest professions of loyalty, "She's just the *sweetest* old lady in the world, of course, but sometimes she's *very* trying." And her son-in-law, whose patience was immense, and whose courtesy was unfailing, had been heard to say with an affectionate smile to his wife, "Granny seems to be aging rapidly these days." Even her grandchildren, of whom there were two, sometimes found themselves exasperated by her, and would say in such cases, "Oh, *Granny,*" or *"Gosh,"* in the tone of voice used by children when words fail them.

Ordinarily, however, everyone loved Grandma Williams almost as much as she loved them, and they ate the custards she prepared so tenderly, and bore with the small surprises she invented for them, and gave her warm scarves and gloves for Christmas, and homemade valentines on Valentine's Day, and gardenias on Mother's Day, and took her out to dinner and the theater on her birthday, and saw that her glasses were found when she lost them, and brought her home books from the lending library, and remembered to kiss her good night, and to be polite to the two or three old friends who still remained to her, and who came sometimes to call. And when Granny announced brightly at breakfast one morning that today she was going shopping, no one criticized her, or even smiled.

"Isn't it something I can do for you, dear?" her daughter asked, looking into the coffeepot. "I may go into town today, and I'd be glad to do any errands you want."

"Happy to get you anything myself," said her son-in-law. "Easy to stop off somewhere on my way home."

Granny shook her head vehemently. "This is important shopping," she said. "I have to do it myself."

"Can I go with you?" asked her younger grandchild, who was eight years old, and who was named Ellen and was commonly supposed to resemble Granny as a girl.

"Indeed you may not," Granny said. "This is a surprise."

If a slight sigh went around the breakfast table, Granny did not notice. "A surprise for everyone," she said. "You remember yesterday?"

Everyone remembered yesterday; yesterday had been an event. Yesterday Granny had received in the morning mail a check for thirteen dollars and seventy-four cents, with a covering letter saying that the sender had owed it to Granny's husband for nearly fifty years, and so was paying it now to his widow, with interest. Granny's son-in-law had figured out the interest for her, and it was quite proper. Granny, today, was rich. "A surprise for everyone," she repeated happily, "with my new money."

Her daughter opened her mouth to protest, and then stopped. Nothing that Granny could possibly buy with thirteen dollars and seventy-four cents would give her more pleasure than surprises for everybody. "I think that's *wonderful*," her daughter said finally, eyeing her family around the table.

"Very kind of you," said Granny's son-in-law.

"I want—" began Ellen.

"Dear," said her mother, "this is to be a surprise."

"But I want to *know*," said Granny. "Robert, will you get me a pencil and paper?" Her older grandchild, who was ten, departed and returned in haste, partly because he had been carefully taught to treat his granny courteously, and partly because surprises did not come every day.

"Now," said Granny, her pencil poised over the paper. "Margaret?"

"You mean what do I want?" said her daughter. She thought. "I don't really know," she said slowly. "A handkerchief, perhaps? Or a box of candy?"

"If I were to get you a bottle of perfume," said Granny with great cunning, "what kind would you most like?"

Her daughter considered again. "Well," she said, "I usually wear a kind called Carnation."

"*Carnation,*" Granny said. She wrote on her paper. Then she looked inquiringly at her son-in-law. "John," she said. "What for you?"

He frowned soberly. "Let me see," he said. "I suppose what I most need is a few good cigars. El Signo, I generally smoke."

"Cigars," Granny said complacently. "A very good thing in a man. Your grandfather used to say that cigarettes were for women and children. What kind, again?"

"El Signo," said her son-in-law.

"I can't possibly write such an outlandish name," said Granny. "What is it in English?"

"The sign," he told her, not looking at his wife.

"*The sign,*" Granny said as she wrote. "You see," she explained, "I can always ask the man what it means, in cigars."

"Now me?" said Ellen.

"Now you, Granddaughter."

"A doll's house with real glass in the windows," said Ellen immediately, "and a bride doll, and a live kitty and—"

"Not a live kitty," said her mother hastily.

"A stuffed kitty?" said Ellen, wide-eyed. "A blue stuffed kitty?"

"Splendid," said Granny. "*Blue cat,*" she wrote. "Robert?" she said.

"Roller skates," said Robert. "Walkie-talkie."

"What?" said Granny.

"Walkie-talkie," said Robert. "It's a sort of telephone, like."

Granny stared at her son-in-law, who smiled and shrugged. "*Telephone,*" Granny said, and wrote it down. Then she leaned back and looked farsightedly at her list. "*Carnation,*" she read. "*The sign. Blue cat. Telephone.*" She smiled around the table at the family. "Now me," she said. "*I* want a ring."

"A ring?" said her daughter. "Granny, you *have* rings. You have your diamond ring, and the little one set with a cameo, and Dad's silver seal ring, and—"

"Not any of those," said Granny, shaking her head vigorously. "I saw a little ring I wanted, in the five and ten the other day. It cost twenty-nine cents, and it was silver-plated and it had on it two hearts set together. I *liked* that ring."

Her daughter and son-in-law exchanged glances. "If you'll wait till your birthday," said her daughter, "perhaps you might have the same ring in real silver; if it's something you like, we could easily have it made."

"I want this one," said Granny. She rose from the table, picked up her list, and put it carefully into her pocket. "Now," she said. "Now I am going shopping."

She departed for her room to get her coat and hat, and her daughter said anxiously to her son-in-law, "Do you think it's all right? I could insist on going along."

"She's getting so much pleasure out of it," said the son-in-law, "it would be a real shame to spoil it. And of course she'll be all right."

"Everyone's always glad to help an old lady, anyway," said the daughter. "If she gets into any difficulty, that is."

Granny, stylish in her neat black coat and a small rakish hat trimmed with violets, set out at precisely ten o'clock, an hour after her son-in-law had gone off to his office, and an hour and ten minutes after her grandchildren had climbed noisily into the school bus. Her daughter stood in the doorway and waved to her as she went down the street; Granny had insisted upon traveling into town on the bus, instead of taking a taxi, and her daughter stood in the doorway until she saw Granny reach the corner, signal competently to the bus driver with her umbrella, and climb aboard, helped, as she always was, somehow, by the driver and two friendly passengers. People would be taking care of Granny like that all day, her daughter thought, and, with an admiring smile, she turned back inside to finish the breakfast dishes. I'll just dress later, she thought, and run into town myself. I might meet her somewhere and bring her home.

Granny sat proudly in the bus, perfectly aware of the attention she was attracting. Her son-in-law had kindly cashed her check, and Granny had thirteen dollars and seventy-four cents in her pocketbook. Her list, she thought, was safely tucked into her pocket, but, as a matter of fact, it had slipped out, and lay unnoticed on the seat when Granny alighted in the center of town, assisted by the bus driver, a kind gentleman, and two schoolgirls.

Not everyone had had such a pleasant two days as Granny had. Miss Edith Webster, for instance, had put in forty-eight hours (and this the first week of her vacation!) of unpleasant and fruitless argument. Edith loved her mother quite as much as Granny's daughter loved Granny, but Edith's mother was perhaps a shade more selfish than Granny—Granny, as Edith would have pointed out if she had known about it, had at least allowed her daughter to get married. Edith's mother was explicit upon this point.

"If you marry this Jerry fellow," she told Edith—as she had gone on telling Edith, over and over, for three years—"you will be leaving your poor old mother all alone, not that I think you *care* about me— no, by now I know better than to think my only daughter *cares* about what happens to her poor old mother—but you'd always have it on your conscience, I hope, that you left your poor old mother to starve."

"You wouldn't starve," Edith had pointed out over and over for three years, although by now the words had no meaning, from being said so often. "Aunt Martha has been wanting you to come and live with her for a long time, and Jerry and I could always give you enough money to get along."

"Aunt Martha? What would I want to live with Aunt Martha for? You certainly couldn't have much respect for my *comfort* if you tried to make me go and live with Aunt *Martha*."

On the morning that Granny set out so blithely, Edith had finally said with more anger than she had ever shown her mother before, "I have every right in the world to get married and have a family of my own, and it's not fair for you to try and stop me."

"You're my daughter," her mother retorted, "and you owe me all your education and all the care and love I've given you all these years. And I'm not going to let you throw yourself away on some good-for-nothing, and leave your poor old mother to starve."

At that point Edith snatched up her hat and fled from the house, leaving her mother still talking, dwelling lovingly upon the symptoms of starvation, and how Edith might possibly remember to show up at her deathbed—not, however, to be forgiven.

Walking down the street, Edith, who was actually an agreeable and pleasant girl, and who did not enjoy quarreling, told herself firmly that a decision must be reached, and immediately. Her mother did not show any signs of ever changing her mind, and, no matter how hard she tried to ignore it, there was the telling fact that Jerry, who had waited patiently for three years, was beginning to remark restlessly that all his friends were married, that a man expected to settle down before he was thirty, that he personally thought that Edith's mother would never give in, and that *he* thought the thing to do was up and get married, and let the old lady give her consent afterward. Edith thought he was right, if she tried to be impartial about it, but still the courage required to defy her mother was more than she could muster.

Going down the street (and she was at this time approximately two miles from Granny Williams, who was just then marching boldly down her own street on her way to a different bus), Edith, in her neat dark blue coat and red hat (as opposed to Granny, who was wearing a black coat and a hat with violets), sighed deeply, and thought: If I only had an idea of what to do; if only somebody, something, somehow, would show me the way, make up my mind for me, give me an omen.

All of which is, of course, a most dangerous way of thinking.

Edith, on her own bus, reached the center of town almost the same time Granny did, and, by an odd coincidence, Edith even passed Granny on the street without noticing her; nor did Granny notice Edith. Perhaps, indeed, Edith thought swiftly: *look at the nice old lady in the hat with flowers;* perhaps the thought passed through Granny's mind: *look at the pretty girl with the sad frown.* These things happen daily, among the thousands of people who pass one another in crowds. At any rate, Edith, whose ultimate destination was the home of a girl friend on the other side of town (someone to whom Edith could pour out her troubles, and who would give her sympathy, if no kind of help), got on the wrong bus. She was worried, and thinking about something else, and there were a lot of people waiting at the bus stop, and Edith did not look up in time to see the sign on the front of the bus, and a man in the crowd near her said loudly, "It's the Long Avenue bus," which was the one Edith wanted, so Edith got on, and paid her fare, and sat down in the first seat she came to, which was the seat vacated by Granny not long ago, and on the seat, Granny's list was waiting to be an omen to Edith. Edith picked it up and put it into her pocket, thinking it was something she herself had dropped, such as a transfer or a scrap of envelope with an address on it; she did not even look at it as she put it into her pocket.

Edith was not the sort of person who, realizing suddenly that she is on the wrong bus, immediately stands up and screams and reproaches the driver for taking her in the wrong direction, and insists upon being put off on a strange street corner at once. She was annoyed at herself for her mistake, but was not inclined to think that the bus company had deceived her. It was not vitally important, after all, for her to reach her girl friend's house before lunch: she was in a strange section of town, and she knew she could easily get out of the bus, have her lunch in the first restaurant she came to, and then proceed in a leisurely manner. So, at the first stop, she got down from the bus and stood while it roared away, regarding her surroundings.

Now, at this point began a series of events that might easily have been a dream of Edith's except for its conclusion. For, as Edith stood on the corner, she realized first that she was in a part of town she had never seen before, and second, that there was no landmark in sight, not even a sign saying RESTAURANT or COFFEE SHOPPE or EAT or DINER or LUNCHEONETTE or FOUNTAIN; in other words, no place where a girl alone could ask for information about where she was without looking foolish. Then, with that enjoyable feeling of anonymity that comes when you are a little lost, with plenty of money in your pocket, and the secret feeling that you can always get home by calling for a taxi, Edith thought that for a little while anyway she had escaped the problem of her mother and Jerry, for the simple reason that neither of them could at present find her to remind her of it. The next thing that happened was her shocking discovery that she did not have any money after all. The change purse she had slipped into her pocket contained, instead of several one-dollar bills and a five—which she now recalled having spent for the hat she was wearing on her head at the moment—only four nickels and approximately seven pennies. Thus was Edith marooned.

It seemed wise, at first, to retire to a secluded spot and wonder what to do. A bus back to the center of town? Then where was the bus stop? Edith craned her neck, but could not find a familiar sign. She fumbled in her pockets, and at that moment found Granny's list. Staring at it uncomprehendingly, thinking for a minute that it was a stray dollar bill in her pocket, Edith read: *"Carnation. The sign. Blue cat. Telephone. Ring."*

"What on earth?" said Edith out loud, and a child passing stopped, stared at her, and then said, "Huh?"

"Nothing," Edith said quickly. "Just an omen."

The child stared further, and went off, looking back at her.

Edith was intelligent enough to know that when she asked for an omen and got it, the least she could do was obey it. Reading it again—she stopped, this time, to admire the queer, old-fashioned handwriting, so much like a voice from a sweet and simple past—it occurred to her that since her omen told her *"carnation,"* a carnation was obviously indicated. Smiling at herself, although not with so much amusement as she might have felt if this omen had not arrived exactly on schedule, she started down the street, in the general direction of the center of town, looking for a carnation. At this time she made her first discovery about omens: that their requirements are usually much more difficult than they seem to be; fewer carnations were in evidence than one might have expected in early summer. For instance, a florist shop seemed a possible place to look, although it did seem rather like cheating, until Edith, scrutinizing carefully the window display of a mangy-looking shop that advertised itself as a FLO-RIST SHOP, found that there were no carnations. Roses, yes. Lilies, violets, ferns, horrid-looking daisies. But not carnations. Puzzled, Edith went on. There were paper flowers in the window of a funeral parlor, and they might as well have been carnations as anything else, but Edith thought that perhaps paper flowers were not allowed, par-ticularly since a funeral parlor seemed no place for a self-respecting omen to lead her. Then, as she had begun to despair, and had gone about four blocks, someone said, "Pardon me, but are you Miss Mur-rain?"

Edith turned; the words were addressed to her. Her mind did not take in the sense of them for a minute, because the man speaking to her was wearing a white carnation in his buttonhole. Edith realized that the omen had said not *"carnations"* but *"carnation,"* and she said, "I'm sorry?"

"Are you Miss Murrain?" the man asked again very politely.

"No, I'm afraid not," said Edith.

"Are you sure?" said the man.

"Yes," said Edith.

"Are you *positive*?" said the man.

Edith stared. "I am not the lady you are looking for," she said as firmly as she could. (Am I? she wondered suddenly.) "I'm sorry," she added when she saw that the man was troubled.

"I wish you were," he said, and sighed.

"Don't you know the lady?" Edith asked.

He laughed. "Come and see," he said. He took her politely by the arm and led her farther down the block to where a group of people were standing around a store window. The store was a grocery, and this was apparently its grand opening day, for bright-colored flags draped the doorway, and signs saying FREE SODA FOR THE LADIES stood upon the sidewalk. The crowd of people standing before the store window separated as Edith and her guide came up to the window.

"See?" said Edith's guide, and Edith's mind registered *"sign,"* the second word on her omen.

FIND MISS MURRAIN, the sign entreated. FIND HER, FIND HER, FIND HER. And, in smaller letters: SOMEWHERE IN THIS NEIGHBORHOOD TODAY, MURRAIN BROTHERS, FINE GROCERIES AND DELICATESSEN GOODS, HAVE A LADY FRIEND WHO IS WALKING ALONE, WAITING FOR SOMEONE TO COME UP

TO HER AND SAY: "ARE YOU MISS MURRAIN?" IF YOU ASK HER THIS, SHE WILL ANSWER: "MURRAIN BROTHERS ARE THE FINEST GROCERS IN TOWN." IF YOU FIND MISS MURRAIN AND BRING HER TO THIS STORE—MURRAIN BROTHERS, FINE GROCERIES AND DELICATESSEN GOODS—WE WILL GIVE YOU ONE HUNDRED DOLLARS IN TRADE. SPECIAL GRAND OPENING OFFER, TODAY ONLY. And, at the bottom of the sign, in very small letters, were the words: SPECIAL HINT: MISS MURRAIN IS WEARING A HAT THE COLOR OF THE BAGS IN WHICH MURRAIN BROTHERS PACK THEIR SPECIAL COFFEE.

"Red," said her guide when he saw Edith lean forward to read the small letters on the bottom of the sign, "it means red, they pack their special coffee in red bags."

"I see," said Edith, who was of course wearing a red hat. She turned and smiled at her guide. "I wish I could help you," she said.

"So do I," he said. They made their way out of the crowd again and stood on the sidewalk. "I could use a hundred dollars' worth of groceries."

"If I see Miss Murrain, I'll try to catch her for you," Edith said.

"Catch her for yourself," he said seriously. "They mean it about the groceries." Abruptly he looked at his watch. "Good Lord," he said, "I'm late."

"By the way," Edith said as he turned to go, "if you don't mind my asking you, why are you wearing the carnation?"

"That?" he said, looking down. "Oh, *that*. Oh, I'm getting married in ten minutes." He was gone, hurrying madly off down the street.

"Congratulations," Edith said weakly after him. Bewildered, she stood for a minute. "*Sign*," she told herself, "*carnation, sign, sign, carnation, carnation, sign, sign, car*—" Realizing that she was beginning to babble, she tightened her lips and reached into her pocket for the slip of paper.

"*Carnation*," it said. "*The sign. Blue cat*."

"Blue cat?" Edith frowned. "Blue cat? *Blue* cat? Blue *cat*?" She was babbling again. She set her shoulders firmly and stepped positively out toward what she guessed was the nearest traffic artery to the center of town.

"Excuse me, are you Miss Murrain?"

She turned; it was a lady, and Edith was sorry for a minute that she was *not* Miss Murrain—the lady so obviously thought she had collared her hundred dollars' worth of groceries, and she looked, moreover, as though a hundred dollars' worth of groceries would not come at all amiss.

"I'm sorry," Edith said. "I wish I were," she said.

"You were wearing the hat, is why I asked," the woman said. She smiled politely, and walked on.

If I go home now, Edith was thinking, Mother will be after me again about Jerry. If I go on wandering, sooner or later I will have to go back and then the whole problem will—

"Are you Miss Murrain?"

"Sorry, I'm not."

"Just thought I'd ask."

Or else, Edith thought, if I went back and told her once and for all—

"You Miss Murrain?"

"Sorry."

"You sure?"

"Positive."

"O.K."

Probably the best way would be to put off deciding for a while yet, and maybe somehow—

"It's Miss Murrain! Are you Miss Murrain, hey?"

"No, I'm sor—"

"It's Miss Murrain—hey, I caught her, it's Miss Murrain!"

Looking around, Edith saw with dismay that she was surrounded by a crowd of people. They were mostly women, housewives out doing their morning marketing, several pushing baby carriages, and there were a few men; all of them—men, women, children—were staring at her, and at the stout, red-faced woman who had her by the arm.

"I got her, I got her!"

"Look," Edith said quietly to the red-faced woman, "I'm terribly sorry, but I'm *not* Miss Murrain. People have been asking me the same—"

"Hundred bucks' worth of groceries, golly!"

Edith, trying to pull away, found that the red-faced woman had hold of her much as she would have held a rebellious child. "Please," Edith said urgently, "believe me—"

"George—Maggie—Earl—I got her, look, it's me caught her, the girl with the groceries!"

"Let me *go,*" Edith said, and pulled harder. "Listen," she said to the crowd, making her voice as reasonable as she could, "if I were this Miss Murrain, I would have *had* to say so, wouldn't I? Because I'm *really* not."

"She's trying to get away, Missus," one of the men observed impartially. "If she goes, your groceries go with her."

"Look," said the red-faced woman to Edith, shaking her. "You're not going to get those groceries away from *me,* you understand?"

"But I can't *get* you any—" Common sense came back to Edith, and she relaxed and said reasonably, "Why don't you take me along to the grocery? *They* can tell you I'm the wrong person."

"Take her to the grocery." The crowd took up the words; they began to move along down the block, and the red-faced woman marched in advance, almost dragging Edith, and shouting right and left, "I got her, I got her, I got the girl with the groceries."

The grocery was some two blocks away; they had gone only a block or so when they were met by a pack of children coming shrieking away from the grocery.

"Miz Eaton got it," they were howling, "Miz Eaton got all the groc'ries, Miz Eaton got the groc'ries, Miz Eaton found the girl with the red hat, Miz Eaton . . ."

The red-faced woman holding Edith stopped, stared, took one deep breath, and then turned to look at Edith, her face, if possible, redder than before.

"You mean to say," she began in a voice obviously restrained to make her imminent wrath the more terrible, "*you mean to say* you told me you were that girl and you *aren't?*" She let go of Edith to put her hands on her hips and in that moment Edith, all dignity lost, turned and ran.

She darted down a side street, thinking for a moment that the red-faced woman was after her, but in a minute, from the sound of voices going up the street she had left, she realized that the red-faced woman had gone on with her following to the grocery, probably to dispute the decision. Breathing fast, Edith slowed down to a walk and began to look out for a place where she could spend one of her nickels on a cup of coffee and a chance to catch her breath. Ahead, she saw a dingy sign that hung over the sidewalk: it read KITTY'S LUNCH. Gratefully she hurried to it and, as she stepped inside, saw that Kitty had, with odd humor, chosen to adorn the window of Kitty's Lunch with a large painted blue cat.

"*Blue cat,*" said Edith to herself. "Kitty."

Not bothering to try to think anymore, she went inside. Kitty's Lunch was nothing more than a long counter with sugar bowls and catsup bottles set at intervals along it, and Kitty herself—presumably—enthroned in vast state on a folding chair at one end of the counter. Edith sat at one of the counter stools and Kitty roused herself much as though Edith had been a mouse, and moved slowly down the counter to serve her, although it did not actually seem possible for there to be enough space behind the counter for Kitty to pass.

"Coffee," said Edith as Kitty almost reached her. "Black coffee, please."

Kitty nodded, and looked Edith up and down.

Edith tried to smile. "If you think I'm that Miss Murrain, I'm not," she said. "They've already found her."

"I'm mighty glad they did," Kitty said. "What is mismurrain?"

"Never mind," said Edith gratefully. "Do you know anything about omens?"

"Omens," said Kitty. "Mismurrain. No."

"Good," said Edith. "If you *did* find an omen, would you follow it?"

"I wouldn't follow a rainbow for a pot of gold," Kitty said obscurely.

She went with dignity to fetch Edith's coffee, which she set down before Edith with a queenly gesture.

By now, Edith thought, it had become inevitable. After Kitty had gone back to her chair at the end of the counter, Edith took the slip of paper out of her pocket and consulted it, although she already knew what it said. "*Telephone,*" she said softly to herself, and then more loudly to Kitty, "Telephone?"

Kitty did not look up from her comic book, but gestured with a large thumb at the wall telephone at the end of the counter. It was not in a booth, it was not even remotely private from Kitty or from anyone else who might happen to come in, but the omen had been explicit so far, and Edith, two more of her precious nickels in her hand, hurried down to the end of the counter.

She dialed the number from memory, and waited interminably until they answered.

"Gambel's Garage."

"Is Jerry there?" said Edith timidly.

"Wait and I'll see." The voice echoed, far away. "Jerry? Jerrrrry? Lady onna phone."

After another deadly wait, during which Edith could hear her nickels washing away, he said, "Hello?"

"Jerry?" she said. "This is Edith."

"Edith?" His voice sounded surprised. "Is something wrong?"

"Jerry," she said weakly. "I'm sorry about keeping you waiting. I mean, I know what to do now. I mean, I guess if you want me to I'll marry you."

"Yeah?" She thought hopefully that he sounded rather more pleased than not. "Good," he said, and then she realized that he had known all the time that someday she would call him like this and tell him.

"Can you come and meet me?" she asked.

"I'm off for lunch in ten minutes. Where?"

"I'm in a blue cat," she said. "I mean, what does it matter! I mean— Just a minute. Where am I?" she turned to ask Kitty. Kitty lifted her face and gave Edith one long look.

"Corner of Flower Street and East Avenue," she said. "How long'd it take you to make up your mind?"

"Three years," said Edith. "Corner of Flower Street and East Avenue," she said to Jerry.

"Right," he said. "About twenty minutes, then. Who's going to take care of your mother?"

"She'll have to take care of herself," Edith said. "*I* need someone to take care of *me*."

"I'll go along with *that*," said Kitty from the background.

"Right," Jerry said.

"And, Jerry," Edith said. "Listen, will you bring—I mean—the omen says—I mean, do you have—can you get—"

"What?" said Jerry.

"*What?*" said Kitty.

"A ring," said Edith helplessly.

"I've already got it," Jerry said.

"What'd he say?" inquired Kitty with interest.

"He says he's got it," Edith told her.

"What?" Jerry said.

"Smart man," Kitty said.

"Goodbye," Edith said to Jerry, and listened, smiling, to his answer. Then she hung up, made a face at Kitty, and said, "I'm not going to tell you."

Kitty grinned. "Three years to make up your mind," she said. "You must be crazy."

. . .

Granny Williams arrived home in style by taxi just as dinner was ready to be served, and just as her daughter had announced for the third time that she was going to call the police right *now*, and just as her son-in-law had said for the twentieth time to give Granny a chance, she had been taking care of herself for eighty-seven years and could hardly get into trouble now.

"Well," said Granny as her son-in-law and both grandchildren ran forward to take her packages, "what a day *I've* had." She smiled happily at everyone and added, "No surprises, now, till we all sit down."

"Are you all *right*?" said her daughter. "I was so worried."

Granny stared. "Of course I'm all right," she said. "Did you think I was arrested or something?"

When everyone was sitting in comparative quiet at the dinner table with dessert dishes (both grandchildren, in their excitement, had almost refused chocolate pudding) cleared away, and coffee cups set out, Granny leaned back in her chair and said with relish, "Now." She waved at her grandchildren and added, "You get my packages, but be *careful*."

Hastily the grandchildren gathered the packages, not at all carefully, and brought them to Granny's lap. "Now," she said, drawing out the suspense as long as possible. "Are we all ready?" The grandchildren signified hysterically that they were all ready. Cautiously Granny lifted one package, turned it over and over, and set it down on the table. Her grandchildren, nearly expiring with curiosity, cried at once, "For me? Granny, for me?" Granny shook her head. "You just wait," she said. Finally she selected another package, poked it experimentally, and then formally handed it to her daughter. "For you," she said.

No one breathed while her daughter opened the package, with all due care for folding the wrappings, winding pieces of string, drawing out the operation. Finally, incredibly, a box appeared.

"Candy," said her daughter. "Granny, how *nice* of you!" She showed the box around appreciatively.

"Open it, open it," shouted the grandchildren.

"After Granny is through, we will all have a piece."

Next, the son-in-law opened his present. "A tie," he said with great enthusiasm. "Look, everyone, a beautiful blue and red and orange and green tie!"

The younger grandchild, the little girl who was supposed to look like Granny as a child, received a set of dishes and set immediately to serving everyone a second portion of chocolate pudding upon them. The older grandchild received a cowboy gun.

"Gee, Granny," he said. *"Gee."*

"You see," Granny explained, regarding her family lovingly, "I went and *lost* my *list.*"

"Too bad," said her daughter, opening the candy box.

"A shame," said her son-in-law, regarding his tie dubiously.

"And," Granny went on, "I had to try to remember what you all wanted."

"This is what *I* wanted," said her older grandchild immediately. "Hands up," he added to his father.

"And," Granny said to her daughter and son-in-law, "I met the most surprising young man. Right about lunchtime, when I was just going into a restaurant for a cup of tea, he rushed right past me, and nearly knocked me down. It was very rude of him, but he was in a *great* hurry." Granny stopped and laughed at the expressions on the faces of her daughter and her son-in-law. "He stopped and apologized to me," she went on, "and would you believe it? He said he was going to be married. He said," she continued, sighing romantically, "that after three years of courting his lady had finally consented."

"Amazing," said her son-in-law.

"Charming," said his wife.

"It was positively *sentimental,"* said Granny happily.

THE VERY STRANGE
HOUSE NEXT DOOR

𝕯

*published originally as
"Strangers in Town," in*
The Saturday Evening Post, *May 1959*

I DON'T GOSSIP. IF there is anything in this world I loathe, it is gossip. A week or so ago in the store, Dora Powers started to tell me that nasty rumor about the Harris boy again, and I came right out and said to her if she repeated one more word of that story to me I wouldn't speak to her for the rest of my life, and I haven't. It's been a week, and not one word have I said to Dora Powers, and that's what I think of gossip. Tom Harris has always been too easy on that boy anyway; the young fellow needs a good whipping, and he'd stop all this ranting around, and I've said so to Tom Harris a hundred times or more.

If I didn't get so mad when I think about that house next door, I'd almost have to laugh, seeing people in town standing in the store and on corners and dropping their voices to talk about fairies and leprechauns, when every living one of them knows there isn't any such thing and never has been, and them just racking their brains to find new tales to tell. I don't hold with gossip, as I say, even if it's about leprechauns and fairies, and it's my held opinion that Jane Dollar is getting feeble in the mind. The Dollars weren't ever noted for keeping their senses right up to the end, anyway, and Jane's no older than her mother was when she sent a cake to the bake sale and forgot to put the eggs in it. Some said she did it on purpose to get even with the ladies for not asking her to take a booth, but most just said the old lady had lost track of things, and I dare say she could have looked out and seen fairies in her garden if it ever came into her mind. When the Dollars get that age, they'll tell anything, and that's right where Jane Dollar is now, give or take six months.

My name is Addie Spinner, and I live down on Main Street, the last house but one. There's just one house after mine, and then Main Street kind of runs off into the woods—Spinner's Thicket, they call the woods, on account of my grandfather building the first house in the village. Before the crazy people moved in, the house past mine belonged to the Bartons, but they moved away because he got a job in the city, and high time, too, after them living off her sister and her husband for upward of a year.

Well, after the Bartons finally moved out—owing everyone in town, if you want my guess—it wasn't long before the crazy people moved in, and I knew they were crazy right off when I saw that furniture. I already knew they were young folks, and probably not married long, because I saw them when they came to look at the house. Then when I saw the furniture go in I knew there was going to be trouble between me and her.

The moving van got to the house about eight in the morning. Of course, I always have my dishes done and my house swept up long before that, so I took my mending for the poor out on the side porch and really got caught up on a lot I'd been letting slide. It was a hot day, so I just fixed myself a salad for my lunch, and the side porch is a nice cool place to sit and eat on a hot day, so I never missed a thing going into that house.

First, there were the chairs, all modern, with no proper legs and seats, and I always say that a woman who buys herself that flyaway kind of furniture has no proper feeling for her house—for one thing, it's too easy to clean around those little thin legs; you can't get a floor well-swept without a lot of hard work. Then, she had a lot of low tables, and you can't fool me with them—when you see those little low tables, you can always tell there's going to be a lot of drinking liquor going on in that house; those little tables are made for people who give cocktail parties and need a lot of places to put glasses down. Hattie Martin, she has one of those low tables, and the way Martin drinks is a crime. Then, when I saw the barrels going in next door, I was sure. No one just married has that many dishes without a lot of cocktail glasses, and you can't tell me any different.

When I went down to the store later, after they were all moved in, I met Jane Dollar, and I told her about the drinking that was going to go on next door, and she said she wasn't a bit surprised, because the people had a maid. Not someone to come one day a week and do the heavy cleaning—a maid. Lived in the house and everything. I said I hadn't noticed any maid, and Jane said most things if I hadn't noticed them she wouldn't believe they existed in this world, but the Wests' maid was sure enough; she'd been in the store not ten minutes earlier buying a chicken. We didn't think she'd rightly have time enough to cook a chicken before suppertime, but then we decided that probably the chicken was for tomorrow, and tonight the Wests were planning on going over to the inn for dinner and the maid could fix herself an egg or something. Jane did say that one trouble with having a maid—Jane never had a maid in her life, and I wouldn't speak to her if she did—was that you never had anything left over. No matter what you planned, you had to get new meat every day.

I looked around for the maid on my way home. The quickest way to get to my house from the store is to take the path that cuts across the back garden of the house next door, and even though I don't use it generally—you don't meet neighbors to pass the time of day with, going along a back path—I thought I'd better be hurrying a little to fix my own supper, so I cut across the Wests' back garden. West, that was their name, and what the maid was called I don't know, because Jane hadn't been able to find out. It was a good thing I did take the path, because there was the maid, right out there in the garden, down on her hands and knees, digging.

"Good evening," I said just as polite as I could. "It's kind of damp to be down on the ground."

"I don't mind," she said. "I like things that grow."

I must say she was a pleasant-speaking woman, although too old, I'd think, for domestic work. The poor thing must have been in sad straits to hire out, and yet here she was just as jolly and round as an apple. I thought maybe she was an old aunt or something, and they took this way of keeping her, so I said, still very polite, "I see you just moved in today?"

"Yes," she said, not really telling me much.

"The family's name is West?"

"Yes."

"You might be Mrs. West's mother?"

"No."

"An aunt, possibly?"

"No."

"Not related at all?"

"No."

"You're just the maid?" I thought afterward that she might not like it mentioned, but once it was out I couldn't take it back.

"Yes." She answered pleasant enough, I will say that for her.

"The work is hard, I expect?"

"No."

"Just the two of them to care for?"

"Yes."

"I'd say you wouldn't like it much."

"It's not bad," she said. "I use magic a lot, of course."

"Magic?" I said. "Does that get your work done sooner?"

"Indeed it does," she said with not so much as a smile or a wink. "You wouldn't think, would you, that right now I'm down on my hands and knees making dinner for my family?"

"No," I said. "I wouldn't think that."

"See?" she said. "Here's our dinner." And she showed me an acorn, I swear she did, with a mushroom and a scrap of grass in it.

"It hardly looks like enough to go around," I said, kind of backing away.

She laughed at me, kneeling there on the ground with her acorn, and said, "If there's any left over, I'll bring you a dish; you'll find it wonderfully filling."

"But what about your chicken?" I said; I was well along the path away from her, and I did want to know why she got the chicken if she didn't think they were going to eat it.

"Oh, that," she said. "That's for my cat."

Well, who buys a whole chicken for a cat, that shouldn't have chicken bones anyway? Like I told Jane over the phone as soon as I got home, Mr. Honeywell down at the store ought to refuse to sell it to her, or at least make her take something more fitting, like ground meat, even though neither of us believed for a minute that the cat was really going to get the chicken, or that she even had a cat, come to think of it; crazy people will say anything that comes into their heads.

I know for a fact that no one next door ate chicken that night, though; my kitchen window overlooks their dining room if I stand on a chair, and what they ate for dinner was something steaming in a big brown bowl. I had to laugh, thinking about that acorn, because that was just what the bowl looked like—a big acorn. Probably that was what put the notion in her head. And, sure enough, later she brought over a dish of it and left it on my back steps, me not wanting to open the door late at night with a crazy lady outside, and like I told Jane, I certainly wasn't going to eat any outlandish concoction made by a crazy lady. But I kind of stirred it around with the end of a spoon, and it smelled all right. It had mushrooms in it and beans, but I couldn't tell what else, and Jane and I decided that probably we were right the first time and the chicken was for tomorrow.

I had to promise Jane I'd try to get a look inside to see how they set out that fancy furniture, so next morning I brought back their bowl and marched right up to the front door—mostly around town we go in and out back doors but being as they were new and especially since I wasn't sure how you went about calling when people had a maid, I used the front—and gave a knock. I had gotten up early to make a batch of doughnuts, so I'd have something to put in the bowl when I took it back, so I knew that the people next door were up and about because I saw him leaving for work at seven-thirty. He must have worked in the city, to have to get off so early. Jane thinks he's in an office, because she saw him going toward the depot, and he wasn't running; people who work in offices don't have to get in on the dot, Jane said, although how she would know I couldn't tell you.

It was little Mrs. West who opened the door, and I must say she looked agreeable enough. I thought with the maid to bring her breakfast and all, she might still be lying in bed, the way they do, but she was all dressed in a pink housedress and was wide awake. She didn't ask me in right away, so I kind of moved a little toward the door, and then she stepped back and said wouldn't I come in, and I must say, funny as that furniture is, she had it fixed up nice, with green curtains on the windows. I couldn't tell from my house what the pattern was on those curtains, but once I was inside I could see it was a pattern of green leaves kind of woven in, and the rug, which of course I had seen when they brought it in, was green, too. Some of those big boxes that went in must have held books, because there were a lot of books all put away in bookcases, and before I had a chance to think I said, "My, you must have worked all night to get everything arranged so quick. I didn't see your lights on, though."

"Mallie did it," she said.

"Mallie being the maid?"

She kind of smiled, and then she said, "She's more like a god-mother than a maid, really."

I do hate to seem curious, so I just said, "Mallie must keep herself pretty busy. Yesterday she was out digging your garden."

"Yes." It was hard to glean anything out of these people, with their short answers.

"I brought you some doughnuts," I said.

"Thank you." She put the bowl down on one of those little tables—Jane thinks they must hide the wine, because there wasn't a sight of any such thing that I could see—and then she said, "We'll offer them to the cat."

Well, I can tell you I didn't much care for that. "You must have quite a hungry cat," I said to her.

"Yes," she said. "I don't know what we'd do without him. He's Mallie's cat, of course."

"I haven't seen him," I said. If we were going to talk about cats, I figured I could hold my own, having had one cat or another for a matter of sixty years, although it hardly seemed a sensible subject for two ladies to chat over. Like I told Jane, there was a lot she ought to be wanting to know about the village and the people in it and who to go to for hardware and whatnot—I know for a fact I've put a dozen people off Tom Harris' hardware store since he charged me seventeen cents for a pound of nails—and I was just the person to set her straight on the town. But she was going on about the cat. "—fond of children," she was saying.

"I expect he's company for Mallie," I said.

"Well, he helps her, you know," she said, and then I began to think maybe she was crazy, too.

"And how does the cat help Mallie?"

"With her magic."

"I see," I said, and I started to say goodbye fast, figuring to get home to the telephone, because people around the village certainly ought to be hearing about what was going on. But before I could get to the door, the maid came out of the kitchen and said good morning to me, real polite, and then the maid said to Mrs. West that she was putting together the curtains for the front bedroom, and would Mrs. West like to decide on the pattern? And while I just stood there with my jaw hanging, she held out a handful of cobwebs—and I never did see anyone before or since who was able to hold a cobweb pulled out neat, or anyone who would want to, for that matter—and she had a blue jay's feather and a curl of blue ribbon, and she asked me how I liked her curtains.

Well, that did for me, and I got out of there and ran all the way to

Jane's house, and, of course, she never believed me. She walked me home just so she could get a look at the outside of the house, and I will be everlastingly shaken if they hadn't gone and put up curtains in that front bedroom, soft white net with a design of blue that Jane said looked like a blue jay's feather. Jane said they were the prettiest curtains she ever saw, but they gave me the shivers every time I looked at them.

It wasn't two days after that I began finding things. Little things, and even some inside my own house. Once there was a basket of grapes on my back steps, and I swear those grapes were never grown around our village. For one thing, they shone like they were covered with silver dust, and smelled like some foreign perfume. I threw them in the garbage, but I kept a little embroidered handkerchief I found on the table in my front hall, and I've got it still in my dresser drawer.

Once I found a colored thimble on the fence post, and once my cat, Samantha, that I've had for eleven years and more, came in wearing a little green collar and spat at me when I took it off. One day I found a leaf basket on my kitchen table filled with hazelnuts, and it made me downright shaking mad to think of someone's coming in and out of my house without so much as asking, and me never seeing them come or go.

Things like that never happened before the crazy people moved into the house next door, and I was telling Mrs. Acton so, down on the corner one morning, when young Mrs. O'Neil came by and told us that when she was in the store with her baby she met Mallie the maid. The baby was crying because he was having a time with his teething, and Mallie gave him a little green candy to bite on. We thought Mrs. O'Neil was crazy herself to let her baby have candy that came from that family, and said so, and I told them about the drinking that went on, and the furniture getting arranged in the dark, and the digging in the garden, and Mrs. Acton said she certainly hoped they weren't going to think that just because they had a garden they had any claim to be in the Garden Club.

Mrs. Acton is president of the Garden Club. Jane says I ought to be president, if things were done right, on account of having the oldest garden in town, but Mrs. Acton's husband is the doctor, and I don't know what people thought he might do to them when they were sick if Mrs. Acton didn't get to be president. Anyway, you'd think Mrs. Acton had some say about who got into the Garden Club and who didn't, but I had to admit that in this case we'd all vote with her, even though Mrs. O'Neil did tell us the next day that she didn't think the people could be all crazy, because the baby's tooth came through that night with no more trouble.

Do you know, all this time that maid came into the store every day, and every day she bought one chicken. Nothing else. Jane took to dropping in the store when she saw the maid going along, and she says the maid never bought but one chicken a day. Once Jane got her nerve up and said to the maid that they must be fond of chicken, and the maid looked straight at her and told her right to her face that they were vegetarians.

"All but the cat, I suppose," Jane said, being pretty nervy when she gets her nerve up.

"Yes," the maid said, "all but the cat."

We finally decided that he must bring food home from the city, although why Mr. Honeywell's store wasn't good enough for them, I couldn't tell you. After the baby's tooth was better, Tom O'Neil took them over a batch of fresh-picked sweet corn, and they must have liked that, because they sent the baby a furry blue blanket that was so soft that young Mrs. O'Neil said the baby never needed another, winter or summer, and after being so sickly, that baby began to grow and got so healthy, you wouldn't know it was the same one, even though the O'Neils never should have accepted presents from strangers, not knowing whether the wool might be clean or not.

Then I found out they were dancing next door. Night after night after night, dancing. Sometimes I'd lie there awake until ten, eleven o'clock, listening to that heathen music and wishing I could get up the nerve to go over and give them a piece of my mind. It wasn't so much the noise keeping me from sleeping—I will say the music was soft and kind of like a lullaby—but people haven't got any right to live like that. Folks should go to bed at a sensible hour and get up at a sensible hour and spend their days doing good deeds and house-work. A wife ought to cook dinner for her husband—and not out of cans from the city, either—and she ought to run over next door sometimes with a home-baked cake to pass the time of day and keep up with the news. And most of all a wife ought to go to the store herself, where she can meet her neighbors, and not just send the maid.

·   ·   ·

Every morning I'd go out and find fairy rings on the grass, and anyone around here will tell you that means an early winter, and here next door they hadn't even thought to get in coal. I watched every day for Adams and his truck, because I knew for a fact that cellar was empty of coal; all I had to do was lean down a little when I was in my garden and I could see right into the cellar, just as swept and clear as though they planned to treat their guests in there. Jane thought they were the kind who went off on a trip somewhere in the winter, shirking responsibilities for facing the snow with their neighbors. The cellar was all you could see, though. They had those green curtains pulled so tight against the windows that even right up close there wasn't a chink to look through from outside, and them inside dancing away. I do wish I could have nerved myself to go right up to that front door and knock some night.

Now, Mary Corn thought I ought to. "You got a right, Addie," she told me one day in the store. "You got every right in the world to make them quiet down at night. You're the nearest neighbor they got, and it's the right thing to do. Tell them they're making a name for themselves around the village."

Well, I couldn't nerve myself, and that's the gracious truth. Every now and then I'd see little Mrs. West walking in the garden, or Mallie the maid coming out of the woods with a basket—gathering acorns, never a doubt of it—but I never so much as nodded my head at them. Down at the store I had to tell Mary Corn that I couldn't do it. "They're foreigners, that's why," I said. "Foreigners of some kind. They don't rightly seem to understand what a person says—it's like they're always answering some other question you didn't ask."

"If they're foreigners," Dora Powers put in, being at the store to pick up some sugar to frost a cake, "it stands to reason there's something wrong to bring them here."

"Well, I won't call on foreigners," Mary said.

"You can't treat them the same as you'd treat regular people," I said. "I went inside the house, remember, although not, as you might say, to pay a call."

So then I had to tell them all over again about the furniture and the drinking—and it stands to reason that anyone who dances all night is going to be drinking, too—and my good doughnuts from my grandmother's recipe going to the cat. And Dora, she thought they were up to no good in the village. Mary said she didn't know anyone who was going to call, not being sure they were proper, and then we had to stop talking because in came Mallie the maid for her chicken.

· · ·

You would have thought I was the chairman of a committee or something, the way Dora and Mary kept nudging me and winking that I should go over and speak to her, but I wasn't going to make a fool of myself twice, I can tell you. Finally Dora saw there was no use pushing me, so she marched over and stood there until the maid turned around and said, "Good morning."

Dora came right out and said, "There's a lot of people around this village, miss, would like to know a few things."

"I imagine so," the maid said.

"We'd like to know what you're doing in our village," Dora said.

"We thought it would be a nice place to live," the maid said. You could see that Dora was caught up short on that, because who picks a place to live because it's nice? People live in our village because they were born here; they don't just come.

I guess Dora knew we were all waiting for her, because she took a big breath and asked, "And how long do you plan on staying?"

"Oh," the maid said. "I don't think we'll stay very long, after all."

"Even if they don't stay," Mary said later, "they can do a lot of harm while they're here, setting a bad example for our young folk. Just for instance, I heard that the Harris boy got picked up again by the state police for driving without a license."

"Tom Harris is too gentle on that boy," I said. "A boy like that needs whipping and not people living in a house right in town showing him how to drink and dance all night."

Jane came in right then, and she had heard that all the children in town had taken to dropping by the house next door to bring dandelions and berries from the woods—and from their own fathers' gardens, too, I'll be bound—and the children were telling around that the cat next door could talk. They said he told them stories.

Well, that just about did for me, you can imagine. Children have too much freedom nowadays, anyway, without getting nonsense like that into their heads. We asked Annie Lee when she came into the store, and she thought somebody ought to call the police, so it could all be stopped before somebody got hurt. She said, suppose one of those kids got a step too far inside that house—how did we know he'd ever get out again? Well, it wasn't too pleasant a thought, I can tell you, but trust Annie Lee to be always looking on the black side. I don't have much dealing with the children as a rule, once they learn they better keep away from my apple trees and my melons, and I can't say I know one from the next, except for the Martin boy I had to call the police on once for stealing a piece of tin from my front yard, but I can't say I relished the notion that that cat had his eyes on them. It's not natural, somehow.

And don't you know it was the very next day that they stole the littlest Acton boy? Not quite three years old, and Mrs. Acton so busy with her Garden Club she let him run along into the woods with his sister, and first thing anyone knew they got him. Jane phoned and told me. She heard from Dora, who had been right in the store when the Acton girl came running in to find her mother and tell her the baby had wandered away in the woods, and Mallie the maid had been digging around not ten feet from where they saw him last. Jane said Mrs. Acton and Dora and Mary Corn and half a dozen others were heading right over to the house next door, and I better get outside fast before I missed something, and if she got there late to let her know everything that happened. I barely got out my own front door, when down the street they came, maybe ten or twelve mothers, marching along so mad they never had time to be scared.

"Come on, Addie," Dora said to me. "They've finally done it this time."

I knew Jane would never forgive me if I hung back, so out I went and up the front walk to the house next door. Mrs. Acton was ready to go right up and knock, because she was so mad, but before she had a chance the door opened and there was Mrs. West and the little boy, smiling all over as if nothing had happened.

"Mallie found him in the woods," Mrs. West said, and Mrs. Acton grabbed the boy away from her; you could tell they had been frightening him by the way he started to cry as soon as he got to his own mother. All he would say was "kitty," and that put a chill down our backs, you can imagine.

Mrs. Acton was so mad she could hardly talk, but she did manage to say, "You keep away from my children, you hear me?" And Mrs. West looked surprised.

"Mallie found him in the woods," she said. "We were going to bring him home."

"We can guess how you were going to bring him home," Dora shouted, and then Annie Lee piped up from well in the back, "Why don't you get out of our town?"

"I guess we will," Mrs. West said. "It's not the way we thought it was going to be."

That was nice, wasn't it? Nothing riles me like people knocking this town, where my grandfather built the first house, and I just spoke up right then and there.

"Foreign ways!" I said. "You're heathen, wicked people, with your dancing and your maid, and the sooner you leave this town, the better it's going to be for you. Because I might as well tell you"—and I shook my finger right at her—"that certain people in this town aren't going to put up with your fancy ways much longer, and you would be well advised—very well advised, I say—to pack up your furniture and your curtains and your maid and cat, and get out of our town before we put you out."

Jane claims she doesn't think I really said it, but all the others were there and can testify I did—all but Mrs. Acton, who never had a good word to say for anybody.

Anyway, right then we found out they had given the little boy something, trying to buy his affection, because Mrs. Acton pried it out of his hand, and he was crying all the time. When she held it out, it was hard to believe, but of course with them there's nothing too low. It was a little gold-colored apple, all shiny and bright, and Mrs. Acton threw it right at the porch floor, as hard as she could, and that little toy shattered into dust. "We don't want anything from you," Mrs. Acton said, and as I told Jane afterward, it was terrible to see the look on Mrs. West's face. For a minute she just stood there looking at us. Then she turned and went back inside and shut the door.

Someone wanted to throw rocks through the windows, but, as I told them, destroying private property is a crime and we might better leave violence to the menfolk, so Mrs. Acton took her little boy home, and I went in and called Jane. Poor Jane; the whole thing had gone off so fast, she hadn't had time to get her corset on.

I hadn't any more than gotten Jane on the phone, when I saw through the hall window that a moving van was right there next door, and the men were starting to carry out that fancy furniture. Jane wasn't surprised when I told her over the phone. "Nobody can get moving that fast," she said. "They were probably planning to slip out with that little boy."

"Or maybe the maid did it with magic," I said, and Jane laughed.

"Listen," she said, "go and see what else is going on—I'll hang on the phone."

There wasn't anything to see, even from my front porch, except the moving van and the furniture coming out; not a sign of Mrs. West or the maid.

"He hasn't come home from the city yet," Jane said. "I can see the street from here. They'll have news for him tonight."

That was how they left. I take a lot of the credit for myself, even though Jane tries to make me mad by saying Mrs. Acton did her share. By that night they were gone, bag and baggage, and Jane and I went over the house with a flashlight to see what damage they had left behind. There wasn't a thing left in that house—not a chicken bone, not an acorn—except for one blue jay's wing upstairs, and that wasn't worth taking home. Jane put it in the incinerator when we came downstairs.

One more thing. My cat, Samantha, had kittens. That may not surprise you, but it sure as judgment surprised me and Samantha, her being over eleven years old and well past her kitten days, the old fool. But you would have laughed to see her dancing around like a young lady cat, just as light-footed and as pleased as if she thought she was doing something no cat ever did before; and those kittens troubled me.

Folks don't dare come right out and say anything to me about my kittens, of course, but they do keep on with that silly talk about fairies and leprechauns. And there's no denying that the kittens are bright yellow, with orange eyes, and much bigger than normal kittens have a right to be. Sometimes I see them all watching me when I go around the kitchen, and it gives me a cold finger down my back. Half the children in town are begging for those kittens—"fairy kittens," they're calling them—but there isn't a grown-up in town would take one.

Jane says there's something downright uncanny about those kittens, but then, I may never speak to her again in all my life. Jane would even gossip about cats, and gossip is one thing I simply cannot endure.

A Great

Voice Stilled

𝒟

Playboy, *March 1960*

THE HOSPITAL WAITING ROOM was an island of inefficiency in the long echoing and white-painted and silenced stretches of the hospital. In the waiting room there were ashtrays and crackling wicker furniture and uneven brown wooden benches and clearly unswept corners; the business of the hospital did not go on with the intruders waiting restlessly, and with every bed in every wing of the hospital filled, it was perfectly all right with the hospital administration to see the wicker chairs and wooden benches in the waiting room empty and wasting space. Katherine Ashton, who had not wanted to come anywhere near the hospital, who had wanted to stay at home in the apartment on this dark Sunday afternoon, who had wanted to cry a little in private and then dine later in some small unobtrusive restaurant—perhaps the one where they did sweetbreads so nicely—and linger over a melancholy brandy; Katherine Ashton came into the waiting room behind her husband, saying, "I wish we hadn't come. I tell you I hate hospitals and death scenes and anyway how does anyone know he's going to die today?"

"You'd always be sorry if you hadn't come," Martin said. When he saw that the waiting room was empty, he turned back and looked hopefully up and down the hospital hall. "You think we could go upstairs right now?"

"They won't *possibly* let us upstairs. Not *possibly*."

"We got here first," Martin said reasonably. "As soon as they let anyone go upstairs, it ought to be us, because we certainly got here ahead of the rest."

"I'm going to feel like a fool," Katherine said. "Suppose he doesn't die? Suppose no one else comes?"

"Look." Martin stopped walking back and forth from the window to the door and came to stand in front of her, as though he were lecturing to one of his classes. "He's *got* to die. Here Angell is flying down from Boston. And practically the whole staff of *Dormant Review* up all night working on obituaries and remembrances, and his American publisher already getting together a *Festschrift,* and the wife flying in from Majorca if they weren't able to stop her. And Weasel calling every major literary critic from here to California to get them here in time. You think the man would have the *gall* to live after that?"

"But when I tried to call the doctor—"

"In my business," Martin said, "you've got to be in the right places at the right times. Like a salesman or something. Just by being here I get a chance to meet Angell, for instance—how long could I go, otherwise, trying to get to meet Angell? And if I swing it right *Dormant* could even—"

"Here's Joan," Katherine said. "She's still crying."

Martin moved swiftly to the doorway. "Joan, dear," he said. "How *is* he?"

"Not . . . very well," Joan said. "Hello, Katherine."

"Hello, Joan," Katherine said.

"I finally got hold of the doctor," Joan said. "I called and called and finally *made* him talk to me. It sounds pretty . . . black." She put her hand across her mouth as though she wanted to stop her lips from trembling.

"A matter of hours," she said.

"My God," Martin said.

"How awful," Katherine said.

"Angell's flying down from Boston, did you hear?" Joan sat tentatively on the edge of a bench. "Anybody upstairs with him?"

"They won't let anyone go up," Katherine said.

"Maybe they're giving him a bath, or something. Or do they bother, if it's only a matter of . . ."

"I don't know," Katherine said, and Joan sobbed.

"But it's pretty certain to be today?" Martin asked with a kind of reluctant delicacy.

"You know how doctors talk." Joan sobbed again. "They had to take me home this morning and give me a sedative, I was crying so. I haven't had any sleep or anything to eat since yesterday, I was right here all the time until they took me home this morning and gave me a sedative."

"Very touching," said Martin. "Katherine and I thought it would look better if there weren't so many people around, so we haven't come until today."

"John Weasel said he'd bring in some sandwiches and stuff later. I plan to stay right here, now, until the end."

"So do we," Martin said firmly.

"The Andersons are coming over, and probably those people he was visiting last weekend, they're probably coming down from Connecticut. And—we all thought it was so sweet—the bar, you know, the one where he had the attack, well, they're sending over flowers. We all thought it was so sweet."

"It was nice of them," Katherine said.

"I only hope Angell gets here in time. Weasel's got the Smiths and their car at the airport and he even called the police station to ask for a police escort, but of course you can't ever make *them* understand. I'm still crying so I can't stop. I haven't stopped since yesterday."

"Someone's coming," Martin said, and Joan sobbed. "Weasel," Martin said. "Weasel, dear old fellow. Any news?"

"I called the doctor. Katherine, hello. Joan, my dear, you shouldn't be here, you really *shouldn't,* you promised me you'd try and get some rest. Now I *am* cross with you."

"I'm sorry." Joan looked up tearfully. "I couldn't bear it, not being near him."

"What a *day* I've had." Weasel sighed and sat down on a bench and let his hands fall wearily. "The *police,* honestly! I told them and *told* them the light of the literary world was going *out* right here, and so could we *please* just get some kind of an escort to bring the country's foremost literary critic over from the airport to hear his last words and close his eyes and whatnot, but I swear, darling, it's exactly like talking to a pack of *prairie* dogs. Calling me 'sir' and asking me who *I* was, and"—he sat up and slapped his forehead violently— "the *wife,* great Bacchus, don't *ask* me about the wife! Cables to Majorca all day yesterday and phone calls to Washington and clearance on the plane and all those cousins of hers pulling strings just simply *every*where and she's arriving with absolutely *no* baggage!"

"You mean his wife *is* coming?" Joan stared, openmouthed.

"Darling, she'll be here practically any *minute;* I kept *pleading* with the woman, I swear I did, positively *entreating* her—no place to put her up, no one free to take care of her, we're *perfectly* capable of making all arrangements this end, and she literally would not listen to a word I said, I swear that that woman would not listen to a blessed word I said. I *knew* you'd be *furious,*" he said to Joan.

Joan wailed. "Naturally we'd send her the *body.*"

Martin was pacing back and forth again, from the door to the window. "When will they let us go upstairs?" he demanded irritably.

Joan looked at him, surprised. "You think *you're* going upstairs?"

"We were here first," Martin said.

"But you didn't even *know* him."

"Katherine knew him exactly as well as you did," Martin said flatly. "Besides, he had dinner with us Tuesday night."

"Katherine certainly did *not* know him as well as I did," Joan said.

"He did *not* have dinner with you," Weasel said. "Not *Tuesday.* Tuesday he—"

"I certainly did," Katherine said. "If you care for a public comparison—"

Joan opened her mouth to interrupt, then sobbed and turned as more people came into the waiting room. "That's Philips, from *Dormant,*" Martin said in Katherine's ear. "The woman is Martha something-or-other; she writes those nasty reviews. I don't know the other man." He went forward, so that Weasel would have to introduce him, but more people came in, and he was suddenly involved in a group, talking in lowered voices, asking one another how long it would probably take, telling one another the names of people in the room. Through and around the quiet conversations went the soft half-moan that was Joan's crying.

Katherine, unable to leave the bench where she was sitting, turned and said to a strange man sitting next to her, "Someone told me once how you could train yourself to endure physical torture without yielding."

"Could it have been Neilson?" the man asked. "He did a nice piece on torture."

"You pretend it's happening to someone else," Katherine said. "You withdraw your own mind and you just leave your body behind."

"Did you know *him?*" the man asked, gesturing. "Upstairs?"

"Yes," Katherine said. "I knew him very well."

Somebody seemed to have brought a paper milk carton full of

vodka, and somebody else went into the hospital hall and came back with a stack of paper cups. Martin pushed through the crowd to bring Katherine a paper cup with vodka in it, and said, "Angell's here. He did make it. No one knows anything about the wife. The man in the blue suit by the door is Arthur B. Arthur, and the dark-haired girl next to him is that little kid he married."

Near Katherine, Weasel was explaining to someone, "—stopped off in the chapel to pray. He's thinking of being converted, *anyway,* you know."

The man next to Katherine leaned over and asked her, "Who's doing the Memorial Fund?"

"Weasel, probably," she said.

"Don't *ask* me," Weasel said beside her. "Simply don't ask *me.* Any more dealings with that shrew of a wife, and I will positively be ready to die my*self.* I will simply *have* to get back to Bronxville for a long rest after all this; it's been perfectly *frightful* ever since Friday morning; I haven't been home since he had the attack, I came right down from Bronxville and I've had to stay in the Andersons' place over on the West Side and it's been just *awful.*"

From the little group by the door, there was a little rustle of quick, hushed laughter.

"I want Angell to do the Memorial Fund, anyway," Weasel said. "His name always looks so much *better* on a thing like that."

Joan was crying loudly now, struggling in the arms of the tall man in the blue suit. "I want to go to him," she was shouting. Vodka from her paper cup spilled onto the floor of the hospital hall.

"There's a nurse," someone said. "They're not trying to offer her a *drink?*" someone else said. "Be *quiet,* everybody," Weasel said, struggling to get through to the doorway.

"Is he dead?" the man next to Katherine asked her, "Did the nurse say he was dead?"

"About three minutes ago," someone else said. "About three minutes ago. He died."

"We missed *every*thing?" Weasel's voice rose despairingly. "Because this just *finishes* it, that's all. They promised to *call* us," he said wildly to the nurse. "That's just about the lowest *I've* ever seen."

"You wouldn't let me go to him," Joan said to the nurse; her voice was heartbroken. "You wouldn't let me go to him."

"We weren't even *there,*" Weasel said. "This poor child . . ." He put an arm tenderly around Joan.

"Mrs. Jones was with him," the nurse said.

"What?" Weasel fell back dramatically. "They sneaked her in? No one let me know? She got here?"

"Can we go up now, anyway?" Martin asked.

"Mrs. Jones is with him," the nurse said. "Mrs. Jones will no doubt want to thank all of you at another time. Now . . ." she gestured, slightly but unmistakably; she was indicating the hall that led to the outside doors of the hospital.

"Well." Weasel tightened his lips. "How about the service?" he said. "I suppose Mrs. Jones wants to run *that,* too? She's never read a *word* of his work, *naturally.* I was planning to read the passage on death from his *Evil Man,*" he explained to Angell, "you remember: it begins with that marvelous description of the flies? He used to recite it when he was drunk. Mrs. Jones will simply *have* to come down here," he said to the nurse. "How can we make any *arrangements?*"

"Mrs. Jones will no doubt be in touch with you," the nurse said. She stood back a little, and this time her gesture was a shade more emphatic.

There was a minute of silent hesitation, and then Angell said, " 'Within the twilight chamber spreads apace the shadow of white Death, and at the door invisible Corruption waits . . .' "

"A great voice has been stilled," Weasel said reverently.

"My only, truest love," Joan mourned.

"He writes now with a golden pen."

"A great writer is a great man writing."

"It was worth coming down for," Martin said, coming over to take Katherine's arm. "I talked to Angell for a minute, and he said to call him tomorrow." Impatient now, Martin led Katherine through the crowd to the doorway and out into the hall.

"Goodbye," the nurse said.

Slowly, a little ahead of the others, who lingered, laughing a little now, gathering around Joan, listening to Weasel, Katherine and Martin went down the hospital hallway. "He might have a spot for me now in that lecture series," Martin said. He gestured upward. "Now that *he's* gone, I could do a talk on *his* work. His personal tragedy, maybe."

"It was hot in there," Katherine said.

Weasel caught up with them, and said quickly, "We're all going on to Joan's. I don't think she should be alone right now. You two come along?"

"Thanks," Martin said, "but Katherine's pretty broken up, too. I'm going to take her directly home."

Weasel glanced quickly at Katherine and said, "Terribly sad, the whole business, wasn't it? I nearly *died* when I heard he was gone, and absolutely *no* one there who cared! I mean really *cared*."

"We paid him what tribute we could," Martin said.

"The responsibility of the intellectual," Weasel said vaguely. "Come over to Joan's later if you can make it?"

He pattered away, back down the hall to Joan and Martin, and Katherine came down the steps of the hospital into the unexpectedly dark afternoon.

"My only, truest love," Katherine said.

"Hmm?" said Martin. "You ask me something?"

"No," said Katherine, and laughed.

"Anyplace special you want to go for dinner?" Martin asked.

"Yes," Katherine said. "That nice little place where they make sweetbreads, I was thinking about it earlier."

ALL SHE SAID

WAS YES

𝔇

Vogue, *November 1962 (Other titles:* *"Cassandra"; "Not a Tear"; "Vicky")*

WHAT CAN YOU DO? Howard and Dorrie are always telling me I'm too sensitive, and let myself get worked up about things, but really, even Howard had to admit that the Lansons' accident just couldn't have happened at a worse time. It sounds awful when you come right out and say it, but I'd always rather be frank and open than mealy-mouthed, and even though it was a dreadful thing to happen *any*time, it really made me *furious* to have our trip to Maine ruined.

We'd lived next door to Don and Helen Lanson for sixteen years, since before our Dorrie and their Vicky were born, and of course, living next door and with the girls growing up together, we'd always been friendly enough, even though you don't have to get along with people *all* the time, and frankly, some of the crowd the Lansons knew were a little too fancy for us. Besides, they were never secret about things and expected us to be the same, and it bothered me sometimes when I stopped to think that for sixteen years we hadn't had a day's privacy; I like friendly neighbors as well as the next one, but it was a little too much, sometimes. I used to tell Howard that Helen Lanson always knew what we were having for dinner, and of course it worked the other way around, too; whenever the Lansons had one of their fights we had to close the windows and go down to the cellar to keep from hearing, and even then Helen Lanson was sure to be over the next morning to cry on my shoulder. I hope the new neighbors are a little more—well—reticent.

Howard and I felt terrible when it happened, naturally. Howard went out with the State Police, and I offered to go over and tell Vicky. It wasn't the kind of thing I relished, you can imagine, but someone had to do it, and I'd known her since she was born. I was thankful that Dorrie was away at camp, because *she* would have been heartbroken, living next door to them all her life. When I went over to ring the doorbell that night I really couldn't think how the child was going to take it; I never did think much of parents going out and leaving a fifteen-year-old girl alone in the house—you read all the time about men breaking into houses where girls are alone—but I supposed Helen always figured Vicky was all right with us home next door; we certainly don't go out nearly every night like the Lansons did.

But then, Vicky was never much of a one for minding things, anyway; I know that she opened the door that night right away, without even asking who it was or making sure it wasn't some man; I never let Dorrie open the door at night unless she knows who is on the other side. Well, I might as well come right out with it—I don't *like* Vicky. Even that night, with all the trouble ahead for her, I couldn't make myself like her. I was terribly sorry for her, certainly, and at the same time all I could keep thinking was what I was going to do when she heard the news. She was so big and clumsy and ugly that I really couldn't face the thought of having to put my arms around her and comfort her—I hated the idea of patting her hand, or stroking her hair, and yet I was the only person to do it. All the way over from our house I had been wondering how I was going to say it, and then when she opened the door and just stood there looking at me—and never a "hello" or anything from her; she just wasn't the kind who offered things, if you know what I mean—I almost lost my courage. Finally I asked her if I could come in, because I had to talk to her, and she only opened the door wider and stood away, and I came in and she closed the door behind me and stood there waiting. Well, I know that house almost as well as I know my own, and so I walked into the living room and sat down and she came along after me and sat down, too, and looked at me.

Well, there was nothing like getting right to it, so I tried to say something gentle first; what I finally settled on was looking very serious and saying, "Vicky, you're going to have to be brave."

I must say she didn't help me much. She just sat there looking at me, and I suddenly thought that maybe all the unusual excitement, with Howard driving off in the middle of the night like that, and all the lights on in our house and my coming over the way I did, might have let on to her that something was wrong, and she might even have guessed already that it had to do with her parents, so the sooner she heard the truth, the better, I thought, and I said, "There's been an accident, Vicky. Corporal Atkins of the State Police phoned us a few minutes ago, because he knew you were alone here and he wanted someone to be with you." It wasn't much of a way to go about it, I know, but I would much rather have sat there talking all around the subject than tell her what I had to say next. I took a deep breath and said, "It's your mother and father, Vicky. There's been an accident."

Well, so far she hadn't said a word, not a single word since I came through the door, and now all she said was, "Yes."

I thought it must be shock, and I was glad that Howard had thought to call Doctor Hart before he left, to come and help me with Vicky, and I began to wonder how long it would be before the doctor came, because I'm simply no good with sick people, and would be sure to do the wrong thing. I was thinking about the doctor, and I said, "They always drove too fast—" and she said, "I know." I sat there waiting for her to cry, or whatever a girl like that does when she finds out her parents have been killed, and then I remembered that she didn't know yet that they were killed, but only that they had been in an accident, so I took another deep breath and said, "They're both—" I couldn't say it, though, just couldn't bring out the word. Finally I said, "Gone."

"I know," she said. So I needn't have worried.

"We're so sorry, Vicky," I said, wondering if now was the time to go over and pat her head.

"Do you think they really believed they were going to die?" she asked me.

"Well, I guess no one ever really *believes* . . ." I started to say, but she wasn't listening to me; she was looking down at her hands and shaking her head. "I told them, you know," she said. "I told my mother a couple of months ago that it was going to happen, the accident and their dying, but she wouldn't listen to me, no one ever does. She said it was an adolescent fantasy."

Well, that was Helen Lanson for you, of course. *Adolescent fantasy* is the way she talked, and pretended she was being honest with the child. It wasn't any of my business, of course, but I can tell you that Dorrie got spanked when she did something wrong, and none of this psychological jargon to make her think it was my fault, either. "I guess everybody told them," I said to Vicky. "You can't drive the way they did without asking for trouble. I spoke to Helen about it once myself—"

"That's when I got over being sad," she said, as though she thought she ought to excuse herself. "I told her, and she wouldn't believe me. I even told her I'd have to go and live with Aunt Cynthia in London, England." She smiled at me. "I'm going to like London, England; I'll go to a big school there and study hard."

Well, as far as I knew, Aunt Cynthia in London, England, hadn't even been notified yet, but if this child could sit there coolly not five minutes after hearing that her parents had been killed in an accident and make plans for her future—well, all I could say is that maybe some of Helen Lanson's psychology paid off, in a way she might not like so much, and I just hope that if ever anything happens to me, *my* daughter will have the grace to sit there and shed a tear. Although it's probably kinder to believe that Vicky was in shock.

"It's a terrible thing," I said, wondering how long before the doctor could make it.

"Aunt Cynthia will get here on Tuesday," she said to me. "The first plane will have to turn back because of engine trouble. I'm sorry about your trip to Maine."

I was touched. Here was this girl, after the most terrible disaster that can happen to a child, and she could spare a thought for our trip to Maine. It was certainly just the worst luck in the world for us, but you can't always expect a child to see things from a grown-up's point of view, and even if the news about her parents didn't bring a tear, I was pleased to see that the girl could still feel for somebody. "Try not to worry about it," I told her. Of course we just couldn't take off for Maine the morning after our next-door neighbors had been killed in an accident, but there was no point in Vicky's bothering about that, too. "Please don't be upset," I said.

"You won't be able to go later in the year because it will be too cold at the lodge. You'll have to go somewhere else, but please don't go on a boat. Please?"

"Of course not," I said; I didn't want the doctor to come in and find us talking about my worries, so I said, "You'll come over and stay with us until your aunt comes."

"In Dorrie's room," she said.

Well, I hadn't really planned anything yet, but of course Dorrie's room was the best place for her; you never know when you're going to need the guest room for company, and Dorrie would be away at camp for the next two weeks. "We'll pretend that you're my little girl for a while," I said, and wondered if it was the right thing to say—it certainly sounded silly enough—and then thought that after all, I had had as much of a shock as she had, and then I heard the doctor's car outside and I confess it was a relief. I still don't think it was natural for a child to sit there and listen to news like that and not even jump.

I left her with the doctor and went upstairs—as I say, I know that house as well as I know my own—and tried to find some things for her to bring over with her; I could come over in the morning and get anything she wanted, of course, so I just took a pair of clean pajamas out of the drawer and one of her good school dresses out of the closet; she was going to have to see a good many people in the next day or so and there was no harm in her looking as neat and clean as I could make her. I got her toothbrush out of the bathroom—and I'm no stickler for housework, but I'd be ashamed to keep a bathroom the way Helen Lanson did—and then I thought that maybe she had some kind of a toy dog or doll or something to comfort her; Dorrie may be fifteen years old, but she still has a little blue lion I gave her when she was small, and you can always tell when Dorrie's upset about something because she takes her blue lion to bed with her. But in this girl's room there was nothing. You would have been shocked. Books, of course, and a picture of her mother and father, and a set of paints and a game or so, but nothing . . . well, soft. I finally lifted her pillow and underneath it was a little notebook with a red cover, like a school notebook or something, and since it was under her pillow I thought it must be something she valued—I've seen Dorrie's diary under her pillow, like that, and even though of course I've never looked inside it I know how excited she gets if she thinks someone's gotten to it. I thought maybe Vicky might want to keep this little book safe, so I folded it in with the nightgown and a pair of clean socks, and after thinking for a minute (after all, wouldn't I want someone to do the same for Dorrie?) I took the picture of her mother and father and put that in, too. When I went downstairs she was still sitting there and the doctor was sitting with her, and when I came in he looked at me and shrugged, so I suppose he hadn't gotten any more tears from her than I had. I went out into the hall with the doctor and he said he had given her a sedative and I said I was taking her right next door and would put her to sleep in Dorrie's bed. "She doesn't seem to care one way or another," I told him.

"Sometimes it takes a while," he said. "It's a terrible thing; too much, probably, for her mind to take in all at once. I expect that by tomorrow she'll be feeling it more, and I'll stop in and see her in the morning."

Well, I saw that all the lights were turned out and the doors locked and then I took Vicky's things and we went next door and it was a relief to me to be back in my own house, even though I admit I felt a good twinge when I saw our suitcases all packed and standing in the hall. We had planned to get a good early start in the morning, and now here I had to unpack everything again. I asked Vicky if she would like a cup of cocoa and she said yes—I never did see that girl when she wouldn't eat—so I left her in the kitchen with her cocoa and a piece of my good chocolate cake and I went upstairs and fixed up Dorrie's room for her. I took out a lot of Dorrie's things because somehow—and I don't want to sound nasty, but it's true—you couldn't think of that great dull girl sleeping with Dorrie's pretty little pictures and dolls and necklaces and dance souvenirs all around her; she fit in Dorrie's room like Dorrie would fit in a dollhouse. I made the bed all neat, and I put on Dorrie's blue comforter, because it would have to be cleaned anyway before Dorrie came home, and then I brought her upstairs and waited while she got undressed. When I went in to tuck her in I had made up my mind of course that I wasn't going to be hesitant or anything, and I was going to kiss her good night, because after all the girl was alone in the world now, except for the kindness of neighbors who took her in. When I came in she was in bed and I think the doctor's sedative—or my hot cocoa—was affecting her, because she looked sleepy and kind of full, like a big cat that's had a mouse. She looked much too big for Dorrie's bed, I can tell you that. She was trying to be brave, though; when she turned her head on the pillow and looked at me she gave a little smile, and I thought maybe she was getting ready to cry, but she only said, "I *did* tell them. I've known about it for two months."

"I'm sure of it," I said. "Try not to think about it anymore to-night."

"They wouldn't believe me."

"Well, it certainly wasn't your fault, and it won't do you any good to keep brooding on it; right now you've got to sleep."

"I knew all about it," she said.

"Shh," I said. I turned out the light, and went over to kiss her good night and she looked up at me and said, "Don't go in any boats." She had some strange connection in that odd mind between me and boats; she must have mentioned it half a dozen times during those first few days, when her thoughts were so confused and dazed.

I suppose she had heard something, or perhaps Helen and Don had said something—maybe one of the last things they said to her; people always remember something like that—and it could have been about me; they talked about us enough, heaven knows. Anyway, I told her not to worry about boats anymore, that everything was going to be all right, and I finally leaned over and gave her a little kiss on that big white forehead and said, "Good night."

"Good night," she said. I turned on Dorrie's night-light in case she should wake up in the night and forget she was in Dorrie's room and then closed the door and came downstairs to wait for Howard.

When he came in he was feeling pretty awful, so I made him some cocoa and while he had it we sat and talked about our trip to Maine. "There's certainly no chance of it *now*," I told him. "The girl's right upstairs. We can't do a thing until the aunt comes."

"They notified the aunt," Howard said. "Sent a cable from the police station."

"What makes me hopping mad is having to unpack the bags. And my nice green sweater I bought just for the trip."

"Well, it wouldn't look very good if we just took off and left the girl alone."

"No," I said. "It's a terrible thing," I told him, "a terrible thing to happen *any*time, of course, but wouldn't you just *know* they'd go and do it now?"

"No help for it. We'll have to try and plan something else. Is she asleep?"

"I think she must be. I gave her some cocoa. You know, that's another thing that bothers me. That girl hasn't cried a single tear."

"Kids like that sometimes feel it worse inside."

"Maybe," but I didn't think so. "No early start tomorrow, I guess."

I really felt like crying, seeing Howard take those suitcases upstairs, but he told me to cheer up. "It's rotten bad luck," he said, "but we'll think of something else."

There was a lot to do the next day. First, I had to unpack those suitcases and put everything away so it wouldn't wrinkle. Also, I thought I kind of ought to go over to the Lansons' and straighten up—Helen Lanson always left things in a mess, and I certainly wouldn't have been surprised to find her dinner dishes still dirty in her sink; that girl wouldn't lift a finger to wash them, I know now, after having her in my house. Not one thing did she do. I can't quite picture Helen Lanson picking up after her, so I guess Vicky kept that room of hers at home looking so swept and bare, but in my house she never made Dorrie's bed once, never got out of her chair to take a dish to the kitchen, never offered to dust or vacuum even though half the mess was on her account.

I had to forgive her, of course, because of the sad blow she'd had, but I'd just like to see my Dorrie act like that no matter *what* happened. I mean, even if I was dead it would give me comfort to know that my daughter didn't forget her training, and the nice manners I taught her.

Half the time Vicky never bothered to answer at all when she was spoken to. That morning I asked her what she wanted me to bring her back from her own house and she just looked at me. Maybe there was nothing there she wanted. I just decided the aunt would have to look over everything. Helen Lanson had some lovely china, and a set of wineglasses I would have given my right arm to own; she'd inherited them from her grandmother, and you'd think even a child like Vicky would have some sense of their value, but when I mentioned them and said how much I coveted them, she only stared at me. I straightened things up around the Lansons' house and got some clothes for Vicky, and then locked everything up tight and brought the keys home and set them on the mantel, where I could find them right away when the aunt came. If I had been another kind of person, I could have those wineglasses today and no one would ever have known.

I was pretty sure that along during the day people would be coming in; the Lansons being as popular as they were, it seemed a lot of their friends might drop over to see if Vicky was all right and I wasn't starving her or beating her or something. You'd think with all the friends the Lansons had, someone might have come forward to take the girl so we wouldn't be tied down with her, but of course we were right on the spot when someone was needed, and as Howard said, it still wouldn't look right to go off so soon. The doctor said Vicky was fine; she spent most of the morning up in Dorrie's room reading Dorrie's books, and after lunch I told her to dress nicely and comb her hair and come downstairs to sit. I just wanted her there looking proper if anyone came; lucky she had a dark dress to wear. Mrs. Wright came by early; she lived down the street and had only just heard. She was kind of sniffling, with a handkerchief over her face most of the time, and she patted Vicky's hand and said it was heartbreaking, just heartbreaking, and Vicky looked at her. After a minute or so of this she gave up and followed me out to the kitchen to get a cup of tea and said, "Has she been like this ever since *it* happened?"

"No," I said. "All night she was asleep."

"Has she been crying?"

"Not a single tear."

I got the cups out; one thing about Mrs. Wright, you don't get off easy. Tea and chocolate cake were the least she expected, and I supposed if the Lansons' fancy friends dropped around later it would mean cocktails and potato chips and crackers and olives and whatnot. "It's a heartbreaking thing," Mrs. Wright kept saying, "simply heartbreaking. Were they killed instantly?"

"I suppose so. I don't know anything about it." I knew what she wanted to ask me, but I wasn't going to help her out. It's not good for people to think about such things; I never asked Howard a word about it and he never offered to tell me, because I always think that a person has enough everyday troubles without going looking for the horrible details of what happens to other people. "They hit a truck," I said. "That's all I know."

"Anyway, it will be in the paper tonight. That poor little girl. Who told her? You? How did she take it?"

"About as you'd expect," I said. I didn't want Mrs. Wright blaming *me* for the way Vicky acted; she might think I'd broken the news wrong, or something, so I started back into the living room with the tea tray and of course she had to follow me and couldn't ask any more about it with Vicky sitting right there. She tried to make bright conversation instead, I guess to cheer Vicky a little, although I could have told her to save her breath.

She told about Mrs. Haven at the grocery forgetting her lamb chops and how the grocer had to come down from his dinner and open the store for her and she told about the Actons' cat getting run over, but she stopped herself in the middle of that and looked at Vicky to see if she had said anything wrong and then she started quickly to tell about her grandson, who just got admitted to medical school.

"He's going to be a doctor," she explained.

"He'll be caught with a girl in his room and expelled pretty soon," Vicky said suddenly.

"Vicky!" I said. I couldn't think of anything decent to say; I mean, I couldn't punish her, her not being my child and all, but I did think I ought to do something, with Mrs. Wright sitting there with her mouth open. "Young ladies should speak politely in company,

Vicky," I said. Dorrie would never have said a thing like that about Mrs. Wright's grandson.

"I'll overlook it," Mrs. Wright said, "considering your present circumstances, Vicky, although you ought not to have that kind of thought with your parents lying there—" She stopped, and took out her handkerchief again, and Vicky stared at the wall, and I thought it would be a pleasure to tan that young lady's hide.

Later some of the Lansons' friends did come, as I expected, and it was cocktails and potato chips and crackers and pickles and everything; we could have had a party of our own, and invited our own friends, for what it cost us to entertain the Lansons' friends, although I must say that one of the men took the Lansons' keys and went over and got a bottle of gin because, he said, it was the least the Lansons would want us to do, and I thought that was probably true. Everyone tried to say something nice to Vicky, but it was hard. I heard one conversation that shocked me, because if I heard Dorrie talking like that to her elders, I would have washed her mouth out with soap. A Mr. Sherman, whom I hadn't met before, was telling her what a fine man her father had been—I suppose he thought he ought to, although anyone who knew Don Lanson knew better—and Vicky came right out and said, in that flat voice of hers, "Your wife finally has the evidence to divorce you." You can imagine how that sounded, right to an old friend of her father's, and he was surprised to hear it, you could tell; I don't think my Dorrie even knows the *word* divorce. Later I heard her telling her father's lawyer that the papers in his office were going to be burned up in a big fire; he had been talking to her about her father's will, and I suppose somehow the idea of a will got through to her—a little thing like that will, sometimes, you know—so she reacted like a spiteful baby. I thought it was extremely rude of her, driving her father's friends out of my house like that, and I was going to tell her so, but there was always someone there talking to her, patting her hand and telling her to be brave. Tell Vicky to be brave—tell the ocean to keep rolling.

Well, it was like that till her aunt came. She was delayed getting here—some trouble with the plane—and so she missed the funeral, but I saw that Vicky was there in a dark blue dress and black shoes and her hair combed, and all, and never a tear did that child shed. They had a nice attendance, I must say. You would have thought the Lansons were the most popular people in town, but I suppose people thought it was a friendly gesture to Vicky, and of course since Howard and I were kind of in charge, I guess a lot of people came out of courtesy to us. Once during the ceremony Vicky leaned over toward me and whispered, "You see that man over there, the one with the bald head and the gray suit? He stole some money and they're going to put him in jail," which I thought a disrespectful and silly remark to make during her parents' own funeral, particularly since a lot of people thought she was getting overcome and looked to see if I was going to have to take her out.

The day the aunt arrived was the day of the big fire downtown that destroyed almost a whole block of offices, so I didn't have a chance to introduce her to many of the people who had been dropping in nearly every day. I had Vicky's clothes all clean and neat—I could hardly send her home dirty, after all—and packed ready to take back. I must say I wasn't sorry to see that girl turned over to her own relatives; it was hard, having her in Dorrie's room all the time, and Howard was getting so he could hardly eat, looking at her sitting there at the dinner table every night and stuffing herself. The night before she went to her aunt—they were going to stay next door for a day or so, arranging for things to be sold and to be stored and to be given away, and I must say I had half an idea that the aunt might have thought of me when it came to the wineglasses, Vicky knowing how I wanted them so much, and after all I'd done—the night before she left, when I went in to say good night, she gave me her little red notebook. "This is for you," she said. "I want you to have it because you've been so kind to me."

Well, it was the only word of thanks I was ever to get. Not one word was ever said about those wineglasses. I knew she prized the little book and thought she was giving me something precious, so I took it. "Stay away from boats," she said, and I laughed at her, I really had to, and then she told me to take good care of the little book and of course I promised her I would.

"I'll remember you when I'm in London, England," she said. "Tell Dorrie to write to me sometimes."

"I surely will," I said. Dorrie is the sweetest child in the world, and if she thought it would give Vicky any pleasure to get a letter from her, she'd sit right down. "Now, good night," I said. I had gotten used to kissing her good night, but I never looked forward to it.

"Good night," she said, and went right off to sleep, as she always did. Well, they left, and I hear the house has been sold and someone new was coming to live there. I took a look at Vicky's little red notebook, thinking it might be a little book of poems like Dorrie gave me once, or even pictures of something, but I was disappointed; the child had been amusing herself writing gossipy little paragraphs about her neighbors and her parents' friends—although what else would you expect, considering the way Don and Helen used to talk about people?—and horror tales about atom bombs and the end of the world, not at all the kind of thing you like to think about a child dwelling on; I wouldn't have Dorrie thinking about things like that, and I threw the little book in the furnace. She must have been a very lonely child, I thought, to spend her time writing sad little stories. I hope she's as happy in London as she expected to be, and meanwhile we've decided what we're going to do to make up for our lost trip to Maine. We'll keep Dorrie out of school for a couple of weeks—she's always at the top; she can miss a little work—and we're all going to go on a cruise.

HOME

Ladies' Home Journal, *August 1965*

ETHEL SLOANE WAS WHISTLING to herself as she got out of her car and splashed across the sidewalk to the doorway of the hardware store. She was wearing a new raincoat and solid boots, and one day of living in the country had made her weather-wise. "This rain can't last," she told the hardware clerk confidently. "This time of year it never lasts."

The clerk nodded tactfully. One day in the country had been enough for Ethel Sloane to become acquainted with most of the local people; she had been into the hardware store several times—"so many odd things you never expect you're going to need in an old house"—and into the post office to leave their new address, and into the grocery to make it clear that all the Sloane grocery business was going to come their way, and into the bank and into the gas station and into the little library and even as far as the door of the barber-shop (". . . and you'll be seeing my husband Jim Sloane in a day or so!"). Ethel Sloane liked having bought the old Sanderson place, and she liked walking the single street of the village, and most of all she liked knowing that people knew who she was.

"They make you feel at home right away, as though you were born not half a mile from here," she explained to her husband, Jim.

Privately she thought that the storekeepers in the village might show a little more alacrity in remembering her name; she had proba-bly brought more business to the little stores in the village than any of them had seen for a year past. They're not outgoing people, she told herself reassuringly. It takes a while for them to get over being suspicious; we've been here in the house for only two days.

"First, I want to get the name of a good plumber," she said to the clerk in the hardware store. Ethel Sloane was a great believer in getting information directly from the local people; the plumbers listed in the phone book might be competent enough, but the local people always knew who would suit; Ethel Sloane had no intention of antagonizing the villagers by hiring an unpopular plumber. "And closet hooks," she said. "My husband, Jim, turns out to be just as good a handyman as he is a writer." Always tell them your business, she thought, then they don't have to ask.

"I suppose the best one for plumbing would be Will Watson," the clerk said. "He does most of the plumbing around. You drive down the Sanderson road in this rain?"

"Of course." Ethel Sloane was surprised. "I had all kinds of things to do in the village."

"Creek's pretty high. They say that sometimes when the creek is high—"

"The bridge held our moving truck yesterday, so I guess it will hold my car today. That bridge ought to stand for a while yet." Briefly she wondered whether she might not say "for a spell" instead of "for a while," and then decided that sooner or later it would come naturally. "Anyway, who minds rain? We've got so much to do indoors." She was pleased with "indoors."

"Well," the clerk said, "of course, no one can stop you from driving on the old Sanderson road. If you want to. You'll find people around here mostly leave it alone in the rain, though. Myself, I think it's all just gossip, but then, I don't drive out that way much, anyway."

"It's a little muddy on a day like this," Ethel Sloane said firmly, "and maybe a little scary crossing the bridge when the creek is high, but you've got to expect that kind of thing when you live in the country."

"I wasn't talking about that," the clerk said. "Closet hooks? I wonder, do we have any closet hooks."

In the grocery Ethel Sloane bought mustard and soap and pickles and flour. "All the things I forgot to get yesterday," she explained, laughing.

"You took that road on a day like this?" the grocer asked.

"It's not that bad," she said, surprised again. "I don't mind the rain."

"We don't use that road in this weather," the grocer said. "You might say there's talk about that road."

"It certainly seems to have quite a local reputation," Ethel said, and laughed. "And it's nowhere near as bad as some of the other roads I've seen around here."

"Well, I told you," the grocer said, and shut his mouth.

I've offended him, Ethel thought, I've said I think their roads are bad; these people are so jealous of their countryside.

"I guess our road is pretty muddy," she said almost apologetically. "But I'm really a very careful driver."

"You stay careful," the grocer said. "No matter what you see."

"I'm always careful." Whistling, Ethel Sloane went out and got into her car and turned in the circle in front of the abandoned railway station. Nice little town, she was thinking, and they are beginning to like us already, all so worried about my safe driving. We're the kind of people, Jim and I, who fit in a place like this; we wouldn't belong in the suburbs or some kind of a colony; we're real people. Jim will write, she thought, and I'll get one of these country women to teach me how to make bread. Watson for plumbing.

She was oddly touched when the clerk from the hardware store and then the grocer stepped to their doorways to watch her drive by. They're worrying about me, she thought; they're afraid a city gal can't manage their bad, wicked roads, and I do bet it's hell in the winter, but I can manage; I'm country now.

Her way led out of the village and then off the highway onto a dirt road that meandered between fields and an occasional farmhouse, then crossed the creek—disturbingly high after all this rain—and turned onto the steep hill that led to the Sanderson house. Ethel Sloane could see the house from the bridge across the creek, although in summer the view would be hidden by trees. It's a lovely house, she thought with a little catch of pride; I'm so lucky; up there it stands, so proud and remote, waiting for me to come home.

On one side of the hill the Sanderson land had long ago been sold off, and the hillside was dotted with small cottages and a couple of ramshackle farms; the people on that side of the hill used the other, lower, road, and Ethel Sloane was surprised and a little uneasy to perceive that the tire marks on this road and across the bridge were all her own, coming down; no one else seemed to use this road at all. Private, anyway, she thought; maybe they've talked everyone else out of using it. She looked up to see the house as she crossed the bridge; my very own house, she thought, and then, well, *our* very own house, she thought, and then she saw that there were two figures standing silently in the rain by the side of the road.

Good heavens, she thought, standing there in this rain, and she stopped the car. "Can I give you a lift?" she called out, rolling down the window. Through the rain she could see that they seemed to be an old woman and a child, and the rain drove down on them. Staring, Ethel Sloane became aware that the child was sick with misery, wet and shivering and crying in the rain, and she said sharply, "Come and get in the car at once; you mustn't keep that child out in the rain another minute."

They stared at her, the old woman frowning, listening. Perhaps she is deaf, Ethel thought, and in her good raincoat and solid boots she climbed out of the car and went over to them. Not wanting for any reason in the world to touch either of them, she put her face close to the old woman's and said urgently, "Come, hurry. Get that child into the car, where it's dry. I'll take you wherever you want to go." Then, with real horror, she saw that the child was wrapped in a blanket, and under the blanket he was wearing thin pajamas; with a shiver of fury, Ethel saw that he was barefoot and standing in the mud. "Get in that car at once," she said, and hurried to open the back door. "Get in that car at once, do you hear me?"

Silently the old woman reached her hand down to the child and, his eyes wide and staring past Ethel Sloane, the child moved toward the car, with the old woman following. Ethel looked in disgust at the small bare feet going over the mud and rocks, and she said to the old woman, "You ought to be ashamed; that child is certainly going to be sick."

She waited until they had climbed into the backseat of the car, and then slammed the door and got into her seat again. She glanced up at the mirror, but they were sitting in the corner, where she could not see them, and she turned; the child was huddled against the old woman, and the old woman looked straight ahead, her face heavy with weariness.

"Where are you going?" Ethel asked, her voice rising. "Where shall I take you? That child," she said to the old woman, "has to be gotten indoors and into dry clothes as soon as possible. Where are you going? I'll see that you get there in a hurry."

The old woman opened her mouth, and in a voice of old age beyond consolation said, "We want to go to the Sanderson place."

"To the Sanderson place?" To us? Ethel thought, To see us? This pair? Then she realized that the Sanderson place, to the old local people, probably still included the land where the cottages had been built; they probably still call the whole thing the Sanderson place, she thought, and felt oddly feudal with pride. We're the lords of the manor, she thought, and her voice was more gentle when she asked, "Were you waiting out there for very long in the rain?"

"Yes," the old woman said, her voice remote and despairing. Their lives must be desolate, Ethel thought. Imagine being that old and that tired and standing in the rain for someone to come by.

"Well, we'll soon have you home," she said, and started the car. The wheels slipped and skidded in the mud, but found a purchase, and slowly Ethel felt the car begin to move up the hill. It was very muddy, and the rain was heavier, and the back of the car dragged as though under an intolerable weight. It's as though I had a load of iron, Ethel thought. Poor old lady, it's the weight of years.

"Is the child all right?" she asked, lifting her head; she could not turn to look at them.

"He wants to go home," the old woman said.

"I should think so. Tell him it won't be long. I'll take you right to your door." It's the least I can do, she thought, and maybe go inside with them and see that he's warm enough; those poor bare feet.

Driving up the hill was very difficult, and perhaps the road was a little worse than Ethel had believed; she found that she could not look around or even speak while she was navigating the sharp curves, with the rain driving against the windshield and the wheels slipping in the mud. Once she said, "Nearly at the top," and then had to be silent, holding the wheel tight. When the car gave a final lurch and topped the small last rise that led onto the flat driveway before the Sanderson house, Ethel said, "Made it," and laughed. "Now, which way should I go?"

They're frightened, she thought. I'm sure the child is frightened and I don't blame them; I was a little nervous myself. She said loudly, "We're at the top now, it's all right, we made it. Now where shall I take you?"

When there was still no answer, she turned; the backseat of the car was empty.

"But even if they *could* have gotten out of the car without my noticing," Ethel Sloane said for the tenth time that evening to her husband, "they couldn't have gotten out of sight. I looked and looked." She lifted her hands in an emphatic gesture. "I went all around the top of the hill in the rain looking in all directions and calling them."

"But the car seat was dry," her husband said.

"Well, you're not going to suggest that I imagined it, are you? Because I'm simply not the kind of *person* to dream up an old lady and a sick child. There has to be some *explanation;* I don't imagine things."

"Well . . ." Jim said, and hesitated.

"Are you sure you didn't see them? They didn't come to the door?"

"Listen . . ." Jim said, and hesitated again. "Look," he said.

"I have certainly *never* been the kind of person who goes around imagining that she sees old ladies and children. You know me better than that, Jim, you know I don't go around—"

"Well," Jim said. "Look," he said finally, "there *could* be something. A story I heard. I never told you because—"

"Because what?"

"Because you . . . well—" Jim said.

"Jim." Ethel Sloane set her lips. "I don't like this, Jim. What is there that you haven't told me? Is there really something you know and I don't?"

"It's just a story. I heard it when I came up to look at the house."

"Do you mean you've known something all this time and you've never told me?"

"It's just a story," Jim said helplessly. Then, looking away, he said, "Everyone knows it, but they don't say much, I mean, these things—"

"Jim," Ethel said, "tell me at once."

"It's just that there was a little Sanderson boy stolen or lost or something. They thought a crazy old woman took him. People kept talking about it, but they never knew anything for sure."

"What?" Ethel Sloane stood up and started for the door. "You mean there's a child been stolen and no one told me about it?"

"No," Jim said oddly. "I mean, it happened sixty years ago."

Ethel was still talking about it at breakfast the next morning. "And they've never been found," she told herself happily. "All the people around went searching, and they finally decided the two of them had drowned in the creek, because it was raining then just the way it is now." She glanced with satisfaction at the rain beating against the window of the breakfast room. "Oh, lovely," she said, and sighed, and stretched, and smiled. "Ghosts," she said. "I saw two honest-to-goodness ghosts. No wonder," she said, "no *wonder* the child looked so awful. Awful! Kidnapped, and then drowned. No *wonder*."

"Listen," Jim said, "if I were you, I'd forget about it. People around here don't like to talk much about it."

"They wouldn't tell me," Ethel said, and laughed again. "Our very own ghosts, and not a soul would tell me. I just won't be satisfied until I get every word of the story."

"That's why *I* never told you," Jim said miserably.

"Don't be silly. Yesterday everyone I spoke to mentioned my driving on that road, and I bet every one of them was dying to tell me the story. I can't wait to see their faces when they hear."

"No." Jim stared at her. "You simply *can't* go around . . . *boasting* about it."

"But of course I can! Now we really belong here. I've really seen the local ghosts. And I'm going in this morning and tell everybody, and find out all I can."

"I wish you wouldn't," Jim said.

"I know you wish I wouldn't, but I'm going to. If I listened to you, I'd wait and wait for a good time to mention it and maybe even come to believe I'd dreamed it or something, so I'm going into the village right after breakfast."

"Please, Ethel," Jim said. "Please listen to me. People might not take it the way you think."

"Two ghosts of our very own." Ethel laughed again. "My very own," she said. "I just can't wait to see their faces in the village."

Before she got into the car she opened the back door and looked again at the seat, dry and unmarked. Then, smiling to herself, she got into the driver's seat and, suddenly touched with sick cold, turned around to look. "Why," she said, half whispering, "you're not *still* here, you can't be! Why," she said, "I just looked."

"They were strangers in the house," the old woman said.

The skin on the back of Ethel's neck crawled as though some wet thing walked there; the child stared past her, and the old woman's eyes were flat and dead. "What do you want?" Ethel asked, still whispering.

"We got to go back."

"I'll take you." The rain came hard against the windows of the car, and Ethel Sloane, seeing her own hand tremble as she reached for the car key, told herself, don't be afraid, don't be afraid, they're not real. "I'll take you," she said, gripping the wheel tight and turning the car to face down the hill, "I'll take you," she said, almost babbling, "I'll take you right back, I promise, see if I don't, I promise I'll take you right back where you want to go."

"He wanted to go home," the old woman said. Her voice was very far away.

"I'll take you, I'll take you." The road was even more slippery than before, and Ethel Sloane told herself, drive carefully, don't be afraid, they're not real. "Right where I found you yesterday, the very spot, I'll take you back."

"They were strangers in the house."

Ethel realized that she was driving faster than she should; she felt the disgusting wet cold coming from the backseat pushing her, forcing her to hurry.

"I'll take you back," she said over and over to the old woman and the child.

"When the strangers are gone, we can go home," the old woman said.

Coming to the last turn before the bridge, the wheels slipped, and, pulling at the steering wheel and shouting, "I'll take you back, I'll take you back," Ethel Sloane could hear only the child's horrible laughter as the car turned and skidded toward the high waters of the creek. One wheel slipped and spun in the air, and then, wrenching at the car with all her strength, she pulled it back onto the road and stopped.

Crying, breathless, Ethel put her head down on the steering wheel, weak and exhausted. I was almost killed, she told herself, they almost took me with them. She did not need to look into the backseat of the car; the cold was gone, and she knew the seat was dry and empty.

The clerk in the hardware store looked up and, seeing Ethel Sloane, smiled politely and then, looking again, frowned. "You feeling poorly this morning, Mrs. Sloane?" he asked. "Rain bothering you?"

"I almost had an accident on the road," Ethel Sloane said.

"On the old Sanderson road?" The clerk's hands were very still on the counter. "An accident?"

Ethel Sloane opened her mouth and then shut it again. "Yes," she said at last. "The car skidded."

"We don't use that road much," the clerk said. Ethel started to speak, but stopped herself.

"It's got a bad name locally, that road," he said. "What were you needing this morning?"

Ethel thought, and finally said, "Clothespins, I guess I must need clothespins. About the Sanderson road—"

"Yes?" said the clerk, his back to her.

"Nothing," Ethel said.

"Clothespins," the clerk said, putting a box on the counter. "By the way, will you and the mister be coming to the P.T.A. social tomorrow night?"

"We certainly will," said Ethel Sloane.

I . O . U .

🕭

Gentleman's Quarterly, *December 1965*

M ISS HONORIA ATHENS WAS outraged, discouraged, offended, and stiff in every muscle. Furious, she hobbled back and forth across the tiny living room of the little house that had belonged to her for only three weeks; if she tried to sit down, shooting pains went up her back; if she tried to stand still, her legs ached. Walking up and down gave her at least some means of stamping out her anger, but the desire for revenge was deep within her. "I could have bought a house on the side of a volcano," she told herself, storming. "I could have found a cottage in the middle of a forest filled with bears; I could have settled down smack in the middle of a superhighway, but *no*." She tried to stamp her foot, and groaned. "I had to pick a really *unpleasant* place to buy my little house," she thought. "I had to get the one place in town on the shortcut to school!" She raised her hands to her head and groaned as a pain shot across her shoulders.

After forty-one years of teaching school, Miss Honoria Athens had retired, to live happily alone and grow a little garden. Her little house stood on a block of similar little houses, in a town of little houses, and almost everyone had gardens, and almost everyone had children. Miss Athens, who was still actually fond of children after forty-one years of teaching, had been pleased to think of living in a community full of youngsters, with their liveliness and fun. That was before she discovered that the only, the practical, shortcut from her neighborhood to the school led over her back fence, across her backyard, over the front lawn next door, and to the street. As a matter of fact, it led straight through Miss Athens' garden.

She hobbled out to the kitchen to look once more upon the patch of ground it had taken her all day Saturday and all day Sunday to dig, and smooth, and clear; every twinge in her aching muscles had come from that garden, and she had consoled herself with dreams of vegetables brought to her table in a miracle of split-second timing, so fresh she could still taste the sunshine on them, tomatoes picked in the cool of the evening and eaten right from the vine, carrots and radishes and squash brought into her little kitchen in a rich, plentiful harvest. Now, looking out her kitchen window, Miss Athens wanted to cry. The shortcut to school crossed what would have been the vegetable garden, and the earth Miss Athens had so laboriously prepared yesterday was, today, trampled and muddied beyond belief, by what must have been an army wearing sneakers.

After teaching school for forty-one years, Miss Athens had no reason to put faith in signs reading PRIVATE or NO TRESPASSING or even PLEASE KEEP OUT OF MY GARDEN. She had, too, a pretty good idea of what might happen to her garden in the future if she started carrying tales to parents in order to get the shortcut routed along the sidewalks; she also knew perfectly well that no boy who ever lived would walk sedately along a sidewalk to get anywhere if there was a possibility of getting to the same place by climbing a fence and shuffling through a backyard full of mud. Bitterly, Miss Athens thought of a shotgun loaded with buckshot, or a lion trap.

At three o'clock that afternoon, Miss Athens was in her backyard, ingloriously hiding behind a bush. She watched as a group of half a dozen boys, whistling and shouting, turned across the lawn next door and made for her yard. Because her aching back was still giving her a good deal of trouble, Miss Athens caught only the last boy, just as he was giving himself a boost over the fence; she caught him by the back of his jacket, but, forty-one years of experience behind her, she immediately shifted her grip to his belt and held on.

"Hey?" the boy said, struggling. "Hey?"

"Come down from there," Miss Athens said.

"Why?" said the boy, but his grip on the top of the fence loosened and he slid slowly to the ground beside Miss Athens. "Let go of me," the boy said.

"What's your name?" Miss Athens said.

The boy's gaze shifted; all of Miss Athens' actions so far had been aggressive and her voice sounded downright unfriendly. "George Washington," the boy said.

"All right, George," Miss Athens said, "why were you trampling my garden?"

"*I* didn't know this was anybody's garden. We *always* come this way. To school," he explained. "This is the way to school. And I got to go home now. My mother—"

"You may come inside and telephone your mother—her name, I suppose, is Mrs. Washington—and tell her that you will be busy this afternoon. You are going to dig my garden over again."

"I *can't*," the boy said, wriggling. "Let *go* of me."

"I'm sorry," Miss Athens said. "I know you weren't the only one, but you're the only one I caught. And heaven knows *I* can't dig that garden again. So you boys who ruined it will have to fix it."

"Golly," the boy said. "I *can't*. But I'll tell the other guys. I'm sure some of *them* would help."

"I'm sure, too," Miss Athens said. "That's why I'm holding on to *you*."

The boy relaxed a little. "Look," he said, "all right, you say I helped wreck your old garden, so sure, it's fair I help fix it up again. Only I just can't *today*. I promise you I'll come on Saturday, for sure, and work in your garden. Okay?"

Miss Athens thought. "How good is your promise?" she asked at last.

"My promise is *good*. Why, if *I* promise, I *always* do it. Word of honor, even if I forget."

"Wait," Miss Athens said. "I have an idea. Come inside with me." Half pulling the boy, she took him in through the back door of her little house, holding on to his belt tightly while she searched one-handed through the kitchen drawers for a pencil and a memo pad. "Now," she said, putting the pad down on the kitchen table, "you write what I say."

"O.K.," said the boy, looking at her out of the corners of his eyes.

"You write . . . let me see. Write: I. O. U."

"What's that mean?"

"Just what it says. It says 'I owe you,' and it's a promise to pay what you owe me."

"I.O.U. O.K."

"I.O.U. two hours' garden work. And sign it. With your real name, please, George Washington."

The boy giggled. "Allen Stuart is my *real* name," he said.

Miss Athens looked over his shoulder at the paper. "Cross your t's," she said; she had been a schoolteacher for forty-one years. "Very nice handwriting, Allen. Now, this slip of paper means that you owe me two hours' work in the garden. When you pay me the work, I give you back the paper and you can tear it up. It's just a written promise."

Allen looked at the paper respectfully. "You going to get the other guys to sign papers, too?" he asked.

"When I catch them," Miss Athens said. "Help yourself from the cookie jar before you go, Allen. Oh, and one more thing: this paper is negotiable."

"What?"

"That means that I can turn it over to someone. For instance, suppose I met someone—your mother, say—who wanted you to work in *her* garden for two hours, and suppose that person offered me some kind of trade for this paper. I could give that person this paper you have signed and you would then owe the two hours' work to whoever held the paper. You see?"

"Yeah," Allen said uneasily. "Can I go home now?"

"Dad?" Allen Stuart, after his customary manner, hung heavily over the back of his father's chair in order to carry on a casual conversation. "Dad, you know that old lady just moved in down the street? Old lady Athens?"

"Miss Athens?" His father stirred irritably. "Stop breathing down my neck," he said.

Allen moved himself a fraction of an inch farther along the back of the chair. "You know what she did?" he demanded. "You know *what?*"

His father sighed and put down the evening paper. "Well?"

"I met her in the grocery the other day," Mrs. Stuart said. She held up a pair of torn blue jeans and sighed. "No animal would treat its skin the way a twelve-year-old boy treats clothes," she told her husband.

"Dad, you know what?"

"Allen," Mr. Stuart said, "go across the room and sit down in a chair. I cannot talk to you unless I can see you and even then I find it difficult. I—"

"She's got a swell idea. Really *swell*. She was mad at me, see, but when I told her I'd pay for it, she—"

"Pay for what?" said his father.

"Mad at you? Why?" said his mother.

"Oh, never mind *that*." Allen spoke with some haste. "Just she was mad at me, is all. And I only said 'pay for it' because, I mean, how could anyone pay for a thing like that, anyway? I just meant I'd do the work over—"

"What did you break?" said his mother.

"What did you ruin?" said his father.

"Oh, nothing, *honest*. Just her old garden, and I *said* I was sorry. But she said I could do the work over again and what I'd got to do was sign a paper—"

"Do *what*?" said his father, half rising.

"Just a paper. All it said was that I promised to work for her two hours. I'm going over on Saturday and work in her garden. I owe her, see? Two hours." Allen spoke patiently.

His father sat back, frowning. "Are you sure that was all the paper said?" he asked. "No other promises of any kind? No commitments for your *parents* or anything? No responsibilities assumed? Of course you're a minor, but I don't want to be liable for any contracts."

"An I.O.U.," Allen said.

"Wait," said his mother, leaning forward. "Allen, do you mean that in return for something you broke at Miss Athens' house, you wrote a promise to work for her for two hours?"

"Sure," Allen said, pleased at this unusual perception from one whom he regarded as ordinarily almost subnormal in understanding.

"I wonder." Allen's mother was thinking hard. "Would you do the same thing for me? For instance, if you want to go to the movies and your allowance is gone, and you want me to advance you the money to go to the movies, will you then sign one of these I.O.U. things for me? For two hours' work, or perhaps some special job? That broken back step, for instance?"

"I still got money for the movies this week," Allen said, going to the heart of the problem. "But yeah, I guess. I could make a paper promising you something."

"But suppose I advanced you the movie money and then you broke your promise on the I.O.U.?"

"Mom!" Allen was deeply shocked. "That would be *cheating*."

Late on Tuesday afternoon Miss Athens, walking almost normally now, came down the street toward her little house. She had spent a hard day shopping, and she wanted a cup of tea. When she came to her own front walk, she was first startled and then annoyed when she saw a boy come hastily from her backyard, but then she recognized Allen Stuart and she said, "Why, hello, George Washington."

"Hi, Miss Athens. I'll carry your packages." Allen was clearly very pleased with himself. He followed Miss Athens up the walk and brought her packages in and set them down on the kitchen table. Then, turning in suppressed delight, he said, "I came to get that paper back, please."

"Oh, dear." Miss Athens sat down abruptly on a kitchen chair.

"Look," Allen said happily, waving at the kitchen window. Miss Athens got up and looked out. "My *goodness,*" she said weakly.

"I been working all afternoon, ever since school," Allen said, "and I bet it looks even *better* than it did before."

"It's certainly very nice." Miss Athens came back and sat down again. "Allen," she said, "this is very embarrassing."

Allen opened his eyes wide. "Something *else* wrong?" he asked.

"Allen," Miss Athens said, "help yourself from the cookie jar. I'm afraid I did something very foolish."

"Why?"

"Well," Miss Athens explained, "I stopped by the grocery on my way home, and—well, I *thought* I had enough money. I distinctly recall thinking this morning that unless I bought too much in the department store I would have *plenty* for the grocery. I was even going to cash a check. But Mr. Smith said—"

"Did you lose my paper?"

"No," Miss Athens said sadly. "I sold it. I was going to go back and redeem it tomorrow morning," she went on earnestly. "It was only because I ran short of money and I *needed* the tea, and all I had in my pocketbook was your I.O.U. So Mr. Smith said he would take that instead. He saw your name and said he knew you."

"I *bet* he knows me," Allen said darkly. "Last Halloween—"

"What?"

"Nothing," Allen said.

"I'll tell you what I'll do," Miss Athens said. "I want to be fair about this. Since you did the work you promised, and since I lost possession of your paper, the only thing for me to do is pay you back."

"You mean," Allen said very slowly, "*you'll* make *me* a paper saying that *you* will work for *me?*"

Miss Athens smiled. "After all," she said, "I did teach school for forty-one years. I imagine I could cope with most of your work. I can write a very neat, well-thought-out theme, for instance. I can do arithmetic, or spelling, or geography. You ought to be able to find two hours of work for me." She laughed. "It's only fair, after all."

A light of the purest, most disinterested wickedness, a light possible only in the eyes of a twelve-year-old boy presented with an opportunity beyond his wildest anticipations, touched the earnest face and wide, truthful forehead of Allen Stuart. "Well," he said, "I don't know what my mother would say, but if *you* think it's fair, Miss Athens. But only if you're sure you *really* think it's fair."

"I would be a very poor sort of person, Allen, if I asked something of you and then refused to take my turn." Miss Athens took up the pad of paper. "What shall I say? Just 'I.O.U. two hours' selected work'?"

"Oh, yes," Allen said. "Oh, yes, that will be perfectly fine."

"There." Miss Athens signed her name with a flourish and handed the paper to Allen. "All fair and legal," she said.

"Thank *you,*" Allen said, picking up the paper with some haste. "Miss Athens, thank you very, *very* much."

And that was how Miss Honoria Athens found herself committed, on her word of honor, to two hours' playing shortstop for the Rockville Rockets baseball team.

Mr. Smith, the grocer, possessed of Allen Stuart's promise to work for two hours upon demand, brought the I.O.U. home to his wife, who took it very seriously. "You see," she explained to her husband, "this is as real as any promise. The little boy has given his word to do the work."

Mr. Smith grinned. "You remember last Halloween?" he asked.

"Was that the same little boy? But you put back the doors of the garage long ago."

"He must be an agile young fellow," Mr. Smith said. "I took this paper only as a kind of a joke—thought it might keep him in line for a while if he knew I had it."

"But I can *use* him." Mrs. Smith was eager. "If he will push a wheelbarrow with rocks in it, I can use this two hours of work from him and make my rock garden, since"—and her voice became reproachful—"I have been three weeks asking *you*—"

"All right," Mr. Smith said, "but just remember, I had to *buy* this paper."

"Indeed?" said Mrs. Smith. "Will you next charge me for groceries out of the store?"

"What will you give me for it?"

Mrs. Smith thought, regarding her husband dubiously. Then, amused, she said, "I will make *you* a little paper. Just like this. Only instead of pushing the wheelbarrow I will promise you a stuffed cabbage with sour cream. I will sign my name on the bottom."

"The big baking dish?" said Mr. Smith.

"The big baking dish."

"Butterball," Mr. Smith said, "you have made yourself a deal."

It might, perhaps, have stopped there if Mrs. Watkins from Willow Street had not come into the grocery store the next morning, collecting for the P.T.A. food sale. Mr. Smith, who ordinarily contributed half a dozen cases of soft drinks to the food sale, took it into his head, this time, to contribute Mrs. Smith's I.O.U. for one big baking dish of stuffed cabbage and sour cream. Mrs. Smith was understandably upset when she heard, and pointed out to Mr. Smith that not everybody was so foolish about what they ate as to prefer Mrs. Smith's stuffed cabbage to good ordinary food, and Mr. Smith would be hopelessly humiliated when everything at the food sale was sold except for Mrs. Smith's stuffed cabbage, left sitting there alone on the table because no one would buy it. Mr. Smith promised to go himself to the food sale and personally buy every scrap of Mrs. Smith's stuffed cabbage, and Mrs. Smith said that if he did, she would never forgive him, because that would *prove* that nobody liked her stuffed cabbage.

Allen Stuart, as it turned out, shortsightedly spent his movie money on a water pistol, which was confiscated almost at once by the seventh-grade teacher, and in order to get to the movies with the rest of his friends on Wednesday night (two cartoons and a serial, in addition to a double feature), he had to sign two further I.O.U.'s for his mother, one promising to help his sixteen-year-old sister with the dishes every night for a week, and the other for an hour's free babysitting, which his mother did not need for herself, but which she used as a bribe in a trade with *her* sister, to get a sweater pattern and an I.O.U.—her sister having been captivated by the I.O.U. notion—for help with the hard part of the sleeves.

Mrs. Stuart got home, read over the directions for the sweater, and decided it was too hard for her after all, so she traded the directions and the I.O.U. for help around the sleeves to her daughter, who gave her in exchange an I.O.U. promising to help Allen with his arithmetic homework every night for two weeks. Mr. Stuart, dazzled by the sight of his older daughter bending her bright head over her younger brother's arithmetic, made, of his own free will, an I.O.U. to foot the bill for a steak dinner for four at the Rockville Inn. "It's such a blessed miracle," he explained to his wife, "to see the two of them sitting next to each other in peace and quiet."

Miss Athens, lying in wait morning and afternoon, captured and signed up eleven more twelve-year-old boys.

Frances Stuart was only human, and her golden head was sadly bowed. What girl could live, she wondered, what girl could positively, absolutely *live* when Florence Crain had drawn the name of Jeff Rogers out of the hat for the Grab Bag Dance? Actually, how could anyone *bear* it? It was simply too much. Naturally, no one would dream of hinting that Florence Crain had been peeking, but really, the whole thing was just too *obvious* a coincidence. Frances Stuart believed with all her heart that she would never, just *never*, live through Friday evening, and naturally Florence would wear the black dress, which was *ages* too old for her, and probably look utterly evil in it, and it was just all of it too *much*. For twenty-four hours Frances Stuart contemplated her own sudden death from a broken heart, and consoled herself with the picture of her stricken parents, and even a contrite younger brother bending over her deathbed, while somewhere—perhaps on the bank of a raging river or on a high cliff miles above cruel, jagged rocks—Jeff Rogers breathed her name just once before hurling himself to destruction. For twenty-four hours this was satisfactory. Then Frances Stuart, being not only human but of a certain shrewdness, armed herself with her aunt's sweater pattern, the I.O.U. for helping with the sleeves, her father's I.O.U. for a steak dinner for four at the Rockville Inn, and an unopened bottle of cologne, and made for Florence Crain.

Florence was a hard bargainer, but by throwing in a yellow skirt that was too big, anyway, and a further I.O.U. for two sodas at the drugstore, Frances came off with Jeff Rogers for the Grab Bag Dance, and an I.O.U. from Florence promising the black dress for the first dance of the fall season.

. . .

The P.T.A. food sale was held on Wednesday evening, and Mr. Smith got there too late. On Friday morning Miss Athens met Mrs. Stuart and her sister in the grocery, all converging upon Mr. Smith and intent on more of Mrs. Smith's stuffed cabbage and sour cream. "Good morning," Mrs. Stuart said to Miss Athens as she edged toward the counter. "I've been meaning to stop in and say hello. And of course to apologize for Allen's causing you so much trouble."

"No trouble at all," Miss Athens said. "He very kindly helped me with my garden."

"So I heard," Mrs. Stuart said. "Actually, I was wondering if you had any I.O.U.'s you would care to trade. Allen is signed up to the absolute limit of his credit, and I *still* have no one to fix our broken back step. I thought perhaps one of the other boys . . ."

Miss Athens opened her pocketbook. "As a matter of fact," she said, "*nothing* seems to stop them from using my yard as a shortcut, although they do seem to be *trying* not to step in the garden. I have more promises of help than I can ever use, though it has occurred to me that I could put up a little summer house, or a terrace or something, to use up all these hours of work." She leafed through a little package of I.O.U.'s signed more or less legibly with the names of various young gentlemen, who still optimistically believed that Miss Athens' backyard was the shortest way to school. "What kind of boy would you like?" she asked.

"Let me see." Mrs. Stuart was, in turn, unfolding a little collection of slips of paper. "You have no use for baby-sitters, do you?"

"I can take the baby-sitting ones," her sister put in. "I have one from my husband promising to put up a television aerial. Or I can trade my own promise to help you with those curtains, Grace."

"I'm very clumsy with curtains," Miss Athens said shyly. "I can't seem to get mine to hang straight."

"Well," said Mrs. Stuart's sister, "I can certainly use a couple of those boys, Miss Athens—I want to build an outdoor playpen for the baby."

"Fine," Miss Athens said. "I have four windows in my living room—would three boys at two hours each sound right?"

"Splendid," Mrs. Stuart's sister said.

"Wait," said Mrs. Stuart. "Don't trade away all your boys, Miss Athens."

"I get more every day," Miss Athens said cynically.

"How about dusting?" Mrs. Stuart asked. "My daughter, Frances, has promised half an hour of dusting every day for a week." She laughed. "Here's one I don't suppose you need," she said. "It's from Allen, promising to get a haircut every two weeks until fall. It cost me a bag of marbles. How about one promising to substitute for chaperon at the dance Friday night? Or here's one from the little Atkins girl promising not to give us any of their kittens for one year. Leaf-raking next fall? Snow-shoveling? Allen has been getting desperate. And here's one from Mrs. Williams promising to make one of those sweet little knitted caps. I got *that* one from Frances, and she got it from the Williams girl in exchange for a home permanent, and the Williams girl got it from *her* mother for doing the family marketing and carrying home the packages. Dear me." And Mrs. Stuart sighed, regarding her handful of papers.

"I could use the dusting," Miss Athens said. "Is she careful of old china?"

"She will be," Mrs. Stuart said. "She'll be fine after the dance on Friday night."

Mr. Smith spoke hesitantly. "My wife's been after me," he said. "I can't find time to do things, much, and I thought I heard one of you ladies mention a television aerial."

"Yes, indeed," said Mrs. Stuart's sister.

"Only thing is," Mr. Smith went on, "I don't know how to go about trading. What do I offer you in exchange?"

Mrs. Stuart's sister smiled happily. "Stuffed cabbage with sour cream."

Miss Athens and Mrs. Stuart stopped for a minute to talk, in front of the grocery, and stepped aside as an unfamiliar young woman approached; she started to go into the grocery, hesitated, and then turned to Mrs. Stuart. "Excuse me," she said, "but isn't your name Stuart?"

Mrs. Stuart laughed. "Children are the world's best newspapers," she said. "I am Mrs. Stuart, I live directly across the street from you. Your name is Boone, you moved in yesterday, and you have two children, one a little girl about four and the other a baby."

"A boy," Mrs. Boone said. "Three months old." She was pretty and smiling and breathless and clearly in the middle of unpacking: her hair was mussed and she was wearing blue jeans. "I'm ashamed of myself," she said, gesturing at her clothes, "but we ran out of milk for the baby, and I've been trying to get dishes put away, and linen out so I could make the beds, and I can't *find* anything."

Mrs. Stuart nodded sympathetically, but Miss Athens, businesslike, took out her package of I.O.U.'s. "Exactly," she said. "You sound like you could use four or five of my boys."

Mrs. Boone looked puzzled. Then she said, "Why, *I* have one of those papers." From the pocket of her blue jeans she took Mr. Stuart's I.O.U. promising a steak dinner for four at the Rockville Inn. "I don't understand it at all," Mrs. Boone said. "Yesterday a very pretty dark-haired girl—"

"Florence Crain," said Mrs. Stuart with admirable courtesy.

"Yes, of course. Florence. Mrs. Smith here in the grocery suggested that she might be able to watch the babies for me while I unpacked, and she was really terribly sweet about it, but *you* know how girls are—she came across a necklace of mine, nothing but costume jewelry and of no value at all, and actually I haven't worn it for years, but *she* seemed to think it was just exactly the thing to wear with a black dress she has—"

"I know the black dress," Mrs. Stuart said grimly.

"Much too old for a girl her age, *I* would think," said Mrs. Boone, accurately interpreting Mrs. Stuart's expression. "I told her I would be delighted to give her the necklace, because she had been so very nice with the babies, but she gave me this paper. She said it was a trade. But I believe it belongs to you."

Helplessly, Mrs. Stuart shook her head. "Not at all," she said. "It belongs to *you*. Would Saturday evening be convenient?"

Every year Mrs. Boone made ginger marmalade from a recipe left her by her great-grandmother. One jar of Mrs. Boone's last-year's ginger marmalade was a more than adequate trade for two hours of baby-sitting by Frances Stuart, on an I.O.U. earned by Mrs. Stuart by putting new curtains in Frances' room. The Boones dined so pleasantly at the Rockville Inn with the Stuarts that they felt enthusiastically that they must reciprocate, and Mrs. Boone and Mrs. Stuart eventually became close enough friends for Mrs. Boone to pass on the recipe for ginger marmalade. Mr. Smith was so pressed by requests for Mrs. Smith's stuffed cabbage with sour cream that he bought half a dozen boys from Miss Athens and used the accumulated labor to build in a small counter across one corner of the grocery, where Mrs. Smith began a little catering service, which expanded in time to such an extent that the Smiths gave up the grocery and took to spending their winters in Florida. Allen Stuart's sternest case of hero worship took an abrupt fall when Jeff Rogers stopped him on the street after school and offered to pay his way into the movies for a week in return for one of Allen's I.O.U.'s, the one from Allen's sister promising to help him with his arithmetic homework every night for two weeks. Bewildered, Allen argued that Jeff did not even take arithmetic, and all that would happen if he had the I.O.U. was that he would have to sit with Allen's crazy old sister every night. Jeff said yes, he knew. When Allen, disgusted, reported this evidence of the disintegration of a fine mind and a good football player to his sister, he was further confused by her gift of a dollar and the promise to *do* his arithmetic homework for two weeks. Murmuring, Allen retreated to the Boones' house to work out an I.O.U. helping Mr. Boone unpack his fishing equipment.

On Saturday afternoon the weather was clear and warm, and the entire town turned out to see Miss Athens, grim-faced, the soul of honor, wearing an undersized gray cap and the number thirteen on her back, select a bat, and walk balefully into the batter's box. The Rockville Rockets won, one to nothing, and everyone in town remembered, forever after, that unbelievable moment when Miss Athens, seeing the first pitch coming at her, shut her eyes and swung.

THE POSSIBILITY

OF EVIL

☙

The Saturday Evening Post,
December 1968

MISS ADELA STRANGEWORTH STEPPED daintily
along Main Street on her way to the grocery. The sun was
shining, the air was fresh and clear after the night's heavy rain, and
everything in Miss Strangeworth's little town looked washed and
bright. Miss Strangeworth took deep breaths, and thought that there
was nothing in the world like a fragrant summer day.

She knew everyone in town, of course; she was fond of telling
strangers—tourists who sometimes passed through the town and
stopped to admire Miss Strangeworth's roses—that she had never
spent more than a day outside this town in all her long life. She was
seventy-one, Miss Strangeworth told the tourists, with a pretty little
dimple showing by her lip, and she sometimes found herself thinking
that the town belonged to her. "My grandfather built the first house
on Pleasant Street," she would say, opening her blue eyes wide with
the wonder of it. "This house, right here. My family has lived here
for better than a hundred years. My grandmother planted these roses,
and my mother tended them, just as I do. I've watched my town
grow; I can remember when Mr. Lewis, Senior, opened the grocery
store, and the year the river flooded out the shanties on the low road,
and the excitement when some young folks wanted to move the park
over to the space in front of where the new post office is today. They
wanted to put up a statue of Ethan Allen"—Miss Strangeworth
would frown a little and sound stern—"but it should have been a

statue of my grandfather. There wouldn't have been a town here at all if it hadn't been for my grandfather and the lumber mill."

Miss Strangeworth never gave away any of her roses, although the tourists often asked her. The roses belonged on Pleasant Street, and it bothered Miss Strangeworth to think of people wanting to carry them away, to take them into strange towns and down strange streets. When the new minister came, and the ladies were gathering flowers to decorate the church, Miss Strangeworth sent over a great basket of gladioli; when she picked the roses at all, she set them in bowls and vases around the inside of the house her grandfather had built.

Walking down Main Street on a summer morning, Miss Strangeworth had to stop every minute or so to say good morning to someone or to ask after someone's health. When she came into the grocery, half a dozen people turned away from the shelves and the counters to wave at her or call out good morning.

"And good morning to you, too, Mr. Lewis," Miss Strangeworth said at last. The Lewis family had been in the town almost as long as the Strangeworths; but the day young Lewis left high school and went to work in the grocery, Miss Strangeworth had stopped calling him Tommy and started calling him Mr. Lewis, and he had stopped calling her Addie and started calling her Miss Strangeworth. They had been in high school together, and had gone to picnics together, and to high school dances and basketball games; but now Mr. Lewis was behind the counter in the grocery, and Miss Strangeworth was living alone in the Strangeworth house on Pleasant Street.

"Good morning," Mr. Lewis said, and added politely, "lovely day."

"It is a very nice day," Miss Strangeworth said as though she had only just decided that it would do after all. "I would like a chop, please, Mr. Lewis, a small, lean veal chop. Are those strawberries from Arthur Parker's garden? They're early this year."

"He brought them in this morning," Mr. Lewis said.

"I shall have a box," Miss Strangeworth said. Mr. Lewis looked worried, she thought, and for a minute she hesitated, but then she decided that he surely could not be worried over the strawberries. He looked very tired indeed. He was usually so chipper, Miss Strangeworth thought, and almost commented, but it was far too personal a subject to be introduced to Mr. Lewis, the grocer, so she only said, "And a can of cat food and, I think, a tomato."

Silently, Mr. Lewis assembled her order on the counter and

waited. Miss Strangeworth looked at him curiously and then said, "It's Tuesday, Mr. Lewis. You forgot to remind me."

"Did I? Sorry."

"Imagine your forgetting that I always buy my tea on Tuesday," Miss Strangeworth said gently. "A quarter pound of tea, please, Mr. Lewis."

"Is that all, Miss Strangeworth?"

"Yes, thank you, Mr. Lewis. Such a lovely day, isn't it?"

"Lovely," Mr. Lewis said.

Miss Strangeworth moved slightly to make room for Mrs. Harper at the counter. "Morning, Adela," Mrs. Harper said, and Miss Strangeworth said, "Good morning, Martha."

"Lovely day," Mrs. Harper said, and Miss Strangeworth said, "Yes, lovely," and Mr. Lewis, under Mrs. Harper's glance, nodded.

"Ran out of sugar for my cake frosting," Mrs. Harper explained. Her hand shook slightly as she opened her pocketbook. Miss Strangeworth wondered, glancing at her quickly, if she had been taking proper care of herself. Martha Harper was not as young as she used to be, Miss Strangeworth thought. She probably could use a good, strong tonic.

"Martha," she said, "you don't look well."

"I'm perfectly all right," Mrs. Harper said shortly. She handed her money to Mr. Lewis, took her change and her sugar, and went out without speaking again. Looking after her, Miss Strangeworth shook her head slightly. Martha definitely did *not* look well.

Carrying her little bag of groceries, Miss Strangeworth came out of the store into the bright sunlight and stopped to smile down on the Crane baby. Don and Helen Crane were really the two most infatuated young parents she had ever known, she thought indulgently, looking at the delicately embroidered baby cap and the lace-edged carriage cover.

"That little girl is going to grow up expecting luxury all her life," she said to Helen Crane.

Helen laughed. "That's the way we want her to feel," she said. "Like a princess."

"A princess can be a lot of trouble sometimes," Miss Strangeworth said dryly. "How old is her highness now?"

"Six months next Tuesday," Helen Crane said, looking down with rapt wonder at her child. "I've been worrying, though, about her. Don't you think she ought to move around more? Try to sit up, for instance?"

"For plain and fancy worrying," Miss Strangeworth said, amused, "give me a new mother every time."

"She just seems—slow," Helen Crane said.

"Nonsense. All babies are different. Some of them develop much more quickly than others."

"That's what my mother says." Helen Crane laughed, looking a little bit ashamed.

"I suppose you've got young Don all upset about the fact that his daughter is already six months old and hasn't yet begun to learn to dance?"

"I haven't mentioned it to him. I suppose she's just so precious that I worry about her all the time."

"Well, apologize to her right now," Miss Strangeworth said. "*She* is probably worrying about why you keep jumping around all the time." Smiling to herself and shaking her old head, she went on down the sunny street, stopping once to ask little Billy Moore why he wasn't out riding in his daddy's shiny new car, and talking for a few minutes outside the library with Miss Chandler, the librarian, about the new novels to be ordered, and paid for by the annual library appropriation. Miss Chandler seemed absentminded and very much as though she was thinking about something else. Miss Strangeworth noticed that Miss Chandler had not taken much trouble with her hair that morning, and sighed. Miss Strangeworth hated sloppiness.

Many people seemed disturbed recently, Miss Strangeworth thought. Only yesterday the Stewarts' fifteen-year-old Linda had run crying down her own front walk and all the way to school, not caring who saw her. People around town thought she might have had a fight with the Harris boy, but they showed up together at the soda shop after school as usual, both of them looking grim and bleak. Trouble at home, people concluded, and sighed over the problems of trying to raise kids right these days.

From halfway down the block Miss Strangeworth could catch the heavy accent of her roses, and she moved a little more quickly. The perfume of roses meant home, and home meant the Strangeworth House on Pleasant Street. Miss Strangeworth stopped at her own front gate, as she always did, and looked with deep pleasure at her house, with the red and pink and white roses massed along the narrow lawn, and the rambler going up along the porch; and the neat, the unbelievably trim lines of the house itself, with its slimness and its washed white look. Every window sparkled, every curtain hung stiff and straight, and even the stones of the front walk were swept and clear. People around town wondered how old Miss Strangeworth managed to keep the house looking the way it did, and there was a legend about a tourist once mistaking it for the local museum and going all through the place without finding out about his mistake. But the town was proud of Miss Strangeworth and her roses and her house. They had all grown together. Miss Strangeworth went up her front steps, unlocked her front door with her key, and went into the kitchen to put away her groceries. She debated having a cup of tea and then decided that it was too close to midday dinner-time; she would not have the appetite for her little chop if she had tea now. Instead she went into the light, lovely sitting room, which still glowed from the hands of her mother and her grandmother, who had covered the chairs with bright chintz and hung the curtains. All the furniture was spare and shining, and the round hooked rugs on the floor had been the work of Miss Strangeworth's grandmother and her mother. Miss Strangeworth had put a bowl of her red roses on the low table before the window, and the room was full of their scent.

Miss Strangeworth went to the narrow desk in the corner, and unlocked it with her key. She never knew when she might feel like writing letters, so she kept her notepaper inside, and the desk locked. Miss Strangeworth's usual stationery was heavy and cream-colored, with "Strangeworth House" engraved across the top, but, when she felt like writing her other letters, Miss Strangeworth used a pad of various-colored paper, bought from the local newspaper shop. It was almost a town joke, that colored paper, layered in pink and green and blue and yellow; everyone in town bought it and used it for odd, informal notes and shopping lists. It was usual to remark, upon receiving a note written on a blue page, that so-and-so would be needing a new pad soon—here she was, down to the blue already. Everyone used the matching envelopes for tucking away recipes, or keeping odd little things in, or even to hold cookies in the school lunch boxes. Mr. Lewis sometimes gave them to the children for carrying home penny candy.

Although Miss Strangeworth's desk held a trimmed quill pen, which had belonged to her grandfather, and a gold-frost fountain pen, which had belonged to her father, Miss Strangeworth always used a dull stub of pencil when she wrote her letters, and she printed them in a childish block print. After thinking for a minute, although she had been phrasing the letter in the back of her mind all the way home, she wrote on a pink sheet: *Didn't you ever see an idiot child before? Some people just shouldn't have children, should they?*

She was pleased with the letter. She was fond of doing things exactly right. When she made a mistake, as she sometimes did, or when the letters were not spaced nicely on the page, she had to take the discarded page to the kitchen stove and burn it at once. Miss Strangeworth never delayed when things had to be done.

After thinking for a minute, she decided that she would like to write another letter, perhaps to go to Mrs. Harper, to follow up the ones she had already mailed. She selected a green sheet this time and wrote quickly: *Have you found out yet what they were all laughing about after you left the bridge club on Thursday? Or is the wife really always the last one to know?*

Miss Strangeworth never concerned herself with facts; her letters all dealt with the more negotiable stuff of suspicion. Mr. Lewis would never have imagined for a minute that his grandson might be lifting petty cash from the store register if he had not had one of Miss Strangeworth's letters. Miss Chandler, the librarian, and Linda Stewart's parents would have gone unsuspectingly ahead with their lives, never aware of possible evil lurking nearby, if Miss Strangeworth had not sent letters to open their eyes. Miss Strangeworth would have been genuinely shocked if there *had* been anything between Linda Stewart and the Harris boy, but, as long as evil existed unchecked in the world, it was Miss Strangeworth's duty to keep her town alert to it. It was far more sensible for Miss Chandler to wonder what Mr. Shelley's first wife had really died of than to take a chance on not knowing. There were so many wicked people in the world and only one Strangeworth left in town. Besides, Miss Strangeworth liked writing her letters.

She addressed an envelope to Don Crane after a moment's thought, wondering curiously if he would show the letter to his wife, and using a pink envelope to match the pink paper. Then she addressed a second envelope, green, to Mrs. Harper. Then an idea came to her and she selected a blue sheet and wrote: *You never know about doctors. Remember they're only human and need money like the rest of us. Suppose the knife slipped accidentally. Would Doctor Burns get his fee and a little extra from that nephew of yours?*

She addressed the blue envelope to old Mrs. Foster, who was having an operation next month. She had thought of writing one more letter, to the head of the school board, asking how a chemistry teacher like Billy Moore's father could afford a new convertible, but all at once she was tired of writing letters. The three she had done would do for one day. She could write more tomorrow; it was not as though they all had to be done at once.

She had been writing her letters—sometimes two or three every day for a week, sometimes no more than one in a month—for the past year. She never got any answers, of course, because she never signed her name. If she had been asked, she would have said that her name, Adela Strangeworth, a name honored in the town for so many years, did not belong on such trash. The town where she lived had to be kept clean and sweet, but people everywhere were lustful and evil and degraded, and needed to be watched; the world was so large, and there was only one Strangeworth left in it. Miss Strangeworth sighed, locked her desk, and put the letters into her big, black leather pocket-book, to be mailed when she took her evening walk.

She broiled her little chop nicely, and had a sliced tomato and good cup of tea ready when she sat down to her midday dinner at the table in her dining room, which could be opened to seat twenty-two, with a second table, if necessary, in the hall. Sitting in the warm sunlight that came through the tall windows of the dining room, seeing her roses massed outside, handling the heavy, old silverware and the fine, translucent china, Miss Strangeworth was pleased; she would not have cared to be doing anything else. People must live graciously, after all, she thought, and sipped her tea. Afterward, when her plate and cup and saucer were washed and dried and put back onto the shelves where they belonged, and her silverware was back in the mahogany silver chest, Miss Strangeworth went up the graceful staircase and into her bedroom, which was the front room overlooking the roses, and had been her mother's and her grand-mother's. Their Crown Derby dresser set and furs had been kept here, their fans and silver-backed brushes and their own bowls of roses; Miss Strangeworth kept a bowl of white roses on the bed table.

She drew the shades, took the rose-satin spread from the bed, slipped out of her dress and her shoes, and lay down tiredly. She knew that no doorbell or phone would ring; no one in town would dare to disturb Miss Strangeworth during her afternoon nap. She slept, deep in the rich smell of roses.

After her nap she worked in her garden for a little while, sparing herself because of the heat; then she went in to her supper. She ate asparagus from her own garden, with sweet-butter sauce, and a soft-boiled egg, and, while she had her supper, she listened to a late-evening news broadcast and then to a program of classical music on her small radio. After her dishes were done and her kitchen set in order, she took up her hat—Miss Strangeworth's hats were prover-bial in the town; people believed that she had inherited them from her mother and her grandmother—and, locking the front door of her house behind her, set off on her evening walk, pocketbook under her arm. She nodded to Linda Stewart's father, who was washing his car in the pleasantly cool evening. She thought that he looked troubled.

There was only one place in town where she could mail her letters, and that was the new post office, shiny with red brick and silver letters. Although Miss Strangeworth had never given the matter any particular thought, she had always made a point of mailing her letters very secretly; it would, of course, not have been wise to let anyone see her mail them. Consequently, she timed her walk so she could reach the post office just as darkness was starting to dim the outlines of the trees and the shapes of people's faces, although no one could ever mistake Miss Strangeworth, with her dainty walk and her rustling skirts.

There was always a group of young people around the post office, the very youngest roller-skating upon its driveway, which went all the way around the building and was the only smooth road in town; and the slightly older ones already knowing how to gather in small groups and chatter and laugh and make great, excited plans for going across the street to the soda shop in a minute or two. Miss Strangeworth had never had any self-consciousness before the chil-dren. She did not feel that any of them were staring at her unduly or longing to laugh at her; it would have been most reprehensible for their parents to permit their children to mock Miss Strangeworth of Pleasant Street. Most of the children stood back respectfully as Miss Strangeworth passed, silenced briefly in her presence, and some of the older children greeted her, saying soberly, "Hello, Miss Strangeworth."

Miss Strangeworth smiled at them and quickly went on. It had been a long time since she had known the name of every child in town. The mail slot was in the door of the post office. The children stood away as Miss Strangeworth approached it, seemingly surprised that anyone should want to use the post office after it had been officially closed up for the night and turned over to the children. Miss Strangeworth stood by the door, opening her black pocketbook to take out the letters, and heard a voice which she knew at once to be Linda Stewart's. Poor little Linda was crying again, and Miss

Strangeworth listened carefully. This was, after all, her town, and these were her people; if one of them was in trouble, she ought to know about it.

"I can't tell you, Dave," Linda was saying—so she *was* talking to the Harris boy, as Miss Strangeworth had supposed—"I just *can't*. It's just *nasty*."

"But why won't your father let me come around anymore? What on earth did I do?"

"I can't tell you. I just wouldn't tell you for *any*thing. You've got to have a dirty dirty mind for things like that."

"But something's happened. You've been crying and crying, and your father is all upset. Why can't *I* know about it, too? Aren't I like one of the family?"

"Not anymore, Dave, not anymore. You're not to come near our house again; my father said so. He said he'd horsewhip you. That's all I can tell you: You're not to come near our house anymore."

"But I didn't *do* anything."

"Just the same, my father said . . ."

Miss Strangeworth sighed and turned away. There was so much evil in people. Even in a charming little town like this one, there was still so much evil in people.

She slipped her letters into the slot, and two of them fell inside. The third caught on the edge and fell outside, onto the ground at Miss Strangeworth's feet. She did not notice it because she was wondering whether a letter to the Harris boy's father might not be of some service in wiping out this potential badness. Wearily Miss Strangeworth turned to go home to her quiet bed in her lovely house, and never heard the Harris boy calling to her to say that she had dropped something.

"Old lady Strangeworth's getting deaf," he said, looking after her and holding in his hand the letter he had picked up.

"Well, who cares?" Linda said. "Who cares anymore, anyway?"

"It's for Don Crane," the Harris boy said, "this letter. She dropped a letter addressed to Don Crane. Might as well take it on over. We pass his house anyway." He laughed. "Maybe it's got a check or something in it and he'd be just as glad to get it tonight instead of tomorrow."

"Catch old lady Strangeworth sending anybody a check," Linda said. "Throw it in the post office. Why do anyone a favor?" She sniffed. "Doesn't seem to me anybody around here cares about us," she said. "Why should we care about them?"

"I'll take it over, anyway," the Harris boy said. "Maybe it's good news for them. Maybe they need something happy tonight, too. Like us."

Sadly, holding hands, they wandered off down the dark street, the Harris boy carrying Miss Strangeworth's pink envelope in his hand.

Miss Strangeworth awakened the next morning with a feeling of intense happiness and, for a minute, wondered why, and then remembered that this morning three people would open her letters. Harsh, perhaps, at first, but wickedness was never easily banished, and a clean heart was a scoured heart. She washed her soft, old face and brushed her teeth, still sound in spite of her seventy-one years, and dressed herself carefully in her sweet, soft clothes and buttoned shoes. Then, going downstairs, reflecting that perhaps a little waffle would be agreeable for breakfast in the sunny dining room, she found the mail on the hall floor, and bent to pick it up. A bill, the morning paper, a letter in a green envelope that looked oddly familiar. Miss Strangeworth stood perfectly still for a minute, looking down at the green envelope with the penciled printing, and thought: It looks like one of my letters. Was one of my letters sent back? No, because no one would know where to send it. How did this get here?

Miss Strangeworth was a Strangeworth of Pleasant Street. Her hand did not shake as she opened the envelope and unfolded the sheet of green paper inside. She began to cry silently for the wickedness of the world when she read the words: *Look out at what used to be your roses.*

Epilogue

✥

FAME

Writer, *August 1948*

T WO DAYS BEFORE MY first novel was to be published, while I was packing to leave the small Vermont town in which I live to go to New York, the telephone rang, and when I snatched it up irritably and said, "Hello," a sweet old lady's voice answered me, "Hello, who's this?" which is a common enough Vermont telephone greeting.

"This is Shirley Jackson," I said, a little soothed because my name reminded me of my book.

"Well," she said vaguely, "is Mrs. Stanley Hyman there, please?"

I waited for a minute and then, "This is Mrs. Hyman," I said reluctantly.

Her voice brightened. "Mrs. Hyman," she said, pleased, "this is Mrs. Sheila Lang of the newspaper. I've been trying to get in touch with you for days."

"I'm so sorry," I said. "I've been terribly busy—my book, and all."

"Yes," she said. "Well, Mrs. Hyman, this is what I wanted. You read the paper, of course?"

"Of course," I said, "and I've been sort of expecting . . ."

"Well, then, surely, you read the North Village Notes column?"

"Yes, indeed," I said warmly.

"That's *my* column," she said. "I *write* that column."

"Of course, I'm a North Village resident," I said, "but I rather thought that for a thing of this importance . . ."

"Now, what I'm doing is this. I'm calling up a few people in town who I thought might have items of news for me . . ."

"Certainly," I said, and reached for one of the numerous copies of the book jacket lying around the house. "The name of the book . . ."

"*First* of all," she said, "where exactly in town do you live, Mrs. Hyman?"

"On Prospect Street," I said. *"The Road Through the Wall."*

"I see," she said. "Just let me take that down."

"That's the name of the book," I said.

"Yes," she said. "Which house would that be, I wonder."

"The old Elwell place," I said.

"On the corner of Mechanic? I thought the young Elwells lived there."

"That's next door," I said. "We're in the *old* Elwell place."

"The old *Thatcher* place?" she said. "We always call that the old Thatcher place; he built it, you know."

"That's the one," I said. "It's going to be published the day after tomorrow."

"I didn't know *any*one lived there," she said. "I thought it was empty."

"We've lived here three years," I said a little stiffly.

"I don't get out much anymore," she said. "Now, what little items of local news do you have for me? Any visitors? Children's parties?"

"I'm publishing a book next week," I said. "I am going down to New York for my publication day."

"Taking your family?" she asked. "Any children, by the way?"

"Two," I said. "I'm taking them."

"Isn't that nice," she said. "I bet they're excited."

"You know," I said madly, "I've been asked to do the Girl Scout column for your paper."

"Really?" She sounded doubtful. "I'm sure you'll enjoy it. It's such an *informal* newspaper."

"Yes," I said. "Would you like to hear about my book?"

"I certainly would," she said. "Anytime you have any little newsy items for me, you be sure and call me right up. My number's in the book."

"Thank you," I said. "Well, *my* book . . ."

"I have so much enjoyed our little talk, Mrs. Hyman. Imagine me not knowing anyone was living in the old Thatcher place!"

"The Road Through the Wall," I said. "Farrar and Straus."

"You know," she said, "now that I don't get out anymore, I find that doing this column keeps me in touch with my neighbors. It's social, sort of."

"Two seventy-five," I said. "It'll be in the local bookstore."

"You probably find the same thing with the Girl Scout column," she said. "Thank you so much, Mrs. Hyman. Do call me again soon."

"I started it last winter," I said.

"Goodbye," she said sweetly, and hung up.

I kept the column that appeared as the North Village Notes of the newspaper the next day. Several people remarked on it to me. It was on the last page of the four.

NORTH VILLAGE NOTES

Mrs. Royal Jones of Main Street is ill.

Miss Mary Randall of Waite Street is confined to her home with chicken pox.

One of the hooked rug classes met last evening with Mrs. Ruth Harris.

Hurlbut Lang of Troy spent the weekend with his parents in North Village, Mr. and Mrs. R. L. Lang.

The food sale of the Baptist Church has been postponed indefinitely due to weather conditions.

Mrs. Stanley Hyman has moved into the old Thatcher place on Prospect Street. She and her family are visiting Mr. and Mrs. Farrarstraus of New York City this week.

Mrs. J. N. Arnold of Burlington spent the weekend in town with Mr. and Mrs. Samuel Montague.

Little Lola Kittredge of East Road celebrated her fifth birthday on Tuesday. Six little friends joined to wish her many happy returns of the day, and ice cream and cake were served.